AFTER ALICE

after · alice

a novel

KAREN HOFMANN

NeWest Press

After Alice is available as an ebook: 978-1-927063-47-7

Library and Archives Canada Cataloguing in Publication

Hofmann, Karen Marie, 1961–, author
After Alice / Karen Hofmann.

(Nunatak first fiction series : 37) Issued in print and electronic formats.
ISBN 978-1-927063-46-0 (pbk.). — ISBN 978-1-927063-47-7 (epub). — ISBN 978-1-927063-55-2 (mobi)

I. Title. II. Series: Nunatak first fiction 37

PS8615.O365A37 2014   C813'.6   C2013-906950-X
                                               C2013-906951-8

Editor for the Board: Anne Nothof
Cover and Interior Design: Natalie Olsen, Kisscut Design
Author Photo: Julia Tomkins

First Edition: April 2014

NeWest Press acknowledges the support of the Canada Council for the Arts, the Alberta Foundation for the Arts, and the Edmonton Arts Council for support of our publishing program. We acknowledge the financial support of the Government of Canada through the Canada Book Fund for our publishing activities.

NeWest Press
#201, 8540 – 109 Street
Edmonton, Alberta T6G 1E6
www.newestpress.com

No bison were harmed in the making of this book.

Printed and bound in Canada

This book is for my maternal grandparents,
Ikey and Lillian Hillaby.

STYX

The 5:40 from Calgary, descending to the runway a kilometre to the south, rattles her roof and screams, all throat and flash, over the little frozen lake. Explosions of scarlet and green light track down the lake, pulse through the ice. The leafless aspens flare silver, copper, and are reabsorbed into darkness. The jet's scream drops an octave, glissando. A spectacle of dragons, a kind of Valkyrie ride.

It's her signal to close her laptop, abandon her work for the day.

She stretches and blinks, tumbles from the tight interlocking puzzle of her mental work, of her reading and writing, into the jet's destruction of silence, into the late afternoon of her empty house, as some component might peel from a shuttle and spin out into the void.

She had not thought, signing the papers for the house purchase, about the runway. Had not thought — entranced by the house, which in August had been full of light and space; entranced by the green and breeziness of the valley, a long slip of light, air, shade, and Montreal sultry and crowded; entranced by the real estate agent's phrases: deer, ducks, lake path — she had not thought. She had seen only the lake, sparkling; the bobbing waterfowl.

She had forgotten how, even as a child, she had thought this area a bleak pinch of the landscape, a dark and dismal passage. The hills in this stretch of the valley low, blocky, not pleasing. A sort of rocky knob, just to the south and west of the lake, scattered now with dead and dying pines, blocking the light, the sun setting behind it by early afternoon. The least desirable land in the whole of the valley.

Reserve land, of course: what was given back to the original inhabitants as least valuable. Rocky, boggy land; the little lake, shallow and muddy, an afterthought in a valley famous for its lakes. Given back in treaties, this unprepossessing twist of the valley. A shameful illiberality. And now she has bought a house here, a bargain because on leased land.

Normally at this time, she begins to prepare her evening meal, to dress a little salad, slice cheese, heat up a prepared dinner. But tonight she is going out. The invitation is for seven. She had forgotten, returning to the valley, how early people in this western part of the country dine. It's inconvenient, at the least. Not really time to eat before, though she doesn't remember a mention of dinner in the invitation. She is not confident that there will be dinner. And yet, there is scarcely time to eat now, before the children collect her. She must change her clothes, find the bottle of wine she has bought to take along as a gift.

She has not wanted to go out, anyway. She had not wanted to go to this party. It's our family, her niece Cynthia had argued. She had pointed out to Cynthia, reasonably, she thought, that family relationships were arbitrary, that a few congenial friends always made better company. But Cynthia had insisted, showing some temper, retreating into an assumed or real inability to understand her. And the boy had seemed to want to go, to want her to accompany them. So now she must go: she will hope that there is something to eat. No time to eat now: no time to eat properly.

She puts on her black wool trousers and a black turtleneck pullover, combs her hair. Adds her good gold chain with its locket, then takes it off. Too showy; too festive.

The wine is on the built-in rack in her kitchen. A good local red. Is that appropriate? She hopes so. She has not yet developed a sense of the local opinions about the valley vintners. Should she have bought Italian? Chilean, perhaps? But this wine proclaims itself award-winning, and cost thirty dollars. It must be an acceptable gift.

Unless, of course, Stephen and Debbie are not wine-drinkers. But she'd have heard that, wouldn't she, from Cynthia?

She finds a long, narrow paper bag for the wine — one bought for the purpose, dark purple, with a cord handle. It had been difficult to find, in the heaps of holiday-themed packaging. She had not wanted to bring her wine in a bag decorated with either snowmen or gilt stars.

The Feast of the Epiphany. That's what today is, January 6th. Is the party a religious celebration? She recalls now that Debbie's family name was Ukrainian. Is it a Ukrainian Christmas party that she is going to? Have Stephen and Debbie reverted to some tradition?

Surely Cynthia would have said. But now she is doubly uneasy. Why had she agreed to go along? And why had she not insisted on driving herself? She does not like waiting for rides. People are rarely punctual.

At 6:45, she is waiting in her basement-entry vestibule, coat and boots on, wine bottle in its purple bag dangling from her gloved hand.

On either side of the highway, the orchards, the rows of trees gnarled and fingery in the vapour lights, casting blue shadows. For a few days there was hoarfrost, and the trees were transformed, ethereal. Now they are merely skeletal, bereft of their leaves and fruit. The trees have cauterized black sockets around themselves in the patchy snow. Skeleton trees, ghost trees. Familiar, and yet not, seen now after so many years away. Familiar in the way of something lost and then rediscovered, something whose appearance no longer matches the image in the memory.

In a clearing along the highway, where the trees have been cut and not yet replanted, figures are silhouetted against bonfire flames.

An atavistic scene: the hair rises, slightly, on the back of her neck. But it's only pruning time, and the prunings, the small lopped-off limbs, being burned. She knows that: while the trees are dormant, the last year's growth is trimmed to channel the tree's sap more efficiently into the fruit, to make picking fruit more efficient.

Now woodsmoke in the air, insinuating itself through the car's heating system. Apple smoke. Her smell-memory conjures Mr. Tanaka climbing down from the tractor, his big iron fork lifting the tangles of twigs, of suckers, onto the trailer. Herself and her sister Alice and the other children, made to pick up the prunings. Her fingers numbing inside the ice-stiffened mittens, her nostrils raw under their mucous crusts as she tramped and scrambled and bent in the snow. (Was it deeper then?) The crackle of green twigs, burning; the scented smoke. The apricot tinge of the sky on days when the sun barely broke over the horizon. The gloss on the white tread marks left by the tractor wheels; the blue light in boot prints left in deep snow.

It's a short trip, much shorter than she remembers. They are already nearing the little village, now. "Turn left at the lights," Cynthia, who has been to Stephen's before, directs from between the seats. Justin is driving, gracefully, alert but relaxed. Too relaxed? He has only his N license, and the highway is slick in patches, with black ice twinkling back the orange glow of the streetlights. After a New Year's chinook, a thawing and dispersal of snow, there has been a sudden freeze. The highway is likely unsafe.

She watches Justin's profile, as always, covertly. Does he look like anyone? Besides Cynthia and her family, of course?

Her grandnephew is wearing a shirt and tie, the cashmere sweater she has given him for Christmas under his overcoat. His hair is smooth, becomingly cut. Very appropriate, she thinks, approvingly. None of that baggy denim and fleece that young men seem to favour this decade. The costume of a spurious anti-establishment pose. No; Justin looks proper, grown-up, a mature eighteen-year-old. And he seems to be a very good driver. She ought to relax.

Now they are climbing from the highway up the steep ridgeback hill. The narrow black road glitters. On either side, the spindly hedge of saskatoon berry, waxberry, Oregon grape clambers the bank, the stripped boughs like dark scratches against the snow.

She recognizes this road, which has changed very little in forty years. This is the landscape of her childhood. She doesn't recognize the name of the streets in the neighbourhood where Stephen lives, which Cynthia is reading from the map. Squirrel, Marmot, Badger. The lesser fauna of the dry Interior. Stephen lives on Jackrabbit. *Jackrabbit.*

It must be a new development. She has left it to Cynthia to navigate, though it's awkward for Cynthia, who is in the back seat, and has to see their faces to lip-read. She perhaps should have taken the back seat herself, but in Cynthia's small Japanese import, there is not really enough legroom for her except in the front. Cynthia must lean forward between the seats like a child, trying to read the infrequent road signs.

"Is your seatbelt fastened?" she asks Cynthia.

"Yes, Auntie Sid."

"Mother!" Justin says, then, mockingly, "Have you washed your hands and buttoned your coat?"

Cheeky boy. "Perhaps you ought to slow down," she tells Justin.

"What is the Feast of Epiphany, anyway?" Justin asks, cocking her a grin. So he has noticed too. A sponge for information: a boy after her own heart, her grand nephew.

He adds, "I didn't think we went in for this stuff. And *do* I want to know my cousins?"

"You see?" Cynthia complains in her flat, guttural voice. "You set a bad example, Auntie Sid, and then I have to deal with him."

It's an old subject of discussion.

She says, "There's nothing wrong with celebrating holidays, Justin. Rituals are important. . . ."

"Yeah, yeah," Justin says, impatiently.

Another thing: she objects to "Auntie Sid." She had always been called Sidonie, emphasis on the first syllable. She had been named after a harpist, Sidonie Goosens, whom Father saw perform in Vienna in 1921. Sidonie had been astonished to hear, in 2004, that her namesake had just died. She had been still living in Montreal, and listening to CBC 2, when she heard the announcement. How could Sidonie Goosens have been still alive, in 2004? It couldn't be the same woman, she had thought. But it was: Sidonie Goosens had lived to be a hundred and five. She had come out of retirement to perform when she was in her nineties. "Imagine that," Tom Allen had said, in his sweet, erudite, conversational voice. Sidonie had taken her namesake's longevity as a good omen.

The car takes a tight bend and fishtails. She grabs the door handle. Cynthia yelps from the back seat.

Cynthia herself ought to be driving. But she has had her license hardly any longer than Justin. In Montreal, Cynthia had not bothered to learn to drive.

"You might want to slow down," Sidonie says, as mildly as she can. "There are more hairpin turns on this road."

"Sorry," Justin says blandly.

She should have driven them herself.

Then from the bank of bleached orchard grasses flanking the road, an apparition rises: a slim-waisted woman in a long, fluttering white dress — a nightgown? — arms taut behind her, as if bound at the wrists, head with its fluttering pale hair flung backward in a posture of desperation. In the few seconds she's caught in the headlights, the woman dashes, jerkily, away from the road, toward the rows of winter-stripped apple trees, flings herself against a lower limb, clings.

It's only as the car passes, as the headlight beam glides on, sucking all light with it, as her angle of vision shifts, as the beams of the vehicle behind them catch the white flash again, that Sidonie, her neck cranked sharply around, comprehends.

A long strip of white plastic — perhaps the torn packaging of an insulation batt — blown from a construction site. A twisted strip of white plastic, caught in a gust from a passing car. That's all.

Justin, at the wheel, says, "What was *that*! I thought it was a white deer for a second!" Sidonie's heart an earth compressor, thudding.

Her nephew Stephen will be forty-seven this year: is that right? Yes; he was born in November of 1959. A middle-aged man now. (How has that happened, that her nephew, her sister's son, can be forty-seven? And she hasn't seen him since his wedding, which must have been more than twenty years ago.)

Of course, Stephen is much changed. He has less hair, his face has blurred, as if a wax model of a face had been pressed with a warm hand; he is fleshier. But also, somehow, he has soured. He looks a little morose, disappointed, ashamed, even as he opens the door and stands smiling. Hangdog, her mother would have said. He has the thick, beetle-like torso of a man who has performed physical labour for thirty years. The set mouth of someone who had hoped for a different life, perhaps.

Stephen is wearing his hair long, over his ears, though it is receding in front, and a graphic T-shirt with gothic lettering, images of skulls and flames. Rock music is playing from a sound system somewhere in the house, and can be heard, or rather not quite heard, in disharmonic counterpoint to the conversations, to the voices of the guests, and of Stephen and Cynthia.

And here's Debbie, Stephen's wife, who has surely nearly doubled in size in the last twenty years. She looks alarmingly hot, though the house is cool to Sidonie's skin. Debbie's face is red, and the tendrils of curled hair on her forehead are damp. Sidonie stiffens as Debbie moves closer, her arms stretching out. She does not enjoy being hugged.

But Debbie's skin, when she embraces Sidonie, is surprisingly cool and dry, and she smells lightly of vanilla.

"So you've come back here after over forty years!" Debbie says. "That's amazing!"

How is it amazing, she wants to ask, but does not.

They are not permitted to join the rest of the guests right away, but are shepherded into a sort of library, where she is introduced to Stephen's children, her grandnephew and niece. They are grown — the boy is in his mid-twenties; the girl around Justin's age — but they seem graceless, diffident. They have a Slavic look, from Debbie's family, no doubt: coarse, dirty-blond hair (though the girl's is dyed black, with light roots), broad cheekbones, pale, slightly almond-shaped eyes. The two of them, brother and sister, look askance at Justin. None of the three of them speaks.

The conversation quickly devolves onto the subject of the children, Stephen and Debbie's offspring and Justin, their resemblances, their accomplishments, their plans. She asks the girl if she is planning on taking courses at the university after she graduates from high school. Her grandniece turns bored, black-outlined eyes toward her. (Hostile? Or just wary?)

"Maybe," the girl says. "I want to go somewhere else, though."

"What are you planning on studying?" Sidonie asks.

A flicker of something in the pale eyes. "I don't know," she says. "I mean, I'm still trying to decide. I don't know if I'll go."

Stephen says, "It's a lot of money if you want to go somewhere else. You need to pull up your grades, get a couple of scholarships. Maybe get a part-time job."

The girl (what is her name?) sighs as if Stephen has suggested she take on a shift at the mines, and surreptitiously plugs small earphones into her ears. One of the new small, flat digital music devices protrudes from the pocket of her jeans.

Justin has been reading the back of a DVD package, but is at last paying attention to the conversation. He appears about to speak to his cousin, but then closes his lips, turns away. She does not blame him; it is tough going, making conversation with these two.

"And Alex?" Sidonie asks. "What program are you in?"

Alex, with his shaggy hair, his beard, his baggy jeans and plaid flannel shirt, is possibly out of university already. But she has not heard that he has entered a profession.

Stephen says, "Oh, Alex is taking a break from university."

"Dropped out, you mean," his sister says spitefully. Apparently she can hear them, in spite of the earplugs.

"Well, now," Stephen says, carefully, "Alex hasn't found something he's interested in yet."

"Except sitting in his room all day downloading songs," the girl says.

Justin's eyes widen; an only child, he has not experienced sibling hostility, she thinks. Sibling rivalry. The unconscious urge to destroy the nest-mate.

Once, she remembers, as a child made to pick up stones in the garden, she had lobbed a fist-sized rock backward, underhand, meaning to hit the clothes-line post, but instead clipping her sister Alice squarely on the chin. She'd stood up straight, then, gaping. Couldn't have done that again if she'd tried; she'd laughed out loud at the absurdity of it. Then Alice was on her, kneeling on her back, seizing her two braids like reins in one hand and whacking her face up and down into the mud. Alice, five years older than her, and much larger — there was no resisting Alice.

Alice'd had three stitches, Dr. Knox driving out from town to do the job. A little white scar, ever after, in the von Täler chin-dimple.

The appalling feeling of the grit in her teeth, of the clay-slime on her lips. Though when she was younger still, she had cheerfully eaten dirt, according to Alice.

She thinks that Justin feels rather afraid of his older cousin, Alex, who has a beefy body, bushy hair and beard.

Alex says, "I actually have a temporary job at the city recycling yard." His voice is oddly high; he coughs and it drops an octave. "I work the chipper. Chip up the Christmas trees and prunings."

Again, the guarded eyes, the impression of withholding, of caution. Wary, like his sister.

Debbie and Steve smile, stiffly. She realizes then that this is one of those social occasions — she has experienced them with her staff — in which the shy parents display the children as currency. Transactional.

Perhaps not wariness, then, but ambivalence. As if their real lives might be going on elsewhere. As if they're waiting for something worth their real attention.

Or perhaps they're just embarrassed.

"Is it dangerous?" Justin asks, of the chipper, and then flushes, but Alex grins.

"If you're stupid, it is," he says.

That comment seems to finish the conversation. What is wrong with these children—these not-really-children-anymore? They seem disconnected from something. Dependent, perhaps, and resenting the cage of their dependence.

At the girl's age, she had already been in university for a couple of years. By the time she was Alex's age, she had finished her first degree, was married, working at her doctoral studies. Had settled to the business of life. It makes her anxious, this disconnection. This indirection.

They move from the library into a roomful of strangers: just the sort of thing she likes to avoid. Stephen and Debbie hover near her a little nervously. Are they afraid of what she will say? She has nothing to say. The conversation is about cooking and house decorating, as it would be (to be fair) at a party given by one of her younger colleagues back in Montreal. Or rather, the conversation is about television shows about cooking and house decorating. The first names of celebrity decorators and builders and chefs are invoked. Someone tells an incident involving a friend who had her house revamped as part of a television series. There is much interest in this anecdote, as if this television personality were an important political or religious figure. (She remembers the Anglican Archbishop visiting Marshall's Landing in the 50s. The general mood of self-improvement that had preceded, and succeeded, the visit. There is something of that in the tone of this conversation.)

The new religion of the middle classes, she thinks. Consumerism dressed up in a deceptive new costume of aesthetics, even environmentalism. More than one of her colleagues has carted off a whole kitchen's worth of appliances and cabinets to the landfill to make room for new, environmentally-friendly fittings.

Stephen's new house is quite grand; inside all is light and gloss: the ceilings high, the walls painted deep serious shades, the mouldings wide and elaborate, the dark hardwood floors glistening. The furniture and cabinetry, the fixtures and collections all oversized and authoritative, public, almost. Nineteen-forties mobster, her husband Adam would have said.

She has seen this style before in the homes of colleagues. New money. She is surprised and perhaps a little disappointed at the normalcy of the house. But what had she expected: something like the shack Stephen and Cynthia's parents, Alice and Buck, had lived in, in Horsefly? They have moved forward, Stephen and Debbie. There is nothing in this house to betray the past, or Stephen's family history. They have worked hard; they have achieved things.

There is no sign of the type of talk she remembers from her childhood, of local politics, fruit yields, machinery on the part of the men, gossip and disapprobation of the neighbours, by the women. But neither has anyone become drunk, and nobody has shouted or swung at anyone else.

What had she expected?

She drifts back into the library. An odd room. What she had taken for floor-to-ceiling bookshelves are actually repositories for row on row of VHS and DVD cases. There must be thousands of titles. A set of cabinets houses several electronic machines with winking blue lights. A semicircle of high-backed, overstuffed leather chairs — rather *Star Trek* — with cup-holders in the arms, confronts the cabinets. No doubt a large screen lurks somewhere, for the viewing of these various media. Yes, there, at the juncture of the wall and ceiling, an aperture.

The library, a sort of combination of chapel and command station, is oddly purposeful and decadent, simultaneously. What can be its purpose? Surely they do not have a room dedicated just to watching movies?

No evidence of any of the Kleinholzes, Stephen's and Cynthia's family on their father's side, at the gathering.

She asks Cynthia, "Do you ever see your aunt Lottie? Your uncles?"

Cynthia gives her a glittering, far-away sort of smile. "Have you tried the food? Go eat something."

She is hungry: there are only hors d'oeuvres in the buffet, not a meal. She should have eaten before she came. She marches over to the long table upon which food has been spread. It is all, at first glance, alarming: more like an art installation or lab experiment than *food*. On oblong ceramic platters rest deep-bowled ceramic spoons holding viscous coils of material: black, coral, acid green. Is this meant to be eaten? Does one insert that entire, rather large spoon into the mouth? Or slurp the substance from it? A phalanx of small square glass vessels like votive holders contains matchstick-like stalks of what she realizes are vegetables — unfamiliar, raw, vegetables — propped in a glob of what might be purple mayonnaise.

She looks around wildly, sees, at last, little crusts of bread, heaped with something she can recognize as a sort of tomato purée, though it has been adulterated with unidentifiable green and black fragments. She bites in, hungrily. Onion and olive and garlic: it is good. But the brittle crust shatters at the onslaught of her teeth, and a large fragment of bread and tomato sauce leaps to the tablecloth.

She dabs and dabs, but Debbie is suddenly there, moving a plate smoothly to hide the stain. "Never mind," she says, kindly.

She must eat, especially now with Debbie at her elbow. She looks around again: there is a basket of crackers — small brown crackers, innocuous, recognizably food. She picks one up, bites gingerly. Her mouth fills gratefully with saliva. Wheat, the comfort of wheat. She picks up a couple more crackers. Debbie hands her a little glass plate. "Pâté?" she asks. But no. Sidonie does not want the pâté, which seems to be liverwurst with pimentos. She only wants to eat the good brown crackers.

They are both rescued by Stephen making his way purposefully toward them through the crowd, like a police boat in a shoal of drifting yawls.

Stephen fetches her a glass, says, "So you've retired from psychiatry."

"I have never been a psychiatrist. I design experiments for psychological research."

Stephen's face falls, as if he has suddenly been presented with a difficult task. But then Debbie is at his elbow, staying his flagging arm, Sidonie thinks.

Debbie says, "But you're retired from your profession now?"

"Officially," she says. "But I hope to continue writing in my field for some time." This is true. She is connected to her institution, still. She has the internet; she lives close to the airport. She intends to continue her work. She has only let go of the extraneous bits, the tediousness of administrative work. She feels, now, the surge of pleasure, of warmth, at the thought of the projects she has still going.

The girl, who has been lurking behind her parents, says, "You design experiments? What does that mean? Like, with rabbits and monkeys?" Her brows are drawn together, her voice is accusing. A typical teenager, fired up with some idea she knows little about. Sidonie could take her on. But it's a fool's errand, arguing with the impassioned young. And she is a guest.

She says, "Not really. Most of my design work is in meta-statistics. I work with computer-generated mathematical models."

Then she has the pleasure of seeing their faces — Stephen's and Debbie's — freeze over, go blank, like stone.

She notices now that the Gothic lettering on Stephen's shirt reads *Styx*. Styx, she seems to remember, was the name of an American rock band from the later 1970s, or perhaps the 1980s. That makes sense. A band of Stephen's generation. As well as being, of course, the name of the river into which Achilles was dipped, imparting him invincibility. Near-invincibility, to be precise. And the river of the Underworld. Coincidentally, she has been listening, today, to her very good Deutsche Grammophon recording of Monteverdi's *L'Orfeo*.

Stephen excuses himself to take a phone call.

"That was from Kev," he says, when he returns. "He couldn't book off work this weekend." He says it significantly, as if Kevin's non-visit, his phone call, were greatly important.

Cynthia says, "I know; he told me he was really disappointed that he couldn't make it."

So Cynthia is in touch with her brother Kevin, too. Sidonie had not known that. But why should she? She stands outside this family group, for all that she half-raised Cynthia. And now, of course,

Cynthia and Justin have a separate house, their own house, in the city. (She should perhaps have bought a place closer to them, downtown, rather than on the outskirts. It had been cheaper to buy, on the outskirts, and was closer to the airport. But it is not very close to Cynthia's house. And she had not thought that it was so close to the village where she had grown up.)

Stephen and Cynthia's brother Kevin, she seems to remember, is working as a cook in a restaurant franchise in Vancouver. He has some sort of family; he had married a woman with children of her own. She has not kept in touch.

There is no mention of Paul. Paul is lost, Paul, their other brother. He, of course, would not be expected to call or to arrive.

She remembers, now, Stephen and Kevin loitering aimlessly, as children, at a buffet. Was it after a funeral? Her father's, she thinks; they hadn't had a reception after her mother's funeral. Nor after Alice's.

Alice had called them *the savages*. The boys were wild, her mother had said. Stephen eleven or twelve, suddenly plump (when was a von Täler ever plump?), anxious, clinging. Intent on getting Alice's approval and attention. Kevin, at nine or ten, chattering ceaselessly, teasing, picking fights, running around aimlessly, careening off walls. And Paul, who was a couple of years younger yet, seven or eight, who had looked exactly like Alice, a young Alice: he had an angelic face, a perfect oval, with delicate beige brows, large, long-lashed blue eyes, a sweet mouth. His fair hair curling below his ears. And he had gone upstairs, at his grandparents' house, during the funeral reception, and opened Sidonie's suitcases, and taken out her things. Had come downstairs with some of her underwear on, over his clothes. And, she'd discovered later, after she'd returned home, had scribbled through all of her books.

How angry Buck had been, when Paul had appeared in his costume — shaking to punish the child. *I'll kick the shit out of you,* he'd said. Alice's tight smile: see what you've done now. Her eyes, turned to Sidonie for a split second: murderous. *See what you've brought on us.*

Of course, they must have all been reacting to the shock of her father's death. He'd been close to his grandsons, especially Paul. Had taken a great deal of time with them. They must have been shaken when their grandfather had died so suddenly. She hadn't been able to see that, hadn't thought of that at the time. She had not liked the children, had not attempted to engage with them, to talk to them in an auntie-ish (what is the feminine form of avuncular?) way, as she did her husband Adam's nieces, Clara's little girls. Had she been afraid? She had certainly not felt that Alice would have welcomed any interaction; she can say that in her own defense.

Then there had been Cynthia, the baby. Who had not really been a baby, but perhaps two years old. "I'm not sure that there isn't something wrong with her," Mother had said, without explanation. But Sidonie could see that, anyway; Cynthia didn't appear to talk at all, but made odd grunting noises. Didn't respond to Alice calling her until Alice walked over to her, turned Cynthia's face toward her (a little roughly, Sidonie thought) and spoke directly to her. She had an odd little face; not really appealing. A troll's face, with tufty beige hair, red-rimmed eyes, pouchy lower lids, a broad, squat nose, a wide, narrow-lipped mouth. A troll baby.

But she had seemed to like the gift Sidonie had brought her, a set of nesting wooden Russian dolls, brightly painted. She had turned the big outer doll over and over in her hands, not shaking it as most children would have, but running her fingertips over the painted flowers, returning to the seam between the head and the body.

Stephen had tried to take the doll away, to show Cynthia how it worked, and she set at him with her fists, keening in a high-pitched, anguished voice that was almost unbearable to hear. And Alice's face: a grimace of dislike.

A far cry now, of course. Look at Cynthia now. She is, in her late thirties, quite a pretty woman, wearing a little wrap dress of some silvery jersey and very high silver sandals. She is laughing, her eyes sparkling, talking to one of Stephen's friends, animatedly, using a combination of sign language and speech. She looks down at her pendant, the translucent white stone pendant, holds it up. She says something. Sidonie can read her lips across the room. *Moonstone*, she says.

That's something. She has given Cynthia a decent chance at life. Whatever she has neglected, she has done that. There is Cynthia, interacting with guests, enjoying herself, almost normal.

The man Cynthia has been talking to leans in closer; suddenly, his wife appears at his side, her hand on his arm, smiling proprietarily. Cynthia's face, like a young girl's. Defenseless.

It is perhaps a shame that Cynthia has not married. It had not seemed a good idea. What sort of man could be expected to take her on? She is managing fine now, with Justin nearly grown. But Justin will need to leave one day, will need to break those ties. And Cynthia needs someone to look after her. Sidonie can't be there for her forever.

She had taken early retirement to follow Cynthia out here to the valley, when her niece had taken it into her head to move back. It had been unthinkable that Cynthia should do it on her own, and she'd been resistant to reason. It would have been better for Justin, for example, to have the choice of universities back East. But Cynthia had kept repeating only that she wanted, above anything, to go back to her roots. Cynthia had found herself a job, had started packing.

Sidonie had sold the house in Montreal — it had been a good time; she'd gotten a good price for it — and made the move, too. She couldn't really let the two of them move across the country alone.

Cynthia and Justin together, now. You would think them brother and sister. (But who did Justin resemble, besides Cynthia?)

She is hungry still, and the crackers are all gone. But here is her grandniece, tipping a fresh heap of the little brown crackers into the basket. The girl meets her eye, almost; makes an invitational movement with her chin. Sidonie pinches up several crackers, puts one into her mouth. There. There. The enticing salt, sweet taste.

The girl winks, and is suddenly subversive, self-possessed. Sidonie warms to her. She asks, "What do you call these, these little bread crusts, with the tomato? I've had them before."

The girl tells her. She elaborates: she names all of the dishes. She reveals that the food (this bizarre, sculptural collection of *hors d'oeuvres* she had assumed had been catered) has been in fact prepared by Stephen and Debbie. The little delicacies — all made here. All made by Stephen and Debbie, with the help of this girl, *Tasha.* Short for Natasha, she remembers now. She had received birth announcements when Stephen's children had come along.

All made by hand, and with such skill. She sees then that she has missed the whole point: how has she not known this beforehand? For here is something admirable, something clear and interesting about her nephew and his wife. That they have cooked all this! And she has been oblivious. (But how to make conversation on this topic, anyway? How can it be a point of connection? She does not, herself, cook.)

"Your grandmother, my sister Alice," she says, "was good at this sort of thing. Fancy cooking. Sewing. She won prizes."

The girl nods, is possibly, though not likely, interested.

Tasha has Alice's eyes, she sees now: or not quite. The irises too pale, the epicanthic fold not pronounced enough. But there is something about the shape of the eyes, something about the lift of the eyebrow. Alice in a certain mood. Alice detached, or assuming detachment, over some impressive accomplishment: that air of self-mockery that mocked others by extension.

She's taken by an impulse to somehow recreate Alice in the girl's imagination. To lure, make an offer, to claim. Not a sensible impulse. Item: it has been on the tip of her tongue to mention the boxes, to intrigue the girl with the mention of Alice's boxes. Foolish, foolish. The girl is not likely to be interested, and Sidonie herself has reasons for avoiding opening the boxes in company. Not to mention that Cynthia has been asking about them for several months now.

What is she doing? What has gotten into her? She does not want to raise the ghost of Alice to impress this girl. She will not raise Alice's memory in this cheap way.

She says, "Ah, but young women these days have better things to do with their time and energy."

She slips out of the French doors onto the deck to collect herself.

Where is she? Can she locate herself in this knot of tall, dark houses, of nested streets? (Badger, Jackrabbit. What names. But the streets of her own neighbourhood, she realizes, carry the names of local birds. She herself lives on Quail Circle.)

Ah, yes, she recognizes this place now, this curve in the main road. It's a road she walked, or was driven along, hundreds of times as a child. A stand of ponderosa, Oregon grape, balsam-root, then. Her home a kilometre or so just over the ridge, on the flanks of the hillside. Her family's closest associates, the Inglises, a kilometre in the opposite direction. And across the road, here — yes — the cemetery road: a shortcut to the ponds, the pickers' camps, the old gold mine where she and the other children had often hiked or played, dangerously.

This little development where Stephen lives seems unattached, not the site of anything in particular. In her childhood, just a little area of land only defined by not being anyone's orchard. Who had bought it, developed it?

It must have no view: it is not close enough to the hill's slopes, but tucked into a shallow fold. But neither do the houses have yards, or only tiny ones, and they are not convenient to shops or services. Why *here*?

But of course: the orchard land is mostly still in the agricultural land reserve, and can't be developed. This new housing development has been squeezed into a small pocket of non-arable, or at least non-cultivated land.

Driving up the hill from the highway, she had seen only the familiar orchards, apparently unchanged in the twenty years since she had last visited. But are all the wooded slopes above the lake developed now?

An ache of nostalgia, of loss.

A youngish middle-aged man, one of Stephen's friends, apparently, who is smoking outside on the deck, sidles up, offers her a cigarette. She does not smoke, though she does not mind the smell of tobacco, especially outdoors. She had smoked, for a little while, in the 1960s, before the habit had resurrected her childhood asthma. In Montreal, of course, smoking is still an acceptable social activity.

Stephen's friend addresses her. "So, you grew up here," he says. "That's amazing."

"Why is it amazing?"

He must have had a few drinks, as he seems a little dazed by her reply. He says, finally, "You must have known my dad, Len Platt. I guess he was kind of a wild young guy then, eh?"

She recognizes the Platt look now: rabbit-white eyelashes, sharp, hooked chin. Shifty eyes.

"Him and Steve's dad. I guess they pulled a lot of dumb stunts. Left a trail of destruct. . ."

Her fingers curl, and he stops mid-word. His realization, the playing out of social terror in his expression, are almost comic. Almost.

He mutters an expletive, then apologizes. "Better not go there, eh?" He's squirming now, his pale Platt complexion suffused. He looks at her helplessly.

She lays her words down as cards in a hand. "Never mind," she says. "I don't think Len Platt's chronic car theft and occasional arson were in the same class as what Buck Kleinholz got up to."

"Got up to," the man echoes, automatically. His pale eyes slide sideways. He backs away.

Ah, the Platts. She should have asked after the man's aunt Lily, with whom she used to play as a small child.

When she goes back inside, Justin joins her. "Do you like the music?" he asks. Is he being mischievous?

"It's a bit cacophonous for my taste," she says. Then, not to discourage him: "I'm too old to understand your generation's music, you know."

Justin laughs. "This old stuff? I thought it was *your* music."

How strange, that a whole generation could lie between them.

"No good rock after 1973, right?" Justin asks.

Standing there in his pullover and tie, his short shining hair, he seems suddenly a little smug. Is there something a little precious about him?

But no. He's just young.

"Maybe not after 1969," she says.

She had hoped they'd leave early, but she can see that Cynthia is determined to see the party to its end. They linger and linger while the other guests are disgorged from the house. She wanders into the kitchen, where Justin is surreptitiously reading the spines of cookbooks on a shelf. There don't seem to be many books in the house. His cousins have also retreated to the kitchen; Alex is making himself a sandwich out of the buffet skewers, while his sister picks the strawberries out of the half-full punch bowl.

She recalls other parties she has attended where the hosts' grown children and their friends were a lively presence. Why has neither Alex nor the girl invited any of their own friends? They seem so uncomfortable, displaced.

Stephen comes into the kitchen, rubbing his hands together like a cartoon maître d'. "Are you kids hungry? Can I make you something else?"

No, they both say.

Stephen, she thinks, looks sad. Or perhaps just tired, disappointed.

But when Stephen leaves the room, Alex looks directly at her. "Dad says you still have some land, an orchard, here in Marshall's Landing," Alex says.

She nods.

"I'd like to see it," Alex says. His eyes are shining; his teeth flash white under his sandy beard. Of whom does he remind her? "I've asked Dad, but he isn't interested. Can you tell me which orchard it is? I've been all along the road, but I can't figure it out."

"You're interested in orcharding?" Sidonie asks. His enthusiasm is a pleasant change from the earlier diffidence.

"My great-grandparents were orchardists," he says. "Both sets, on Dad's side."

Well. That's true, in a way. But she wouldn't have put the Kleinholz's smallholding in the same category as her father's estate.

"And my great-grandparents on my mother's side were orchardists, in the Ukraine," Alex adds.

She had not known that, and it's interesting, in a way, to put Debbie's family into historical context.

"It's on the left, around the first bend, after you crest the hill," she says.

"Do you know the street number?"

She doesn't. There had not been street numbers in her time. She has not visited the orchard since her return.

Justin says, "I didn't know you still owned land here. And I can't believe you haven't been out to see it in twenty years."

She doesn't want to see it. It is being taken care of. She doesn't need to go back.

"What do you do with it?" Alex asks, speaking at the same time as Justin. (Or has he said, "What are you doing with it?" which would have meant something different, less innocent?)

She decides to answer him as if it has been the first question.

"The orchard is leased out. The house itself is empty. It's not habitable."

"You're an absentee landlord, Auntie Sid," Justin says, smirking.

Now that *is* annoying. She is getting so tired of the new versions of the local history that she has been hearing since she moved back from Montreal. It sounds almost colonial: British investors, a stratified society, indigenous and Asian labourers working for pennies a day. It wasn't quite like that.

And the land, her land — it's almost worthless. There's not enough left to be called an estate, even, now. She's just holding onto it.

Holding onto it in hopes that one day it will be worth selling, or rebuilding as an estate. (But that is a daydream, and none of this new grandnephew Alex's business.)

"It's what, a fifteen-minute drive from your house," Justin says. "I can't believe you don't go to see it! The place where you grew up!"

She shakes her head, frowns at Justin. The young don't understand about the past. To them, it's a foreign country, clearly demarcated, walled off. You have to be middle-aged before time begins its collapsing trick and you realize that the past, even the distant past, is just next door, a short walk down a grassy slope. That all of your mistakes, your regrets, your wounds and grievances have collected there, piled up. That all of the people and places you have lost are camped out there, displaced, out of reach, but just in view.

Alex says again, "I'd like to see it. Would you go with me? Would you show it to me, the house and the orchard?"

"I'm very busy," she says, discouragingly. She ought not to have engaged in this discussion to begin with. She has no interest in taking Alex to Beauvoir. Alice's children have had their share. She has been dutiful there. What is left is Sidonie's only.

Cynthia finally looks into the kitchen, says "Ready?" and Justin (who has taken off his tie and sweater; he must have been too warm) gets off his stool so hastily that it rocks and he has to catch it to prevent it from falling over. The girl laughs, not kindly.

Sidonie catches sight of herself in the simple maple-framed mirror in the hall. In her black trousers and sweater, her still-dark hair in its precise bob, she is too angular; a dark slash, a discontinuity, in the room. Nobody else is wearing black; the men are in jeans or khakis, checked shirts; the women in little coloured dresses; they look like young middle-aged party-goers in any North American city. She looks frightening, witchy. But that is not her fault. She does not belong here.

Why have Stephen and Cynthia insisted? She has nothing to offer, no connection to recover, with these middle-aged offspring of her sister's, or with their children. This would have been Alice's world, this world of houses and domestic arts. It is not hers. She is not good at it; she has repudiated it. She is not Alice. She cannot be Alice for them. And Alice is gone.

A memory, then, of the apparition on the highway this evening. Certainly not a good sign after the many years of therapy expended after Alice's death.

Who even remembers Alice now? Alice's children. Hugh would, and Walter Rilke, her old neighbour, who manages Beauvoir. Masao, if he is still alive; perhaps a smattering of other former classmates or old friends. (Alice's old friends! She could look them up. That would be a project. But why? What would be the use?)

Better to let go: to accept the loss. To sever, to amputate, to prune away. For after all, in this country of her past, the dead outnumber the living. Alice, Mother, Father, Graham, Mrs. Inglis. No doubt also most of her teachers, her parents' friends, her neighbours, who would otherwise be very elderly. If she begins to visit, she will be pulled in; the weight of losses will pull her under.

She should never have come. (She should never have come back.)

She has nothing in common with this nephew and his family; they belong to different worlds. Cynthia can visit if she wants; Sidonie need not. She does not need this sort of social contact, this forced familial interaction. There is no bond, here. She barely remembers Stephen; saw him two or three times as a child, attended his wedding twenty years ago. She would not know him, if not for the accident of birth.

She has not avoided family entanglements these four decades to be trapped by them now. More reasonable to create one's own family out of congenial company, as she had been thinking earlier.

They say protracted goodbyes at the door, only Stephen's and Cynthia's to each other sounding sincere. She feels a reprieve. She will refuse any subsequent invitations to this house.

She waits for Cynthia and Justin on the top step, outside the door. The moon has risen and is visible behind the messy twist of pine branches, through the dead pines at the edge of this new subdivision. It is caged in a snarl of broken, dead limbs.

How has she made this mistake, to return here? But she will draw herself in; she will regroup, rethink. She begins to descend Stephen's front steps.

And then, turning to look back for an instant, she slips, her weak ankle, the ankle she has favoured since the winter before, when she had sprained it in Montreal, turning under her, her foot twisting in a sudden, irrevocable wrench and crack.

She clutches the heavy iron railing and manages to fall on her bottom and not her face. But the pain: waves of it traveling up though her leg, her trunk, and spreading (she can feel it, from the inside) across her face and scalp.

Stephen's wife Debbie says "Oh, Auntie!" with what sounds more like exasperation than alarm, and gets a bag of frozen peas from the refrigerator, and Stephen and Cynthia try to haul her to her feet and back into the house. But she will not go back inside; no, no. She is being unreasonable. She is making more trouble. But she will not go. Cynthia wrings her hands; Debbie flutters. She is a dead weight on Stephen; she hears him grunt, feels her own mass press down cruelly on his meat and bone.

Then more arms are under her, around her: Alex and Justin have moved in to assist Stephen. Under many arms, she is hoisted, supported more evenly. Now she can find her balance, put down her good foot, help support herself.

She allows herself to be hobbled to the car and sits on the passenger seat, the car door open, the frozen peas burning her instep.

Beyond the pain, rage. She had not wanted to go to Stephen's for dinner, but Cynthia had made a fuss. *Family*, she had said, playing that trump card. Why should it matter? Old guilt, old burdens and omissions. She is captive to them still; they all are. She had given in, against her better judgment, thinking: it is only for one evening. And now she will pay much more than she had bargained for. Stupid, stupid.

BRIDGE

She has broken one of the bones in her foot: a small bone, called the lateral cuneiform. The emergency-room doctor who sets the bone shows her a diagram. "It's the bridge of your foot, between your heel and your toes," he says. "It connects all of these parts and makes them articulate: see? If it were one of these long bones, the phalanges, or one of these little cuboid bones of the heel, we would not worry so much. But with the bridge broken, the foot can do nothing. It must be put in a cast, and it must not bear weight."

She will be, she calculates, out of commission for six weeks. The pain, at first, is excruciating, but more so, the thought of being immobile. She is able to hobble around her house with crutches; can even manage the stairs, clutching the railing, hopping. But she can't drive her car, which has standard transmission. She can't go out walking along the little lake.

Stupid. Stupid.

Cynthia has said: call anytime. But she does not call. She will not be supplicant. She will tough it out.

She lasts five days.

Justin calls her. (Cynthia can hear a little, can lip-read, but can't manage on the phone.) "You must be out of groceries."

She is, she admits painfully, nearly out of groceries. And other things, too: toilet paper, reading material. But she will not bother Cynthia, who works such long hours. She can wait until the weekend. She is making things more difficult, she knows, but cannot stop herself from this demurring.

But no: here is Cynthia, within a couple of hours, with Justin, carrying bags of lettuce and lemons and hothouse tomatoes; steaks and eggs; a loaf of crusty, chewy, acidic bread, which Sidonie tears into, wolf-like, when they have barely left.

She is subjected to the indignity of Cynthia poking through her refrigerator and cupboards, scolding, not so much as a potato in here! But this officiousness is amusing, too: it seems only a few years ago that their roles had been reversed. She herself, or more likely Adam, scolding: how will you take care of yourself? Do you think food magically appears in the cupboards?

Cynthia says, "I've signed you up for the local paper to be delivered."

No no no. "I don't need it, thanks. I get *The Globe and Mail*."

But Cynthia has turned her face, pretending not to hear.

Her neighbour knocks on her front door, the classic casserole dish in her hands. She has avoided this neighbour: the woman in the other half of the duplex, whom she sees often coming down her mirror-steps, carrying one of those flat-faced, owl-eyed, blonde dogs that look at you like autistic children. (Is it her imagination, or does this woman always leave her house just as she does herself? Does she watch from behind those sheer drapes for another human being to appear?)

"Beef and noodle," the woman says. "I hope you're not vegetarian?"

"No," Sidonie says. "I am not."

"I didn't think so," her neighbour says. "I can smell meat cooking sometimes."

The irritation of being watched: she feels herself grimace.

"Your daughter and grandson, I see them come visit," the woman says.

"My niece and grandnephew."

"Oh? Right then. It looks like you have someone taking care of you."

"Yes."

"Well, that's good. Your grandnephew, he's a nice-looking boy. I couldn't think who he reminded me of. Then it came to me, in the checkout at Safeway. He's the image of that young actor, what d'you call him, that Leonardo."

Sidonie shifts her weight. She will need to put down her crutches to receive the casserole dish, but she will not invite her neighbour over the threshold if she can help it.

"He's at the university, is he? What a nice-looking boy he is, and so polite."

"Yes." The exposure. She wonders perversely: is Justin too polite? Is it a bad sign?

"Here," her neighbour says. "I'll just put it in your kitchen for you." And she kicks off her rubber clogs, moves through the doorway and past Sidonie, jostling the door open a little as she goes with her elbow, bustling down the hallway in her stockinged feet to the kitchen, as if she knows exactly where it is. Of course she does. Her house is a mirror image of this one.

Then she leaves, pulling the door shut behind her carefully, and Sidonie breathes again. There's something almost too chipper about her neighbour. Too casual. A prairie accent. She is not used to the informality of the West, now. Familiar, that's the word. She does not like having a stranger whisk through her house like that. She does not like the thought of someone making her way, on the other side of the walls, around a space that is a mirror-image of her house. She will admit this. It makes her occupancy of her semi-detached house seem even more random, unintentional than it already does.

But the casserole is tasty, laced with sour cream and paprika, juicy with mushrooms.

The things she has had shipped from Montreal — the contents of her apartment — do not fill up the rooms of her new house, and neither do they seem to belong in it. Her odd bits of furniture, her rugs and pictures, which in her Montreal flat had seemed rich, layered, polyphonous, organic, seem here only unrelated and shabby. Light and openness have disconnected objects from one another, so that the effect has been unpacked, disassembled. Her tables and chairs and rugs are stranded; the house looks like a sparsely-stocked second-hand store. She hasn't even hung her pictures, for when she took them out of their crates, they had seemed too dark, too strong, and yet too small to hang on the pale walls.

She could get rid of all her furniture and pictures, buy new. Or she could tear out the kitchen, with its pale cabinets, its cold faux-marble surfaces, put in something darker, more sober. Paint the interior some deeper, more substantial colour, to suit her furnishings. Such waste, though, to dismantle an almost-new house. And the exterior, which she may not alter, would be disharmonic.

She doesn't know how to make this house seem right, intentional.

Her sister, Alice, had known that sort of thing. It had been her province. Alice won competitions in the sewing of piles of flowered flour sacks into ruffled café curtains and slipcovers with coordinating piped cushions. Sidonie had not been able to sew a straight seam. And it had been Clara who had arranged the furniture and pictures in Sidonie's Montreal flat. Clara and Anita, her sisters-in-law: they had descended on her, after she had left their brother, and had struggled and heaved, thumped and shaken her new place into that richly-coloured and textured nest. Clara had taken her down to Jaymar to buy that sofa, for Adam had insisted on keeping the le Corbusier pieces. Clara had dickered with Adam for the other furniture, the Barcelona chairs, the Eames lamps; Sidonie wouldn't have bothered. And Anita had selected the paintings and photographs out of the collection that Sidonie and Adam — but mostly Adam — had bought, over their twenty years together. Anita had selected the ones that she thought would do for Sidonie, an assortment that Adam had agreed to relinquish, and Anita had painted the walls of Sidonie's new apartment oxblood and teal and plum.

While Sidonie had sat and watched, passive, dazed, exhausted by the effort of having left Adam, dazed and exhausted perhaps by the change itself.

Strange to think that time is twenty years in the past.

In the blue winter light of her new house, her flat in Montreal seems in retrospect a jeweled tent, a Shangri-la from which she has been evicted. Though she has chosen that eviction, chosen exile.

Perhaps she needs Clara and Anita here to orchestrate her new place. She misses Clara, whom she saw weekly in Montreal — Clara with her indefatigable willingness to analyze any subject, to test it with anecdote and counteridea, to joke about it and weep over it, to wear it down to a few bright shreds. Clara, always arriving with a box of éclairs, a new book, tickets to the play that everyone would be talking about. She misses Anita, too; Anita, cut from the same cloth as Adam and Clara, but always a little mysterious; quiet, then surprising. Anita, who out of silence made a pronouncement that had one thinking for days. Anita who, looking at a picture, a building, a street scene, would point out the object or pattern that suddenly shifted the whole into a new frame.

She needs Clara and Anita here to make sense of her domestic arrangements, her new neighbourhood. To define and delineate them.

Though she had wanted to get away from Clara and Anita. Had wanted to escape.

Perhaps. Perhaps she will admit that. Otherwise, it is all like shipwreck. Arctic shipwreck. She is Franklin, marooned by bad decisions and hubris. A ship in ice; a stone, half-buried in frozen mud.

She has not enough warmth to light her life up on her own. It is chill; a cold hearth. It has been a mistake, this house.

It has been a mistake to come back. No, not a mistake: too inconsequential a word, implying that there will be other mistakes, other opportunities. It has been a grievous error, the sort of error that, as she grows older, she realizes cannot be undone, contrary to the reassurances, in her youth, of articles in popular magazines, of

Sunday School teachers. Miss Erskine, with her tweed skirts and knee socks, her shapeless sweaters — jumpers, she called them — the heavy soft valise of her breasts resting on her abdomen, even though she must have been young, in her late twenties or early thirties at most. Daphne Erskine, with her smooth, earnest girl's face, her overbite, her thin, straight, beige hair. She'd be dead now. Or would she? Perhaps not; she had not been that much older than Sidonie. Miss Erskine, Sunday School teacher and Girl Guide leader: the two roles blended into one, somehow, with Jesus asking after the state of their fingernails and teaching Good Sportsmanship, and Lady Baden-Powell inquiring after the state of their souls. Miss Erskine, all fuzzy layers of woolen vests, saying, *Girls, there is no mistake you can't undo.* An odd idea for the sister of a Protestant vicar, surely.

But this error that has cost her too much, in its enacting, to reverse, and that will thus bend and distort the rest of her life, will strew small and large items of regret along her path from now on. She can't go back; she has retired from her profession, sold her apartment, accepted farewell gifts from her friends and colleagues, and ignored the advice of those closest to her. She has bought a house, moved her furniture and books across the country. There is no going back. It is an irreversible error.

Clara calls, says, "You sound like you're waiting for something. Not living your life. What are you waiting for?"

The bone in her foot to heal, obviously.

"No, before your accident, even, you've had this tone. You're just marking time."

"I'm waiting for spring," Sidonie says.

Clara makes a disapproving tongue click down four thousand kilometres of optic fibre cable. (Or is it all microwaves, now?) "You're willing to spend half of the year waiting for the weather to change? Does everyone do that, out there?"

"No," Sidonie says. "Some ski."

"Or maybe you are procrastinating over something," Clara says.

Clara, her conscience, who has been keeping tabs on her, keeping her on a leash, these decades; who has hung tight to Sidonie, even after Adam let go his hold.

Sidonie thinks, not for the first time, that possibly it was to move further out of Clara's range that she has moved back, after all these years.

She doesn't try to explain what she is doing with her days.

Her other former sister-in-law, Anita, telephones a day later: obviously Clara has put her up to it. "But I approve of you having some downtime," she says. She believes that Sidonie has fallen intentionally, as a way of leaving the rat race. "It's all about the mind-body connection. Have you thought of trying yoga?"

But her body has betrayed her; she does not want to pay it attention. She does not tell her former sisters-in-law how she fills her time; she does not quite know herself. Before her accident, she had filled two hours a day marching around the little lake, her boots bristling with spikes and springs, ski poles probing for hidden ice. She had marched around the lake, a forced march, staving off stagnation. Now she hasn't even that.

What she should be doing, in fact, is working. She has work: chores not completed when she left the Institute. Books she has been asked to read and review for journals. An article she is supposed to be writing for JASC, a conference paper with a near deadline. She had made a good start, too, rattling through a couple of unfinished reports in the first few weeks in the fall. She had thought: at this rate, I'll be at loose ends in about twenty-one months. But since then, she has been unable to submerge in her work. She limps about the house, picking objects up and replacing them, checks her email, follows esoteric and irrelevant internet links. She has not written more than a few hundred words.

Why should it be difficult? She has read and digested and written all of her adult life. She has produced dozens of articles and conference papers, and two books. She has years of research material to write up, still: has looked forward for years to a fallow period, a break from the endless jostling and chatter of work to be able to write it all up. She is no undergraduate to be stymied by the empty page (or screen).

The sorting of data, the assembling of information, of observations, into meaningful order, the selecting and presenting that is required, seem all beyond her just now. It is as if a break has opened between one part of her brain and the other. A new stoppage somewhere in the processing room. She has the material, but she cannot seem to conceive of a use for it, a way of disseminating it. Her mind lies unproductive, stalled.

She gazes out of the window, which needs cleaning; she glances at the clock. (It seems always to be four p.m., surely the most useless time of day.) She stumps around on her crutches. She opens the refrigerator and shuts it. She checks her email. She looks at various internet sites that sell classical recordings. It is shameful, to be in this state. She is guilty of sloth.

Sidonie's mother would have found chores for her to do. She had been a great believer in manual labour. Neither Sidonie nor Alice had ever dared admit to boredom. When they had free time, they escaped, made themselves scarce, in order to have the luxury of dawdling, of lallygagging. Or Sidonie had: she can't speak for Alice, can't swear now to Alice ever seeking solitude. Though she surely must have tried to escape chores. Even Alice must have occasionally ducked chores.

Plucking stones from her mother's garden plot, she remembered as the azimuth of childhood ennui and ill-usage. Blue clay lay below the loam, below the thin topsoil coaxed with its yearly feedings of compost and rotted horse manure. The blue clay spat up stone after stone, dribbles of granite, quartz-speckled eggs, which they must gather in galvanized tin buckets, spring after spring, gumbo agglomerating on gumboots, bent-over back seizing, leaping sixty years forward in its cramps and spasms. Cold-stiffened fingers bruised by the stones; nails, already chewed and chipped, further reduced to splinters. And the stones never stopped surfacing. Father, striding by in his leather breeches that never wore out, his knit-by-mother wool socks, his boots: *Ah, the labours of Hercules, girls! Good work, good work!*

Her mother, like the medieval Christian monks, like the Buddhists, had believed in the efficacy of manual work as a grounding exercise. And she herself has designed experiments in manual activity for specific kinds of developmental issues. Digital manipulation, the working of the palms and fingers in sand boxes and sinks, miniature gardens, Lego and Meccano sets. Standard ideas in her field, now, but she had been a pioneer researcher. And she had been unique in prescribing goals, so that the activities resembled work, rather than open-ended play. (She wonders, now, briefly, if anyone has used her ideas in conjunction with large motor stimulation — labour, in other words — and has given subjects large plots of earth to dig up, floors to scrub. Probably some ethical difficulties there. People of her parents' generation, of course, had no qualms about child labour.)

But her mother, her father: they would not have, had not, recognized much of what she has been engaged in as *work*. Is that the issue? She had produced a lot of work at the Institute. She had kept on target. She had kept her division on target, ahead of target, month after month (however the junior staff might complain). She and her team had designed and tested and created computer models for dozens of experiments each year, and these experiments had been performed, and knowledge gained.

She has designed experiments to test the learning, which is to say the memory, of mice and men and mutant fruit flies, of monkeys and dolphins, newborn humans and those with senile dementia. She has seen her experiment designs used to discover the growth of neuron paths in flatworms, fireflies, houseflies and helmetless bicycle-accident victims. She has provided the means to test hundreds of premises, and dozens of potential therapeutic remedies. She has seen, as a result of her work, cautious results of reversal (more precisely, adaptation to) profound brain trauma. She has seen results of her work used to etch, with lasers, unhappy memories in the brains of fruit flies.

Work of the eyes and brain: of the head. Had she limited herself too much, there? She has practiced the discipline of putting ideas to paper, of assembling and compiling information for decades;

it is in her bones. Are her bones now rejecting it? For they refuse to move into the rhythm of reading and writing. She feels this resistance as an actual stiffness, she notices: an inability to flex muscles, to bend, to incline: a disinclination. She is unproductive, unable to move forward.

It does not make sense: she has time now to work, and she does not work. Perhaps she has needed the pressure of the group, after all? But she had been a loner, an intellectual *coureur de bois*. (That was not her term: her director, Dr. Haephestes, had used it, beaming with apparent genuineness, in his speech at her retirement dinner in the fall. She is not sure now that the term was meant entirely as praise.) She had led teams, given direction. (She had not been particularly good at working in a team, but she had led teams.) Is it that she misses her assistants, her researchers and technicians, the way a paraplegic misses limbs?

She has been happy, since her move, only when working, she realizes. And now she does not work.

Is she wallowing? She is wallowing. *Accidie*. Another sin.

"I have a question," her niece Cynthia announces, in her thickened speech. They are eating at a popular franchise restaurant off the highway, in the strip that extends now ten kilometres north from the city. It's noisy, and Sidonie has to lean forward to understand her. (Perhaps she is starting to lose her own hearing?) She has been expecting a question or request. Cynthia doesn't often take lunches during the week; she says she doesn't have time. She is an art teacher at an elementary school, and expected to do extracurricular things at noon hour. And here it's a Wednesday, and she has asked to meet Sidonie for lunch.

Cynthia, in her late thirties, looks younger, as women of her generation seem to do. Prolonged adolescence: women in their forties dress like teenagers. Well-off women, at least. Entering the restaurant, Sidonie had seen her first from the back, her shoulder-length blonde hair, her puffy silvery parka, her slim, low-slung jeans, and had not recognized her. Had thought she was a young girl, at first.

"Go ahead," she says. A habit of Cynthia's childhood, to announce formally that she has a question, before asking it. Even if the question is minor. Perhaps it is something she was taught at her school for the deaf; an aid to being understood more precisely.

"The question is about my mother," Cynthia says.

She is wearing a very thin T-shirt with an odd screen-printed image of the moon, and a lot of silver jewelry — three chains, one with a silver arrow pendant, one with a bluish translucent stone, and a silver bracelet set also with semi-precious blue stones. Cynthia is fond, Sidonie notices, of a certain kind of hand-made, artisanal costume jewelry.

"Yes; go ahead." She keep her voice calm; doesn't show irritation at her niece, who is fiddling with her fork. Why can't Cynthia ever broach a subject naturally? It is not as if she ever says no. *You spoil her,* Clara has said, on many occasions. *You don't have to make everything up to her.* But apparently she does.

"I wanted to ask you," Cynthia asks, "if you've thought some more about letting me look at my mother's things?"

Cynthia has asked this of her, now, a few times. An ingenious answer is needed, to buy time: all of her alarm bells are going off. Sidonie says, "I've been busy. . . ."

What is there, besides Alice's little boxes of keepsakes, of schoolwork and party invitations, that Cynthia might be interested in? There are, in fact, two dozen or more large boxes and trunks from Beauvoir, and they have been in storage for four decades. She does not know what is in them, precisely. Or rather, in part of her brain there is a precise index of those boxes, but she is not, at present, willing to access it.

Cynthia says, "You said once that you had kept her personal things, and you would give them to me when I was grown up and had a place of my own."

Had she said that? But she must have. And now, certainly, Cynthia is grown up. Grown up, with a nearly grown child of her own. She is not likely to carelessly leave something behind in a move, or to let small children spoil things. Sidonie has been procrastinating, avoiding, locking her mind against it. Though she hasn't succeeded in forgetting about it.

"Yes, you should have them," Sidonie says. Why is she so reluctant to admit this? A relief, surely, to have them taken off her hands. "They're mostly things from her childhood, you understand. You might not find them that interesting. Our mother, your grandmother, kept everything Alice ever. . ." She had been about to say 'touched', but that sounded off, in her own head. ". . . everything Alice ever wrote, and all of her little ornaments and bits of jewelry. Nothing of value, of course."

"Except to you and I," Cynthia says.

She can't resist deflecting the point with a correction. "You and *me*," she says. "To you and *me*. They're all in a muddle, the boxes from the old house. It will take me some time to get them out for you. They should all be sorted."

This is true. She had retrieved the boxes from the storage facility, when she moved back. They need to be sorted; most of what is in them needs, likely, to be thrown away. She has been procrastinating. She has had some idea about sorting the papers — she knows that there are invoices, letters, ledgers from the orchards — with a view to donating them to a local archive. That sort of thing is, apparently, useful. There are even university courses in the history of orcharding. And she ought to go through the photographs, too.

"Where are the boxes?" Cynthia asks. "Are they here, in town? I think you said they were in a storage unit?"

She had not meant to admit it, but she is powerless against direct questions.

"In my basement now."

"Oh," Cynthia says, in her slightly guttural speech. Then: "I wonder if you would be willing to let Justin or I help you sort the things out."

Justin or *me*, not Justin or I. But she does not correct her niece this time.

"I'll think about it," she says.

What Alice has left behind. Well, it's out of her control, except for those boxes in her basement, the little odds and ends of a life. Those she can deal with. She will take them on. It is her duty. She sees, too, that what is required of her is something more than sorting through the boxes that half-fill her basement. What Cynthia wants is a history, a background, a past. Understandably, perhaps. Sidonie has always been taciturn on the subject of Cynthia's parents. With good reason, of course.

But now more is required. Sidonie can understand that, though she herself is suspicious of this kind of investigation. What one is likely to turn up is rarely useful, and usually only what one already knows. It is the nature of human beings, as well as other sentient things, to try to fit anything new into the patterns they already know.

Yes, a dubious exercise, this knitting up of narratives. Very few have the perception, the curiosity, the courage, perhaps, to really discover anything useful.

But she will begin to sort through the boxes. She hasn't the excuse of a shortage of time, and it would be churlish not to. Also, she would very much prefer, now that she thinks of it, to do this herself, rather than to have Cynthia or one of her reprobate brothers, or any of their children, take it on, either before or after Sidonie's demise. She might as well face facts: she will not be around forever. At some point, someone will have to deal with these things. And there are things that she wants to protect them from, things they likely should not see. As well as things she wants to protect from their eyes.

She allows Justin to fetch her in Cynthia's car, drive her to the mall, where they may rent, for a nominal sum, a wheelchair, and travel up and down the corridors with their polished stone floors: temples, she thinks, to materialism and conspicuous consumption. She can see that even to someone Justin's age, there is something faintly embarrassing about the mall; something bourgeois. Clara and Anita disapprove, highly, of shopping malls. Yet how open and accessible, compared to the fusty department stores of the city when she had been taken to shop here, as a child. Fulmerton's, Bennett's, with their smell of rubber boots, their utilitarian racks of drab dresses, their supercilious sales clerks. At the mall, she buys socks, underwear. Buys herself some blue jeans, which she has not worn in nearly fifty years, so long ago that they were called dungarees.

She sits with Justin, in the long afternoons when he has no classes, in cafés, as she and Adam — or more precisely, Adam — had sat with Cynthia in cafés twenty years ago, and lets him talk. Justin, like other eighteen-year-olds she knows, does not know what he "wants to do," as he puts it. He gets good marks in all of his subjects, he says. None appeals to him more than the others. She sees that there is a gap, a disconnect, between his sense of what he likes to do and what he knows or imagines work to be. This state, too, is not uncommon in his generation — a generation of dilettantes, she thinks. We have provided too much. They have not learned the discipline of work.

She recalls her parents and their friends saying the same thing.

In the mall, she sees Justin surreptitiously looking at displays of clothing with skull decorations, loose, long, hooded jackets, and short pants and high-topped sneakers.

"What is it?"

"Nothing. The hoodie, there."

"Do you want to go in and look at it?"

"No. . . no. It's too young for me."

"Oh, for crying out loud," she says, surprising herself, her mother's voice rising through her. She makes him turn around, wheel the chair into the store, between the electronic sensors. He explains to her the motifs of skateboarding culture. She offers him the word "iconoclasm," watches him store it carefully. She buys him the jacket. She supposes that she feels an attachment for Justin because of those early months of close association, when he and Cynthia had lived under her roof, when she had helped to care for him. She does not think of this time often — it was a short time, less than two years. It had been difficult for various reasons, including the practical difficulty of having a baby under the same roof. She had not been used to babies. She had been a great deal worried about Cynthia at that time, and about other things.

It is not especially fondness or pride or protectiveness that she feels, though. She perceives him, necessarily, as healthy and thriving in a transparent bubble. An odd conceit. She has never spoken of it to anyone. She is careful not to speak of Justin to anyone except Cynthia, and then only cautiously. She does not wish to invite scrutiny or censure, or to encroach on someone else's territory. She will not be proprietary.

She had, many nights, walked Justin, a colicky infant, up and down the length of her apartment while Cynthia, still more or less a child herself, had slept. She had tried not to become attached to him, knowing that the arrangement was temporary, that Cynthia would finish her degree and leave. And believing or suspecting at some level that Justin represented some deep, unimaginable betrayal.

She has Justin drive downtown, right to Water Street, to see how the new bridge is progressing. She has seen, in the newspaper, the architectural drawings, the proposed span — an arc like a flattened bell curve, an unusually broad distribution, in statistical terms. Now there is only a great deal of metal grid work, like a spiky, angular sculpture: reinforcement or scaffolding, she cannot tell.

"I remember the old bridge, the first bridge, being built," she says to Justin. "It had the largest floating span in North America."

"Yes, I have heard that," Justin says. Politely.

"The middle section, the part that rises, was also innovative. People used to drive up to watch it open, at first. It would open at regular times, I believe, to let sailboats with their tall masts through. It was very modern."

"It looks very steampunk," Justin says. "The counterweight and so on. Like a drawbridge. What did people do before the bridge?"

"There was a ferry."

"That must have been *slow*," Justin says. "I can't imagine a ferry transporting all this traffic."

Of course, there had not been nearly so much traffic. The bridge had made the expansion, the travel across the lake feasible. And the new, wider bridge would, presumably, open the floodgates even more.

A phenomenon she has seen in her lifetime: the proliferation of the automobile, and the attendant *growth*, if that is the right word, of cities, towns. What will happen, then, to the land, the earth and trees, the countryside that lies at the feet, is known through the feet? What will happen to the small catchments of humans who recognize and are recognized by each other, in the context of the folds and valleys, the plants and trees? Will it matter?

How will people properly locate themselves in this man-made world? But what effort, what great effort to try to preserve a little paradise. How much planning, how great a cost, how much reliance on timing and fruition.

Justin says, sounding middle-aged, "I think all of this development spoils the landscape. Where is it going to end?"

His fine-boned neck and jaw emerging from the heavy hooded cotton jacket, the one she bought him. His long, fine fingers on the steering wheel.

As a child, she had not known what the valley looked like, in geological terms. The big ordnance maps that the high school geography teacher had unrolled for them — school atlases, in those days, hadn't contained detailed maps of British Columbia — had shown the irregular outlines of the lakes, and the meandering canals that connected them. The flattish foreshore of the smallest lake, where she now lives, marked in the three-stemmed symbols that represent marshland.

But the maps' contour lines had not translated themselves in her imagination into the landscape she knew: the steep arid hillsides with their gullies, their sparse ponderosa, rabbit bush, yellowed bunchgrass; the marshaled green rows of fruit trees, their lush understory; the flat bottoms of the valleys, where rows of tomatoes and cabbages and onions grew from the black soil, and cottonwoods shaded the lakeshores. And later, flying in or out of the valley, she'd caught only glimpses: the plane slipping below the clouds to reveal a slab of lake and sparse forest and the rows and loops of streets like diorama miniatures.

But now she has seen the whole of the valley, its clefts and tendons, its coloured-resin bodies of water, spread in a patchwork of satellite photographs across her computer screen. She has flown, virtually, across and along the valley, skimming trees, rooftops, the wrinkled cobalt surfaces of the lakes. Has seen that the three smaller lakes, in their chain, are one lake, interrupted. Or were, a few millennia ago. That all the lakes were one, even further back in time: a single inland sea, filling the whole valley, extending further south, where now still more small lakes form a kind of coda as the valley drains into the Columbia basin.

The peaks and highest ridges must have been islands in a great blue expanse. Then, as the lake slowly receded, arms and inlets forming where now the smaller lakes lie, cut off. Or had it happened suddenly: a cataclysmic rush as the glacial stopper at the valley's southern neck suddenly popped? Roaring water scouring deep holes, carving a channel through to the Columbia, and then south and west to the sea?

Justin has downloaded the link, set up the icon, the little blue and white marble on the screen. She has flown up and down the valley, has skimmed in over the long central ridge, has searched out the grids of green dots that are the orchards, the patches of random scrub and ponderosa, the yellow grass of the slopes. She has found out the gullies, the rock outcroppings. She has found out the dips where natural springs hide — the thickets of willow and fir and saskatoon that burrow there for water. She has followed the paths of the alkaline ponds, the unlikely turquoise and emerald of the ponds, as they string across the hillsides, drawing up bitter salts, giving back no life. She has discovered how green spreads up from the valley basins, from the lakes, carried artificially by the hidden arterial pipes. How the green stops abruptly at the edges of steeper slopes and gullies, where the natural arid life of the region reasserts itself.

She has spent much time in this virtual travel. She is grateful to Justin for his enablement.

She thinks, sometimes, that Cynthia does not appreciate Justin as she should, that she doesn't see what a miracle it is for grace and intelligence to come together in so young a person. How unusual, how valuable the boy is. Her mother and father would have seen him as she does: the heir to all they built.

It is not reasonable to make a boy the anointed one. She can attest to that. But he will be the one to take it on. If not Justin, then who?

"Can you drive a manual shift?" she asks.

"I can," Justin says, with, she thinks, more bravado than accuracy.

She arranges for him to be dropped off at her house by Cynthia, gives him the keys to her new BMW, lets him drive around the town-house complex, then up and down the highway, to show her that he can change gears without taking his eyes off the road. With great effort, she maintains a calm posture, a relaxed expression.

"You can use the car," she says, "in exchange for driving me around."

His joy fermenting, sealed down, only his widened eyes speaking. She breathes deeply through the adrenaline-rush of her risk-taking.

Mid-February: St. Valentine's Day. The 5:40 jet shakes her windows. She crutches her way to the kitchen, slides the black plastic dish into the microwave oven.

The ringing of the phone startles her; for a few seconds she confuses it with the sound of the microwave timer, so unused is she to the phone ringing, so unexpected a call, and answers only on the third ring.

"Took you long enough," Hugh says. "Six rings. I almost hung up."

"Three rings," she says.

"At least five. Do you always go to bed this early?"

"Hugh. It's not even six o'clock here. I am making my supper."

She is not so surprised to hear from Hugh. They had kept in touch, as people do, via Christmas cards and then Christmas emails, for the last few decades. But now, since her move back to the valley, he has been calling every few weeks, has promised to visit. He's consulting on the new bridge, or claims to be, though she has not seen his name connected with the engineering companies mentioned in the newspaper articles. Still, Hugh is supposed to be retired.

She wonders, though, what it is Hugh wants of her.

"I am watching the news on the Internet," Hugh says. "I tried to Skype you, but you aren't online. Why don't you leave the computer on like a normal person?"

"Distraction," she says. "What's on the news, Hugh?"

"Have you been paying any attention to what's going on in Rhodesia?"

"You mean Zimbabwe?"

He ignores this. "Three thousand percent inflation, for god's sake. What do you think it's like to live with that economy, Sidonie?"

He sounds like he's accusing her of something, but she knows him too well to take his tone personally. "I can't imagine," she says, "although my father could have told you."

Hugh is distracted for a moment. "Eh? Oh, yes. Well, that makes it worse, doesn't it, seeing where it can lead. I'm just back from Harare, you know. What a mess. I tell you, I'm alarmed."

Why is he telling her all this? She feels it is nothing to do with her. Hugh is addicted to the Internet news.

But she remembers then: his youngest daughter lives in Zimbabwe still, with her mother. Hugh likes to talk about his offspring; he has five or six. It is the kind of topic she finds boring, from friends or colleagues. Almost as bad as stories about dogs.

She changes the subject. "How is the work on the bridge progressing?"

He growls, and there's a tirade against the other engineers, the city council, the province, and the whole bridge project. She doesn't understand half of his terminology, but he isn't paying much attention to whether she's following him, anyway. She can picture him, pacing his apartment, wearing his headset, his lower jaw thrust out, his clipped ivory mustache, like an Eskimo carving, riding his lip, twitching. She can hear in the background what sounds like two competing voices; either he has two computer screens on or one and the television.

"The work seems to have started," Sidonie says. "They're building the on-ramp on the town side. I've seen photos on the news. Do you like the design?" she asks, and Hugh stops his rant abruptly.

"Yes. Very much!"

She does not know why he should sound so surprised by her question.

Surprising to her, still, that Hugh is part of her life again. Hugh, solid, blunt, grounded. She cannot remember not knowing Hugh, though he claims to remember a time before her advent. Not the same Hugh, of course: Hugh-the-boy, who is now erased by the white hair and leathery arms of Hugh-the-man.

Her earliest memories must be of the back of Hugh: his tow head, his grey knit shirt and short pants ahead of her. She has always known him, and he has always taken charge of her. "No dawdling, now!" he'd always called to her, over his shoulder, as they'd trudged up and down the hills. "No faltering, men!"

Hugh is the bridge to her earliest self. He is the only one left, she thinks, who knew her, who remembers growing up in the orchards, remembers the hills and the lakes as they were, remembers the small universe of their school and playmates, their childhood pleasures. Hugh remembers her parents and Alice — as she remembers his parents and Graham. She does not think about the past often, but she does not like to think that she alone remembers it. Hugh is necessary for that connection. But what does he want from her?

She has kept her distance from him these past few months; it has been Hugh who has initiated all the conversations. But now, housebound, on crutches, in the cold dirty end of winter, the uncertain, messy beginning of spring, she finds herself taking somewhat more of an interest in his calls. She can see that if she pays too much attention, she will step over some invisible line, and then the existence of Hugh will begin to take up too much of her time.

The time she divides, now, between randomly springboarding between Internet sites — videos and blogs and obscure articles — and hanging out with Justin in malls and cafés. She has become a disaffected youth, to use the term popular in her own youth.

Which had been not at all disaffected.

"I'll be out next month," Hugh says. "April at the latest."

Her microwave oven beeps for the third time. How long has she got before the ragout dries out? Should she just say to Hugh, I'm cooking my dinner right now; I'll ring you back?

She finds cooking only for herself boring and pointless: she does not think much about food. The refrigerator that came with the townhouse has a capacious lower freezer drawer in which she keeps neat stacks of prepared entrées in plastic and cardboard boxes, from the frozen food section of Safeway. They can be warmed quickly in the microwave, and are not at all unpleasant, though of course they do not compare with the meals she was accustomed to in Montreal, which she usually bought at the deli on her way home. Every two weeks, she buys a dozen different entrées and stores them: it's much more logical for one person than obtaining ingredients and cooking.

It is true that when Cynthia and Justin have come for dinner, Sidonie has had to buy great quantities of dishes. She sees that mini-meals might not be a feasible option if she were to have guests on a regular basis. Her cupboards, though, contain the necessities: coffee, wine, olives. Apples in the refrigerator, and cheese. And packages of pre-washed lettuce and greens. (Her mother's astonishment and disapproval if she were to see a handful of baby arugula and butter lettuce leaves packaged in a cellophane tub and sold for six dollars.) But how convenient, how easy, to open the tub and mound the leaves on a plate. How easy it is to be nutritionally virtuous, with vegetables already washed, sorted, and de-bugged.

She knows what it means, too, that she doesn't cook her own meals, that she eats raw things, or food pre-cooked and packaged. She has read her Lévi-Strauss.

"Well, I thought I'd just touch base with you," Hugh says, and then, adds, surprisingly, "A happy St. Valentine's Day to you," before he rings off, finally. But she has not been paying attention, the past few minutes, to his call. It is too late for the ragout; it's lukewarm, and reheating it creates a sticky, scorched, rubbery mess. She eats a few bites, puts the rest in the trash, makes some toast, feeling unsatisfied and a little aggrieved. She could heat another meal; but the spoiling of the first makes another seem distasteful.

She should cook food for herself. All this packaged food is likely very high in preservatives. There is something wrong with it. It will rot her insides, give her cancer. The packaging — which is Styrofoam, she notices, though disguised with some sort of black colouring (and is that also carcinogenic? It looks as if it might be) — will not break down in the landfill. (Does the landfill still lie to the west, off the back road, an old alkali pond shedding sprays of effluvia and gulls? Or has it filled up, now, with Styrofoam packaging and disposable diapers?)

In her youth, before the landfill, everyone had to deal with their own garbage. But there hadn't been so much then. Less packaging, less of everything. Anything combustible went into the boiler, anything organic into the compost. Everything that could be clothing or container or conveyance recycled. Broken things ended up in the attic, or, if they couldn't be mended in any scheme of winter ingenuity, in the gulley to the north of the house. (What a midden that gulley must be now — decades of broken bicycles — wheels and gears removed, of course — of shattered china — though that might have been used to line the walk — of tin cans, perhaps. What would be in it?)

She eats the toast, and then the heel of a triangle of brie cheese. There is much rind in proportion to cheese, and she chews it hungrily, pressing the cold, floury, sour coating into her palate. Disgust and pleasure, both.

After the brie, she thinks of pears: pears yellowing, gritty, freckled, on the windowsill; pears hanging like hard green promises in the orchard. They'd only a few pear trees: a half acre, perhaps. Soft fruit was so unprofitable in its ephemeral-ness. But Father had loved pears. They'd had them through the winter, canned, their white slices glowing like quarters of moon through the glass jars. But for a couple of weeks in the fall, there would be fresh, juicy pears, bursting with flavour on the tongue.

No pears now: if she were to buy one, it would soften and brown before it ripened.

ITALY

Hugh has colonized her house: his laptop open on the new desk, his pill bottles lined up on the dresser in the spare room, his ablutions kit next to the sink in the guest bathroom. Hugh in her house. What an odd thing.

And yet not. As children, they had been in each other's houses nearly every day, but for half a century, they have barely known each other's location in the world.

Hugh is comfortable. He is tidy, quiet at the right times (when she is working, thinking). In the evenings, he puts on music, grunting (approval?) at her collection; choosing Fauré, then Fleet Foxes, without comment. He mixes drinks, which they sip standing at the window, admiring the little lake, or seated with newspapers. (She remembers his mother's gin-and-tonic ritual, but Hugh, it seems, is a rum man.)

Moreover, he cooks. He takes her to buy groceries, occupies himself when she is busy, entertains her when she is not. He takes out the trash, and she sees him from the window chatting with her neighbour, who appears animated, even roguish. What are they saying?

He wipes up the kitchen and his shaving ends, and brings her magazines (travel and architecture) that she would not buy herself, and a walnut torte from a European bakery.

A good guest. Although she is not used to sharing her house.

While Hugh is off during the day, doing whatever it is he is doing ("I come in at the end," he has said, mysteriously, of his consulting work for the new bridge), she finds herself suddenly energetic, alive. In this space (or path? for it seems to be about motion, staying in motion) she finishes her JASC article, easily, clearly: it has not been so convoluted after all. It is merely a small item. She reviews a couple of new books for journals, and surprises herself by finding unsuspected merit in them both. She is pleased with the resulting pieces: she has, she believes, achieved a good tone, wry, matter-of-fact, detached, but with enough wit to engage readers.

She tells Hugh about Beauvoir, about finding a new lessee or tenant, about leaving it to Justin. He advises her to sell. She could get a handsome price for the orchard. Enough money that she could travel, buy another apartment in Montreal, so she'd have a pied-à-terre there. Enough perhaps to endow a scholarship. To take Clara and Anita on a Greek cruise, no expense spared. She would leave Justin the money, rather than the land. He would start out on his life with many advantages.

Hugh says, "What a nice sensible, reasonable woman you have become, Sid."

Sensible? As compared to whom? Herself, younger? Hugh's former wives?

"You're so balanced, so logical," he says. "Why didn't we get together? We'd have made a good pair, don't you think?"

Ah, so it is in comparison to his most recent ex-wife, the one in Zimbabwe, with whom he is still having arguments over her not leaving, not encouraging their daughter to leave. Not about her, really.

Hugh asks one night if she has any old photos of his family. "I've lost mine, somehow," he says, "between my moving from continent to continent and my various marriages. I had been thinking that you might have your family photos still, and that there would be some with my parents and Graham in them."

She says no at first, then thinks that there must be photo albums, though she had not come across them in her preliminary excavation.

Hugh is much more direct than Cynthia had been. "Do you think you could look them up for me?"

She had been too conditioned in early childhood to resist Hugh's directions. She must look.

Hugh tells Justin about his daughter Ingrid, apparently enlisting his help as a peer of Ingrid's, and Justin seems fired up by the idea. He has a lot to say about colonialism, to which Hugh doesn't respond much. She apologizes after Justin leaves: it's the university. Young men always pick up these Marxist ideas.

The photo album is, after all, not difficult to find. It's not in the boxes from the storage unit, but on her bookshelves: she has kept it with her these decades. Intact, though when she opens the cover, the photographs spring from the stiff yellowed pages like a shower of dry leaves. The little black gummed corners that have held them in place have lost their adhesion. She will have to be careful of order, mindful that she does not lose the connections of the pictures to their captions.

But between them, she and Hugh can identify most of the scenes and the figures in them.

"Flower show," says Hugh. "Circa 1950."

A group of women in print dresses and broad-brimmed hats: Mrs. Inglis presenting a ribbon to Mrs. Koyama; Sidonie's mother in the back row of the group, tall, angular, her short dark hair parted on the left and slicked back behind her ears. She looks odd among the other women with their fair or grey hair, their light cotton dresses. Mother is wearing an Air Force blue (Sidonie remembers — it's grey in the photo) gabardine skirt, a checked shirt that might be a man's, except for the buttons going the other way. All around her, Mrs. Ramsay and Mrs. Inglis, the Misses Thompson, and Mrs. Hubert, and especially Mrs. Koyama and Mrs. Tanaka and Mrs. Imaku, are shorter. It's a pleasing scene: the dark spike of

Mother among the pink and lilac and maize, like a deep blue delphinium in a pot of petunias. "Formidable women," Hugh says, "my mother, yours, Mrs. Clare, Mrs. Protherow. They ran Marshall's Landing like an English country village."

This is true, Sidonie thinks. The Women's Institute teas, the Red Cross projects, the Hospital Auxiliary, the Parent-Teacher Association. Dispensing order and education — and conformity — throughout the community. But many of the women, by the time this photo was taken in the mid 1950s, would have been German or Polish immigrants. A tenuous grip the "English" ladies must have had, at best. Why had they bothered? For it seems to her now that the photos, the concert programs, the cards are records of a fading empire. Why had they bothered to keep up all of the dusty rituals?

And the Japanese women? "Did they end up here as part of relocation during the war?" she asks. "All those little cabins beside the road, when you come around the bend by the park — was that a relocation camp? Where Masao and Mr. Tanaka lived?"

"You know it wasn't," Hugh says, severely. "It was just a workers' camp."

"I couldn't remember, exactly. I'm five years younger than you."

"The Japanese families came in the early part of the nineteen-hundreds. Before the first war."

The grave markers in the cemetery: *Sachiko Tanaka Born 1921 Died 1924.* Tragedy in six words.

"I remember the farms in the bottom land," Sidonie says. "Mother bought cucumbers there; it was too hot at our place for growing cucumbers. I remember the soil, so black. It still is, isn't it? And the Chinese farmers with their conical straw hats. We called them Chinamen."

In the playground, a little ditty: *Chinese, Japanese, dirty knees, see these.* There were accompanying hand gestures, of course. On "Chinese," you pulled the corners of your eyelids up; on "Japanese," you pulled them down. On "dirty knees," you touched your knees, and on "see these," you plucked out the front of your blouse or shirt with the thumb and index finger of each hand, so that you made tenty little breasts there. The ditty was considered objectionable, but not for the racial stereotyping.

Where had the Chinese farmers gone? There were only Japanese family names by the time she was in her teens.

"The Japanese assimilated better," Hugh says.

What does that mean? How much loss behind that word? She thinks, then forces herself not to think, about Masao.

Photos of themselves as children: dressed up for Hallowe'en, perched in boats, posed for comparison against newly-planted saplings. In one early photo, Graham, Hugh, and Alice are lolling, apparently naked, in a large tin washtub. Alice, in the centre, is looking directly at the camera. Her fair hair falls over her shoulders; her chin rests on her knees. Her gaze is assured, evaluative. Sidonïe is standing beside the tub, holding onto — possibly holding herself up by — the rim. She is very small, and is wearing a diaper and sunbonnet. She is howling.

Hugh says, "Is there a picture in which you are not howling?" He says it affectionately, as though it is a natural and pleasing thing that Sidonie should be always in extremis, and himself always ready to rescue. To be gallant.

Photos of school concerts, of plays: children in costume. Class photos: the fair and red-haired children, the dusky. All varying shades of grey in these photos, of course. She and Hugh identify most of the children. Hugh gets the ones that she doesn't. In the earlier photos, the von Tälers, the Inglises, the Clares, all stand at the back, taller, with better haircuts, clothes that, even in these old photographs, look like they fit better, are of better cloth. In later photos, the others have caught up in size, though. They are indistinguishable by appearance.

"A history of immigration and assimilation there," Hugh says, surprisingly.

A snapshot of a group of children in shorts and button-down shirts, all wearing kerchiefs tied in square knots at the throat. "The hiking club," Hugh says.

Sidonie turns the photo over. On the back is written in ink faded to the colour of tea: *Rainbow Hill Hiking Club.* "Yes," she says. "You browbeat half the kids of Marshall's Landing into learning how to find edible roots and track antelope in the dark."

Hugh says, "I think I must have been a tyrant. Did we have badges?"

"Yes, badges. Not armbands, at least."

A badge, sewn of layers of felt and embroidered by hand: Rainbow Hill Hiking Club. That sort of thing was popular then: children were always starting clubs.

Hugh's hiking club: Hugh of course, Graham, Alice, Masao, Sidonie. A couple of others? Walt, later, definitely. His brother. Children from their side of the hill, from the few square miles or so that encompassed Beauvoir and Sans Souci and the smaller orchards around.

"We all had to wear hats and carry rucksacks with water canteens — mostly jam jars," Sidonie says. "Though you and Graham had real tin ones, with olive canvas carriers. . ."

"And rations," Hugh says.

"We were soldiers," Sidonie says.

"We were at war," Hugh says, "against all of the newcomers. It would have been, what — 1953 or so, when this photo was taken. How old were you?"

"Nine," Sidonie says.

"We'd been going a couple of years by then. So Alice and Masao and I'd have been twelve, Graham about fourteen, when we started it."

"Alice had probably been made to take me along," Sidonie says.

They had marched up Rainbow Hill and all over Spion Kopje, which must have been miles. Sidonie's legs would ache, but she never complained: to complain was to be a poor soldier, to endanger the unit.

It was called a hiking club to placate and lull the parents, though children normally ran around the hills unsupervised all summer, anyway. But it was a paramilitary operation. They were drilled, gave complete allegiance to Hugh. Not to Graham, who was older, who invented everything, who imbedded the jokes, but Hugh, who worked out the practical details and chivvied them along.

There was a tree fort, built in a thick copse of poplar that had sprung up where a piece of pine forest had been logged out, then left to sit. Hugh had drawn the plans to scale, pages of them. They'd all been commissioned to borrow or steal lumber scraps, saws, hammers, spikes.

Hugh had trained them in elaborate combat schemes: they were divided up — diplomatically — into armies with historical names: the Danes and Geats and Jutes, she remembers, at one time. Hugh had said (but that must have been later, when more children had joined or been conscripted, and Hugh was the oldest left) that the war was just an exercise in politics: the Germans and Japanese were obviously on the same side as the British. Hard working; good at fighting and keeping order and inventing things appreciative of culture. It was the Polacks and Bohunks, lazy and incompetent and shifty, who were the real enemy.

Revisionist Hugh.

Graham, perhaps because he was older, had treated it all ironically. There had been no sign, then, of the illness that had ambushed him in his later teens. No lapses in judgment, no blurring of fantasy and reality. Had there?

Names: Hugh was Major Sinclair; Graham was also a major, but had to be called The Sandman. What were the others? Richard, she thinks, was Lieutenant Clare, though there was some dispute over that, wasn't there? He wanted to be a major too. So he was allowed to keep his own name, though the rule was that one must assume a *nom de guerre*.

Walt was Sergeant Jones: Graham named him. Masao was Lieutenant Smith.

Masao, the orphaned nephew of the von Täler's foreman, the only dark face in the group.

Alice was Lady Pomona Vere de Vere. Graham's idea again.

Sidonie was called May Day. She had not, then, seen the joke. Mayday. *M'aidez.* Graham had said she was a heroic Japanese double agent. The others had been apt to leave her behind sometimes — to run on and leave her crying, her short, fat legs unable to keep up. Once they had tied her to a tree to stop her from either following them or tattling to their mothers.

It was Hugh who noticed Sidonie missing, after Alice and Masao and Richard Clare had captured her and tied her up; Hugh who had found her. She had untied herself, though. He had offered to carry her on his back, but she had refused, had stalked resolutely behind him.

Hugh says that he does not remember that. He says, "In those days, we children had our own parallel world, didn't we? Apart from the adult world. Not created by adults. And we wandered pretty freely."

Yes.

They were, as children, permitted to wander the countryside pretty freely. It was theirs — by virtue of their fathers' ownership of the orchards, by virtue of their having tramped all over it, following Hugh.

Hugh says, "Remember Mussolini?"

Yes.

Mussolini, who lived in a tumble of rough slate blocks on the south face of Spion Kopje. (Spion Kopje: they didn't know how to spell it, and called it Spine Cop, or Spy Cop. A South African name, clearly; one of the first managers for the land company must have been fresh from the Boer War.)

Mussolini: enormously fat, as big around as Sidonie's arm, and probably long as she was tall. He had a good territory; the hill was pocked with groundhog and vole tunnels. He liked to sun himself on the largest boulder near the peak. Coming up the hill, they would stamp and smack their walking sticks on the ground, to give him warning. That was the safe thing to do. But Mussolini wouldn't hide or retreat; he merely coiled his dull-grey, diamond-patterned body tighter, watched them pass with glass-bead eyes. Alice and the other girls would shriek; even the boys went pale. Walt said the hairs all down his spine stood on end. Masao said that Mussolini smelled like hot metal.

Graham and Hugh had argued about whether their response to the snake was conditioned or innate. Sidonie thought she would like to watch Mussolini, to memorize his flat blunt snout, the scales, the graduated ivory beads of his rattle — to fix him in her mind as Richard Clare did with his charcoal pencil in his sketch book. Mussolini was simple energy, she thought — not evil, but not good either — only a length of thick muscle.

When he left for his boarding school — he'd have been fifteen, maybe? — Hugh had called Sidonie and Walt for a meeting. He marked each of them on the inside of their elbows with a sooty thumbprint and told them to be observant. They should continue patrols, recruitment, training, and report to him. And especially keep an eye on Mussolini.

Hugh laughs. "The serpent in the garden. It's a wonder none of us died a premature death, hiking up Kopje, with those rattlers."

And then he's abruptly silent, as if realizing what he has said.

Hugh drives her here and there, up and down the valley, from Vernon to Oliver, north to Sicamous and Salmon Arm, west to Kamloops.

When Adam had come here with her, on their honeymoon in 1963, he had said: It looks like Italy. But it's all too new and temporary. Like people never meant to stay. None of the buildings are over thirty years old.

She supposes that there hadn't been the materials or the labour fifty or a hundred years ago to build permanently. Not the money. Adam had been concerned, as a young architect, with matters of culture and structures. What is culture, he had asked, if it does not leave permanent artifacts? What can be measured?

"What would you say is the culture of the valley?" she asks Hugh.

"I suppose it's let me do my own thing; everyone else can sink or swim. Look how the ridings have always voted."

"That's an ethos, Hugh, not a culture."

"You're right. Though ethos is part of culture, of course. That's a hard one. I guess the culture has changed. When we were young, it was all transplanted English village, wasn't it, Sidonie? Women's Institute teas and flower competitions."

"Colonial, then. Your mother's hats," Sidonie says.

"Exactly. And the schoolteachers and doctors always Scots."

"Terrible," she says to Hugh, "when you think of it. The way we were raised, privileged Europeans. The snobbery. It was like a plantation."

"Do you think so? Aren't all societies the same, conquering, transplanting, then finally giving in to the local rootstock, getting assimilated? And anyway, how're you going to do something like orcharding without cheap labour? That means immigration and infrastructure, and the Europeans do that better. Democracy is a European idea. It's lucky the British were in charge. It could have been much worse."

"But there were lots of German-speaking people around. The Knopfs, the Klopfs, the Getzkes and Bolskes and Mannskes."

"They came later," Hugh says. "In the early 50s. Don't you remember?"

Yes.

She remembers now — she would have been perhaps nine, in fourth grade, in a school that has suddenly expanded to include dozens of new arrivals. Who were these children? She remembers them as alarming, because strangers. The younger ones spoke English without an accent, but the older ones had heavy accents, and limited vocabulary. Strange clothing sometimes — cut-down women's and men's woolen things, and strange names, though these were quickly shortened and altered to Mike, John, Betty. For a while, they were regarded with suspicion, but after a few months, only the poorer of the original children, those partially marginalized themselves, kept up the term *bohunk*. But even people who considered themselves well-bred used the term DP.

Germans expelled from Poland, she guesses they must have been.

She remembers, in the spring, when she walked up the hill from the school, the sounds of saws and hammers, the odours of fresh timber, are everywhere: a spring chorus, like the frog ponds. A businesslike sound, a let's-get-down-to-it sound. A clean sharp smell, like the smell of the bath house, only yellower.

Her father had been pleased: good clean immigrants, he'd said. They'll contribute to society.

But Sidonie and Alice both pretended, suddenly, that they did not understand German, when the new children spoke to them.

A shame presses on her. The past is not a comfortable place to visit.

They picnic on a steeply sloping hill planted with vines above the blue, blue lake. It's only March, but the earth is already pleasantly warm, the sun like heated honey. They have stopped at the European deli and bakery, have bought cold meats, bread, chocolate: have purchased wine from the same vineyard they are looking over.

She says, "Adam thought it looked like Italy."

"It does look like parts of Italy, here," Hugh says. "Also parts of Chile. And Turkey. And California. The lake and the hills and the orchards and vineyards. Even the houses, the way they're built on the hillsides, and all stucco. And the tourists."

"A culture of sunshine."

He laughs. "*Oh, for a beaker of the warm South,*" he says. "Look, Sidonie: the buttercups."

So there are, a slope of buttercups, shimmering in the bone-coloured, snow-bleached grass.

She recites their botanical names from memory.

"You should have been a botanist," Hugh says. "You should have come back here and worked in botany. You should never have left us."

He has stretched himself out perpendicular to her on the tartan car blanket, and put his white head in her lap. She doesn't move.

"Hugh, you left long before I did," she says. Sensibly.

"You used to tell my mother that you wanted to go to Italy,"

Hugh says. "It must have been a little after you told her that you were going to marry me."

Yes. She remembers. Mother, her mother, sewing new drapes for Mrs. Inglis's new picture window. The Inglises' house had been undergoing renovations: a new wing added, the mullioned windows replaced with plate glass and the hardwood floors covered with lino-leum and wall-to-wall carpeting. Everything painted too, and the old dining-room table and sofa and chairs, with their curvy legs ending in wonderful, terrifying animal feet, being sold at the auction and replaced by new Danish wood.

Mrs. Inglis was getting wall-to-wall carpeting in a shade called "Siena Wood," which Mr. Inglis says is rust, really. The drapes Mother was sewing were a complementary blue: the blue was called "Lake Maggiori," and Sidonie had thought it was the colour of *their* lake on a certain kind of day: an overcast day in September, when the cloud was very high and pearly.

Mrs. Inglis had said that Siena and Lake Maggiori were places in Italy, that she had been to Italy; she was on holiday there once, as a girl. "Napoli!" she had said — Sidonie can see her now, rolling her eyes upward, clasping her hands, parodying herself. "The art! The architecture! The beautiful young men!"

Napoli was Naples, she had known. Father has been there, too. Father had his pocketbook stolen by bandits in Naples. They are all bandits there, he had said. Father was attacked by the bandits in an alley where he had parked his motorbike. But Mussolini cleaned up the bandits, Father says. That was a long time ago that Father was in Italy: before he came to Canada.

Italy was in books, but Canada isn't, very much. And Marshall's Landing, never.

That shade of blue could be called Okanagan Lake blue. But who would know what that meant?

Mrs. Inglis had said, "Sidonie, dear, come and sit by me," and Sidonie had realized that she had somehow crept under the machine and was holding onto the iron supports.

She remembers that it was difficult to refrain from mentioning that Mrs. Inglis had eaten four Nice biscuits. She knew not to do that, though she hoped Mrs. Inglis wouldn't eat the whole row that Alice had arranged, overlapping like fish scales, on the plate. Nice were Sidonie's favourite biscuits, with their odd vanilla-almond flavour, which called so much attention to itself and then disappeared, just as you tried to identify and hold onto it. And Mother didn't buy Peek Freans very often, so the old blue tin with its pictures of King George V and Queen Mary was only brought out for company.

"I think I'm going to go to Italy one day," the little girl Sidonie had said to Mrs. Inglis.

"Fancy!" Mrs. Inglis had said. "What is it about Italy, all of a sudden? Graham wants to go there too." Her glance, Sidonie noticed, was fixed on the last Nice biscuit. Sidonie couldn't help herself. Her hand shot out and snatched the biscuit, and it was entirely in her mouth before she knew what has happened. Mother had been mortified.

But Mrs. Inglis had laughed.

There was something sweet and lush and glowing about Mrs. Inglis: a warmth, like an orchard in the sun. Sidonie had wanted to grow up to be like Mrs. Inglis, with her auburn hair, her soft, curvy front and slim legs, her easy laugh, her lack of fear. She remembers thinking: Mother likes Alice best. But I have Mrs. Inglis. I am hers, and she is mine.

Sitting among the buttercups with Hugh's head in her lap, she thinks: I must be careful not to confuse my affection for Hugh's mother with my friendship with Hugh.

That night, she is awakened by a noise: something like a stone dropping and rolling across the floor has disturbed her. She can hear, then, Hugh's bed shifting, Hugh muttering, his feet padding on the hardwood. He has knocked something off his nightstand — likely a pill bottle, a water glass. More muttering, and shuffling, as if he has gotten down on his hands and knees to retrieve something from under the bed.

Should she go knock on his door, offer to help? But the image of the two of them, in pajamas, hair awry, minus glasses and bridges and who knows what, crawling around the floor, alarms her. She stays where she is, in her high firm bed. But then she can't sleep.

It occurs to her now that she does not quite see the point of the reminiscing on which she and Hugh spend so much of their evenings. What is it that Hugh wants? A pleasant story? She is not the right companion for him, in that case. She has serious misgivings. She enjoys Hugh's company: he is intelligent; they can have a conversation. But she does not see eye to eye with him.

Then Hugh leaves, flying back to Toronto. They have had a pleasant time, she thinks, but she is glad to see him go. She is glad to be on her own again.

Heading out for a walk, she meets up with her neighbour, and thinks again: she timed her leaving to intercept me. The little flat-faced dog licks her ankle.

"I see your husband is off again," the woman says, chattily.

"He is not my husband."

Perhaps her tone has been too abrupt, for the woman colours and says, a little sharply, "Boyfriend, then."

Sidonie waits. She is good at waiting, making people say more than they intend to.

Of course, for both Alice and her, there must have been a kinship taboo in place. They had grown up too much with Hugh and Graham to consider them as romantic partners. And vice versa. Though there had been other objections, other barriers, as well. She remembers the odd conversation with Mother, in Mother's last illness: *Alice could have married anyone,* Mother had said. *We didn't need Betty Inglis trying to foist off that Gordon Defoe on us. She thought she was better than us, you know. But Cecil Inglis came here as a manager for the land company. Somehow he arranged to get paid in shares when the company was doing badly in the 30s, and he traded those shares for that big parcel of land that they called Sans Souci. Really, they weren't anyone. Betty was a soldier's wife, and Cecil was just an officer in India. They'd had to leave. They were fresh off the boat.*

Fresh off the boat: she remembers her mother using that phrase. She can remember what her mother said almost perfectly, she thinks.

She had been horrified, appalled. It had seared into her. Her mother complaining in an unfamiliar, petulant voice: *but they always had a little more money than us, and Betty acted like Hugh and Graham were headed for Oxford. It was her idea to send them to that private school in Vancouver, you know. And they sent Graham off to the one in England when he was fifteen. But he got sick and had to come back, and then Betty said that the air here was healthier. But it was because Graham was not right, even then. She had it in her head that the boys would both marry upper-class girls. She thought Alice wasn't as good as them, though Alice was the prettiest girl around, and your father would have been titled, back in Europe.*

Mother, rambling, displaying unattractive grudges and jealousies, letting loose some old secrets, in her last weeks. She had been in pain, and the morphine had disinhibited her, of course. But a shock to find all of that festering, when she had grown up knowing Betty Inglis as her mother's closest friend. A shock to have secrets revealed.

Revealed and not revealed. She had thought, then, that Mother had meant that Alice should have married Graham or Hugh. But Graham had become ill in his early twenties, and Hugh, who was Alice's age, had never seemed like a possible partner for her. He had been a boy still, when Alice was already grown. And they'd all grown up as siblings. There had been no possibility of romance between them. Had there?

And she herself had been too much younger, had left the valley before she was grown up, so the question had not arisen. There had been no possibility of romance between herself and Graham, or herself and Hugh.

Had there?

ᛏᛟᚤᛟ

POMONA

She could have found her way on her own, but Walt Rilke is waiting for her in the long, rutted driveway, in his green gabardine work clothes, his leather work boots planted squarely on the centre ridge, among the colonizing dandelions and plantain and a dwarfish, determined race of mustard, as though nothing has changed in two decades.

Though as she gets out of her car and walks toward him, she thinks, for an instant: *No, not Walt.* White hair tufts out from under his cap, at the sides; the skin of his neck and face has leathered to a permanent tobacco-brown, is shirred around his prominent blue eyes, stretched taut and shiny at his knobby cheekbones. Moles of various species cultivate his cheeks and forearms. His grin as usual — full curving lips pulled back over serviceable teeth, eyes disappearing into their puckered lids. Who is this old man?

She would not have recognized him, except that he resembles his father. Then the images of him, past and present, serigraph in her mind and he is just Walt, whom she has known nearly all of her life. Trusty sidekick Walt, trudging after her in his short pants and gumboots, his red cheeks, his white-blond hair like milkweed silk, transparent against the sun.

He stretches out both hands. "Sidonie. Long time no see. How the heck are you?"

"Walter," she says. "Good to see you."

And here Walt's son Jack — looking like the image she'd had of Walt, a middle-aged man now, his tow hair darkened, but tufting out in the same way under his cap.

"Dr. von Täler."

Firm grip; callouses. She remembers Jack as a small boy, remembers Walt at the same age, and at the age Jack is now, remembers Walt's father, old Mr. Rilke, at the age of Jack and the age of Walt. Layers of memory: the images all ranged one behind the other, like one of those stylized watercolours of mountain ranges. Only instead of retreating into mistiness, her memory-images become sharper the further they are in the past.

But how like his father Jack is — the stocky build of him, the sturdy neck, the face all knobs and creases. She sees all of her images merging into just this one, this genotypical Rilke.

The Rilkes breed true, her father had said.

"It's been what, a dozen years?" Walt says.

"Twenty-one this June," she says.

They stand about in the driveway, grinning at each other. The Rilkes are not talkers. She is not a talker. They commune by standing still, shuffling their boots. It's faintly ridiculous. She could have found her way by herself. And really, it wasn't necessary for her to drive out at all. She does not need to see the orchards — Walt's usual annual report, delivered over the telephone, would have been sufficient.

But it's a ritual, she recognizes. An important one, for two grown men to take half a day from whatever else they might be doing. The message is that they have been working hard. She must fulfill her seigniorial role, and acknowledge, adjudicate their hard work.

Jack clears his throat. She wonders about Jack, who must be in his late thirties now, perhaps forty. Still living at home, working for his dad. Hadn't he taken a heavy mechanics course just out of high school and gone north to work at one of the big mines? But he's been back some time. Not married any longer, or so she'd been informed in one of Christina's Christmas cards. The type of man who might find it difficult to meet a girl. Shy, a hard worker, but something of a plodder. The Rilkes are a race of garden gnomes, Alice had said.

"It's a beautiful day," Jack says.

It *is* beautiful, this April day: bright and clear and warm, the sky cloudless, the lake cobalt. The hills, which will be sere and yellow by July, are green. The trees are all in blossom or fresh leaf. A day of spring. Beautiful and bucolic, here in the countryside. On either side of the driveway, the rows of mature Delicious, each tree grown to its full extent, the circumference of a room. Wrinkled purple-grey limbs; bronze-green branches in full leaf now. Soft clear-green of spring leaves; their silvery-grey undersides; the blossoms just peaking, their rounded cups unfolding, Schiaparelli-pink sepals and white, white petals.

On this day of her appointment with Walt, she has awakened with an unusual sense of purpose, put on her jeans and Gore-Tex boots and layers: T-shirt, pullover sweater. Hiking gear, because she doesn't own orcharding clothes these days. She knows they will start their walk in a cool morning wind, damp air rising off the lake, and then, as they march up and down through the trees and the sun rises in the sky, they will get warmer and warmer, and finish off in Walt's kitchen, which will be hot from his wife Christina's baking. She must layer on and be prepared to layer off.

Her foot has healed, as the emergency-room doctor had said it would, in the six weeks since the accident. She is able to walk again, a little more each day. She does not attempt the lake path, but she can drive herself, walk about the stores. She has retrieved her car, which is unscathed: only the radio station settings have all been changed. She has had to reset the buttons to CBC One and Two.

She has driven north along Highway 97, past the new super-markets and gas stations, the Esso and the Petro-Canada, the A&W, the McDonald's. Past the old plaza, built in the early 60s, with the

CIBC, the IGA, the bakery and liquor store, the little one-storey buildings re-fronted, patched up, painted, this decade, beige and burgundy, bearing new signs, but still recognizable. Plain, even ugly buildings, she sees now, the old and the new. Not planned; built of necessity. Strung along the highway, the most basic way stations. On the side roads, more modernization: the high school tarted up with a glassed-in entry; some frou-frou apartment blocks. But there is more sameness than change.

On the side roads below the highway, the old fruit packing houses, with their red asphalt shingles standing in for brick, the creek with its scrim of cottonwoods, the rich-soiled bottom lands of pasture and vegetable gardens. And above the highway, the slopes with their orchards, their scarves of saskatoon-berry bushes and red-osier dogwoods, their little stands of ponderosa pines.

Turning left off the highway by her old school, she followed the narrow road with its rutted shoulders up the hill and over the crest and down again. All along the roads, the saskatoon, the wax-berry, in their sharp, tender green leaves, vulnerable, dangerous. The Oregon grape, evergreen, glossy; its blooms deep-yellow plumes. In the orchards, the trees in their rows, pale green and white, like lace tossed on a lawn.

So beautiful, so beautiful.

She has not been back for over twenty years, but the landscape is familiar to her as her own body: the valley itself, with the big lake mediating the climate, daubing something almost Mediterranean on this Canadian landscape. The lake, like a great creature rolling out its own bed, undulating from the foot of the cool, damp Monashees in the north a hundred kilometres south to the desert, with its Blue Racers and scorpions, its petroglyphs, its prickly pear.

And within the central part of the valley, a ridge of steep hills, wrinkled by dry gullies, pinched into a few peaks: Knox, Dilworth, Spion Kopje. The ridge divides the valley into two. In the west fork of the valley, the main lake, the thick, open-mouthed blue serpent of it. In the east fork, a string of sister lakes, draining, diminishing from north to south: turquoise, green, brown. The sides of the ridge draped with the orchards, the fruit trees so well adapted to the surfeit of sun, to the lengthened summer, the ameliorated winter of the valley.

This particular orchard, even after four decades mostly of absence, familiar as the terrain of her own hands. This plot of land, this section of west-facing hillside, where she was born and raised, and where she has now returned. She feels bathed in light. She feels oriented, grounded.

They set off up the driveway, its ruts and potholes (she must ask Walt if he will grade it again this year), between the stands of trees. Mature trees with strong limbs and scaly, purple-grey bark: Delicious, Golden Delicious, Spartans. She can see here the years of neglect, some years the trees were not pruned. The symmetry off; some narrowness of the basal limbs. But they seem healthy, after all. The leaves held out to the sun, small hands. The blossoms, thick, clotted, and (listening for a moment) active with bees. Row on row, the trees: variations of themselves. Like machines, they produce the fruit: hundreds of pounds for each tree. But they are organisms: livestock, rather than crop. They must be tended: pruned, thinned out, sprayed for pests, protected from frosts, visited by bees. Their limbs, in late summer, in early fall, growing so heavy with the fruit that wooden posts must be propped under them to prevent their cracking off at the joints.

The texture of tree trunks asserts itself, remotely, in her fingertips. Slubbed satin of the younger cherry; sketchpad-sheets of the curled apple bark. A body memory. Her fingers recognize the texture as if it is their cradle tongue, not heard for half a century.

Along the driveway, deeper into the orchard. Now, a clearing, an acre or two of outbuildings and yard. They pass the old house, her old house. She does not look at it closely, only sideways, out of the corner of her eye, registers the boxy mass of it, its honey-hued stucco, tile roof, boarded-up windows. The house she grew up in, the house built to her father's specifications, the house containing all of her childhood, and Alice's. It's an odd house: built not to take advantage of the view of the lake, but to repel the southern sun, to create a refuge, a well of cool shadow. The windows are high, small;

the walls thick. It's larger than most houses of its vintage in this village — larger and more European-looking. It tells, she thinks now, the story of her father's youth: part Bavarian castle, part Alpine chalet, part Italian villa.

And now a wreck, a smashed box, though the outside, of course, betrays little of the havoc. She does not think about what's inside; her mind skulks around the edge of it.

"Do you want to go inside, have a look around?" Walt asks. "I brought the keys down in case."

No. No, she does not. She does not want to go into the house. She had been in on her last visit, twenty years ago. She does not want to see it now.

Though she will have to deal with it, some day.

She strides on.

Past the old wash house, past the chicken shed, past the Quonset where the tractors and other equipment live. The sweet-sharp smell of pesticide. The landscape of her very early childhood, when she had not ventured beyond her mother's garden. All in good repair. The dry climate preserves. That and, she supposes, Walt's assiduous stewardship. What decay, what wreckage has infiltrated, must have arisen in the years when Walt was absent, when the house and orchard stood unattended.

Then past the yard, and a turning of the double track of the driveway, this rough road used by the tractors and pick-up trucks. Now they're in a sheltered rise, a section always planted with the tender fruit, the peaches and the less hardy cultivars of the cherries. The cherry trees with their delicate, narrow, translucent leaves, their pink blossoms like Japanese watercolours. The peach trees with their deep forks, their narrower limbs: some are damaged, torn nearly in two, and bearing great scars, and there are spaces where trees have been removed. The peaches have not fared well during their decades of neglect. An unpruned peach tree, or one too heavily laden, is a vulnerable being.

"A battle zone, eh?" Walt says. "This section should be replanted in two, three years."

They walk the rows of Golden and Red Delicious, the Spartans (how she misses Spartans, which are really only grown in this province!), Macs (cheap, not good keepers, but popular, Walt half-sneers: the orchardman's bias), the gnarled, finicky Red Havens, the tall Bings, purple in the spring light.

They cut north and eastward, through the trees, as the tractor path swings wide here to avoid a rock outcropping, a steep-sloped gully of pine. Here a section of very old trees, gnarled and blackened.

"Still producing," Walt says. "But they'll have to go in a year or two."

They talk prices: Granny Smiths, *Grannys*, Walt says can be relied on to bring in about eight-and- a- half grand an acre; Spartans, only around seven. Cherries are holding at ninety-five cents a pound, but with a shelf life of about two days, they're volatile. Peaches, free-stones, will gross four grand an acre — hardly worth the trouble, and they ripen in series, so they're labour-intensive. And if they end up going to processing, the orchardist takes a loss. Everyone grows some peaches — they fill the space between cherries and apples — but only a block. Soft fruit's a gamble.

Then the new saplings, chest-high, their trunks the thickness of two thumbs, still bearing the graft scars. But they've all taken — purple buds swell the twigs.

Scions, they're called, the new grafts. All apple cultivars in this part of the world are grafted onto root stock of the Transparent, a tough Russian breed. Somehow, the tree bears the fruit of the graft. The root stock provides hardiness. It's a kind of miracle.

"The new grafts look healthy," she says. She reads the plastic tags: Pink Lady, Honeycrisp, Ambrosia. Fancy names.

"Experimenting," Jack says. "See what grows best on this slope." Gingergold, Jazz.

"Jazz, now," Jack says, "That's a cross of Gala and Braeburn." Healthy young trees, all.

"It's the middle generation that's missing," Walt says. "You'll have a gap in your production."

It is true. The orchard looks well cared for: pruning completed, last-year's props and sprinkler pipes stacked in the shed, sulfur powder from the dormant oil visible in the cracks and crotches of the trees. The obedient rows of trees, pleasing variations on the theme of trunk, branch, twig. (Could this be represented by a formula?) But there is an absence of young trees, those that should have been planted out and grafted in over a decade or two ago. Perhaps they should plant some earlier-producing varieties to catch up, fill the gap. More peaches, which reach puberty at two or three years. The tradeoff will be a shorter lifespan, of course. But it might work out. They will have to do some calculations.

She points this out; it's not Walt's fault, of course, as he wasn't responsible for the orchard during that time, but it will affect his and Jack's yield in the next decade or two.

Jack says nothing, only tosses his father a look.

What was that? But she has missed it.

Such satisfaction, that Walt and Jack are leasing Beauvoir, that they are caring for this place. They are orchard men, the Rilkes: it is in their bones. And they know Beauvoir. The Rilkes have been neighbours of Beauvoir, they have worked at Beauvoir for half a century, off and on. The stir, now, of the cultivator's instinct, the same she has felt in starting a new research project. A combination of gambler's euphoria, that locking-in of attention and optimism, and a sort of curiosity, and a third element: energy. A surge of endorphins. How it all floods back — the knowledge of the profession, the body-memory of seasonal tasks, the sensory triggers of the timing and shape of tasks. Pruning and spraying, thinning, picking — all these she would know when and how to do by the angle of the sun, the warmth on her forearms, the size and colour of the buds and fruit, the form of the tree on the screen of her mind.

She must be careful. She must not become too involved in this: it is not her occupation. Not her business. She is only maintaining Beauvoir, husbanding it for the future. She has never wanted to run an orchard, to be tied brain and limb to the work. It is only for the future.

Only body memory, trip-alarmed by walking among the trees.

The look between Jack and Walt, back there. But if something is amiss, it will come out later at the kitchen table, where they will negotiate new terms, and discuss what Jack will plant this year, what will be grafted in. For now, they will perform this inspection of the trees, the sloped land, on foot. It is not necessary; it is a ceremony of some kind. Nevertheless, it must be done.

Up the hill (her newly-healed foot paining her a little), to the highest part, the most exposed shoulder of the slope. From here she can see for miles the sweep of the east shores, the pine-topped hills, the fans and rectangles of fruit trees.

But it is all altered. Where the little village along the highway had seemed only slightly changed, this slope above the lake has changed alarmingly. Dozens, hundreds of new houses have sprung, toadstool-like, from the ground, eating away at the meadows, the pine brush, and even, here and there, at the orchards themselves. And what she has taken to be orchard, she sees, is actually something else: not the dotted rows of trees, but the wavy lines of vine plantings. Fully two-thirds of the orchards along this ten-kilometre slope, she judges, have been turned into vineyards.

"So much new development," she says to Walt and Jack. This — crowding — is unsettling, threatening. Who are all of these newcomers, pushing up their clusters of new houses where her memory plants woods, meadows? But what has she expected? Everywhere the cities are spreading to the countryside, the old villages taken over by new houses.

"Must be a real change," Walt says.

Yes.

"The orchards are hanging on, most of them," Walt says. "ALR keeps that going. A lot switching to grapes, of course."

Again, the half-look, the almost imperceptible signal between Walt and Jack. Some conflict between them, maybe? Walt's thirty acres, with its heave southward, would be good for a vineyard. Maybe Jack is pushing to switch. Well, she'll find out soon enough.

All changed. The proliferations of new houses, the breaking up of the orchards. Why is this upsetting to her? She has not lived here, has chosen to live elsewhere, for nearly fifty years. She is not, in principle, opposed to change, to development. People have to live somewhere.

It is the evidence the changes give of newcomers, of strangers moving in, appropriating what she had thought was hers.

But what had she thought was hers?

"Beauvoir is still producing," Walt says. She notices, with pleasure, that Walt uses the old name, pronouncing it the old way: *Beaver*.

She remembers the great orchard estates of her childhood: Eagles' Rest to the north and west, Robinson's Dingle to the south, San Souci north and a little east, shoulder to shoulder with Beauvoir.

In Marshall's Landing in the 1940s, when she was a small child, there had been perhaps seventy families, half a dozen orchard estates. The estates had anchored the landscape, economically and socially. Eagles' Rest, where the Protherows lived, the biggest, and fittingly: Major Protherow (who she had been surprised to discover, at nine or ten, was also Father Christmas at the community children's party), the unofficial leader of the community. Mrs. Protherow, who smelled of violets and wore long, dusty-looking silk dresses and opened the Ladies Auxiliary Tea. Their spinster daughter Margaret, who gave piano lessons and painted. The name Eagles' Rest, Father had said, came from the ospreys that nested in the tops of the tallest ponderosas and plummeted into the lake, where the shore was steep and the water transparent, dark green, to pluck out the rainbow trout. Though by the time Sidonie's father had told her this, the ospreys had already vanished, prey to the DDT used in the orchards back then, or else the mad son Lorne Protherow's gun.

Next door to Beauvoir was Sans Souci, where the Inglises lived: Mr. and Mrs. Inglis and Graham and Hugh, who were older than Sidonie, as old as her sister Alice. The Inglises, their tweed suits and tea rituals, Mrs. Inglis's herbaceous borders, the high hollyhocks and delphiniums, the peonies and Michaelmas daisies and dahlias as big as a child's head.

She thinks of mentioning to Walt that she is back in touch with Hugh Inglis, but does not. Hugh, whom she had followed about from the time she could walk, and who had books she might look at but not take away, and Meccano that she might not touch. What is she doing, now, with Hugh?

Eagles' Rest and Sans Souci, Beauvoir and Rainbow and Robinson's Dingle. Ridgetop, Rainbow, Pixie Beach. North Star, Gordon's Brae, Davidson's, Campbell's, Reynolds', Farquarson's. This had been the community in the 1940s and 1950s — a group of families, well-enough off to enjoy books and concerts, music lessons, teas. The men had organized irrigation systems and marketing cooperatives and school boards. The women had raised money for a library, a community hall. The children had finished high school and worked in the orchards in the summers, taking the hottest part of the day off to swim, to socialize. They had gone on to university. Several Olympic rowers and swimmers had come out of the area.

An ideal time. A time of achievement, of prosperity. Of general happiness. Had it not been? She could stride about this part of the valley as a young woman, and know that it was her place.

Of course, the tradition of the estate has long died out. Even by the late 1950s, the names had become tarnished with a patina of embarrassment, an aura of silliness, anachronism. When Major Protherow had died and the Eagles' Rest had been broken up and sold, suddenly it wasn't the fashion to have an estate, a name.

Eagles' Rest had been partitioned, parts sold off for smaller orchards, the beach and house section bought by the United Church for summer camp — when was that? 57 or 58. The name had not been kept. Sans Souci had been sold in the mid-80s, and Beauvoir had not been inhabited by von Tälers since 1974. And only forty acres left of the original one hundred.

And the smaller plots, the ten-acre plots. How are those sustainable, these days? Not enough income from them to support one family, and too much work for them to be purely hobby farms. How are they managed?

But here she is, with Walt Rilke, who is — perhaps miraculously — keeping Beauvoir alive. She still has Beauvoir. It is still a working orchard. She still has a good chunk of land, and she has Walt Rilke, who was raised on this land, who was trained by her father to look after it.

A stand of pears here, where her father always grew the pears. Bartletts, D'Anjou, Bosc. Old trees: these must be the same trees he planted. A pear tree, you plant for your grandchildren, her father had always said.

She thinks of her father, not much older than Walt, than she herself, when he died. He had walked the orchards every day, unless he was ill. His lists, his mind carrying a map of the trees: not only a snapshot of this year's configuration of the orchard's acres, but also maps from years before and after. What had grown, what could be planted. His mind a map of each slope and hollow, of the idiosyncrasies of each cultivar.

Wearing his hat, always, and his good leather boots, resoled and resoled, and polished each Saturday by Alice, and then herself, on the back step with a tin of gasoline-smelling wax, a stiff brush, a clean scrap of flannel. Her father strolling — he did not stride — between the rows of trees, and always the lists in his head. And a trail of foremen and dogs and children behind him. Father who, as she has come to appreciate, was one of the last of his kind, a gentleman farmer, polymath, as familiar with Schubert on the gramophone as digging out beds for new trees or wielding a pruning hook for twelve hours at a stretch.

How it comes back to her, as she walks the rows of trees.

In spring and summer, Father wears a flat, broad-brimmed hat of tightly-woven straw: it's called a Panama hat, he says. It is worn by gentlemen in hot countries to shield them from the sun. A very practical design, Father says. It's probably been in use since the time of the Spanish Conquistadors. Maybe they got it from the Greeks. In fall, Father wears, not a flat tweed cap like the other men, but a felt fedora, and in winter, a tall fur hat with ear flaps, made of wolf skin, from Russia. Father says that they know how, in Russia, to keep the cold from your ears. This hat is not actually from Russia, though: it was made by an Indian lady in Medicine Hat to replace his original Russian hat, which he bought in Hamburg before embarking for Canada. The replica hat, Father says, is just as good as the original (which was chewed by mice one year, when Father forgot to store it in its tin box). The Indians, Father says, know how to work with animal skins: it is in their blood. The original Russian hat and the original Italian hat he had brought with him for the purpose of protecting his scalp from the harsh Canadian climate. He can still order the Italian hats; they come in big cardboard boxes stamped "*Borsalino Alessandria Italia.*" But no hats may be ordered from Russia, which is now in the Soviet Union, behind the Iron Curtain.

Father needs hats because of his premature baldness. Father says: I had such a thick, curly pelt when I was a young man! I never would have believed I'd go bald!

What had made him go bald?

The gas, he says. The gas, in the war. Not the last war. The one before that. Also, it did a number on my lungs, Father says.

The names of the fruit a currency for conversation. He would cup an apple in his hand, point to a tree not yet in leaf. If you could name it, praise; if not, a patient explanation. See here, the five swellings at the blossom end. By four or five, her legs long enough to keep up, she had begun to learn.

These are the fruit that are grown: apples, pears, plums, peaches, apricots, and cherries. Then the varieties: Red Delicious and Yellow; MacIntosh, Transparent, Gala, Jonathan, Spy, Spartan, Granny Smith, Winesap, Jubilee. Each kind of apple looks a little different than the others, and tastes different, and ripens and ships differently.

Father has a big book called *Pomona* that has paintings of all of the different kinds of fruit and their names. The names are European names, though, and underneath some of them, in Father's tiny scrolling writing, are the Canadian names. Bon Chrétien, for example, has *Bartlett* written under it.

"Pomona," Father says, "was a Roman goddess, the goddess of fruit and orchards." Father shows Sidonie a picture of her in one of his books. She has curly auburn hair and plump, white arms and legs, and a dimpled smile. She has on a yellow wrapper and one of her bosoms is sticking out, but she doesn't seem to notice. In her left hand, she's holding a Gala apple, and under her right hand is a Golden Delicious.

"She looks like Mrs. Inglis," Sidonie says. Father laughs. But Alice says, scornfully, that she doesn't at all.

It is something else that Sidonie means: a feeling she has about Mrs. Inglis, that she will later put the words *abundance, generosity* to.

Father tells them the story of Pomona. "She had lots of admirers," Father says, "but she married one who tricked her with a disguise. He disguised himself as an old woman, and gave her advice." Sidonie doesn't like that story: she likes the stories about the sailor Ulysses. The proper name for those stories is *myths*, Father says.

She learns to identify each cultivar, to see the fine differences among trees. I will be an orchardist like you, Father, she says.

He laughs. And Alice says: no, because you're a girl. It would have to be your husband. And it's going to be *my* husband, because I'm older.

It had not turned out that way, of course. Why not? *Hubris*, her father's stories would have said.

A memory-flood. She must be careful. She does not want to be caught up in this flood. There is no going back: she knows this.

Walt is asking her about being tired. She has not been paying attention. No, she is not tired. She is fit; she walks a good five kilometres a day, now that her break has mended. As well, the orchard seems smaller than she remembers. Of course it is: sixty acres have been lopped off, sold, since she was a child. But what is left has been compressed. The distance from the house to the edge of the wood, an arduous journey in her memory of childhood, now diminished to a brisk ten-minute walk.

"No, I said *retired*," Walt says, grinning, his bright blue eyes disappearing into a tangle of branching wrinkles. "Did they give you a good send-off, your company, out there? A good dinner, speeches, a gold watch?"

Yes. She hears what Walt is up to, now. It is the local form of teasing; a sort of farmer's humour, specific for those who have gone away and returned. It purports to admire how grand, how impressive your life must be! But the subtext is, of course, don't get too big for your boots.

Yes, a grand dinner, she says, entering into the spirit of it. Over the top. Lobster flown in from Nova Scotia. Little birds stuffed with organic wild rice and rare mushrooms. Three hours of speeches. She falls into the appropriate tone: irony, self-deprecation, tempered with a little wide-eyed amazement.

"*Heyyyy*," Walt says. "You must have brought them a lot of dough."

Had she? She supposes. Dr. Haephestes saying, yes, you must have a party. It's for the rest of us who are staying. It's a ceremony to mark a change in regime.

A beheading, she had said to Dr. Haephestes, and he had laughed, but had not denied it.

She had not planned to retire early. But it had seemed the right time — a change in atmosphere, a shifting of priorities at the Institute. She feels, now, the unease of the past couple of years: the growing sense that the world of her research was shifting, becoming something that she did not feel comfortable with. She does not say any of this. She has never, she thinks, had a conversation with Walt about what it is she works at.

"You'll be glad to be back," Walt says.

This is likely true.

She is not quite sure why she has come back. For the boy, perhaps, though she doesn't let herself think of it too much: foolish to pin one's expectations on another human being. But for the boy, if she is honest.

They have reached the northern boundary of the land — here is the camp road, which, she sees, has been recently paved — or repaved, to be precise — looping around to meet the edge of the estate again. Had it not been first paved in the early 1960s? She must fit the memory into a time frame, fit it between her rare visits back. Vineyards are interspersed with orchards along this road.

Gnarled vines haul themselves up on strung cords or cables; it's altogether an unfamiliar look. She can see, though, how the vines have been pruned back, their strength retrenched into a thickened trunk, limbs or whatever they are called. Truncated. All to force new growth. A couple of figures — a middle-aged man and woman — lean against support poles, talking. Walt and Jack lift their hands, and the people in the vineyard salute back.

It appears to be a quieter time of year, in the vineyard as in the orchard. Winter pruning and dormant-spraying completed, and a space of rest before the spraying of the set fruit. Who does this work, now — thins the fruit, picks the grapes when the harvest arrives headlong? She had not thought of this before — that although Walt and Jack run the orchard, teams of labourers must come in seasonally, and do the bulk of the concentrated work.

Vietnamese, she guesses. Cambodians.

"No," Jack says. "That was in the 80s and 90s. It's Mexicans now. Come up from Washington. And Sri Lankans."

There is some guilt in Jack's tone. That's his age. His is a generation schooled to notice, to address, inequities. In her childhood, the orchard workers had been minorities too, a changing force of small brown people from various countries, willing or at least available to take on low-paying physical labour. Refugees from turmoil in other nations often, so that the waves of settlement in the valley might map, as a geological cut would, the international political upheaval, the wars, of the last century. Of course it must have been hard work: she herself had picked up prunings as a child; had thinned the small fruit till her arms ached; had picked cherries and peaches under a relentless sun. It was a hard life. But some would stay, integrate into the community. Their children would go to university. And how could the fruit be grown and harvested without a cheap, seasonal labour force? Even in the 50s and 60s, families weren't big enough to do all of their own orchard work.

Cheap seasonal labour. She has not thought much about it. Walt, of course, would do the hiring, the overseeing.

Along the road, now, treading the gravel shoulder. Above and below, the orchards and vineyards, in their new sharp green leaves, and then the lake — here, a couple of miles wide — and the steep blue rise on the opposite side. The west side of the lake, though, riddled with the chalky geometry of buildings. That's new, too.

In the past, this section of hillside had also been part of Beau-voir — both sides of the road. But now it is not. And around the bend in the road, where the ponderosa woods butt up against Beauvoir at its most south-westerly corner, where they normally would have been able to cut through — a sudden outgrowth of new houses. They are large, with stone facings and wide, Craftsman-style trim, many windows to the view of the lake. Expensive landscaping too, and driveways full of new cars and boats. And high board fences block-ing the route.

"Where is all this money coming from?"

"Alberta oil money," Jack says. "Not a housing lot to be had on any lake in B.C. these days."

Walt only grunts. A sore point? The Rilkes have worked their orchard for over fifty years, but have not become wealthy enough to own a lakeside cottage.

Here is the old access road, now named: Tiefendale Point Road. Was that always its name? The old Tiefendale dairy farm lay just to the south of here, until the 1950s. She had walked there, some-times, to collect an extra pint of cream, if Mother were baking. She remembers the surprise of an escaped cow appearing suddenly in a stand of ponderosa.

They start up the road, which is paved until the last of the new houses, then an earthen track again. Now they must climb back up the hill, through the pine woods. She remembers the climb from childhood, how they would leave the lake in late afternoon, dripping wet, and dry off completely as they climbed the hill under the west-ering sun. Dry off and arrive baked, as if they'd ascended through a kiln. The resin scent of the pines in the hot dry air.

The pines are all dying in this little fold of woods, their bunched long needles bleached or rusty. And small firs, opportunists, already pushing up among the waxberry, the saskatoon and Oregon grape.

Walt makes a *tsk* sound with his teeth at the sight of a pile of sprinkler pipes that have rolled into a gulley, spilled about, fifteen-foot long aluminum tubes. Should have got those picked up, Walt says. And without a further word, they are carrying the pipes up out of the fold in the hill, closer to the tractor road, so that Jack can retrieve them later. She carries up a couple — she can only manage two at a time, though, and gets in Jack's and Walt's way. There isn't room for all three of them to pass on the slope. She stands instead and waits.

Walt in his green gabardine, Jack in jeans and a chunky sweater. Both men in their tractor caps, though Jack's is reversed, the bill over his neck. Good orchard men: solid, stolid. Not imaginative; slow of conversation. But stalwart, utterly dependable.

Walt, showing off, runs up the slope with a bundle of pipes cradled across his arms.

A shift, a slippage in time.

She remembers now Mr. Rilke running toward the house, out of the orchard, a limp and heavy burden carried in front of him. *Bitte, bitte...* his voice like something flayed. What was in his arms was Karl, Walt's older brother, who was what, thirteen, fourteen. Tall, strong Karl, laid out across his father's arms, bucking and writhing for breath. Father had run down the steps: "Put him on the ground. *Am Erde!*" Mother, following, turning back in a whirl of housedress and apron, running in to phone. The Rilkes had no telephone. Father with his mouth on Karl's, as if blowing up an air mattress that writhed and grabbed the dirt and drummed its heels on the ground and then was still.

"I can't," Father said. "I can't put the air in."

Karl's chest crushed — from the step, she could see it, the stoved-in shape, lopsided under his blue jersey. Blood on his mouth and Father's. Karl's blue eyes frozen open.

The keening that was Mr. Rilke. And then Mrs. Rilke, running through the trees, having been fetched by Walt.

It was the tractor, of course, rolling on Karl. He'd tried to turn too tightly on a slope. The tractor had reared like a stallion, and Karl had slipped from the high seat, and the wheel guard had caught him, the heavy green steel slice of it, with the tractor's weight behind it. Walt had seen it all.

She has not thought of that death in years. Does Walt think of it? Did he think of it when his boys, Jack and what's the younger one, Rob, were teenagers, when they drove the tractor, as they must have done?

She remembers Walt at both her parents' funerals. And at Alice's.

In Walt's kitchen, with plates of sticky buns and a strudel full of tart-and-sweet apples and a carafe of deep black coffee, Walt crosses his arms and looks at Jack, and clears his throat and doesn't speak. Christina, who has been bustling around, serving them, says, "Oh, for crying out loud! Just spit it out!"

Walt finally opens his mouth and says, "You see, Sidonie, we've had an offer on our orchard from Rhenisch next door, and considering how little we made the last year out of the two orchards, and how much the work has been, well, we think, that is, Jack and I think, we'll sell. And I will keep this house and half-a-dozen trees, but the rest will go. And so — well, we will have to give up Beauvoir."

Yes, she can see that. Not profitable for them to manage Beauvoir; not enough to keep them both.

"The trees are old, there's going to be a lot of waiting before a new crop," Walt says.

Jack has been chopping rounds of apple trees into firewood outside. Now the sound of the blows, of axe on hard wood, stops. Christina goes to the window, calls out to him: "Come in for a snack."

"Not till he's done the work," Walt says.

The child who remains at home, who works for his father, may not be allowed to grow up.

Walt looks up at Sidonie from under his big sandy-white eyebrows, and she sees that he is nervous. Does he think she is going to scream and throw herself on the ground, as the young Sidonie would have done? But she has grown inward, reserved, since her early childhood; has grown skin like bark.

"Well," she says, for she needs to say something. "After all that work you have done on Beauvoir this past winter."

It is too bad; she will have to look for a caretaker or lessee again, and will be hard-pressed to find anyone, let alone someone as practiced, as knowledgeable as Walter. Someone with the lime earth of Beauvoir in his veins. During the time she had leased out the orchard to other people, it had not been maintained. One tenant had not looked after the trees at all, but had pastured horses there, letting them eat the fallen apples. Some horses had taken colic and died.

But can't Walter manage Beauvoir on his own?

"What are you going to do?" she asks Walter, and he laughs.

"Retire! I will be sixty-two this year, the same as you, Sidonie."

"Retire and do a little traveling, like we've never been able to," says Christina, stoutly, in her voice the common frustration of orchard women.

What about Jack, then?

"Jack is going to be taken on as foreman in the grapes," says Walt. "He's going to learn the grape business."

So — to work for someone else, and not with orchards. Something in her recoils. Yet that is a sensible move. He'll have a steady income, and not the burden of losses in bad years.

"And my younger boy doesn't like the work; he's in computer programming," Walt says.

Ah, there it is, the exacting equation of inheritance. The children must leave to be successful. Some of the children must leave, because the orchard will support only one family; if one doesn't stay, there is nobody to run the orchard. She remembers that Walt has two girls as well, but they are not part of the calculations, it seems.

She and Walt are here, possibly, because their older siblings died young.

She asks, "Do you think Georg Rhenisch will want to buy Beauvoir as well?" She's half-joking; she will have to think what to do now. This applecart well and truly upset.

But Walt takes her seriously. "We did ask him for you; hope that wasn't making assumptions. But he says that they don't need that much more land right now, and Beauvoir slopes north a little too much; not enough sun for grapes."

"If you're thinking about selling though," Christina says, "you know that the old Inglis place above you is nearly all built out now; the developer might be looking for a new property. And people have been having good luck getting the rezoning lately. Tell her what those lots are going for," Christina urges.

Walter shakes his shaggy white head. "Two-fifty."

Two hundred and fifty thousand? *An acre?* That is shocking. She wonders if Hugh knows that.

"No — for a sixth-acre lot."

The amount seems impossible.

"I kid you not!" Walt says.

How much did the developer pay for Sans Souci?

Christina shakes her head. "It's changed hands since Hugh Inglis sold it, and I heard he got two-fifty for the whole thing, back in 86. But there's what, fifty lots in this new subdivision?"

"Holy mackerel, eh?" Walt says.

She doubts it's that easy to get things out of the ALR these days. It was an aberration, back there in the mid-eighties. Different government.

"What about Alice's boys?" Walt asks. "Any chance one of them would take it on? They must be all grown now, eh?"

Alice's boys. "I don't think any of them would be interested," she says, more coolly than she had intended. She does not want to say that she has no idea where one of Alice's three sons is, has not spoken to two of them in twenty years.

"I see Stephen around," Christina says.

She does not reply.

"Well, we just wanted to let you know," Walt says, with a letting out of breath as if for a hard task accomplished. "So that you can plan."

She drives home, south on the highway. Now, by herself, inside the safe shell of her car, she is able to begin to think. Breathe; slow her mind. Let her mind ebb back into her body, her limbs.

What to do with her forty acres: her hillside of fruit trees, what is left of the estate her parents planted and ran? Fruit trees, a willow-choked gully, a few acres of steep slope wracked with pine beetle, a wrecked house, empty for nearly three decades. It's been too much trouble, finding someone to lease or manage the land, these days. She can charge almost nothing for the lease; it's not worth it to anyone to cultivate if they have to pay a large rent. She's been charging just enough to pay the taxes. Even so, she has had difficulty finding someone willing to take it on, to put in the work. But the land should not sit idle; that's a waste.

She has been thinking of her boy, Justin. He is only eighteen. Not ready. She has planned that he would have the university years, would come into the land, as her father had done, in his thirties: mature, seasoned, a man.

It is not for herself. She will never live here again among the trees. She has no illusions about what is required, physically, socially, to run an orchard, to take on the community roles that her father or Mr. Inglis played. But she had wanted that for Justin.

Perhaps it has been stupid to hold that idea, that Justin would want the estate. What were the chances, after all? She had wanted him to become educated, to get his university degree, to travel a little. To become more than a farmer. And then to return and live here, to manage the orchards intelligently — to use his brain, not just his muscle. She had envisioned him at her father's old desk, looking at accounts, discussing plans with his foreman. She had imagined buying more property for him — forty acres, after all, could not support a family in very much comfort — setting him up in some style.

A daydream. *Buddenbrooks,* Clara had said scornfully, when she'd mentioned it once.

But the hills, the lake, the sky, the trees. The apples glowing red among the leaves. Her father walking through the orchard in his

Panama hat, the sun on his shoulders. The dignity of his labour, of making with his hands and eyes and brain a little world.

Her mother with her garden, the jeweled jars of peaches and beets and pickles lining the larder. Herself and Alice running through the tall grass. Alice with her apron full of day-old Rhode Island reds. Alice stepping out to a school concert, often the star, in crinoline and shining pale pageboy. Herself climbing to the height of land, lifting her face, smelling the air, storing the molecular print of the landscape in her bones.

In his speech at her retirement dinner, her director Dr. Haephestes had said, inaccurately, that she was returning to the village in which she had grown up. "Sundrenched, pastoral, fruit-growing village," he had said, actually. And not grown up, but "in which the fruits of her investigative genius had first been nurtured, as tiny seeds," which was botanically inaccurate, as well.

She is not returning to this community, no. She has bought a little house, a townhouse, as they called row houses here, on the outskirts of the city, ten kilometres further south along the highway, near the airport. A much more practical idea. She will continue to write and give conference papers for several more years, with any luck.

But she had envisioned, also, Beauvoir continuing on, at arm's length, under the husbandry of the Rilkes. Herself called in to vet big decisions. Beginning soon to bring Justin with her — he must be introduced to the orchards gradually, so they seemed appealing, not a millstone. At some point, she had planned to hire an architect to look at the house site — for the house itself would have to be bulldozed, likely; it was almost certainly damaged beyond retrieval — and have some discussions about a new place. Justin, of course, would have been part of that.

And yet, without the Rilkes. . . .

It has been an unfeasible dream, perhaps. Clara was right. She cannot practicably live here and run the orchard. She is too out of touch, not strong or young enough to manage it. She would have to work in the trees, and she is not up to that, no matter how fit she is for her age.

She has forfeited the land, perhaps, by her absence, by not having children of her own, by pursuing an intellectual life. By not being born a boy. She hadn't even wanted the estate for many years. She had rejected ties, had given it to Alice. Though it had come back to her, or what was left of it had. She had not wanted it.

But she had not ever thought that it would cease to be, cease to be hers. Cosmic irony, of course. *You don't know what you've got till it's gone,* as Joni Mitchell had sung.

She thinks that it might have been in those early days after Justin's birth, the nights she walked him up and down the short path of her apartment's breadth while Cynthia slept, that she had begun to think again of Beauvoir, of the slope of trees beside the shimmering lake, as something to which she belonged, something of value. Something to pass on to Alice's grandson.

Though perhaps it was more truthful to say that she had seen, in Justin, something of value to Beauvoir. A caretaker for Beauvoir. She has not thought of that.

Something ties her to this place, she sees that. She has not lived here in more than forty years — closer to forty-five — but something in her bones has become magnetized, is pulling her towards the landscape itself. Is it the minerals, the iron and calcium in the well water, long ago laid down in her bones, pulling back to the earth from which they leached? Longing pulls her, lines up her neurons like iron filings. She cannot see how to hold the land. But she must.

HUSBAND

Hugh telephones: he'll be back, he says, in June, with his daughter Ingrid. He seems to assume that he will stay with her again, that they will stay with her. It's a trespass: she resents it, then gives in, weakly, shaking her head at herself.

And now she must get through the boxes somehow, because she'll need space for Ingrid as well as Hugh. She must begin.

It takes her nearly a week before she acquires file folders, some labels, a package of paper dust masks, latex gloves, clear plastic boxes. Before she summons up enough will to descend the stairs to her daylight basement and to dive in, seizing a first box, sitting herself on a low stool beside it, slitting the packing tape.

She is ready to begin. She does not begin.

She turns on a lamp, angles it so the light shines directly into the box. She puts on a dust mask, tucking the elastic thread behind her ears, pinching the metal tab over the bridge of her nose. She puts on a pair of close-fitting latex gloves.

It is not dust she is worried about, or mouse droppings, even. It is the past, the underworld of memory.

About two-thirds of the boxes are labeled *Alice*: some in her mother's copperplate writing, the rest in her own impatient scrawl. She wishes the labeling had been more explicit; then she'd have some idea of where to start. As it is, she must try to guess, by the exteriors alone, what is in the containers. Some boxes are significantly older and marked with pasted-on labels written in thick, browning fountain-pen ink. Those must have been packed or assembled when she and Alice were still girls.

She has no desire to root through all of these things. If they could only be given to Hugh and Cynthia as they are. But no; who knows what could have been slipped into a box. Only she can go in safely, extricate any live fuses.

That's melodramatic. There may well be nothing. At most, only a few notes or letters to disturb the reader, and then only if he or she is alert and has sufficient background knowledge to be able to absorb the implications.

She will start with those that are not marked with Alice's name.

A large carton next, containing two metal boxes, each a foot square by half a foot deep, each with a lid, which has been sealed with duct tape. The tape is brittle, but not broached; what's in the tin boxes should be still intact.

Her mother's work again. She finds two loose paper labels, which must have originally been stuck to the metal; the glue on these has long undergone whatever chemical changes glue does, and is neutralized. One reads "Keepsakes 1940 – 1953" and the other, "Keepsakes 1953 – 1973."

Dating, then, from the year of her mother's arrival in the valley to her death. Mother must have sorted and packed these tins during her last illness; they have been dealt with efficiently, with a view to long storage. They say, now, that Mother didn't trust Alice and Sidonie to do the job properly. Had Mother expunged things as well? Who had she imagined breaking the seal as she taped the lids down? Or had she thought that the boxes might very well be destroyed without being opened?

She has seen the tin boxes before, of course: it comes to her now.

They had lived in the attic, and Mother had brought them down on sentimental occasions to leaf through them. *Here is the program from the war bond concert, when the operatic society did* The Pirates of Penzance, *and Betty and Anne Protherow and I were the sisters... and look; the blue ribbon I got for my dahlias!* And Father would sing a bit of the operetta, and they'd say *do you remember,* and be off for an hour or so, in a place that Alice and Sidonie couldn't follow.

Even then, even in her childhood, Marshall's Landing had seemed a place of past glories: exotic, paradisiacal. Her parents had reminisced: concerts and dances, flower shows and picnics on barges, of Father and Mr. Inglis playing polo, of Mother and Mrs. Inglis and Mrs. Clare and other women who were all now staid and grey dancing the cancan on stage in the community hall. Some of this world still existed, in remnants, in Sidonie's and Alice's childhood; more in Alice's, perhaps, as Alice was five years older than Sidonie and could remember occasions that Sidonie couldn't. But what remained seems a shadow, only, of a more luxurious, a more cultured time. There was always the sense that the best world had passed: only poor rags remained.

And what is this world to her, now? Or the realm of her childhood?

One of the boxes will be full of concert programs and dance cards and tea invitations: that will be interesting to Cynthia, perhaps. The other box will have — what? — school memorabilia, birthday cards, newspaper cuttings, largely featuring Alice. Also interesting to Cynthia, but preferably sorted first. But which is which? The boxes must have been purchased at the same time; they are identical.

She will have to open them.

Perhaps she should be thinking in terms of museum archives. The contents of the boxes will document a time long past and could be valuable. She wonders if she should worry about the age of the contents; perhaps they will crumble, disintegrate, as soon as air enters the container?

She remembers this particular box: this one with the Ogopogo Apples logo pasted on. She has seen it many times, in the attic of her parents' house, and had once or twice rifled through it, removing — and, she hopes, replacing — contents. Borrowing. It appears to contain the bulk of Alice's dozen or so years of schoolwork: her arithmetic and spelling sheets, her coloured maps and pages of numbered notes and exercises, as well as her essays and stories. All with grades of A or above 90%: that was Alice. Even the very early pieces distinguished by the very neat printing and conventional spelling.

She supposes that she could give the box to Cynthia as it is. Let Cynthia sort it out, and keep the more personal, the more expressive work, if she chooses. It's not her duty to compensate, now, for Mother's idolatrous archiving.

To be fair, there had been a similar box of her own infantile emanations, also kept by Mother in the attic. She has to admit that. Her mother had kept her work, too. She herself had burned it, in the late fall of 1973, driving out into a suburb of Montreal where she and Adam sometimes walked along the river. She had built a small, efficient bonfire, using newspaper, matches, fireplace kindling bought from a hardware store. Not easy for urban dwellers to burn things, she had realized. Nobody had real fireplaces anymore. But the fire had caught quickly, thanks to her training in the Girl Guides and Hugh's Hiking Club, and she had burned that box, with its contents, down to grey ash before anyone had noticed the small fire on the river bank.

A satisfying personal ceremony, and one she has never regretted. The objects of the past are contaminated; they hold the dust of all mistakes. She would burn up the lot of this, if she hadn't promised it to Cynthia and now Hugh.

She pages through relics, replaces them in their boxes. Moves on.

A trunkful of Alice's dresses. These had not been packed by Sidonie, hurriedly, with most of Alice's other things, in the days after Alice's death, but by someone else, earlier. The dresses have been folded, meticulously, with twists of tissue in the folds, more tissue and plastic bags around the dresses. Mothballs in the trunk, at one time; there's still a faint odour of naphtha. A professional job, almost museum quality; no evidence of mildew or vermin or even discolouration. Who had done this, archived the clothes so well? Mother, likely; Alice herself wouldn't have been bothered.

She doesn't unseal the bags, doubting that she'll be able to re-pack them as well. Through the tissue, the plastic, she sees swatches of fabric, and with almost no hesitation, her memory fills in the rest. Blue broadcloth, mint-green poplin, white piqué. Candy-pink madras plaid, blue gingham, blue seersucker.

Dresses that Alice had made herself: the last years she was at home, the dining room table was perpetually covered with pattern tissue and fabric yardage, as if it were the back room of a dressmaker's shop. And the dresses were lovely, were confections. All with fitted bodices, full skirts: that was the style. Only the necklines and sleeves and collars changed, and Alice drew and adapted these constantly. It was a serious business. Women's magazines elaborated at length on the correct choice of neckline for face shape. The collars and necklines all had names: Peter Pan, portrait, sweetheart. A whole culture of neck openings.

And Alice's clothes were so much a product of her imagina-tion and labour that they might be justly seen as an extension of her. Though they were also the taste of that particular era. Art and packaging at once. Well, that might say something about a woman's lot. She must remember to ask Clara about it. Clara will explain it to her.

She ought to just pass this trunk on to Cynthia, intact. Cynthia will be charmed to receive something so pretty, so benign, from Alice. She ought to have thought of the dresses before, ought to have searched them out and given them to Cynthia. That might have been enough to satisfy her, might have forestalled this whole quest.

Cynthia can have the trunk of dresses. Cynthia can take respon-sibility for letting in the destructive air.

But if she herself were to undo these sealed bags, preserved in the dry desert air for these fifty years, what would come out? Would they smell of Alice? Would she recognize that smell?

Pandora's box: that was a story Father told her. The moral, he said, was that curiosity could get you into a lot of trouble. But Clara says the real moral of the story is that good and ill are inseparable in human experience. It's not Greek at all, but probably Zoroastrian, by way of the Persians, Clara says.

If she opens any of these bags, she will be in trouble, Sidonie knows.

She takes her X-Acto knife, makes a swift incision across the brittle membrane.

Mrs. Inglis says that she has found a husband for Alice. This, Sidonie, straddling the tall wooden stool, her legs twisted around the stool's legs, her skirt half up her thighs, overhears. Her mother and Mrs. Inglis are in the parlour with tea, Sidonie perched at the kitchen counter doing homework. The curtain between the kitchen and dining room is napped wine-purple flannel, through which anything can be heard.

Husband: this is a verb, Sidonie knows, and she imagines her mother and Mrs. Inglis do not know that. A verb meaning to cultivate or till, to manage prudently, to use or spend wisely. She sees that these meanings of the word are also apropos.

Sidonie's mother makes a sound like a slow bubble rising in stew — a cross between a sigh and a sputter. Then her voice, high and pinched, as if she were letting it out carefully, the way you let the dog out without letting flies in: "Oh?"

Sidonie sways a little over her geography homework, hums randomly under her breath. Important to keep moving, to not set up a sound of stillness, of listening, that might trickle into the other room, where her mother, narrow, but somehow slack, in print rayon, and Mrs. Inglis, a taut bolster in her cotton shirt and gabardine skirt, sit on the sofa.

Mrs. Inglis says, "Cecil is bringing in a new manager. He's from the States — went to agriculture college. He was overseas, but he hasn't got family. He was engaged, apparently, though it was broken off. Cecil's cousin knows the fellow's aunt, so we don't need to worry on those fronts."

Sidonie wonders if any of Mrs. Inglis's statements would qualify as non sequiturs. That is a term she has just learned. It's a useful word. It sounds like what it means: something shadowy, gimpy, loitering on the edge of what is open and frank. The sequiturs standing in their group, casual, dressed in their clean uniforms — togas, maybe — with their spears all polished. Then the non sequiturs, lurking, spurned, for good reason. They make her uneasy, these unspoken connections between things. They are shifty, dangerous. They don't play by the rules.

She hums, pencils in Skeena River on her map. As she writes, she hears the words pronounced in Mrs. Inglis's fruity vowels, feels their stickiness, as if they are globs of preserves falling from a spoon.

"Respectable," Sidonie's mother says, and Sidonie can hear the sound of her mouth again opening so briefly to let the words out. Respectable is not a sticky word, from her mother's mouth. It is a white wall, with a small stained-glass window, like at church. It means, Sidonie knows, going to church, but the right one, not the tiny Catholic one by the highway, nor the painted wooden one where the Lutherans meet and sing loudly and seriously, their somber German words spilling out when the doors are left open on hot Sundays in July. Though that is almost respectable.

Respectable is Mrs. Inglis and Mr. Inglis, who came from England and owned one of the big orchards, and hired workers, and their two sons, Graham and Hugh, and the Protherows and Wentworths, the Smithsons and the Elliots and Erskines. Respectable is also Sidonie's family, though they live in a smaller house than the Inglises, and had a smaller orchard, and though Sidonie's father is not English, because he comes from a titled family, and her mother's parents are Scottish. Respectable is also Dr. MacKenzie, and Miss Thompson and Mrs. Clare, who runs the Ladies' Hospital Auxiliary, and the principal, Mr. Ramsay, who are all Scottish. To a certain extent, it is the German-speaking families that moved here after the war: the Knopfs and Kruegers, the Rilkes and Getzkes and Gormanns.

It is not the Dubrinskys and McCarthys and Platts who are Catholic and have the butcher's store, or the Indians who sell salmon and berries door-to-door in the fall, or the American tourists who stay at the Kal-Oka campground in the summer, and buy the turtles Sidonie and Walt catch in Wood Lake, only to let them go, or the orchard workers who live in the camp up the hill, with its tiny cabins you can see from the road, and the irrigation duct running by on its trestle legs. It is not, somehow, the Japanese farmers who grow beautiful glossy cucumbers and cabbages on the rich black bottom land, though everyone is respectful of them.

Respectable also means being married to someone with white skin and wearing a hat and speaking the Queen's English and a lot of other things that Sidonie can't identify and wouldn't seem to matter, taken on their own, but add up to something important. Alcohol consumption; the colour of women's dresses and hairstyles and their voices, especially outside; what is growing in the front yard; what is taken for lunch by children, and what teenagers do on Friday evenings. All of those things: hard to identify, but easy to recognize, both by the respectable and the not. Some of the immigrant families, for example, have learned English and dress like Canadians and plant proper flowers in front of their houses, while some do not. Sidonie doesn't understand why people who are not respectable don't try harder to become so; after all, it is preferable; more opportunities are available. If, for example, Mrs. Platt were to tidy her hair, stitch up the torn hem on her rayon dress, and press that dress, or better still, exchange it for one in a quiet grey or navy print, she might be included in the Women's Institute meetings, and wouldn't that be nicer for her?

Some parts of being respectable can be helped, but some, like being English as opposed to Indian, cannot. They are simply an accident of birth. That is perhaps not fair, Sidonie can see, but on the other hand, if people have bad genetic traits, they can't cut the mustard. That is a metaphor that Mr. Inglis uses; Hugh Inglis has explained to Sidonie, who doesn't always understand metaphors, that it means "can be relied on to do appropriate things in work or social situations." Sidonie has been learning about genetics in biology class; about Gregor Mendel, who was Austrian. She understands that genes can be passed on, and she can see, in the families in Marshall's Landing, that genes are important. That if you have certain sets of genes from your ancestry, you are more likely to be feckless and dirty, to steal things and fail at math. That is obvious.

It is good to be respectable, because then you will work hard and have good manners and a clean house, and bad things will not happen to you.

And Alice, who not only belongs to this protected and circumspect circle, but is a star, a princess: crowned Lady of the Lake, and voted Most Likely to Succeed in her graduating class, must marry someone of equal stature: someone who will fit in. This is difficult, because there are not very many boys Alice's age here of equal stature.

Sidonie's mother says, "Alice is going to the secretarial college at the coast in the fall," which is news to Sidonie, and on second thought, probably not true. Her mother's voice is all minced up and dry, like the feed cakes that Alice's friend Bonnie gives her horse in the winter. Sidonie can see, in her imagination, her mother's lips pushed out, finicky and velvet, over the words. That is because Alice has disappointed, and Mother is upset and embarrassed. Alice has not fulfilled her potential so far. She has gone to Victoria College on a scholarship, with the idea that she will get her degree and/or meet a nice college boy, but neither has happened. Here Alice is back home, nineteen years old and not even engaged.

Secretarial college? Is it true? Father and Mother have said that Alice won't go back to college, because it was so expensive for her to live in Victoria for a year, and she didn't apply herself. Her marks were not very good. Mother said that Alice should have done the teacher's training program, which was only one year; she could be finished and getting a job. But Father had said that a degree would give Alice more opportunities, and Alice had not wanted to be a teacher.

Sidonie doesn't know what grades Alice got; Alice isn't saying. She is sullen when the topic of college comes up; she says that it was all nonsense, anyway. But Alice isn't happy to be home; she says, repeatedly, that she is bored, that this is a nothing place.

If she is to go to secretarial college, she might be happy. She might be nicer to Sidonie.

Sidonie untangles her legs from the stool quickly, with the sudden thought that she will find Alice, tell her this bit of news. Before she reaches the door, though, she remembers: she should hold still, see if she can learn more. Alice will only be annoyed with Sidonie if she is brought half a tale. And — Sidonie has almost forgotten — there is the matter of the husband whom Mrs. Inglis has found for Alice. Of course it's a joke; Mrs. Inglis has said many times that Alice is too young to be thinking of getting married. It's just her way of teasing Mother, who is very worried about what will become of Alice. But still: interesting to hear about the proposed husband, the newcomer. Perhaps he will be suitable: be handsome and sophisticated, and will fall in love with Alice. It is not just any man who can appreciate Alice, or whom Alice would be interested in. She is not, for example, interested in boys her own age, or in the slightly older fellows with their work-hardened forearms, their sunburned necks, their lingering accents, who moved to Marshall's Landing after the war and drink up their wages. For a man to appeal to Alice, he must be not only flawless, but exotic. And Mrs. Inglis knows that.

She sidles back to her stool, but it is too late. There is a listening quiet, an awareness, from the other side of the curtain. Her mother and Mrs. Inglis have remembered that she is within earshot. They will say no more.

Alice, in Sidonie's imagination, in the place she sorts and stores everything, is a wisteria pod: long, silvery, languidly curved, probably stuffed with silky down. Sidonie can see in her mind a picture of Alice the seed pod: the shimmery white seed hairs lying smooth, tightly packed, all going in one direction. Alice isn't quite as tall as Sidonie is, but is willowy rather than gawky, as Sidonie is. She has hair that is almost naturally platinum blonde and is a beauty.

Alice is treated, now that she has been away, as if she were a little different from the rest of the family, from Sidonie and her parents. She doesn't have to eat the same food and has new clothes and is allowed to visit the friends she has made at college, the town girls, instead of doing chores. The girls Alice has made friends with are Nancy and Diana and Jill. They have the clothes advertised in magazines. They have only to do small chores, like brush the cat or dust the piano. Or so Alice tells Sidonie, when she is in a talkative mood.

And Alice works at Fulmerton's in town, in Ladies' Clothing. She must dress up for work, unlike Sidonie, who wears dungarees or shorts, or her mother, who wears sturdy gabardine skirts and aprons, and puts on dresses when company comes.

Alice is a beauty, and is good at everything that Sidonie is not — sewing and writing and baking and dancing. Sidonie is certainly not a beauty, and is possibly a disgrace. Although she is fourteen, she is still scrawny, knobby, with stick legs. She can't walk across a room without tripping over something. She makes messes when she helps in the kitchen, as she has been expected to do the last year, with Alice gone, and her schoolwork is a disgrace. Also, she slouches, and doesn't look people in the eye when they speak to her.

Alice has come back from college even more impatient with Sidonie's looks and comportment, or lack of it.

One day, she had seized Sidonie by the shoulders, forced her to look at her own face in the little square mirror over the bathroom sink. Sidonie had stared at the two faces: Alice's oval, like a three-quarters moon, with its rows of evenly crimped cornsilk waves, and her own, which she could not bear to look at, which reached out to her, jumping, alarming, as if seen through moving ripples. Alice had squeezed Sidonie's jaw in her hand and turned Sidonie's face to the mirror, and held it there until Sidonie raised her eyelids. And finally, the face had stopped moving, for a few seconds, and she was able to see it: square, brownish, with dark brown, wavy hair escaping from her braids and lying on her forehead, her flattish nose, her grey eyes. For a few seconds, it was only a face. It did not shout out the whole history of her being, did not turn her inside out, like a wound, as she felt. For a few seconds she saw this. Then, something else: her eyes were not round like Alice's, but long and just slightly slant, and her eyebrows made another long line at the same angle and so did her hairline and the edge of her cheekbones. Now her face was a pleasing arrangement of long, slightly arched, lines, like a painting of the sea or cirrus clouds. Only the mouth, with the lips pulled back in a sort of snarl, ruined the effect.

Sidonie is not a beauty, but Alice is: that is what people know of her. It is her job.

Alice must have beautiful clothes, have her hair styled, wear gloves and hats. Sidonie does not wish for any of this. She does not wish to be Alice, only to admire Alice, and for Alice to be kinder to her. And when Alice has found a husband, someone to care for her, to give her what she deserves; then she will be happy.

All the stories say so.

And that is the first she had heard of Mr. Defoe.

Perched on her stool, listening to Mother and Mrs. Inglis plot: what had she learned? More than gossip: she had ingested, with her milk and graham crackers, something more insidious. A sense of separation that had not served her or Alice well. Respectability: how Mother and Mrs. Inglis both had cherished that hothouse plant. So much effort. How they had fought, how much energy they had put into cultivating that glossy thing, for their children. How they had worked to provide for their children something they themselves did not completely understand. And how ephemeral, how untenable it had been, for all of them, and how deadly, in the end, for them all.

Yet she can see what they fought for, and does not know that she would have had it different. Her world has been larger, richer, because she had the opportunities for education beyond the rows of fruit trees. And she does not know how that wider world would have been brought to her without the trappings of culture surrounding it. What was possible in those days?

She shuts up the trunk, poking the billowing cellophane bags back inside, ineffectually. It's too much: What's shut in there is too much.

And now it is May and feels like summer. She takes a trip to Vernon to hear a jazz trio play at the college. (How Vernon has come along!) She'd invited first Cynthia, then Justin, to come with her to the little concert, but both had pled prior engagements. Her own fault; she hadn't thought of asking someone to come along until too late. She leaves her house an hour earlier than she needs to and takes a detour, driving off the highway to find the old track (now paved, and lined with houses) that they had followed to the gold mine. The paving doesn't go all the way though: it stops, perhaps a quarter of a mile short. She is relieved: the hill is still there in its loose curtain of trees, a granite knob rising from the other slopes.

On the way back to the highway, she takes the route that winds up through the orchards, and sees stick-legs of the tall ladders among the rows of trees, men and women thrust head and shoulders into the sharp spring green of the leafy canopy.

Thinning. She has done that. Her fingers, in her sensory memory, twist around small furred fruit: little plush ears. The fruit that will not survive, will not be food. (The fruit that will not reach fruition.) She can remember the last time, fifty years ago.

During thinning, everyone works: most of the kids miss school. Alice has her job, of course, but Sidonie and Mother and Father, Walter and Mr. Rilke are all out in the orchard early, early, in the cool fresh dawn. Walter's cousins Trudy and Anna, who are too young to thin, are conscripted to rake the small hard unripe fruit from the mowed grass under the trees, as Sidonie used to do. Father has mowed before the thinning to make the fruit easier to pick up. If it is left on the ground, it will rot and foster pests.

Sidonie and Walt must each finish half a row per day. Mother and Father and Mr. Rilke can do much more. They work longer, too: from dawn till dark.

Thinning seems to take forever this year. Sidonie worries about missing school, and the apricots, she notices, are a little larger every day. It's almost too late, and the ones left have already had to share too much of the tree's sap and sunlight with their neighbours.

Thinning seems a strange thing to do, if you think about it.

When the bees and warmth have been plentiful during blossom time, and the fruit has set in heavily, as many as eight or nine of the little fruits have to be removed for every one that is left. It seems preposterously wasteful. Mother says, "When I first thinned, coming from the prairies in the Depression time and hardly having seen fruit, I couldn't believe we were supposed to take all of that fruit off. I never thinned clean enough. And then when your father came up here, it was the same all over again." But it seems odd to Sidonie, too, though she's lived in the orchards all her life, and understands that if the fruit isn't thinned out, none of the fruit will grow big and juicy; it'll all be small sour fruit.

The thinners stand on tall A-shaped ladders, dropping the green fruit to the ground below. It makes hardly a sound. Father keeps them spaced when they're thinning, so that they don't chatter and waste time. In the morning, the low sun slants in through the trees, and the orchard is alive with birds and light and the rustling of leaves in the breeze. The big trees are ships tossing gently in a sea: the ladders are rigging. But in the heat of the day, everything is still, silent, deep in the dappled pale green shade of early spring

It's strange to be thinning in such silence. Usually Alice is there, and Masao and the men from the camp. Even neighbours are hired, so that the thinning can be finished in a couple of days. And then everyone moves on to the next orchards. It's always the same order, because the fruit is not all exactly at the same stage. Some orchards face in a more southerly direction; others are sheltered, free of frost pockets; others slope more steeply or are in shadow part of the day. And everyone, people like Mr. Rilke, who have only a dozen acres, and orchardists like Father and Mr. Inglis, who own a hundred acres, knows what order they will come in, and everyone who can works in the orchards for as long as it takes for all the work to be done.

But Mr. Defoe has changed the order of things. He's started thinning earlier, and hired all the people to come and work in Mr. Inglis's orchards who would usually be working in Father's right now. Father was angry — he stopped Mr. Defoe as he drove by in his truck, and said "What are you playing at, my man?" in a loud voice. Mr. Defoe didn't get out of the truck; he said, "Now look here, von Täler, I'm running things now." Then Father talked to Mr. Inglis, and Sidonie didn't know what Mr. Inglis said.

Sidonie doesn't mind the quiet, though for the first couple of days, she is stiff from thinning, and her arms and back so sore she has trouble sleeping. Mother rubs arnica lineament into their shoulders, and the house smells of it; a hot, angry smell. But in the daytime, in the trees with their new sharp green leaves, nobody is angry, only working very hard to snap off the little green nubs. When they come in for the evening, Sidonie tries to do her pages of math and geography and composition. But her fingers cramp up, and won't hold the pen. The muscles for holding the pen are the same muscles as for the tiny twist and pull that snaps off the fruit, Father says, rubbing Sidonie's fingers between his palms, blowing on them. Sidonie does the dishes, even though it's not her turn: the hot water is so soothing.

The thinning is taking too long. Already they should be starting the apples and pears, but the apricots and peaches aren't done. Father says: the children shouldn't be out of school any longer. Father goes to ask Mr. Nakamura, who looks after the Clare's orchard, for some help, but Mr. Nakamura is working as hard as he can. He can't spare anyone.

"It is unfortunate," Mr. Nakamura says, and Father nods.

"A bad business. We will have to do something. I've spoken to Inglis, but he says his hands are tied."

The next morning, Masao turns up, rapping lightly on the kitchen door before they're even all dressed.

"I said I was too sick to work today," he grins. It's a joke: the men in the camps have all been working for Mr. Defoe. But Masao has come to help *them*.

Alice is smoothing her hair back in the mirror over the kitchen sink. When Masao says he's staying, she puts down her hairbrush. "I'm sick too," she says. And on the telephone to Fulmerton's, she sounds so quiet and faint that Sidonie wants to laugh. "Mrs. Lloyd?

I'm afraid I can't come in today. I've got such a headache. . . flu, I think."

So they have two more pairs of hands. Alice and Masao are fast at thinning, even though they talk and laugh and pelt each other with green fruit.

And then they are at the last tree, and the thinning finished, but it is not a triumph, because they are all so dirty and tired, and have not eaten a good meal for days, and it is so late: the spraying has been delayed. People stop by the house every evening to see if there is work, but the orchards are all finished now. Mr. Inglis's orchards have all been thinned, and also the independent farmers. There will be no work until July, when the cherries are ripe.

"And what then?" asks Father. "Will Defoe hire all the pickers at once, too? Pick the green cherries?"

"I'm sure it will all work out," Mother says, but Sidonie thinks she doesn't sound sure. She wonders if Mother remembers that Mr. Defoe is supposed to marry Alice.

Mr. Inglis's truck is stolen, near the end of the thinning season, and found in Vernon. Everyone suspects the Platt boys, but they protest their innocence vehemently (and probably truthfully for once, Father says).

"It was them out-of-town pickers that the new foreman hired, eh? Them *interinits*," Sidonie hears Len Platt saying, in front of the Red and White Grocery.

Mr. Defoe comes to talk to Father and drink whiskey in the parlour. None of the family is allowed in. "Business," Father says. There is no shouting, but after Mr. Defoe leaves, Father seems smaller, in a frightening way.

And then he comes over again two evenings later, driving his red truck up the driveway into the yard. Sidonie has been getting the eggs. He brakes the truck beside her and stops. His sandy hair looks damp, and he smells like soap. Sidonie notices the black hairs on the forearm resting on the open cab window.

"Hello, Sidonie," he says. "Is your sister home?"

Sidonie feels herself scowl. She wants to say no, but Alice has already seen the truck: The back door slams and Alice strides out, wearing a blue skirt and white blouse. Her tanned legs are bare, and she has sandals on her feet, and her pale pink toenail polish looks shockingly nude in comparison to the bright red polish most women are wearing.

Sidonie asks, "Alice! Where are you going?"

"See ya," Alice says, climbing into the truck beside Mr. Defoe. He reverses and turns the truck, nearly crushing the mock-orange bush, and then speeds down the driveway.

If Mr. Defoe marries Alice, he'll be Sidonie's brother-in-law. But maybe it would be a good thing. If he were married to Alice, he couldn't treat Father badly, could he? Perhaps Alice will convince him to change his mind about hiring away all of the orchard workers. Perhaps she is doing that right now: talking earnestly but sweetly to Mr. Defoe, explaining why it's better to cooperate.

Though, to be honest, that doesn't sound like Alice.

When Sidonie brings the eggs into the kitchen, she says to Mother, "Alice went somewhere with Mr. Defoe."

"Shhh, I know," Mother replies. "We don't need to announce it to the world."

Sidonie understands: Father isn't meant to know. Is that right? It seems dubious: Alice ought not to be going around with Father's enemy, especially behind Father's back.

But then, maybe it's going to be a surprise. Alice will convince Mr. Defoe to work with Father, as all of Mr. Inglis's previous foremen have done, and then Father will be very happy and relieved. That must be it.

Mother had burned herself out on Alice, that was the matter. She had expended all of her imagination and energy on preparing Alice for something that was starting, that summer, to look as if it wouldn't happen, and she was panicking. That was it.

And Father? What had he been thinking? What had he hoped for Alice? That seems less clear. Had he left matters like that to their mother?

He had been so much taken up with other things: the orcharding business was at its peak, demand for fresh fruit among easterners and Americans very high, so prices good, but many orchardists entering the market, and labour scarce.

Mr. Defoe. She has not thought of him in a long time, though she supposes now that in some way she has never *not* thought of him. He certainly wasn't what Mother hoped he would be. Not good enough for Alice, anyway. They should have seen that.

VETCH

Cynthia visits one Sunday — on the pretext, or Sidonie assumes
it is a pretext — of bringing Sidonie a large, hanging planter filled
with bright-coral petunias and that ubiquitous little blue flower used
to fill flower baskets.

"Happy Mother's Day," Cynthia says.

Really, it is embarrassing. She is not Cynthia's mother. There is
no need for this sort of thing. She assumes that Cynthia has really
come to check on her progress with the boxes. She feels hemmed
in; she is not ready to hand over her gleanings yet. But then she
thinks, happily, of the dresses: yes, those Cynthia might have
right away. She lugs the trunk up to her living room, opens the lid.
"Go ahead," she says.

Cynthia is so pleased that Sidonie feels guilty, fraudulent. She
sits back, though, while Cynthia begins to lift out the transparent
packages with their pastel folds.

Can she remember the stories behind the outfits? She can. She
names their occasions, briefly, for Cynthia: valedictorian speech,
competition speech, trip to Vancouver, visits to different associations.

Blue poplin, pink shantung, eggshell sharkskin. A floating, ruffled frock in aqua cotton lawn: she remembers Alice and Mother sewing this dress. Fifty-four separate pieces, Mother had said, half boasting, half complaining. Yards of ruffles; a dozen pearl buttons, each with a tiny fabric loop.

A cloud of white inside cellophane packaging; Cynthia exclaims when she sees it, wants to open it. But it's not Alice's wedding dress; it's a short white formal dress with layers of tulle in the skirt, a boned bodice with a deeply scooped neck. Cynthia holds it up by the ruched shoulders: Alice's graduation dress?

No. Her Lady of the Lake gown. Her graduation gown is in another bag, drifts of embroidered, sequined tulle, pale blue. There doesn't appear to be a wedding dress.

I know she had one, Cynthia says. There are photos.

Yes, there are. But what has become of the dress? Sidonie, looking through the album, finds the picture but doesn't remember this garment at all.

"Perhaps it was borrowed," she says.

It was common to borrow a dress, especially if the wedding was a small one, or hurried.

When Cynthia had shaken out the white frock, something small and hard had fallen out of its folds, bounced and rolled under the chair. Cynthia had not noticed; she was looking at the dress, and she didn't, of course, hear the small thud. For no reason, except, perhaps, her own reticence, Sidonie had left it lying.

When Cynthia leaves, she retrieves it, kneeling to feel beneath the sofa. It's a small piece of carved jade, a little stylized cat. It has a hole through it for a cord. She knows exactly what it is: *netsuke*, an ornamental button for a Japanese coat. She has never seen it before, but as she holds it in her hand, she thinks that she knows where it has come from.

It's Masao who shows Sidonie the chocolate lilies and Indian paint, which grow not on the sunny, grassy, hillsides, but on the north-facing slope above the camp, where the spruce trees grow black and scaly, draped with old man's beard, and the irrigation pipe curves its way, galvanized tin on wooden trestles, around the outcrops of the hills. Here the forest is cool, shadowy, unfamiliar. Under the half-pipe, which leaks, mosses and ferns grow, and violets, and a chain of small ponds, thick with cattails and yellow water lilies, painted turtles, frogs.

Masao lives in the pickers' camp with the single men who work the orchards. He is a nephew of Mr. Tanaka, who plays chess with Father. Masao and Mr. Tanaka are not the only men from the camp who come to their place to work, but Sidonie knows them best because of Mr. Tanaka playing chess. But Mr. Tanaka is old: a businessman. He used to be. He wears glasses and speaks very little, and has a kind of harsh voice, grey threads in his hair. Masao is different: his face is round, full of light. He is taller than Mr. Tanaka, and, while they both speak perfect English, he talks like the kids Sidonie knows, while Mr. Tanaka is abrupt and formal. Both Masao and Mr. Tanaka were born in Canada; even Masao's parents were born in Canada, Father says. They are Canadian citizens. What happened to Masao's parents is a disgrace, Father says. But Mother and Mrs. Clare say, you never know; they are different from us. And look what the Japs did to our boys in Asia.

Sidonie is not supposed to go over the hill to the camp, and in fact would not venture on her own, but one day, when Masao and Alice are joking over the sprinklers, Masao invites Alice and her to come and see his house, and so they do, without Alice telling their parents. (How old are they at this point? Alice perhaps fifteen, and Sidonie ten?) One Saturday Alice just says, "Come with me," and they walk up the hill to the top, just where the road curves and begins snaking down the hill again to the lake, and then turn and go into the camp, which is a collection of tiny cabins sheltered under very large pines and fir trees. Sidonie has been before, of course, in Father's truck, when he drives Masao and Mr. Tanaka home after a chess game, in the winter, when it is dark at suppertime and the snow thick on the ground. But she has never gotten out of the truck, only looked through the window at the neat wooden cabins with their green trim and roofs, and the clearings of vegetable gardens and swept dirt yards. Now she is anxious; they are not supposed to go to the camp, are they?

But Alice hurries her along and seems to know where to go. It is the tiny cabin on the end, no bigger, Sidonie sees, than the room she and Alice share. Alice knocks on the door, and it is opened by Masao, who bows a little, the way he does sometimes when he's nervous, and asks them to come in. Sidonie is enchanted by the cabin — a little house, with everything you could want. A little stove, like the one in the wash house, only smaller, black, with a round plate that can be lifted out (there is the little handle that slips into the slot) to put wood inside. On the stove is a kettle, and there is a countertop with a basin, and some shallow shelves holding a blue-and-white teapot and cups, as well as bottles and paper packages all neatly folded. There are two narrow bunk beds with patchwork quilts, and a tiny table, painted with orange and green chrysanthemums, and a calendar and a painting of ducks on the wall. Everything you could want, and so clean.

Sidonie and Alice have to sit on the lower bed, because there are no chairs. Alice spreads out her blue chambray skirt and shakes her hair over her shoulders. She doesn't look around her as Sidonie does, but instead looks at Masao with a sort of mocking look, a challenge. Daring him, Sidonie thinks, or daring herself. Sidonie wriggles and tries to pull her own skirt smooth under her legs. It has ridden up, and the quilt, which is made of hairy thick pieces of wool fabric, as from people's overcoats, is itchy against her thighs.

"Sit still," Alice says. "Stop bouncing!" But Masao, who has been putting crumpled brown leaves from a twist of brown paper bag into the teapot, sits beside Sidonie and smiles at her. "Want to play a game?" He gets off the bed and reaches under it, suddenly, kneeling and bending to the ground to retrieve a box. His shirt slides up, showing the worn waistband of his black trousers, his lean brown back. Sidonie watches his back, which is curiously appealing. She wants to touch it, the smooth lean evenness of it. Then she looks up guiltily, to see that Alice is looking at Masao's back, too.

Masao emerges from under the bed, as if from underwater, smoothing down his hair and clothes, grinning. "Here."

Inside the flat box: a board, like a chess board, only with little curved legs, and made out of wine-coloured wood, and a bag of black and white checkers. The white checkers are made out of something natural — not celluloid or stone — perhaps ivory or shell — and the black pieces are stone, polished like glass marbles. The black pieces, Sidonie sees, are slightly larger than the white in diameter, but from a short distance they appear the same size. Why is that?

"You can play this with an opponent," Masao says, "or by yourself. See?" He moves pieces, his fine fingers not much bigger than Sidonie's own.

"What small hands you have," Alice teases. "Like a girl's." Sidonie thinks Masao will be mad, but he isn't. He laughs and holds his hand, palm out, in front of Alice. She presses hers against it.

"My palms are bigger," Masao says, "but your fingers are longer."

Alice slides her hand up a little so the bases of their fingers meet, and her pink fingertips extend past Masao's. "Yes," she says. And then slides her hand down again, so that once again they are palm to palm.

Sidonie watches for a moment, feeling that she does not quite know this aspect of Alice. Then she turns her attention to the game, which is kind of like chess, but different, too. When she finally manages to figure it out, the light from the small, high window has shifted, and Alice is saying that it's time to go. Beside Sidonie is a small blue-and-white cup half full of pale yellow tea, already cool. She can't remember drinking it, though she recalls its thin, bitter, floral taste.

Sometimes when they walk up the camp road, Masao meets them before they reach the cabins, stepping swiftly out of the shadows under the trestle to intercept them. Once, Sidonie, startled, screamed, and after that Masao would try to surprise her, perching on top of the trestle to dangle the feathery ends of grasses on her neck, or springing out to tickle her sides. Sidonie will then chase him through the trees, laughing and panting. Alice doesn't chase, but laughs at both of them, mocking, but not with her usual meanness.

Alice says, "If you mention this at home, we won't be allowed to visit anymore," which she doesn't need to say; Sidonie understands it. She and Alice are not supposed to go into the pickers' camp, where the workers for Mr. Inglis's and Father's orchards live. Many of them are rough men, strangers. But there is more than that edict behind Alice's concern: Alice does not like to be seen in public to be friends with Masao. Sidonie has noticed that they do not walk home together from the high school bus, and Alice does not go with Masao to the Teen Town dances, or to parties at friends' houses, or sit with him at the beach. Yet Masao comes to their house, and from spring thinning through fall picking, they will see him in their orchard almost every day.

Now, fifty years later, she understands.

She has not seen Masao for years. He'd be living still — not yet seventy. She had not found him at his little shop in the plaza, now that she thinks of it, when she was last here more than twenty years ago. She tries to recall what has taken the shop's place. Is it the insurance broker or the bakery? But the premises have likely changed hands more than once.

It would, in fact, have been 1963 when she saw him at his store, when she had come back with Adam on a kind of honeymoon trip. Mother had said that Masao had opened a shop, a music store, in the new plaza on the highway, and Sidonie and Adam had driven down to where the Canadian Imperial Bank of Commerce, the Red and White food store, the café and drug store and hardware store stood, a small row of false-fronted buildings. And there was Masao's shop: Kobe Music. And Masao coming around from behind the counter, looking surprised, happy, shaking hands with Adam, squeezing Sidonie in a hug.

Adam had wanted to buy a record — a recording that Sidonie knew they could find easily in Montreal. But then Mr. Tanaka had come out from a back area, even smaller than Sidonie remembered (she towered over him, now) and wobbly, and somehow, having forgotten how to speak English, and insisted, in grunted Japanese, in sign language, that the record should be a gift. Sidonie had been paralyzed with awkwardness, but Adam had known what to do: the record was accepted as a gift, with many thanks from Adam, and bows from Mr. Tanaka. And then Adam had to buy another record, which he did, from a stash Masao produced from a back shelf. "Still in its jacket," Adam had marveled. "This is rare. My father will be amazed." But Sidonie had recognized it as one of Masao's own.

After, Adam and Sidonie were beckoned into the back room, where Mr. Tanaka served them green tea in the tiny porcelain cups with no handles that Sidonie remembered from their cabin, and Masao, with an ear for the door chimes, sat and talked to Sidonie in his old teasing way. Has she learned to speak French yet? Does she talk more in French than in English? (That wouldn't be hard!) And has she broken all of her new wedding dishes yet? And has she learned to cook for her new husband, or poisoned him with her awful food, like the last one? Adam had smiled, and Mr. Tanaka had laughed and rubbed his hands together.

Mr. Tanaka, Masao said, had had a stroke. Since his stroke, he can't remember how to speak English, though he still understood it, some of the time. "When he wants to," Masao said, mischievous again, and Mr. Tanaka had chuckled, as if he got the joke.

And Sidonie's father had loaned Masao a good part of the money to get the store started: did Sidonie know that? That was very generous.

Her discomfort, then, that Masao had clowned, and kowtowed to Adam. Or so she had seen it.

He'd likely be living in the same house — the little brown-painted bungalow with its porch and maples that he had bought back in the late sixties. She imagines him there, on his knees cleaning out the peony beds, as old Mr. Tanaka had done, coming inside to make tea, to put something on the stereo. Imagines the sandalwood and jasmine smell of his house, the shade of the bamboo blinds.

Perhaps she could give him a call. He must be in the telephone book.

She will ask Hugh if he has heard from Masao first, perhaps. That'd be the smart thing. She and Hugh could make a visit together, next time Hugh is in town.

But later, she thinks: *foolish, foolish*. What would she and Masao have to say to each other? Even with Hugh there. She has witnessed these conversations between the elderly, on meeting old acquaintances. The shock of alteration, the awkwardness, the inventory of memories, not always shared, the slow trickle-in of grief, the ineffable sense of loss. The descent into the maudlin, if alcohol has been imbibed.

A pointless exercise. Pointless and painful.

She will not speak to Hugh, after all.

Sometimes she and Alice and Masao do not go to Masao's cabin, but instead head through the trees, following the irrigation pipe as it skirts the camp and then makes a line across the ridge of the hill. On the other side is a rough granite outcropping, and from this mass of rock, the lake stretches out for fifty miles in two directions, north and south. The hills on the other side are far enough away to be blue, and the lake is cobalt on sunny days, steel when clouds dull the sky. Sometimes the paddle-wheeler can be seen, traveling between the dock, invisible at the base of the hill a mile below, and Fintry, on the other side, and sometimes little sailboats, white specks moving back and forth.

In the rock outcropping is an old gold mine, like a cave. They must not go inside, Masao says, for the shaft has partially collapsed, and they might fall down and be crushed. The opening is full of spiders' webs and old lumber: Masao lifts a board to show the black widow clinging underneath, shiny as coal. He uses his penknife to flip the spider over; underneath is the red hourglass. Sidonie feels a sort of horror at the mine that extends to the outcropping itself. She shakes when she first sees it, even though Masao shows her the trove of white quartz pieces in front of the mine opening.

Alice and Masao, Sidonie sees, both like the outcropping, with its astonishing vista. Once up there, they relax as if they are at home. Alice sometimes packs a picnic lunch: egg sandwiches, oatmeal biscuits, apples. Masao sometimes brings soda. That's a treat: they don't have it at home. Father says it rots the stomach; Mother says it is too expensive. Masao apologizes for it: he can't bring food, he says, as he doesn't have access to the kitchens. But Sidonie loves the soda: the bottles with their narrow necks, the fizziness, the sweetness, which she thinks of as Masao's sweetness, a kind of honeyed lilting softness that spills over onto Alice and her and the trips themselves.

Sidonie picks the chocolate lilies, with their deep glossy brown and green checkered bells, but only if they walk along the trestles on the way home. Out of water, the lilies don't last half an hour. She picks the Indian Paint, too, for the flash of its orange flame in the shadowy parlour. But on their picnics, she gathers only a certain family of flower, which grows everywhere in a dozen or more varieties, so common and unprepossessing as to be nameless. No: some have names. Vetch, alfalfa, clover, locoweed. But the others are anonymous, overlooked short bushes, tangled vines, tall, hairy stalks. What makes them a family is that they all produce pea-blossom-shaped flowers. Some of the flowers are yellow, some, like those of the alfalfa, blue ranging through lilac and purple, some a striking violet-pink. Some of the blossoms are arranged in long spikes, others in ball-shaped clusters, and still others in single blooms.

She can't say what fascinated her first: that there were so many of these plants, or that there were such subtle variations among them. (That they were related, connected, was a premise *a priori*, apparently.) She has begun, unable to find out their names, to keep track of them in a notebook: drawing in the flowers, numbering them, making cryptic notes about where she has found them, what date. They are intricate to draw, and for some, she has borrowed her father's magnifying glass and gazed at the blooms, nodding to herself, humming, as the familiar flattened trumpet shape, the inner and outer lobes, the furred throats, slip into focus. Some of the blossoms are flatter, some longer, some more pouched, some veined. But all share the base pattern of a flared tube — a tube with nectar at its foot, and the two pairs of symmetrical, fused, cleft lobes, the smaller hooded by the larger, outer — that reminds of her of something she can't quite identify.

Often, Sidonie brings her notebook along on the forays. She remembers now the intensely sweet scent of the little yellow bells. The dark mouth of the mine, the vertigo of the rock peak.

How often had they gone? Had she always been invited, or had Alice and Masao made the excursion on their own?

They had done that hike together for years: until Alice and Masao were in their late teens, maybe. And to her, Masao seemed a childhood friend, familiar as their own orchard, as Graham or Hugh Inglis, as shy tow-headed Walt.

She remembers the lowing of cattle from Tiefendale's dairy farm to the south and west of the picnic hill. Did Alice once or more than once send her down the rutted dirt road to ask Mary Tiefendale, in her droopy print dress, her hand covering missing teeth, smudging her words, for a pint of milk?

She remembers how the light grew thick, and blue butterflies, the same purplish-dusk-fading-to-turquoise as the blossoms of the alfalfa that attracted then, clung to her page, their antennae exclamation points above her pea-flower drawings. The blue butterflies, the little Azures, resting their thread legs, their comma feet, on the page of her sketchbook. Did her eyes close in the heat of the afternoon, the buzz of the insects, and Alice's and Masao's voices fuse into one murmur, as if a clear small spring were trickling over the parched soil, the glittering, broken granite slope?

Hugh returns, as promised, in late June, bringing his youngest daughter, a sturdy girl in her early twenties, with the thick blonde hair and short upper lip that Sidonie associates with the Dutch. She seems natural, wholesome, Sidonie thinks, dressed in khaki shorts and T-shirt. She looks very much like Hugh, and like Mrs. Inglis, whose presence is startlingly conjured up by Ingrid's round hazel eyes and grin.

Her neighbour calls to her over the railing as she's watering her pots of geraniums: "I see you've got your boyfriend's grand-daughter visiting. She's the spit of him, isn't she!"

"Hugh is not my boyfriend," Sidonie says. "Ingrid is his daughter, not his granddaughter."

"She's a lovely girl," the neighbour says.

Sidonie invites Cynthia and Justin for the evening, in order to meet Hugh and Ingrid, and then also invites Alex and Tasha. The arrangements cause some confusion; Justin, who has been anxious to meet Ingrid, Cynthia says, had been put out to hear his cousins had been also invited. But Hugh had thought that Ingrid would like to meet more people her own age. There is much telephoning back and forth, with Justin a sulky go-between, and Sidonie feels annoyed: there must be simpler ways to arrange an evening. The plans expand: now Kevin, who's going to be in town, is invited as well, and Stephen and Debbie. And then, when he arrives, Justin greets Ingrid with what Sidonie can only interpret as shock or great disappointment. Had he been expecting Ingrid to be some-how different? Sidonie can't see that there is anything wrong with her looks.

Hugh makes up for the awkwardness, becoming voluble, almost overbearing. "It's time Ingrid saw a little of her other country," Hugh says. Ingrid's mother, also an engineer, has remarried and remained in Zimbabwe. But the farm on which her family has lived for several generations has been taken over. "Think of that," Hugh says. "A hundred and fifty years, one family cultivated that piece of bush, made it profit, and it's just taken away, *snap*."

This is out of Ingrid's hearing. She and Alex are at the end of the living room, engrossed in Sidonie's music collection.

Justin says, "But they were colonists, exploiters. It's the African people's land. It should go back to them. The British and Dutch had no business there in the first place."

"But Europeans have lived there now for generations," Cynthia says. "The people who lost it, Ingrid's grandparents, weren't colonizers. They had just been born into that life. Why should they lose everything?"

"Anyway," Hugh says, "they've made a mess of it now. The natives can't or won't farm it; this last trip, when I drove out there, everything was dead. Nothing was being cultivated. They'd cut down the trees for firewood. It was all dust blowing away."

"Maybe it shouldn't be farmed," says Justin. "Let it return to its natural state."

"But the blacks there are starving," Hugh says, impatience in his voice. "They are just sitting there, starving, begging their mealie-meal from the local warlords. Nobody grows anything but ganja weed."

Justin says, "If they are starving, it's the white people's fault. They kept the Africans from getting educated or learning to run their country, and made them dependent on Western things. It's a known fact."

Tasha says, "I think it should all go back to the way it was before. The people can go back to living naturally off the land, the way they did before white people came."

"Well," Hugh says, "That's a nice idea, but they all have guns now, and all of the industrialized nations want their natural resources. And they're killing off the game. White rhinos are gone. Elephants nearly gone. Your children will never see those animals."

Justin says, "But the Europeans hunted game. Look at all those movies from the 1950s."

Sidonie suddenly remembers: in 1953, she and Alice and Hugh and Graham had been taken by Mrs. Inglis to see *Mogambo*; she remembers Hugh putting his hand over her eyes just as Grace Kelly and Clark Gable — playing characters married to other people — had been about to kiss, and also when Clark Gable had shot the gorilla. And after, Graham arguing with his mother about the portrayal of the gorilla: humans were much more dangerous to gorillas than vice versa, Graham had insisted, angrily, costing them all a stop for ice cream. Does Hugh remember that?

"The Europeans have a lot to answer for," Hugh says. "And yes, they probably shouldn't have been in Africa at all. But more harm is being done now, and stupidly."

It is a serious discussion, tinged with anger. She wants to shake Hugh: he is too sure of himself, too knowing. Justin is very young. Perhaps he is naïve, but he is young. She remembers something Clara used to say: if you vote conservative when you are under twenty-five, you have no heart, and if you vote liberal after you are twenty-five, you have no head.

Is that what it comes down to?

Cynthia says, "I don't know what's wrong with that boy. It's like he's suddenly become a sullen teenager. I thought we had skipped that stage."

Kevin is also there. Alice's second son. He looks even more startling than Stephen did; he has arrived from the coast on a motorcycle, wearing a ripped and high-smelling leather jacket, and when he shrugs off his jacket and helmet, he reveals a shaved head, a preposterous reddish mustache, and forearms so thickly tattooed that he appears to be wearing printed sleeves. He is ebullient: he bearhugs Sidonie, disconcertingly. His nephews and niece obviously idolize him as a counter-culture figure. Shades of Buck Kleinholz. Sidonie tries not to purse her lips; she glances at Hugh, but Hugh is laughing, delighted.

And she has to admit that Kevin is more likeable than his father. He lacks that permanent sense of grievance, or whatever it was, that Buck had. He seems, she has to admit, quite comfortable in his inscribed skin.

Alex and Ingrid have drifted off to Sidonie's patio and have to be called a second time for dinner, Sidonie notices. Cynthia gives her a raised-eyebrow glance. But Alex has a girlfriend, Jessica, who usually comes to family things, and is out of town now, working at a resort. And Ingrid will not be here in a week or two. It is nothing. She does not see how Alex is preferred, but though Justin seems to have recovered his politeness, and in fact is behaving with charm, Ingrid does not respond to his attention.

Sidonie has contributed to the dinner only the use of her kitchen and what she could find at the German deli: prosciutto-wrapped asparagus, local cheese, wine, of course, and thick chewy bread from the very good local bakery. But now Cynthia serves up watercress soup with watercress picked from the creek, and cream and flecks of something light and smoky. "Nigella's recipe," Cynthia says. "I saw it on TV." What is the smoky meat? "Guess," she says, then tells them. Smoked pheasant, local, bought from a charcutier at the weekend market.

A pan of lake trout: these were swimming this morning, Stephen says.

And a cake for pudding, made by Tasha, with ground almonds and tiny, sweet, intensely flavourful strawberries.

"Hundred-mile diet," Kevin says, and then they are all off again, arguing, interrupting, changing sides. It is a new thing: she does not remember discussions like that happening at the von Täler table, nor at dinners with Adam's family. But she notices how, with Kevin present, the rancor does not grow. He exudes a kind of bonhomie, an openness that is a matrix for all of their interchanges. A kind of confidence that comes, perhaps, from being on his own turf: he is a professional chef.

When her opinion is elicited, she laughs and says that she does not cook at all.

Later, Hugh says that Kevin reminds him of Sidonie's father.

"My father!" She is appalled. No, no.

"Yes,' Hugh says. "That quality of friendliness. Peter had that, I remember."

Possibly. But in her father it had been something of a different caliber, surely.

Hugh is often busy with his work on the bridge, and she feels that she must find activities to occupy Ingrid. She's a quiet girl, given to sleeping late, but otherwise easy to accommodate. She cooks, tidies up after herself, reads, goes for walks, does yoga in her basement room in the morning when the sun shines in. She is quite amiable. But she must not be made to sit in a suburban house for days, and Sidonie needs to work.

It's Alex who comes to the rescue, surprisingly, offering to take Ingrid out on days when he isn't working, which seem numerous, given the time of year and the purported construction boom. But it's a kindness; the girl must want to be with people her own age, and Tasha seems to have a full schedule, while Justin has proved a disappointment as an escort: he's reverted to being surly around Hugh's daughter, as if he has a grudge against her. Even Hugh and Cynthia have noticed this. Cynthia says that she's bewildered by it.

So unlike Justin, to not be a paragon of consideration, of good manners.

So: Hugh drives into town, to oversee whatever it is he is overseeing on the new bridge construction, and Alex comes by most afternoons to take Ingrid out.

In the evenings, Hugh and Ingrid, and often Alex, congregate at her house; they open the French doors, let in the lake breeze. Alex, she sees, is fascinated with her LP collection. Sometimes he'll take Ingrid out again, to a bar, she supposes. It's kind of him. One evening when they stay in, when Justin has come by as well, Hugh makes them look at the photo albums.

Justin is able to pick Sidonie's mother out of the crowd in the photo easily. You look just like her, Auntie Sid, he says. Alex, surprisingly, is the one to spot Hugh's mother.

Sidonie's mother, in this photo, must be fifty, and Hugh's mother is even older. They were old, for mothers of young children.

Hugh says, "This was my parents' second marriage. When they met in India, they were both married to other people. Mother had two children, who she lost custody of, when she ran off with my father."

Sidonie had not known that. She knows little of her own parents' lives before their arrival in the valley, either.

In the early 50s, Mother had taken Sidonie and Alice on the train to visit her family in northern Alberta; they'd visited only that once. Mother's parents and grown brothers had lived in an unpainted wood house on a few acres of scrub land. They had seemed, even to Sidonie's seven-year-old self, very poor. She remembers little of the visit: only Granny showing her a photograph album, which, like everything important in the house, was kept put away in a tin box, wrapped in newspaper. In a photo with "Hastings Photography Studio" written in the corner in white, Father was wearing a suit, and Mother a little skirt and jacket and hat. There was a backdrop of trees and an archway that did not look quite real.

"I guess your ma always wanted to be high class," Granny had said, suddenly. "I guess that's why she went for your pa."

The summer that Mother is dying, Alice mentions that they must telephone Mother's brother Don, let him know. Sidonie asks, "Why were they so poor? It was like the thirties, there, wasn't it? Why were they so poor, still, in the fifties?"

Alice says, "I don't know exactly. There was one more brother, Howard, you know. He was killed in Europe, in the war. Mother always said he was her favourite brother.

"And her parents had a bad start, Mother always said. They were more or less deported from Scotland, you know. Ma's father did something — killed the laird's deer, or something stupid like that. Probably starving. I think he was probably a delinquent of some kind from the start. Mother says he liked horses, but never could hold down a job or make the farm work, and they owed a lot of money. Grandma was supposedly from a more educated class — her father was a schoolteacher — but she never seemed to have it together, did she? Mother always complained that her mother didn't have the sense to stop having children — she said that there'd have been money to put her and Don and Gordon through school, if it hadn't been for the other two being born."

It was not to be answered, Sidonie's question. By this time, both of Mother's parents were long deceased; her brother Ken had moved to Edmonton, and was retired; her sister Mary already dead in a car accident. Don, who'd got the farm, had sold it when the tar sands were being explored, and now lived on Vancouver Island, purportedly a wealthy but miserly bachelor.

When Alice had told her these things, she had thought: that explains a lot about Mother. Now she wonders, as she did not then, why Alice had been told and not her. Mother, confiding in Alice. What else had Alice known?

On one side of the family, a down-at-the-heels, possibly depressive or alcoholic Scots. On the other, European bourgeoisie.

One of the von Tälers had come looking for Sidonie in the late 1970s, had tracked her down in Montreal. Or, to be precise, had not come looking for Sidonie, but for von Tälers in general. This was an American one, from California or Nevada; she can't remember precisely, now. A man younger than herself, looking, as people did then, for his roots. He'd found her in the phone book. He'd wanted to know about the rest of the family, but she hadn't much information for him. Her father had been dead by then. The American was setting up a group, he said. They could all connect with each other. All of the offspring and relations of the old count. Sidonie had declined, but offered him Alice's children. He had not, she thought, been particularly interested in the Kleinholzes.

A patriarchal structure: only the name had mattered, really. Primogeniture, too. Her father, born into a medieval town, his father the *Burgermeister*, his close relatives titled. If his father had been the older son, he'd have had a different life. As it was, when he was eighteen, the Archduke, a distant relative, had been assassinated; his country had been plunged into war. At twenty-nine, without patrimony or profession, he'd decamped for Canada, had used a small legacy from his grandmother to buy an orchard. (A small legacy? the cousin had said. In my family, we say that he swiped grandmother's jewel case.)

Father hadn't had any recent family photos. Her second cousin, though, has offered to share his collection with her. Come to think of it, he had said that they were available online, at the address he gave Sidonie. She must remember her password; that's how it was set up, she thinks, with a password. Possibly Stephen or one of the children will be interested.

Her father had told no stories of his childhood, of growing up in manor houses, visiting grandparents in a castle with an estate. Her mother had mentioned these details to her and Alice, occasionally.

He had told them instead stories of gods and goddesses, of heroic exploits, sirens, sailors bewitched into pigs. She'd thought that he made them up, because none of the other children had known them; they only knew the usual fairy tales, or other popular books, like *Alice in Wonderland*. Though that wasn't really a children's story, she thinks, now. Later, in university, she'd discovered their sources in Virgil, Homer, Aeschylus.

And he'd told them of his walking trips with other young men he knew from university, through the German lowlands, across the Alps, and into Italy. He'd told them about visiting Rome and Naples, about the statues of gods and heroes. About the Italian countryside. He'd said, "You'll go there, one day, you girls. You'll see for yourselves."

But they hadn't: neither she nor Alice. Though she has traveled for work: she has been to England, to France, to Australia and Japan.

She and Hugh and Ingrid drive out to Marshall's Landing; Ingrid must see, Hugh says, the location of her ancestral home.

Hugh turns in at his old home Sans Souci, or what used to be his home: now it's called, as the large, carved wooden sign on the gates to the broad, newly paved road says, Arrowleaf Ridge.

"An appropriate name, don't you think?" Hugh comments.

"*Balsamorrhiza sagitatta*," Sidonie says. Balsamroot arrowleaf. The showy, golden-petalled sunflower indigenous to the dry interior. She glances at the treeless bluffs above them, but they are too late for the blooms. She can see the patches of leaves, pale matte grey-green, but not the deep saffron of the flowers. "Very good," Hugh says.

Of course it had been Hugh who had taught them the Latin names of the indigenous plants, out of a field guide, and had translated the Latin, too. And had tested them all, and rewarded them for correct plant identification.

Hugh parks, and they get out and stand in the broad curved street. Here had stood Hugh's house and his family's orchards; his mother's peony garden and herbaceous borders had draped the landscape: green, well-manicured, civilized. The lawn where they used to play croquet and badminton; the flagstone terrace where Mrs. Inglis had served tea.

All vanished, replaced by this new housing development. That is the way of things, of course. And who is to say that the Inglises' very English establishment was a preferable tenant?

Still: a pang of nostalgia.

Hugh takes a professional interest in the swoops of wide street, the march of new houses, some lived-in, with established landscaping; others more rawly new, or still under construction. All are large, expensive-looking, with stonework, large windows, porches, gables, double or triple garages, sometimes detached.

Sidonie observes that Italianate seems the preferred style.

Hugh laughs. "Yes. We're obviously either in the late Republic, or the south English seacoast in the twenties."

They pass the winery, which has been here for twenty years now, but is new to them. "We'll stop and try the wine and have lunch," Hugh says to Ingrid, "on our way back up." And then down to the beach.

Around the sharp, steep hairpin where Hugh had lost control of his mother's Anglia, fifty years ago. And then to the lake.

Which has not changed; which has changed. The bay flung out in its curve; the narrow strip of cottonwoods between the beach and the road, the profile of the blue mountains on the opposite side of the lake familiar, she thinks, as her own face. The jolt of recognition like electricity, old synaptic connections firing in surprise: *here, here.*

Hugh treads the shingle of small smooth pebbles, skipping flat ones out between the dock and the swimming platform, which are deserted this early in the year, but for a pair of mallards. "The beach has shrunk," Hugh says.

"The water is high."

"But the beach is smaller, too. When did the packing house come down?"

"In the mid-seventies," Sidonie says. "You've surely been back since then."

"But not down to the beach," Hugh says.

Hugh stands scowling at the strip of houses with their private docks, their "No Trespassing" signs, lining the shore just to the south.

"How was this sold? It should have been kept for a park, a public beach." "I wish now that I had kept some of the land," Hugh says. "I could have kept a few acres, have somewhere to come to now."

"To do what with, Dad?" Ingrid asks.

"These monstrosities of houses at Sans Souci," Hugh says. "It's hard to get my head around them. I feel dislocated."

"What do you mean, dislocated?" Ingrid asks.

"Cut off from my own past. My youth. I feel no connection between my roots and all of this."

"It's just time and change, Dad," she says. "You've built yourself grand houses, too. And you've lived where you chose to, all over the world."

Ingrid takes off her shoes and shoulder bag and passes them to Hugh.

"You're not going in!" Hugh says. "The lake's much too cold still!"

But Ingrid makes a running leap, dives into the clear water, comes up with a whoop, water sheeting from her hair and clothing. "It's not so bad," she says, grinning at them.

"You'll get my car seat wet," Hugh grumbles.

But Sidonie smiles, sits down on the shore on her haunches, as she has done so many times in the past. She has a thick tartan blanket in her bag, she says; Ingrid can sit on that. And so she does, wearing Sidonie's cardigan over her wet T-shirt, all the way home.

She has something of her grandmother, Sidonie thinks. A kind of cheerfulness, a kind of fullness. Perhaps it is grace.

Hugh and Ingrid are leaving; Hugh is returning to Toronto, taking Ingrid with him. Stephen — Steve, the family calls him, now — and Kevin, who is visiting again, have made what Sidonie thinks of as an early-summer dinner: there is a salad of various leaves and flowers, mange-tout peas, snappish young radishes; baby carrots and squash and zucchini all lightly roasted; a pilaf with almonds and apricots; a dessert (brought by Sidonie) of strawberries and cream, both from the farmer's market, and flaky *palmiers* from the bakery. Kevin has brought some little pork medallions — organic wild pork, he says — that have been marinating in apple cider all the way from the coast, and are now barbecued. This time, everything but the almonds and rice are local. The day is sparkling, light-suffused, and they sit around the new gas brazier on Steve's patio into the long evening.

Only Alex seems ill at ease; he fumes, uncharacteristically, at the smell of barbecuing, the whine of lawnmowers, the shouts of children from the neighbouring houses (which are always so close, Sidonie thinks, in the newer subdivisions). During coffee and dessert, he clears his throat and leans forward.

"I stopped by the old place the other day, Auntie Sid. Your neighbour said he's giving up the lease. I wondered what you were — you know, planning to do."

They are all quiet. Sidonie's foot, her mended foot, begins to throb.

"I've put ads out for a new lessee," she says. "Walter and his son will work the orchard until I find someone suitable."

In fact, the responses haven't been promising so far. One prospective tenant had wanted to rip out all of the mature trees, plant in slender spindle. She considers that factory farming: trees planted only a few feet from each other, pruned, essentially, to one vertical limb, quickly harvestable. She has heard that the method yields a high return, but it is not orcharding. Other prospective tenants have been discouraged by the information that the house is not habitable.

"Your neighbour said that," Alex says. "What I mean is, well, in the long term."

Debbie says, "Alex!"

"After I die, you mean," Sidonie says.

"Well," Alex says. "Yes. Or before, you know. I mean, why are you keeping the place? Your neighbour must not pay a lot for the lease, or it wouldn't be worth it to run."

Here it is. She has not foreseen this, not worked out the details in her building of sky castles.

She swallows. "It's going to Justin, when he's older. As I have no children of my own, and as I raised Cynthia." There. Logical enough.

Justin's jaw drops, literally.

"Fair enough," Steve says. "I know that we got our mother's share already, that half the orchard has been sold off over the years, so we've had our share."

It is true. Alice had been given land when she married, and Sidonie had sold more after Alice had died, put the money in a trust fund for Alice's sons to live on. But it's suddenly not enough; it's suddenly preposterously unfair.

Justin says, "I don't believe this." He does not sound happy.

"It's not worth all that much," Sidonie says. "The land is in the ALR, you know. It can't be subdivided and developed. It's not such a big thing."

"And if I don't want to run an orchard?" Justin asks. Demands.

Cynthia says, "It's a decision you can make when you're older. You ought to appreciate this, Justin. It's very generous of Auntie Sid."

But she can see that it is at once too generous, and too narrow. What has she done?

They're all talking at once, voices rising.

Justin waves his arm in the air like a fourth-grader. "Can I speak? Can I speak?"

"*May I*," Cynthia says, but the others pause, look at Justin.

"I just want to say that we should all hear Alex out on this before we jump to conclusions," Justin says.

Alex speaks. "I know you all won't go for this. It's just an idea, okay? But I've been thinking about it for a long time, and reading books on orcharding, and taking courses. Now that Auntie Sid's place is available, it seems like the time to start. I think it might work, with a few bugs ironed out. I'd like to take on the lease."

It's impossible, of course. But brave boy, brave boy, son of Stephen and Debbie, grandson of Alice and Buck, great-grandson of Peter and Frances. Alex wants to turn Beauvoir into an organic orchard and market. He wants to live in the house, to renovate it, eventually. He thinks he can manage it on his own. He has thought it out: he wants three years to start turning a profit; then he'll start paying Sidonie.

"I don't think so," Steve says. "You have no idea how hard orchard work is. You've never done it. I have. It kills you. And for what, if your cousin will inherit the lot."

"I thought," Alex says, "that it belonged to all of us."

There's the insoluble problem, of course.

Justin says, "I don't want it! I'll share it with you and Tasha!"

Kevin clears his throat. They all look at him. He raises his eyebrows. Shrugs.

"Can I say something?" Tasha speaks now, putting up her hand like Justin. They are still children, Sidonie thinks. "I'd just like to say that I think Justin and Alex and I should have a say in this because it is our future, as Auntie Cynthia points out. You're all older, and you've made your choices. But this really affects us."

"Are you planning to work on the farm with Alex?" Kevin asks.

"Yes," Tasha says. "In the summers, at least. It's got to be better than waitressing in a crummy sports bar or selling cheap clothes in the mall."

"You won't always be a student," Debbie says. "You'll have a career in a few years. What then?"

Steve says, "You kids don't know how hard, I mean how really hard, farm work is. It's backbreaking and the sun and frost kill you. Kevin should know: he and I worked in the orchards when we were young."

"I liked it," Kevin says.

"Well, I didn't. I hated every minute. Prune, thin, spray, pick, all year round. An endless round of boredom. And Dad screaming at us every minute to hustle our butts."

"It doesn't have to be like that," Kevin says.

But Steve is wound up, and must continue. "Every second it was 'get up that tree and do something.' You try pruning in minus-thirty weather, in the wind. Freeze your fingers off, and all your joints stiff with cold. At fourteen years old, I fell out of a tree because I was too cold to grip the ladder. Fourteen years old! Fell out of a goddamn tree and broke my goddamn arm. And the old man comes and kicks me in the ass. 'Get up that ladder and finish your tree.'"

"It wouldn't be like that," Alex says. "I'm nothing like my grandpa Buck."

Tasha says, "You haven't said anything, Auntie Sid. What do you think?"

What does she think? She doesn't know. She's acutely aware, as she hasn't been in years, of her limitations, her inability to absorb a rush of new information and respond to it at the same time. She is acutely aware of what has been said: that it's a beautiful, grand, brave, impossible idea. That nothing can come of it, of course. That it can't work. But her mind is paralyzed as far as processing any of this.

There is the wood lot: a few acres of steep gully and dead pine and scrub. That would be easy, she thinks, to take out of the ALR. It's what's been done all over the valley, she sees: the housing developments are springing up on the non-arable land, the steep, rocky brush. View lots: a euphemism for houses with steep driveways and tiny, gabion-wall yards and a fortune in engineered foundations. The wood lot could be subdivided. The lots would likely sell for enough to work out some arrangement. To buy out the others.

But they have had their share.

And then there is Paul: Alice's youngest son, brother of Stephen and Kevin and Cynthia. Paul, who is rarely spoken of, who has been missing, or out of contact, for perhaps six or seven years. Last heard of on Hastings Street in Vancouver's Lower Eastside.

He has not been abandoned so much as abandoned them: Sidonie knows that all of the others have made attempts to find him, help him, bring him back. He evades them. It is a sad story. They did not leave him alone out of uncaring, but because there seemed little else to do. They do not speak of him, as they do not speak of their parents, of their murdered mother, of their dead deranged father.

When he had first gone to the streets in the early nineties, Sidonie, in Vancouver for a conference, had made a point of tracking him down — or nearly tracking him down. She had talked to a social worker, had managed to talk to Paul on the phone, had arranged a meeting. But he had not shown up. She had waited in the coffee shop for two hours, had gone back the next day at the same time. But he had not showed. Had he looked in through the windows, she wondered, and not liked the looks of her? She could not lose that thought, though it was irrelevant, a distraction.

Before flying back to Montreal, after that trip (eleven or twelve years ago) she had set up a fund for Paul: monthly installments for the rent on a small apartment, grocery money. Had given the social worker the means of letting Paul access the funds, only (as the social worker had suggested) a little at time. Had asked him to keep her updated. She'd made sure that way, through a succession of caseworkers, that Paul was still alive — though whenever one of his siblings had tried to find him at the apartment, he disappeared. But two or three years ago the current case worker had reported that Paul had not shown up to collect his funds, had not been seen at the apartment, though someone else was living there. And they had not heard of him since, though she had continued to rent the apartment for a year in the hope that the stream of occupants it had were sub-letting, were compensating Paul in some way.

She had let Paul's apartment go and kept a trust fund for him. But if she sells the wood lot, divides things up, she will have to include a portion for him. Wherever he is, he might need a home again some day.

No, the wood lot must not be sold now. She must keep it intact, a resource. Down the road, the cash might be needed to rebuild a house, develop or preserve the orchards. She cannot sell.

Steve says, "I'm nearly fifty. Once you're fifty, you don't get your life back. But I'd like to see Alex set up. If there was some capital, I might contribute. Take another mortgage out on my house. I have lots of equity."

"And what about Tasha?" Debbie asks, with some fierceness.

"I don't know how you're going to buy me and Auntie Sid and Paul out as well," Cynthia says. "Think about the amount we're looking at here, Steve. Millions. It'll be years before Alex turns a profit, and we all know that small-time farming doesn't exactly pay."

"Oh my god, Ma, you're such a fuckin' capitalist!" Justin says.

Cynthia says, "It's about your future, Justin. You want to do things. You want to go to university and you want to travel, and some day you're going to want a house and a studio. This is how we're going to pay for them."

"I don't need all of that shit paid for," Justin says. "I'm willing to work my way. I want Alex to be able to set up his farm." (When has Justin become so coarse in his speech? But he is furious with all of them, acting out some unexpected anger; even she can see that.)

She looks over at Alex. The setting sun back-lights his profile: he does have some of her father's features. His chin, receding a little, shaped finely as by a carver's chisel, under that pugnacious growth of hair.

He's a smart boy; he knows that he has lost. Good for him for trying, though.

She says, "There wouldn't be enough to put into Alex's idea, shared each way. And Alex is too young, too inexperienced, to take the orchard on. It's not practical. I want the orchard to run, not to be sold and broken up."

There it is. It's not about Justin. It is Beauvoir that she cares about. That is suddenly transparent.

Justin gets up abruptly, shoving his chair so that it clatters against the others.

"You're all a lot of fuckin' hypocrites," he says. "You don't see anything. You don't see *who you are*." He slams through the house; they all — except Cynthia — hear Cynthia's car start, pull out of the driveway. As the car rounds the cul-de-sac, throwing up dust, Cynthia looks up.

"Was that my *car*?"

And, astonishingly, everyone laughs.

Kevin says, "I'm forty-five years old, and I'm still cooking for a franchise, and I don't own my own home. And you may not know this, but I'm also supporting a couple of kids. Frankly, if I don't get a bit of cash, I'm going to be pretty well destitute in ten or fifteen years."

Cynthia says, "I do have a pension plan, and I own my own house, or part of it, such as it is. But I'd like to be able to pay for Justin's schooling, help him buy a first house when he's older."

She could sell Beauvoir. The orchard would not bring in a huge amount, but with the wood lot subdivided, there would be enough for all of them. She could make all of their lives a little more secure. She is tempted. But it is not required of her; she has taken care of Alice's children. And Alice had received her share.

BABYLON

In the fall, she books flights and hotels, restaurants and symphony tickets over the internet, consults with Clara and Anita by telephone and email. She is accomplishing things, moving forward. She is planning her escape. She prepares for a long absence: she stops her mail, throws out perishable groceries. She does not give a key to her neighbour. She washes her windows, which have been blasted, it seems, with dust. She stretches an old sock over a broom and winkles cobwebs from the high corners of her vaulted ceilings, from the upper cornices of window frames, from the hidden recesses above her pink kitchen cabinets.

More sorting of the boxes. (Paradoxically, she has energy to do this, now that she has all of these other activities on her agenda.) She sets up her low stool next to an opened carton, and dives in.

A shoebox of letters from Sidonie herself; when she opens the box, realizes what she is seeing, she feels instant shame that there are not more. Fifteen years' worth, but not so many from a child who has fled to the other end of the country.

Leaf through them quickly. She will not read them now. She is a little short of time; she's leaving for Montreal in a few days, and still needs to check a couple of references for her paper. She will keep these letters for later; only skim them now.

Dear Mother and Father, How are you all? I have started all of my classes. It takes me twelve minutes to walk from my calculus class to my physics class, but we have only a ten-minute break...

Dear Mother and Father, I hope you are well. I have been to the swimming pool three times this week...

Dear Mother and Father, Thank you for your care package. It has been twenty below for the past ten days...

Once-a-week letters for the first year. Than more infrequent.

Dear Mother and Father, I have met a girl called Clara who is in one of my classes. She has invited me to hear some jazz music this weekend...

Dear Mother and Father, You will be surprised to hear that I have become engaged...

Dear Mother and Father, Adam and I will be arriving by train in Kamloops on August 11...

Sidonie has told Adam that Alice is considered a beauty, and for the first few minutes after Alice enters the parlour, Sidonie is able to see her with unaccustomed eyes, and sees that she is beautiful, still, at twenty-four. Alice has a classic, oval face, fine, translucent skin; large clear eyes, lake-blue; a small, slender nose; a full-lipped, symmetrical mouth. She is slender, though her face is a little fuller.

She'd be considered a beauty in Montreal, too. But she looks unkempt, somehow: her hair is darker, pulled back into a ponytail; she is wearing a pair of faded cotton pedal-pushers and a loose plaid shirt, which might belong to Buck. What has happened to Alice? Of course, she has three small children, and lives in what Mother has described as a very backward place.

Then the new Alice subsides into the old, and is just Alice, and Sidonie can't see her objectively any more.

Alice is not talkative. She asks no questions of Sidonie, or of Adam, volunteers no information. Adam asks her some questions about the baby, Paul — how old is he? Does he sleep through the night? And Mother asks some other questions: did Alice get the box of cherries and apricots Mother sent up to her? Did she can them?

Silence falls.

Mother says, "Alice was Lady of the Lake a few years ago. She and some of the other girls were presented to Princess Margaret, when she came to open the bridge."

Adam, who has fortunately been illuminated by Sidonie, nods and widens his eyes a little, to show that he is impressed, but at the same time, Sidonie sees it occur to Mother that Adam might not understand.

"It's a beauty pageant," Mother says.

"A local custom," Alice says now. "Like the agricultural fair. Only girls in swimsuits instead of pumpkins."

Sidonie can hear the smile in Alice's voice, but Alice hides her smile behind her hand.

"Alice made a very good speech about — what was it about, Alice?"

"Tea cosies," says Alice.

"About the importance of the domestic arts. And Mr. Buckley praised it."

Mr. Buckley is the local MLA and the premier.

Another silence falls, and Sidonie wonders why Alice hides her mouth, and doesn't open her lips very wide.

Mother says, "Sidonie, I'm sure Alice would like to see your wedding album."

Sidonie is about to say that she hasn't brought it, but Adam jumps up. "I'll get it for you, darling," he says, and is off up the stairs before Sidonie can speak.

Mother takes Paul, who protests, and passes him to Father, who says, "Let's go outside and see the chook-chooks" in a voice Sidonie doesn't remember having heard before. Then Mother puts Sidonie on the sofa beside Alice, and the album on Alice's lap, and sits on Alice's other side.

Alice doesn't touch the album; it is Mother who opens it up. Sidonie feels her cheeks grow hot, and glances at Adam, but he is leaning back slightly, his legs crossed, his hands behind his head.

Clara has put the album together for them, with Anita's photographs arranged on heavy cream-coloured paper, little black gummed triangles at the corners holding the photos in place. Clara's fine script describes what the photographs show. The first photo is of Sidonie in the park, in the fall. She doesn't remember it being taken, but she remembers the day: a Sunday walk with Adam's family. There are leaves on the ground, and her face, under her little rolled felt hat, is in profile, a little blurred, as if she had been turning her head, and the straight horizontal lines of her eyebrows and lips are emphasized. Sidonie likes this photo: she is in motion in it, and Anita has seen what Sidonie sees in her own face: the horizontal planes.

"It's too bad about the blur there," Mother says. "They should have taken another photo, and got one that was still. But I guess it's hard to get Sidonie to hold still. Oh, and look; there's a shadow too. What a shame. It's a funny photo to choose, isn't it?"

The shadow is of Adam's father's wheelchair; it makes an interesting shape across Sidonie's coat, like a design in darker fabric.

Alice doesn't say anything; Mother turns the page quickly. On the next page is another candid, but oddly revealing photo of Adam with his violin. Sidonie likes this one too. Adam is not looking at the camera, and his gaze seems focused on something not seen. Sidonie realizes that she can tell what he was playing from the angle of his body, the expression on his face: Stravinsky's Concerto in D for strings, obviously. She can almost hear it, to look at him.

"Here's a funny one of Adam," Mother says. "He looks completely lost in his music."

There are a few more snapshots of Sidonie and of Adam. Alice doesn't comment. Mother's voice becomes furry, but with an edge, and Sidonie decides this is what people mean by *arch*. Mother says to Adam, "I suppose your sisters took all of these photos and put them in the album to bring you down a notch. Little sisters won't let big brother have dignity, even on his wedding day."

Sidonie squeezes her eyes tight for a second, then glances at Adam, but he is still sitting in that relaxed way, a slight, not unfriendly smile on his lips. He is sending her signals, audible only to her. She can't interpret them, but they are calming, invisible fingers pressing gently on her shoulders.

Here are Sidonie and Adam at Christmas, in the posed photo that they used for the engagement announcement. Adam is seated in an armchair, Sidonie perched on the arm, leaning into him just slightly. And then the one Anita took right after, when Adam pulled Sidonie playfully into his lap. Her knees are up, and a lot of leg is showing, but what feels more exposed is that her hair has fallen over Adam's arm, and he's bent over her, laughing, and she's looking—uncharacteristically—right into his eyes. Adam's gaze, too, is entirely on hers, and somehow, perhaps because of the light, or that they're both in semi-profile, they look connected. She sees that they look similar, even, in the curves of their lips, the angles of their jaws, the shapes of their noses. But it's not just that; there is some energy between them, some almost-visible conduit, taut, between their glances. She wishes that her mother and Alice had not seen that picture.

Then the photos of the wedding day. These are photos everyone will expect to see, Anita had said: Sidonie getting dressed, getting out of the car, going into the church, coming out of the church on Adam's arm, posed in family groups in the park, dancing and having toasts at the reception, and then sitting in the back of Adam's Uncle Lou's open Cadillac, with the "Just Married" sign on the back. In all of these photos, Sidonie thinks that she looks like someone else. She had been someone else all that day. Adam's mother had said, Just be yourself, dear, but Clara had said, No, that doesn't work for Sidonie. She needs to be inside someone else. You're a bride, Sidonie: a glamorous girl from the West, bringing her new blood and nerve to an old East Coast family. This bride, she can pickle cabbage or shoot a varmint, but she's also the top of her class and the toast of the city. Like Carolyn Jones in *How the West Was Won*. Can you do that, Sid?

So Sidonie had; all day she had been that other bride, that character from a movie. She can see it in the photographs. She doesn't look much like herself, she thinks. Her back is very straight, and her head balanced just so on her neck, which looks longer than usual, and she has a little pout on her lips, and her eyelashes lowered, except when she is looking at Anita and smiling. And then the smile is not hers, but the smile of the bride. She looks at the photos and feels cold: someone else is gazing out. Someone other than her carried those flowers, got married to Adam.

"My, you look graceful and elegant," Mother says. "Quite different! Fine feathers, I guess. But I told Alice that you made a beautiful bride." Mother is very interested in describing all of the clothes to Alice — the wedding dress, the dresses worn by Anita and Clara and Adam's mother and all of the aunts and friends. Sidonie is amazed that Mother noticed so much, that she can remember so much detail. "The centrepieces are burgundy roses and stephanotis — you can see what a deep colour the roses are! Brought in from Georgia, I believe. And your going-away outfit is merino crepe — a sort of orange, wasn't it, Sidonie? Not a colour most people would wear, but I guess you need to stand out, in fashionable society."

Mother also identifies all of the people in the photos, and explains who they are to Alice, not in terms of their relationships to Adam or to Sidonie, but rather in terms of their professions, or their husband's or father's professions. "This woman in the blonde mink — isn't she the wife of Adam's dad's business partner, Sidonie? I think she was a Fitzgerald? We had cocktails at their house up the mountain. Such a beautiful house, though I myself dislike a steep driveway."

Alice yawns widely, but behind her outstretched fingers.

"You look like a mannequin," Alice says.

Sidonie knows that Alice doesn't mean this as a compliment, but she is pleased, because that is what she thinks too. "Yes, I do!" she says. "I'm all posed. It doesn't look like me at all." She has expected

Alice to say that this fancy wedding and the nice clothes are wasted on Sidonie, and though Alice has not, Sidonie feels the old tight clench of anxiety paralyzing half her brain. She thinks of Alice's borrowed wedding dress, the shack at Horsefly, and feels shame for her own finery. It's all wrong: this should belong to Alice, not to her. And she waits for Alice to turn on her, for Alice's explosion of bitterness, braces against the cutting voice which is always much crueler than she can prepare herself for.

But there is no reaction from Alice, and Sidonie can't even feel a heat, a resentment, emanating from Alice's person, so close to her on the sofa. Something is turned off, locked away. And that is more alarming than anything. Alice murmurs "Oh?" and "Yes" to Mother's comments, and doesn't even joke.

Alice and Buck and the babies are going to spend the night; Mother has made up a bed for them in Father's office. There is a new sofa in the room which, after much tugging and wrestling, converts to a double bed. Sidonie says "Oh!" because Alice might want her old room; she must usually have it, but Alice mumbles "I'm hardly ever here." Buck is supposed to come back for supper (roast duck, with new potatoes and snap beans, beet salad and thick, rich gravy), but doesn't. Nobody says anything. Adam compliments Mother's cooking fervently and has third helpings, and then two slices of peach pie, as well.

Alice picks at her food. Father says "Eat more; you're feeding a baby," and Mother says "Shhh," and glares at him for mentioning it at the table, and in front of Adam. Mother disapproves of Alice breast-feeding; Sidonie has heard them talking. "You'll ruin your figure," Mother says. But Alice says "I have no way of sterilizing bottles or keeping milk fresh up there. What am I supposed to do?" There is something in the way the words "up there" sound that makes it Mother's or maybe somebody else's fault that Alice can't clean the bottles. Sidonie can tell they've had the argument before.

Painful, even now, to relive the agony of that afternoon. She hadn't possessed a good deal of empathy then, but had intuited Alice's deep rage, Mother's grief.

What it must have cost Mother to be near Alice, to see her, to stand — as much as she could — at arm's length from Alice. She must have given Alice a great deal of room, for Alice wouldn't have put up with anything else — any interference, suggestion, remonstration. And yet, she wouldn't have been able to resist the little ambushes, the low strikes from the underbrush.

She hadn't understood, until Cynthia was a young adult, that frustration: to see one's child's life change for the worse, and to not be able to do anything.

Sidonie has not kept the letters her mother wrote her. She has not thought about it since, but during those years, throwing away the letters, scarcely read, was a gesture, a claim staked on behalf of her own independence, her new identity. But she can remember the mention of Alice in each letter, growing more overtly concerned. "Alice is pregnant again — I do hope she'll take better care of herself this time." "Alice dropped in yesterday. Those boys sure outgrow their clothes and shoes fast!" "Alice should can more — I think she's not getting enough vegetables in the winter." "I wish you would invite Alice for a visit — she could use a real break."

Never a direct mention of Buck: only news of their moves necessitated by his unemployment and failed ventures. Scarcely a mention of the children, except to say that Father had taken Stephen on a fishing trip or that the older ones were running wild: every time they visited, they broke something or hurt themselves.

Kevin cut his lip open on one of Father's chisels. Stephen fell off the shed roof. Paul fell off the shed roof. Kevin tried to climb down the chimney and got stuck in a flue. Paul got a rock in his eye.

On that visit, that Saturday night, Buck didn't come back till past midnight. Sidonie woke to hear shouting, a crash that might not have been the first one, Father getting out of bed and going heavily down the stairs, remonstrations, more shouting. In the morning, Buck, unshaven, undershirted in the kitchen. Alice scrubbing at his shirt in the sink. Buck tossing tiny Paul up in the air, heart-stoppingly high. Alice's sharp rebuke, Buck's surly grin.

Alice and Sidonie and the little boys going to church with Mother; when they got back, Buck honking the truck horn impatiently, rudely, for Alice, while she changed Paul's diaper.

The calm after Alice left, which at least partly answered the question: why did Mother and Father allow it? Why didn't they tell Alice to leave Buck, come back home?

But there are other answers to that question.

On the Saturday evening, after supper, before Buck had come back, Sidonie and Alice had gone up to their old bedroom, sat on their old beds.

"So," Alice said, surprisingly, "you didn't get to have this room to yourself for very long."

It is so exactly what Sidonie had thought that she is shocked, though not so shocked that she doesn't hear the mockery in Alice's voice.

"Is it strange to have sex in your old room?" Alice asks. Then says, "I always found it quite exciting when Buck and I did it in here."

This turn of the conversation is more than shocking: it is aggressively coarse. Sidonie feels her lips purse. Of course she has had much more frank discussions of a sexual nature in her psych classes, and with Clara and with Adam, but it is Alice — Alice, who has always been reserved, prim — who is speaking like this.

"Or *do* you fuck?" Alice continues. "No offense, but it's hard to imagine you getting into bed with anyone without putting their eyes out with your elbow. And your *bridegroom*" — she stretches out the word, so that it sounds both pompous and lewd — "looks like he's used to women more sophisticated than you. But maybe you two just like to cuddle and read all night?"

Sidonie says at last, "You know nothing about my life. Why don't you mind your own business? Why do you have to be so mean?"

She hates that she sounds childish, but she has no defense against Alice.

Alice raises her eyebrows. "Mean? No; you know what, Sidonie? I'm actually concerned about you. I think maybe you're being taken advantage of, and don't even realize it. Who are these people? They've rather taken over your life, haven't they?"

Please don't please don't please don't, Sidonie thinks in misery. She imagines Clara saying, "You must defend yourself," but knows that whatever she says, Alice will use it against her.

"Of course," Alice says, "you rather like that perverted stuff, don't you, little freak? Do you think that I don't know about your games? Your little games with older men, and your poisonous little notes?"

Alice means Mr. Defoe. But how is that Sidonie's fault? It wasn't a game. Alice must know that it was all Mr. Defoe. But she feels unsure, guilty, shamed.

If Adam were to hear this, he would think that Sidonie has something very wrong with her. He would see that she is a freak, dirtied by her own ignorance, her own helplessness.

No. No.

Adam would say that there is something wrong with Alice, something twisted and nasty. Sidonie breathes in and out, willing Adam's face, his voice, into her mind.

"I pity you," Alice says. "You must have a really narrow little life. You must have a lot of restrictions. They can dress you up, but they can't take you out."

And there, her mind is clear enough that she can identify the antidote — the one clue in the whole stream of poison. *Dress you up.* Alice is jealous of her; her nice clothes, the apparent wealth and comfort that Alice must read in those photos. Alice is jealous. Only jealous. A little relief trickles through; she has not fallen into Alice's ambush entirely.

"I pity *you*," Sidonie says, on the strength of that trickle, "because you're married to Buck, who, everyone knows, is a drunk and a bum, and you'll always be poor and have black eyes and get fat."

And then Alice opens her mouth in a sort of grin that is also a snarl, a rictus, and Sidonie sees what Alice has been hiding with her hand, her tight-lipped speech. Both of Alice's upper eyeteeth are gone, pulled out, and dark spaces gape. Alice is missing teeth. How has that happened?

Instantly, her little surge of anger evaporates. She is horrified at herself.

"Oh!" she says. "I'm sorry, Alice. I didn't mean it," but Alice has already gotten up and stalked from the room.

They do not make another trip out to B.C., she and Adam. She returns only after several years for Father's funeral. It is not hard to stay away: she has a new family, her work, a social circle. She and Adam go out to restaurants, clubs, at least three nights a week. And she has become a different person: has shucked off her old self, grown a new, sharp and edgy one, untouchable in her shiny exoskeleton.

"I think," Adam says on the trip back (she can remember this even now, the scenery of Kicking Horse Pass streaming past their windows), "that your family's dynamics are not very good for you." She does not argue this. For weeks after the visit, she reverts, becomes more gawky, more fearful, more anxious, more prone to automatic movements, unable to sustain eye contact. She agrees, numbly: no more trips to Marshall's Landing for a long while. To Sidonie, at nineteen, the long while is perhaps indefinite. But at this point, she doesn't think she cares to see Alice again.

At Christmas of that year, Adam had taken her to the Florida Keys for a fortnight. (You look peaky, Clara had said, when Adam suggested the trip and she had demurred, fearful. Go. Go. You'll love it. A second honeymoon.) In the newness, the exoticness (grapefruit orchards, giant sea turtles, alligators, palm trees) Sidonie had been remade. She had swum every day, lain on the warm sand. Her body had remembered how to relax, to stay still.

No permanent damage.

She gives her paper, and then she has two weeks of holiday, two weeks to visit her old friends, to inhabit, again, the lighted glass city. Her former sisters-in-law have organized her; she stays the first week with Clara, who conducts a seamless itinerary of shopping and lunches and scenic walks and concerts. Even naps are scheduled in, though Sidonie does not nap, but uses the opportunity to prowl, to read, to answer emails. Clara interrogates her: what is she thinking? How is she feeling? And it is a relief to talk, to have her thoughts drawn out, examined, classified, offered back to her tidied and rearranged. Yet there is something exhausting in all of this too — a sense that she has lost autonomy, that she has lost *intactness*, that makes her irritable, that makes her hold back. She knows, for Clara has explained this to her, that her terrible introversion is a pathology, something she needs to outgrow. But she feels that she is a soft-bodied creature, shamefully extracted from its shell.

The second week she spends with Anita. Anita's pace is different than Sidonie's (different than most people's, Clara says). There are no regular meals; she will suddenly announce that it's time to go somewhere, and leave in five minutes or an hour for that place. Sidonie finds the lack of foreknowledge of events both excruciating and bewildering. It is agony to wait, to not know whether to eat or to go for a walk or start a book. When she asks Anita, Anita only says: Do what you like! This is frustrating — she doesn't want to go out or begin work if Anita is planning an outing or has invited people in, but she has to admit, there is freedom in this arrangement. She can come and go as she pleases — Anita will join her or not, as *she* pleases.

Clara says that Anita's habits are ridiculous. It's all about control, about power, Clara says. Anita wants to have everyone adjust to her plans, but won't admit that she has plans. She likes to keep everyone unbalanced.

Sidonie isn't sure about this. But she is grateful for her sisters-in-law, these familiar companions. They are not unchanged; or perhaps more precisely, in being away, she is able to see the changes that have been gradually occurring in the past few years. Both are quite grey, Clara's customary bob a silver helmet and Anita's still-long hair streaked with shades of lightest through darkest grey, like one of her own photographs.

She has known them most of her life.

She had formed an attachment to Clara first: Clara has said many times that she recruited Sidonie, rounded her up. Of course, Sidonie did not see it that way.

She is drying her hair after swimming at the Y pool, and a woman's face appears next to hers in the long mirror: "I see you here a lot, don't I? And at the Thursday night concerts."

The woman is young, as tall as Sidonie, with a short dark bob, dark eyes and brows, narrow features, a wide mouth. She is a more vivid, more pronounced version of Sidonie, though she doesn't notice this until later. Her hair is straight and tucked behind her ears, and Sidonie thinks immediately that she will have her hair cut in the same way: her long braids never fit securely under her bathing cap, so her ends always get wet. And it is such a bother to braid her hair and put it up.

"Yes," Sidonie says. "I swim here on Mondays, Wednesdays, and Fridays, and I go to the concerts."

"Are you a student?" the woman in the mirror asks.

"Yes," Sidonie says. "Yes."

"Me too," says the woman. "What's your major?

Sidonie says, "Psychology," and the woman says, "I'm doing literature," and smiles as if they have just discovered something important. Then she turns and puts out her hand. "I'm Clara St. Regis."

"Sidonie von Täler."

"What have you liked best, in the concert series?"

"Sibelius," says Sidonie. "That was on the 17th. Also Mahler, on the 12th of April, and Bix, the 15th of March."

She realizes instantly that she has been overly precise, and blushes. But Clara says, enthusiastically, "Really? You liked the Sibelius? Most people don't get it. Why did you like it?"

Sidonie explains about the angles, the slip of perspective, the stone edges. She is talking about synesthesia, but Clara thinks she is using metaphors and is very excited. "That's it! That's it exactly." Then: "Do you go downtown on the weekends to hear jazz? Do you ever go to the Yellow Door? No? You must. Come with us this Saturday. No, I'll pick you up. Where do you live? Brilliant."

An odd exchange, seen from almost any perspective. But Sidonie finishes drying her hair and goes on to her Wednesday morning classes in a little cloud of wonder and pleasure. She has not made many friends in her first two years on campus, for a number of reasons. She is, of course, two years younger than most of the other students, and is only now growing into her adult body, filling out. A gangly girl, too tall for her frame, with long braids, huge eyes, a pointed chin, she looks like a child, one of those occasional accelerated students, all intellect and no social or physical development. Then there are the obvious oddities of her personality: her over-precision, her obsession with numbers and arcane facts, her inability to make small talk. She is not the only one like that; she sees others, boys mostly, who carry that mark. She avoids them as if they were pariahs, though she is lonely.

And there is something else; a seriousness that makes it difficult for her to join the other girls in her dormitory over their perpetual hot chocolate and boy talk. There is something more interesting going on in life, she thinks. She has been ready for an adult world for some time, and has been disappointed, generally, in what she has found on campus. Though she would not be able to put her finger on it precisely. She has thrown herself into attending the series of lectures that happen outside of class time, and the foreign films, and the concert series. And she swims. But it has seemed to her that the films and the concerts only hint at a world of people that she has no access to: one in which ideas are important, personal eccentricities are respected, taken for granted, and a kind of intensity of experience not based on personal emotions is a shared goal.

So it is that Sidonie, who up to this point has apparently paid rigorous attention to the dorm's strictures about talking to or accepting rides from strangers, going out after dark, venturing downtown, or going to bars, finds herself climbing into a strange Volkswagen Beetle at the corner of University and des Pins at nine o'clock on a Saturday night. She has forgotten what Clara looks like — she is not good at recognizing faces, and is relieved to find that she is able to identify her new acquaintance in the back seat. In the front seats are a man, driving, of whom she can only see a quarter profile and a corduroy shoulder, and another woman who looks quite a lot like Clara, and is introduced as Clara's sister, Anita.

The driver is Clara's brother, Adam.

Sidonie has never been to a nightclub before. Preparing to go out has cost her some effort and more thought than she is used to putting into her appearance. She remembers from movies that women wear black dresses to nightclubs, but she has not got a black dress. She puts on her good grey dress, but sees that it is all wrong. The dress, with its short sleeves and circle skirt, makes her look like she is going to church. Something more — vertical — is needed. But she doesn't have clothes like that: all of her dress-up clothes, bought or sewn by Mother and Alice, have fitted bodices, wide skirts, little cap or puffed sleeves. Some of them are Alice's hand-me-downs, and are in Alice colours: sunflower, rose, seafoam. And they're all too short: she has apparently grown a couple of inches since leaving home. And her everyday clothes — the skirts and sweaters or white blouses she wears to class or out walking — are also too short, and getting shabby. Most of them were her school clothes; she can remember wearing that tartan skirt, for example, in her grade 11 history class, because she used to trace the pattern with her finger while the teacher droned on about the Stuart kings.

They are familiar and comfortable clothes, and she has not had to think about them. But now she sees that everything she owns is for a different Sidonie, one who at that moment has ceased to exist. Nothing, not her pajamas, not her underwear, not her saddle shoes or little cotton socks, is anything that her new self would have chosen.

And all because of an invitation to a nightclub.

It is not until she is much older that Sidonie understands that most people do not become someone new overnight; do not transform with the flip of a mental switch, and that others find her proclivity for instant transformation disturbing. And she is to do it more than once in her life.

She has an instant conviction that she must go out and buy new clothes, and that the clothes she wants will not come from Mother's sewing machine, or from Ogilvy's. Where will she find them? She will discover this. It will be a research project. In the meantime, it occurs to her that the other girls in her dorm borrow clothes from each other on a regular basis. It seems to be an accepted transaction, though she has never participated in it.

She opens the door to the lounge, announces: "I need something straight and black to wear, right now."

The other girls, who are playing records, eating popcorn, and painting their nails, as usual, on a late Saturday afternoon, freeze and stare at her. Then one of them says, "Woo-hoo, Sidonie!" and before she can escape, she is swept up and showered with garments; someone is pulling out her pinned-up braids, sweeping her hair into a ponytail; someone else is pulling a sweater over her head. In some odd way, she has become accepted, temporarily, into their society, but she must endure a ritual cleansing and robing, she thinks.

The girls buff and comb her and urge her to climb into different articles of clothing, most of which are too wide and short, but eventually they are satisfied, and lead her to a mirror. Sidonie examines herself dispassionately; she has not yet become comfortable with her own reflection, and must look at herself, still, as a compilation of angles and planes. But what she sees pleases her; she has become something sleeker, harder. A package. She has on someone's tight black sweater, and someone else's black pencil skirt, nylons, and makeup, but the final effect is of a dark, sine-curved column with striking horizontal marks — dark-lashed eyes and brows and glossy red lips.

And then she looks again, and is reminded of Alice. Though her eyes and hair are dark, she has somehow grown Alice's cheekbones and brow and oval jaw. How has that happened? She has a nasty feeling that Alice wouldn't like it, would be quite annoyed. But Alice is a long way away. And strangely, she understands something about Alice now. She has put on this understanding with Alice's image. It is this: that Alice has always been in disguise, as Sidonie is now. That it is a useful thing to be in disguise, to assume this sort of protective shell. Sidonie has eschewed artifice, feeling ashamed to attempt it, seeing it as a kind of weakness to be seen attempting beauty. But it is her own raw naked self that she has endangered by doing that. Now she sees that in creating this new image of herself, she has become invulnerable in some way. She remembers that when she was young, she used to see Alice as a seed pod: the brittle exterior, the silky threads inside. She feels some sort of surprise or wonder: she has created in her own mind a sense of Alice as being dry, cool, through to her core. Now she must adjust that image she carries, that sensation.

And inside herself, she feels the new Sidonie start to take form, with not a little contribution from Alice. She feels her edginess still, feels her strangled tongue grow quick, sardonic. Her bones and sinews, her very cells, seem to line up differently.

The other girls are pleased with their achievement. One of them says, "You're really quite pretty, Sidonie," with obvious surprise, and another says, "You look like Elizabeth Taylor in *Cleopatra*. Doesn't she look just like Elizabeth Taylor?" And they all agree she does.

That is how she goes out to meet Clara. And Adam.

It is dark in the club, and Sidonie doesn't take in much about her companions: it's too loud to talk, also. The jazz, she opens herself to (though the cool Alice-shell remains intact; she is still, she is aware of her outer body); it is both the inspiration and detail of her new self, filling out the sketch that she has glimpsed earlier in the evening the way blood pumps through the wings of an adult insect emerging from its nymph state. Imago. The jazz, the little table where she sits with Clara and Anita and Adam, the drink (gin and tonic; horribly, excitingly bitter, but the only mixed drink she'd been able to think of when asked), the low, coloured lights, the smoky atmosphere — they all become her new tissues.

The music says: I am floating apart from the confusion around me. I am seeing and appreciating it and keeping my distance from it. I am a little sad and detached, but surprised or agitated by nothing. I am ordering the world: this room, the wet pavement outside, the neon lights, the red leaves in the park: they all have their place. I am ordering sadness and happiness, tipping them slightly on their edges, spinning them like schnapps glasses. All of the world: the rows of apple trees, the moody lake, Mother's relentless polishing and preserving, Father's weary, calm immersion in whatever space he is in, Alice's cool silky smoothness, the black sewing machine, the battalion of bottled golden peach quarters, Mr. Defoe's hard hurting hands, the sheen of Masao's brown back, Mrs. Inglis's hats and her plummy voice and gee and tee: all of those things are ordered inside me, part of me but not part of me, all winding through their own variations. And calculus and past subjunctive and Dr. Leavis and Dr. Skinner, and all of their ideas, they are lining up to put out their little solos, and it is all about a pattern, and the pattern plays and changes and winds back through itself, but it is only pattern.

She is transformed. It is not to last; the old anxieties and muteness will break through. But she is transformed enough that some of this new vision of self will remain, enough to javelin her, improbably, with amazing luck, into another life, one in which she can expand and bloom; one imminently suited to her oddities, her hybrid culture. Though there is a cost, of course.

A man walks up to her on the path between the Arts building and the Leacock building. He says hello, and ducks under her umbrella. He has dark hair, longer in front, dark eyes, is perhaps in his early thirties. He is also very thin, and walks in an unusual way, as if his arms and legs were too long, too delicate, to bear weight. He holds his head slightly inclined, too. Everything about him, in fact, forms a series of graceful sine curves. But he looks familiar. A prof?

"Adam St. Regis," he says. "We went to the Yellow Door last weekend."

Clara's brother, of course. The new Sidonie doesn't grin in recognition, however, but makes a little inclination of her head, a small laugh at herself. "Out of context," she says.

"Yes!" Clara's brother says, "I always find that too."

Sidonie has seen Clara twice at the pool since Saturday. She notices the resemblance between Clara and her brother. "Where are you off to?" he asks, and for a moment she can't remember, so happy is she to be reminded of Clara.

So it is Clara who is her first friend, and Anita and Adam only Clara's siblings, who often come along on outings, who are at the apartment when Clara takes Sidonie home. But Sidonie adapts to them all with delight. Her new self grows niches in which to absorb and respond to the St. Regis life: the food, the topics of conversation, the tone, the jokes, the habits of concerts and reading and walks on the mountain. All, she thinks, new experiences, though looking back, decades later, she can see that it was a only a slight adaptation she was making, that she had been bred very nearly for this life, even in that far-flung community of Marshall's Landing. Father's gramophone, Mother's Royal Family scrapbook, the omnipresence of the orchard, the Inglises' brand of Britishness, the prim dry Scottishness of Mr. Ramsay and Miss Dobie, the accents and cabbage-roll domesticity and serious Schubert addictions of the Schillers: all of these had been a sort of primordial soup in which she had become a suitable addition to a family like the St. Regises.

But at the time, it had seemed miraculous: her adaptability, their acceptance.

She is persuaded to bring her violin to Sunday dinners at the house on Clarke, and she and Adam play a duet, Clara accompanying them on the piano. Sidonie thinks about how much Mother would like to see this: how to Mother it would be the epitome of Culture. She writes about it in one of her brief, infrequent, laborious letters home, trying, for once, to choose the detail that will convey this image to Mother, both precisely and accurately. (Why does she feel the need to show off to Mother, to gain her approval, at this point of rebirth? She doesn't know.)

Perhaps she is practicing her new voice.

Clara played the piano, while her brother and I attempted a violin duet. We were all very serious, until Clara's mother mercifully interrupted us with the tea-tray.

Who is speaking in these letters? A different Sidonie, one who has transformed herself into the sort of magazine that Mother might like to read.

But there is another story, one that she doesn't tell.

The day Adam ducks under her umbrella, he invites her to lunch at the faculty club. It is a dull, wet Friday in early October. Clara and Sidonie were supposed to go shopping after their morning classes, but Clara has a bad cold. She has suggested that Sidonie go look at the exhibit in the Redpath, instead. And that is where Adam finds her. Had Clara arranged this? Probably, though it wouldn't have occurred to Sidonie, at the time, to wonder.

At lunch, Adam seems nervous. Sidonie has not yet formed much of an impression of him, except that he is quiet, that he listens to and trades witticisms with his sisters, especially with Clara, as if they were equals, something that in her experience boys or young men are not likely to do. She has learned that he plays the violin, as she does. She had thought at first that he was a musician, but, in fact, he is a professor of architecture. And driving home that Saturday night, she'd sat in the front, and they'd talked about turn-over in lakes. He had that sort of detached politeness that reminded her of Graham and Hugh Inglis; a sort of suit through which it was hard to see.

Today, he stammers a little, seems to be sweating. Perhaps it's because students aren't really supposed to be in the faculty club, Sidonie surmises. She is also perhaps unsuitably dressed. She hasn't had time yet to hunt down the sort of clothes she has envisioned for herself, and yet her old wardrobe seems unsupportable — and so she is wearing (and Adam wouldn't have been able to see this until she took off her raincoat) a boy's rugby jersey, striped in olive and cream, a short pleated skirt in rust-coloured Harris tweed, and marigold tights, all borrowed in a forage through her dormitory mates' closets. She likes the abstract effect of the colours and lines of the clothes; up close, she has to admit, they might seem strange.

She says, "Should I keep my coat on? I'm afraid that I'm inappropriately dressed." But Adam says, emphatically, that she isn't.

She asks for eggs and bacon (she has missed breakfast, as usual). Adam orders soup and a clubhouse for himself, but hardly eats. It's warm in the faculty club, and the leather chairs and oak tables gleam comfortingly, substantially. The food is a pleasant weight in her stomach. It is almost as nice as being with Clara. But the new Sidonie, self-aware, remembers to smile pleasantly at Adam and to ask him if he liked the Sibelius piece at the concert the evening before. She knows he goes to these — Clara has mentioned it — but Clara had been ill and Sidonie had not thought to look for Adam.

They discuss Sibelius.

Adam says, "Do you like Italian food?"

"I don't know," Sidonie says. "I've only ever eaten the Marshall Landing version of spaghetti, which has Campbell's tomato soup in it. I doubt that's the real thing."

Adam laughs. He says he knows a little place off St. Denis that's supposed to be good. Would she like to try it? What about tomorrow night?

"Do you think Clara will be up to it?" Sidonie asks.

"I thought just the two of us," Adam says. His voice is odd. Skittish, she would say.

It isn't until Sidonie is getting dressed the next evening that it occurs to her that she has been asked on a date. She has spent Saturday shopping for clothes — an annoying activity, she thinks, when she could have used the time to do homework — except for discovering the St. Laurent discount stores — and has come back with a sleeveless black shift and black tights, new leather boots with Cuban heels (she'll have to go without new books for a month to pay for them) and a long string of improbable, large imitation pearls with a golden cast. One of the girls — Judy? Jenny? She can never tell them all apart — offers to help her with her hair. A chignon, says the girl. Think Audrey Hepburn. It requires a lot of pins, but the effect is correct, Sidonie sees.

"Is it a date?" the girl asks.

"I don't think so," Sidonie says. "Older brother of a friend."

"Is he handsome? Single?"

"Those are irrelevant questions," Sidonie says. She means it humorously, but the old, brusque Sidonie has emerged, and the girl is offended.

"Is he interested in you or not?" she snaps.

She did not know, but it became apparent quite quickly that the dinner was meant to steer their relationship down a specific path. When their engagement is announced in December, people keep remarking to Sidonie, "That was a quick courtship," or some version of that idea. Sidonie thinks that if anyone knew really how quick it had been, they would have been quite shocked. It is a matter of minutes, from the moment she realizes that Adam has asked her on a date, to the time it takes her to finish getting dressed, gather her coat and handbag, and walk downstairs to the lobby to wait for the car, her mind opens to, accepts, embraces the idea of Adam as her lover.

She is perhaps not unusual in this quick decision. Women of her generation were, after all, prepared, not dissimilarly to Mother's Christmas goose, for a certain role. They had to judge all eligible men, all encounters with eligible men, against their certain end of assuming this role. Why not Adam? He is handsome, in his fine-drawn way, funny, intelligent. They both play the violin, and she gets along with his sisters. A sensible choice.

What is different about Sidonie is that she thinks *lover*, not *husband*. Why is this? Possibly because she is still so young: only eighteen. Possibly because of Mrs. Inglis's frequent stories about Alice Keppel, though those were meant for Alice: stories about her namesake. Probably because she has never believed that she is capable of the kind of joining that marriage is believed to embody. She has known, though not chosen, an emotional autonomy, all her life. She cannot envision it changing.

For this reason a man shall leave his parents and cleave to his wife, and they two shall become one. She has heard this passage invoked — how many times? — by Mr. Erskine. She cannot see herself becoming one with anyone.

Sidonie is, at this time in her life, neither especially religious nor irreligious. She has not consciously adopted the atheistic or

Bohemian attitude, the extolling of Free Love, that existed in echelons of Montreal society, though likely not in Marshall's Landing, in the early 1960s.

She decides that she will sleep with Adam as soon as there is an opportunity. (And as soon as she decides this, she feels her body, her arms and legs, her breasts and belly and pubis, grow warm, polarized towards Adam.) She will possibly marry him, but only after they have discussed and agreed on every possible decision. (She will not be her Mother, trapped in a round of exhausting work. Will not be Alice, caught in the net.)

She does not know how, nor has the self-possession, to play coy, as young women of her time are supposed to do. And though Adam is thirty-one years old, an urban sophisticate for his time, he could not have expected Sidonie's response to him: that instant, complete opening to him.

It is Sidonie who says, "I want to go home with you, after," the second time they go out together. Adam has his own place, of course, a bachelor apartment. He doesn't live with his parents and sisters. There is only one thing that statement can mean in their time. On Adam's sofa, they kiss, and given the possibilities, she is nearly swooning. Adam asks, "Are you sure?" before he pulls out the sofa bed and they go further. This is what she would expect; this is gentlemanly. Adam has safes; that is also gentlemanly and mature. She is pleased, somewhere under her insistent drive; she has chosen correctly.

Afterward, she weeps a little; not at Adam's house, but after he has driven her home (for she must be home; she must be in her dormitory, if not by the official curfew of midnight, at least by two in the morning, or she will be disciplined. Her dorm-mates will cover for each other up to a certain time, but will not vouchsafe the entire night. They have a social code to enforce.)

It is not the pain of deflowering, which her dorm-mates dread in hushed whispers, that has hurt her, for that was taken care of years ago. Neither is it the intrusion into her self, the loss of power that women will describe a decade later in group encounters, that upsets her. What is disappointing to her is that the experience is so mundane, over so quickly. That there is no intense, wild pleasure, but only something not too dissimilar from her first occasion. It is disappointing. She is almost transported back into her gangly fourteen-year-old self.

And then she accepts that this is all it is, this perfunctory penetration and bumping.

Another rebirth? No, just the final stages of the first one. Compromised, complicit with her own corruption, she feels that she has emerged into the human world, this time consciously, intentionally. She is an adult now: she fully understands the adult world. She has put away her innocence, which is to say her belief in her own incorruptibility, for good. She feels she is sophisticated, and she is aware of the word's literal meaning.

So she thinks in those heady first weeks. When she is not completely engrossed in her very difficult courses in physics, which for some reason are required of any science student, and which cause her elation, rather than angst.

When Adam announces the engagement to his family, Clara claps her hands as if applauding a performance or the winner of a race. She says, "Oh, good! Now we will never lose you."

Sidonie assumes at the time that Clara means her, Sidonie, but years later, thinking back, wonders if it wasn't Adam that Clara was referring to. For what was Sidonie recruited? To fill a place, really; to ensure that whomever Adam married wouldn't change him, wouldn't change the St. Regis family strain. If so, the whole family must have felt that way. Adam's father said, "Do you mean to tell me that young people are still getting married?" But smiling. And Adam's mother said, "I'm very pleased; you'll be a great asset to our family." That is the main tenor, that she is joining their family, as if it's a company or club. There was the implication that she had been vetted, an offer made.

Later, in her bitterness, she had wondered why he had bothered to marry, at all. But he must have had to: he must have wanted that social enfranchisement as much as she did.

From her own family, a different response: she has not brought in someone new, but has acquired a large, costly possession whose merits have yet to be proven: a bicycle, a horse. The occasion warrants an expensive, long-distance telephone call. Mother says, "Oh, my goodness! Are you sure?" And Father says, "Well, if it's what you want, *Liebchen*."

Sidonie doesn't speak directly to Alice, who is already married, with two babies, and living in a rural place with no phone. Mother tells her that Alice wishes her the best of luck, which Sidonie takes to be a liberal translation.

She declines the offer of a loaned wedding dress (she remembers it: full-skirted, tight-waisted, encrusted like some marine beast with hard, scratchy tulle and lace), and wears, daringly, a little suit of raw silk, in an off-white like light cream. It has an open neckline with a flat, rounded collar, a boxy jacket, a narrow skirt. With it a pillbox hat and a mere reference to a veil.

Mother, seeing her, is disappointed, Sidonie can tell. "That's so very — modern!" Mother says.

What did Sidonie think she was doing? And Adam? What was he thinking?

Those are questions Sidonie has time to gnaw on only much later in her life, and the answers she arrives at in 1983, when her marriage to Adam comes unraveled, are not the same answers that she finds in the decades after that.

In 1962, Sidonie is thinking that it will be a sensible thing to marry Adam, since he has asked her, and since they enjoy each other's company. Marrying Adam will mean that she may move out of her dorm, where it is often too noisy to concentrate on her work, and where the girls — whose names she can never remember — are much too inclined to borrow her things, to leave the bathroom in disarray, and to tease.

And part of her thinks that it is sensible to settle the question of whom she will marry early, so she can get down to the serious business of her life, and not have to devote energy to the activities that comprise the search for a suitable mate.

The foolish virgins and the wise. Miss Erskine had told them it was about Choosing Sensibly. She had congratulated herself, marrying Adam, for choosing so much more sensibly than Alice had.

On her last night of her visit to Montreal, she and Anita and Clara go to a concert, Clara leading them through shining wet back streets. They go down some stairs leading off a side street, shake out their umbrellas, go through dim light and fragmented music: someone is tuning up a bass viol. They find seats in the small, dim room: Sidonie recognizes, and Clara is greeted by, some luminaries she remembers from Clara's parties, or has seen pictures of in magazines. This is a select audience: a private fundraiser.

Everybody hushes, as for a religious ceremony.

The small elderly man, a well-known singer-poet, walks in with just a guitar. He is introduced; there is warm, quick applause, as for a family member; and then he begins, his familiar baritone growling monotonically through the familiar sly, sacrilegious lyrics. (How much had it cost Clara for tickets to this very intimate event, she wonders?)

She remembers that she has heard him sing decades before, in a small room, before his fame and the huge concert halls. She had not been particularly impressed with him, as a young woman; he was not musical, she thought: though his lyrics were sometimes funny, they didn't make sense. And his voice was almost atonal, the music droning, punctuated uncomfortably with patches of nasal wailing, like klezmer music.

On this occasion, she hears the music and lyrics differently: hears the bleakness, the self-deprecation, the loneliness under the layers of wit and black humour.

It's crowded and cold, in my secret life. . . he sings, and it seems that he is looking right at her, into her. It is almost too much to hear; she wants to weep; a storm of regret, longing, despair rises in her chest. She wants to run outside in the rain, to beat her breast, but must sit on her little chair among the other listeners and politely clap.

After an hour the singer takes his break, and the audience stands around talking. They are all old friends of the singer; everyone touches him, Sidonie notices. He is very slight in his jacket. His cropped white head seems to be too large for his body. She retreats to the periphery of the room: Clara and Anita ought not to have brought her here.

The singer's glance falls on her, and returns; he locks gazes with her and she has to fight the urge to look away. She has never learned to meet eyes with a stranger.

On the way home, Clara says, "If we weren't all so old, I'd say he was trying to pick you up," and Anita says, "He was just trying to remember if he'd slept with you."

"He didn't," Sidonie says.

Anita and Clara laugh.

They are sirens; they find more and more to entertain her; they will not let her go.

MUSSOLINI

After her long visit with Clara and Anita, she flies from Montreal to Toronto to spend a weekend with Hugh (Ingrid is away, visiting her older half-siblings). She and Hugh go out for dinner, to a concert, to the new wing of the museum, shopping. Hugh is amiable, urbane. Toronto is interesting. She likes that there is something new to do every evening.

Hugh has got tickets to see the production of *Götterdämmerung* at the Four Seasons. She has seen the entire cycle, of course, at the Bayreuth Festival, but this is a maiden Canadian performance, not to be missed. She suspects Hugh has got tickets for her sake, not out of his own interest; before the four and a half hours are up, she catches him snoring gently at least twice.

After a late dinner, he says, "Do you remember the opera singer? No: you'd have been too young. That was the winter of 49."

But she does remember.

An opera singer is coming to Marshall's Landing. He is a real opera singer, a tenor. But he is also Mrs. Inglis's cousin. He will sing in the hall and anyone can go, and the ticket money is for war orphans, though Father says it had better be kept here — there will be lots of starving here, after this winter.

The outside of the hall is partly brown-stained wood and partly shiny tin. Inside, the walls are cream, with wainscotting in a dense, heavy green, like moss, and the floor made of strips of wood, varnished and shiny. There is a stage at one end of the hall with an orange curtain, and along the adjacent side, a long narrow kitchen with pass-through windows.

Sidonie feels anxious in this room; it feels like a copy of something much grander that she has never seen. It tells her that there are bigger halls in other places, where more important things go on: it tells her that she and her world don't matter. But Alice loves it. Alice is always here, being the princess in the school play, singing in the Christmas concert. Alice is wearing a new winter dress: deep plum velvet, with a gathered skirt and little silver buttons up the front, and a small collar. She has pulled her hair up rather tightly, and her face is winter-pale. Against the velvety plum of her dress, Alice's head looks, Sidonie thinks, as if it were made of frosted or translucent glass, like the vase Mrs. Inglis has with the woman's head on the side of it.

Alice has not wanted to sit with the family, but Mother bought tickets in a block, and the seats are numbered, so she has to. She sits on the very end of the row in the aisle seat, her face turned slightly, as if she has no relationship to the rest of them. Next to Alice sits Father in his best suit, then Mother, and last, Sidonie, who is worried that someone she doesn't know will sit on her other side. But it's only Mr. Inglis, so she has let herself slide back into her chair instead of being scrooched up against Mother. Mr. Inglis says to Mother that Alice looks very beautiful, and then takes Sidonie's hand. "And here is our shy violet," Mr. Inglis says. Sidonie knows she is not beautiful: she has skin that is brown in summer, sallow in winter. And she is wearing an old dress of Alice's that's too big still. The bright blue colour makes her feel awkward, as if she is too shiny. But she likes the way the dress droops on her, the thick heavy wool tent of it. It's like a monk's robe, she thinks: in it she is hidden, safe. It's one of the dresses that had come from Europe in a box, before the boxes had stopped arriving. A hand-me-down from a second cousin, never seen, and too big even for Alice when it had arrived. But then Alice had worn it, and everyone had said Oh! Alice! Because it had matched her eyes exactly. It does not match Sidonie's eyes, which are grey.

You are not supposed to crane your neck around like a yokel, but Sidonie does a little, looking for people she knows. She sees her teacher, the infant teacher, Miss Cavendish, and Miss Erskine, her Sunday School teacher. And Hugh and Graham Inglis, and Mr. and Mrs. Clare with all of the red-haired Clare children in a row, and Dr. Stewart, who came to see her when she had the measles, and old Mr. and Mrs. Schiller, who are the only people in Marshall's Landing whom Father can speak German with, although he says that they have a much different dialect, and are hard to understand.

The hall lights dim. A spotlight shines on the stage. Mrs. Inglis swooshes out onto the stage in a long grey dress and pearls and a smaller hat than usual, and introduces the singer, and everyone applauds, and then the tenor comes out, and bows. Mrs. Inglis and the tenor must know each other quite well, Sidonie thinks, but they are pretending to be grand and formal: there are flourishes. The tenor is not tall, but is widest around the stomach, and has thin legs; he's cone-shaped, like a fir tree. He is bald on top of his head, but has lots of fair curls along the side and back. He is wearing evening dress: a tailcoat with a waistcoat under and a starched shirt front and a little bow tie. He looks shiny, glistening.

When the tenor begins to sing, he opens his mouth wide and his lips make a sort of humped shape, and a high, resonant sound, like nothing Sidonie has heard come from a man's mouth before, soars out into the hall. Sidonie hears some of the children and even adults in the audience titter, and she wants to herself, not because the sound is funny, but because it's so unexpected. But it would be rude to laugh. Instead, she moves the energy of her brain away from the top of her head, where the giggling is, down, down towards her shoulders. She lets her shoulders drop, opens her chest so the music can get inside.

The tenor is singing in Italian: Father has told Sidonie this. She can't understand the words. What does the song mean? Even with her chest and shoulders open, waiting, Sidonie feels perplexed. It is not just the words, but the music itself that seems foreign. What is the music saying? It is a different language than the music she has heard before. It's not like the music of church, which mostly says *Let's be good people together*, or the music Alice likes to listen to on the radio, which says *Quick! Have a good time*, or of Father's gramophone records, which say *Aren't musical notes beautiful*, or even the jazz music heard once at Inglis's, which says *It's lovely to be so sad*.

Sidonie asks Father to read the program to her: the first song is "Questa donna conoscete" from *La Traviata*. Is the song a story, then, like a play? Sidonie thinks it must be. But how can people follow the story if they can't understand Italian? The music, she thinks, is more like Father's Mozart recordings than anything else, but the singing changes it. The piano accompaniment is not very pronounced. The singing is the music.

And then she feels: that's it. The singing *is* the music. The tenor's voice is the instrument, and it doesn't really matter that she can't understand the words. He is making an instrument, like a cello or a horn, out of his lungs and throat and mouth. She glances back: Richard and other children are still looking at each other and giggling. Alice is holding her head at an angle that tells Sidonie she knows people are looking at her.

And then there is intermission, with coffee and cake at the pass-through, and Alice standing a little apart with her friends Bonnie and Coralee, and the ladies complimenting each other on their clothes. Someone else comes up to Mother and says, isn't Alice a pretty girl! But Sidonie thinks that there is something disturbing about Alice: she is too pale, and the plum velvet dress too rich. Something about the way she looks reminds Sidonie of the opera singing. She is too fragile, too beautiful: she is vulnerable. Some danger threatens her.

After the program begins again, the tenor sings some Schubert *Lieder*, which Sidonie has heard before on Father's gramophone, but not like this. The tenor sings the song about the little brook. Father has told Sidonie what the words mean, so she can recognize them: *ever cooler and clearer, the brook rushes along; is this then my path?* And Sidonie can see the little brook, and the young man with his walking stick following it down the mountainside. *Is this my path?* He is going to come down into the valley; he's looking for his destiny. She can see his slim straight back in his green woolen waistcoat, his cap. He's standing on the little crooked path, and the sun is shining on his shoulders through the pines, and he is happy and only a little bit scared, because he's at the beginning of his life. He doesn't know what his life will bring, but he has all sorts of hopes and ambitions. And he's happy because he's free. He's free to follow any little brook he wants.

This time Sidonie is listening so deep in her chest that she isn't aware at first of the movements around her. It's a bump on the back of her chair that makes her eyes fly open, so that she sees a very odd thing: people in the audience are leaving in the middle of the concert. Families and individuals and small clusters of people have risen, in the little space between the songs, and are silently filing out. What is happening? She looks around. Is it a fire? But no. Mrs. Inglis strikes the piano keys and the tenor begins again, after only a little hesitation: this time, "The Huntsman." And people are still leaving. The Davidsons, the Bonds, the Robinsons. The Clares, the McCarthys, the Platts. Other people she doesn't recognize. Alice's friends Bonnie and Coralee get up too, and Alice half-rises, but Father takes her elbow and pulls her back into her seat.

Sidonie tries to hear the song: *Leave your gun in the wood, your yelping dogs at home!* but the bustling around deafens her with distress. She cannot tell what the people who are leaving are thinking; their faces are closed. Mother is rigid beside her: red spots burn on her cheeks, but she doesn't turn her head. Father is intently composed, listening. Behind her, the Schillers stay in their seats. Alice is pale and removed, as if she's left her shell there and gone away.

What does it mean?

Finally, only the Inglises, the Erskines, the Protherows, Mr. Ramsay, Dr. Stewart, the Nakamuras and Mr. Tanaka and Masao, and the Schillers, with their odd clothes and accents, and perhaps a few others remain. The hall is half-empty. The tenor keeps sing-ing, though, and when he is finished, they all clap very loudly, as if to make up for the missing pairs of hands. Nobody says anything. Mrs. Schiller is crying, but whether because of the music or the exodus, Sidonie can't tell. Mr. Inglis shakes Father's hand. Mrs. Inglis brings the tenor from the little room beside the stage, and everyone shakes his hand.

And then Mrs. Inglis says, "Much too early to go home! A party!" and Father says, "Well, why not?" and everyone is going to the Inglises. Sidonie and Alice and Hugh are all allowed a little bit of sherry from a cut-glass decanter (the sherry is the colour of a specific kind of grown-up sadness and confusing behaviour, Sidonie will think forever after), and cake, and then to go up to Hugh's and Graham's playroom and look at Graham's encyclopedia set, while downstairs the adults move onto whiskey and pretend that the con-cert was not disrupted.

Nobody explains to Sidonie what has happened; very late, she finds herself lifted off Graham's shoulder onto her father's, and then is in the cold winter night.

How to make sense of that concert, now?

It's a story of ethnic tensions, obviously. This had been just after the war. But more: some other forces at work. She remembers Father and Mr. Inglis, Mr. Ramsay and Mr. Erskine — and perhaps Mr. Protherow?— all in white jackets (smelling of mothballs, which was a queer smell, interesting and bad at the same time): how they made a row of white jackets shaking the singer's hand, like a scene from a movie. (How long has it been since she has seen a group of men in white dinner jackets? An unexpected thing in that countryside.)

"It was the German songs," Hugh says.

"The *Lieder*."

"Yes. It was still too close to the end of the war. Mother's cousin Harry didn't think of that, I guess. And my mother — I think she believed that Art transcended all, you know."

"Some people stayed. Men with dinner jackets."

"Is that what you remember? For me, it was the low-cut dresses and satin bosoms. Yes; my parents and some of the other Brits trying to hold the class line. Of course, if Harry hadn't been Mother's cousin, if Mother hadn't arranged the whole thing, they might have left, too."

Yes. That had been in 1949, when they had been Swiss. It was later in the fifties, when the other German people had come, the displaced persons from Poland and the other countries in Eastern Europe, that things had changed.

The first day of fifth grade: a new teacher, whom she did not know. This was significant, because she had known all of the other teachers all of her life. But the school had expanded, suddenly: there had been a great influx of children.

On the first day, Miss Beattie makes the children stand up beside their desks and state their names. When it is her turn, Sidonie stands up, says her name: Sidonie von Täler.

"Sidney One Dollar?" Miss Beattie says. "Is your last name, 'One Dollar?' I don't see you on the class list, Sidney. Do you have an English name that you go by, as well as your Indian name?"

Several girls, quick on the uptake, are giggling. Vern Platt says, "One Dollar's a *squaw*," using his trick of not seeming to speak. Sidonie is utterly confused for a few moments, an odd feeling, as if the desks were swirling around her, sucking air from the room. What is the teacher saying? The giggling behind her spreads. Her legs tremble, and she looks around her quickly for help, but even normally friendly faces are contorted, suffused with some sort of mirth. Only Edith Henry is not grinning or laughing, but scowling darkly down at her desk.

Then the penny drops. Sidonie opens her mouth to say her name again, but to her surprise and shame, tears and sobs suddenly burst out of her, choking out the words.

"Sit down," says Miss Beattie.

Sidonie puts her face in her arms and feels tears and mucus slime her cheeks and mouth.

Richard Clare says, "Excuse me, Miss Beattie?" and Sidonie

knows, without turning around, that Richard's arm is waving in the air, his red hair smoothed back, his blue shirt crisp and tidy.

"Yes," says Miss Beattie, her voice a little less impatient.

"Her name is *Sidonie von Täler*," Richard says, enunciating in an exaggerated way, speaking with a neutral politeness that verges somehow on insolence, but only so slightly that it could not be objected to.

"Oh, I see," says Miss Beattie. She gives a little laugh. "Well, there's no need to cry about it, is there, Sidonie?"

After that she has treats Sidonie as if she were mentally and morally defective, speaking to her in a high, unnatural voice, raising her eyebrows and holding the paper out with the tips of her fingers when she hands back Sidonie's assignments. On the assignments she writes: You must check for spelling errors. This is atrocious! And: did you proofread this? She gives Sidonie C, always, on compositions.

Sidonie knows that she can do better: she does not proofread, she forgets letters and even whole words, she scribbles madly. The ideas tumble out of her onto the page, her hand not fast enough to channel them out through the fountain pen. That is another thing: the blots Sidonie makes on the pages of her books and on herself. Miss Beattie says "You look as if you've been trying to dye yourself blue," and also "How do you expect I will read something so untidy?"

But Sidonie never fixes up her work: she can't bear to read her own phrases and sentences. It is as if somebody else had written them, somebody who knows too much about her, whom she knows too much about. The unfamiliar and yet too-familiar voice on the page makes her squirm inside, is like a black gloved hand fossicking around in her gullet.

And her mind is already on something else by the time she has finished a composition. She doesn't want to linger.

Miss Beattie tells the class to tidy their desks, then walks around the classroom, peering inside the desks. When she gets to Sidonie's, she gives a large sigh, then tips the desk up so everything inside splashes out onto the floor: notebooks, textbooks, drawings Sidonie has done on scraps and then crumpled up, an old sandwich, chewed pencils, a broken shoelace.

Humiliation. But it isn't so bad once Sidonie has gotten over the shock, the exposure, and is on her hands and knees, picking things up. Walter Rilke, going by to sharpen a pencil, surreptitiously drops another crumpled scrap on the pile she is gathering. She looks up at him, but he winks, and she smooths it open to find a rough caricature of Miss Beattie wearing a peaked hat, with boots, general's stars, a whip.

Sidonie's pen breaks during an in-class composition and she has no spare. Walter does, though, she knows: he keeps in his desk a little metal box of spare nibs. Quietly, trying for once not to bang into everything along the way, she creeps from her desk up the narrow aisle to Walt's, whispers to Walt, takes the nib, heads back.

Miss Beattie's voice crackles through the scratching of dozens of pens. "Miss von Täler! Stop sneaking around like a dirty Nazi spy!"

How she had burned. How Alice would blame her; how angry Alice would be again that she had shamed them.

They had lost status, somehow, the von Tälers, with the influx of other Germans, with the sudden division of the community along ethnic lines. It had not been the fault of the new immigrants, of course. But she thinks she might have blamed them.

Early spring, 1959: she is in tenth grade, though doing some eleventh-grade subjects; she should be in ninth, but has skipped a year.

Now she must be nice to Lottie Kleinholz, who is as stupid as a Silkie hen, but is Buck's sister. The Kleinholzes are invited to dinner: all of them still at home. Buck's younger brother Gerry, who once pelted Sidonie with pieces of frozen horse manure. His brother John, who has a wall-eye and a lisp. His sister Lottie, who stares like a rabbit in headlights when anyone speaks to her. The parents: nasty Mr. Kleinholz, whose eyes run, and who is famous for trying to touch girls' breasts; nobody will play at Lottie's house. Mrs. Kleinholz, with her pale eyes and overbite, whom Sidonie does not actually dislike. She looks like a rabbit, but she is kind, speaks kindly to all children, in her accented voice.

They all come to dinner. Mother cooks a large pork roast, but with an air of resignation rather than celebration. There is no cake: Mrs. Kleinholz has insisted on contributing some pies. And no garden salad or young peas, for it is too early in spring.

Sidonie is told to take Lottie upstairs. In her room, which she shares with Alice, Sidonie sits on her bed while Lottie wanders around. Lottie seems confused by the pictures, the framed reproductions that hang on the walls: why are these here? Who painted them? Are they of one of your homes? It's as if she's never seen paintings hanging in a house before.

When she bends to examine the rabbit lamp, Sidonie says "Don't touch that," sharply. Then Lottie sits on Alice's bed and stares at Sidonie.

Father has bought wine for the dinner, over Mother's objections. "They'll think it's a party," Mother had said. Father had been sheepish: "Only a little Gewürztraminer. It's customary."

Mr. Kleinholz drinks three or four glasses quite quickly, and begins making lewd references, and Mother gives Father her dark look. But Mrs. Kleinholz's cheeks become pink, and she seems less sad, and almost pretty. During dinner they talk about apples — *Ja, the Gravenstein is a good producer, but hasty to get thrips* — and after dinner Buck's younger siblings and Sidonie are sent outside while the parents and Alice and Buck talk about the wedding arrangements.

On the porch, Gerry Kleinholz lights a cigarette.

"Give me one," says John.

"No."

Give me one."

"No."

"Give me one."

"I'll give you one, alright," Gerry says. He clouts John above the ear, hard. Lottie's mouth hangs open.

Sidonie says, "We don't smoke on the porch. You go out in the yard."

The boys stare at her, then Gerry mimics her, putting on a mincing British accent. Sidonie looks away, straightens her back. It is cold; night has fallen.

"Do you want to take the truck and go down to the Tastee-Freez?" Gerry asks. It's a moment or two before Sidonie realizes that he's talking to her; the others are waiting for her reply.

"No," she says.

John says, "More fun to go down Platt's, get some hullabaloo juice." He capers oddly, a little kicking-up of the heels. Oh: the distaste. She can feel the messiness, the wrongness of the Kleinholzes, like black mildew on the pumpkins.

"Whatchoo staring at?" John says. His face is like a jack-o'-lantern, she thinks: his eyes show nothing but snap, like the desire to punch, to torment; his lips are drawn back over his bad teeth in an appalling grin. It is worse than Lottie's cow-like blankness.

Gerry Kleinholz has become popular in the last year or so. He has a better haircut and clothes — rumour has it that Buck pays for them — and a driver's license. Some of the girls have begun to speak of him as possible.

But he's too dumb, too mean, too unpolished, Sidonie thinks, for anyone to look at.

They wait and wait; finally the boys slouch off, telling Lottie to stay at the house.

Sidonie fumes inwardly. But she holds herself still, pretends she doesn't see Lottie shivering in her thin blouse.

She has noticed that Buck has a suit on tonight, a brownish tweedish suit, and a very narrow tie. It's a cheap suit, too cheap to even be flashy, but new. In it, Buck looks smaller, older, more ordinary. She had seen Alice glance across the table at him with something like disgust on her face. Had noticed Buck catching the tail end of the look, and almost felt sorry for him. It's a very sheepish, worried Buck tonight: not the cocksure young man in the T-shirt, now.

Buck's brothers return, and they are all finally allowed back into the house in order for the Kleinholzes to leave. Mr. Kleinholz leers at Sidonie: You'll be wanting to get this one married off soon," he says. "Overripe by sixteen, remember that."

After, Father pours himself some scotch and lights a cigar, and Mother doesn't say anything about his smoking in the house.

"*Kleinholz*," says Father. "When I was a boy, it was an insult lads tossed at each other. It means "little wood," of course, but it had another connotation."

"None of that vulgar talk," Mother says. "I think we've had about enough of it for one night."

In their bedroom, Alice lies fully clothed on top of the covers, staring at the ceiling. "So what's the scoop?" Sidonie asks. She has learned that approaching Alice with a light, sardonic tone circumvents much of her scorn and disdain.

Alice shrugs. "Nothing I couldn't have predicted. 'You kids don't know how much it costs to live, here's some money to get you started, blah blah blah'."

In fact, Father has agreed to give Alice and Buck ten acres of orchard: the smallest part that may be subdivided off. Mr. Kleinholz will run it for Buck, though. Buck has got a job at a sawmill in the Cariboo, and he and Alice will go live there.

What are the Kleinholzes giving in return? Nothing. A son.

Buck says it will only be for a little while, the living in Horsefly. "Till I can move up to foreman," he says, in an odd earnest voice.

So Alice is caught. As they had tried to catch Mr. Defoe, Alice herself is caught.

And how was it that Alice, in the space of a fall and winter, had gone from bride-elect of the most eligible bachelor in Marshall's Landing to this?

That is another story. That is a story that Sidonie can hardly bear to think about.

In the bright-jacketed paperbacks that Alice smuggles into their room to read (because Father says they're *schmutzig*, smutty), girls who become pregnant before they are married are threatened with horsewhipping. But there is no prospect of Alice being beaten. Neither do their parents put Sidonie under close watch, as is supposed to befall the younger sisters. Rather, Sidonie moves, that spring, to the far periphery of her parents' collective vision. They hardly notice what she does, or even if she is home. Not that she goes anywhere; she is spending her time cramming, cramming. Reading books that she brings home from the high-school library by the bagful, trying to make up for the lost years, the years she had languished, supposedly unteachable, at the elementary school. She has her own project: she is building an escape route.

Alice is married in June, as soon as can be decently arranged; even so, her belly protrudes a little, and she has to wear an empire-waist dress, rather than the tight-bodiced, low-waisted Juliet gown that is the fashion. The wedding takes place in the Lutheran chapel, which the Kleinholzes nominally attend. Mother says, Mr. Erskine will be heartbroken. And Alice says, I doubt that.

The Lutheran chapel is bigger and newer than their church, but plainer. Pine pews, white walls, no stained glass. But on the wedding day, it's full of flowers: roses, peonies, iris, narcissi, some late lilac, boughs of syringe and spirea. There are three giant arrangements at the front, jugs and vases filling the windowsills.

It's as if the whole neighbourhood has stripped its gardens for Alice. It is the doing of the Women's Institute ladies, of course. When she sees all the flowers, Mother cries.

In August Alice and Buck leave for Horsefly, Buck's truck packed with boxes of canned fruit, bedding, dishes, Alice's sewing machine, Buck's gun and fishing rods. Alice seems excited, glad to be leaving. She hugs Sidonie, unexpectedly. Sidonie feels the swell of Alice's belly press against her own flat one, and recoils. Mother wishes that they could have waited until fall, so that she could have sent them up with a box of winter squash.

Alice is twenty. Buck is twenty-one.

The week after Alice leaves, Sidonie begins her final year of high school, attending the new school that has opened on the flat land between the creek and the community hall at the bottom of Berry Road. She is nominally in Grade 11, but has got her teachers to make certain accommodations for her: she challenges certain courses, doubles up in others. As a new school with smaller student body, some combined classes, this is possible to do without inconveniencing the teachers excessively. She begins sending for university application packages, and has them mailed to Graham, who is living at home this year, and who participates in her quest with cynical indulgence: "The fleshpots of Montreal, eh? Sure that's what you want?"

She does not want the packages to come to her house to be commented on and perhaps intercepted by Mother and Father. She doesn't want them to come to the post office addressed to her either: nothing comes through the post office without entering community discussion.

She goes to school, speaks almost to nobody, walks home, does her chores, does homework in her room. She lies low. Mother and Father are subdued; little more is required of her than to be quiet and do her chores.

In June, Father says, "How can you be graduating? You are sixteen!"

Mother says, "I suppose you could have told me in time to make you a dress!"

Sidonie thinks that she has done Mother a favour: to sew a formal gown this spring would have taxed Mother beyond even her immense capability. "I'll wear an old dress of Alice's," she says. "I don't really care about it."

In fact, Mrs. Inglis had bought her a frock from a store in town, a bronze taffeta, she remembers. Nearly the only dress left in the shop, so late in the season, but oddly suited to Sidonie's colouring. It had been cut strangely in the bodice, in a straight line that skimmed the collar bones. *Bateau*: is that what they called it? Banded with brown velvet, and otherwise undecorated. Layers of tulle in the skirt, of course. It probably hasn't been kept. It certainly wasn't in the trunk of Alice's gowns. A pity; she'd like to have seen it again. It was the first thing she owned, she thinks now, that she chose herself, and it was a present from Mrs. Inglis, who became, after Alice's defection, more of a friend to Sidonie than she has probably appreciated.

She had spent much time at the Inglises' that summer. Hugh had only been back on a flying visit; he had got a summer job working on the railway. She had gone for walks with Graham sometimes, when he had been well enough. She had played endless games of chess with him, when he was not as well; the games accompanied by a dark running commentary on the actions of the figures, who spoke to him, were part of some court intrigue. Sidonie did not mind this: it had not been so long since she had been small enough that the animate and inanimate alike had spoken to her in cryptic utterances. Graham had always seemed to know her; that is, he had talked to her with the same theatrical, fantastical persona as always, and she had not seen any difference between them. Mrs. Inglis had not hovered, and had thanked Sidonie — genuinely, Sidonie thought — for her kindness. But it had not been kindness, only self-serving propinquity, for Sidonie had been bored and lonely herself.

Graham had helped her with her applications, and called her the *princesse lointaine*. And she had not thought of him except as someone who was nearly always available and a satisfactory companion. Only Richard Clare had said to her: Be careful, or you'll go insane, like Graham Inglis. It was commonly supposed in their community that too much intelligence would tip the brain over the top into madness, as if intelligence were a chemical agent. Too much of it a very bad thing.

What had they done? Read, played chess, walked. She had not thought of Graham romantically: no. An air of tragedy hung over him, and she was damaged, or thought of herself as damaged, rejecting all sexual thoughts. But Graham must have been practice for her for later: for Adam and others. And also, though she had not seen it, a kind of paradigm of culture and sensitivity.

Once, she remembers, going with Graham and Walt up one of their old hiking club trails. A significant day: they had found Mussolini dead.

She had seen him first, fallen into a crack between two of the boulders.

At first they think he is caught, and debate whether they might be able to pry him loose without coming into striking range. But then they hear the flies, and Walt — cautiously — manages to nudge the end of his stick under the snake's body and flip it out of the crack.

They can see right away that he is really dead. Half of his neck is blown open. Twenty-two, Walt says.

How shocking: first, that someone would shoot Mussolini, who had lived in these rocks for decades; second, that his torn flesh should be the same texture, the same bright red, as a human's flesh. The wound in his neck looks just like the time Father had gashed his hand open between two bins.

Walt cuts the rattle off with his pocket knife and then they scrabble a shallow burrow in the loose shale, edge the body (limp, now, drained of its electricity) into this grave and kick a mound of shale over it.

"Otherwise the magpies will peck it to bits," Walt says.

They do not mark the grave, but Sidonie thinks that she can find it again. Graham had said that the location and details of the burial must be reported to Hugh in person; however, the news of Mussolini's demise must be transmitted right away.

She remembers that urgency. Had she written Hugh a letter? She thinks so.

He would not have kept it, on his many travels.

How strange that they would have called the reptile after a fascist dictator; the snake (who might have been female, actually) had not been, after all, a threat to the world, but only a wild thing. A piece of energy, of sheer being: that had been Mussolini-the-snake. A piece of wildness, of the valley as it had been before orchardists and schoolteachers, before the irrigation pipes had turned the sere, austere slopes into gardens. A piece of dry heat, of muscle and fang and obsidian eye; intrepid hunter and devourer of small wary hairy things; goddess of hot stone and cool secret cleft, alike; collector of the sun's enormous power though her polished diamond-shaped scales, her forked black tongue, her two-chambered heart.

What is left, now, of the wild?

She had left Marshall's Landing in the fall of 1960 to travel as far from her home as she imagined was possible. She had abandoned her mother and father — more than that, she had seized their moment of weakness, of grief and bewilderment — to betray them, to ambush them with her leaving. She had sent them a few letters, which had been kept, though they are solipsistic things, devoid of feeling or authenticity.

She had abandoned Alice, and Graham, and the fragile wild hillsides.

She had escaped Marshall's Landing. She had saved herself.

She would not ever say that it had not been worth it.

FLOOD

She returns from Toronto to rain: not the intermittent, light drizzle typical of the valley, but a dark, heavy maelstrom of weather. The water is bucketing down so hard that she scarcely notices the grader half-blocking the winding driveway. Fixing the hillocky, pot-holed road at last?

She opens her front door to the smell of damp carpet, of damp wood, damp Sheetrock, mould.

In the basement room is a shallow shining lake, and all of the crates and trunks and boxes sitting in it are cubist islands.

"I told you that I should check on the house while you were gone," Cynthia howls. "Why do you have to be so damned stubborn and independent? You make more trouble for everyone in the long run, you know that? You always think you know more than everyone else, but you don't."

Justin says, "Mother," but he too looks as shocked as Sidonie feels.

"Do you ever stop and think," Cynthia shouts, "that other people are intelligent, too? That they might know as much as you? More than you, about some things?"

It is astonishing; she hasn't heard an outburst like this from Cynthia in years, not since she was an adolescent.

"Does it ever occur to you," Cynthia shouts, her speech now garbled further with choked-back crying, "that you might be wrong sometimes? That you should talk to other people? Has it ever occurred to you that other people might worry about you? Might need some kind of interaction with you?"

Oh dear. But she can understand why Cynthia is upset: she's very worried about damage to her mother's things, which are in the boxes, still in the process of being sorted out, retrieved. Sidonie thinks that most of the personal things — anything of value — have been already moved into the Rubbermaid tubs, which are high and dry. She says so to Justin; Cynthia is in no mood to listen, to read lips.

Cynthia drives off, tires squealing, to get new boxes, and returns a little more calmly with stacks of heavy cardboard from the Wal-Mart bins.

Justin says, "I've never seen her this mad before." His voice holds both shock and delight, the delight of the young in drama, in something happening, perhaps in recriminations that are not, for once, directed at themselves.

Sidonie is angry herself for a few days. Cynthia is over-reacting: it's unjust. But then contrite, ashamed. How can she make it up? There is nothing to be done but to tip everything hurriedly into the dry boxes and carry it all upstairs. The wet things are spread out across shower rails, chairs, countertops. But much has been spoiled. The smell of mildew consuming cloth and paper fills the house.

As they're carrying the wet boxes outside, the next-door neighbour suddenly appears. "You've got water, too? I've called my lawyer. We're likely going to have a class action suit." She looks younger, animated; Sidonie at first doesn't recognize her.

Crates and boxes fill her living space now. She has arranged them as best she can to allow entrance and egress to her furniture and doorways, but they obstruct her fifty, a hundred times a day. She feels a pooling of irritation in her stomach. She thinks: I should have had the lot taken directly to the dump.

Justin is busy with classes; Cynthia comes over once, stares at the boxes with dismay, then spends the entire evening looking for the box she has begun to pack, which has been lost in the shuffle.

In the end, it is Steve's wife Debbie who gets the stuff shifted, bustling in from her car with a stack of flattened cartons, with tape, a Jiffy marker. Debbie tucks her stubby person up on a low stool and begins lifting items from one container and placing them into another, an efficient machine. Sidonie is anxious, at first: will things be lost? — but then surrenders into an appreciation of the rhythm. Debbie doesn't speak much, only holds items up or reads titles or labels for Sidonie's deliberation. In three hours they clear half a dozen of the large boxes. Sidonie offers to make tea, belatedly, but Debbie refuses, and bundles herself down the stairs with things they have sorted for disposal: bags for the dump or for recycling. She asks if she may take the boxes of books home to Stephen to look through; Stephen, she says, is a great reader, always picking books up in second-hand stores and flea markets. Stephen has a den in the basement with shelves and shelves of books: a real library. Many of the boxes had held nothing but old clothes — shabby wool coats, worn gabardine work pants, faded print rayon dresses, tattered nightwear and underwear — that must have been in dubious condition even before having been soaked and mildewed. Why had those been kept? They must have been boxed up, stored in the attic by Mother, and moved into storage by Sidonie without being checked after Alice had died. Of course, there had been little time.

It is dreadful, unbearable. And Cynthia is impossible; furious. She knows that Cynthia does not stay angry long, but that once riled, she makes implacable decisions, is resolute.

Her house has been disturbed by Furies, it seems. She cannot settle. She cannot eat or sleep; something has infected her. Cynthia's anger or Debbie's re-packing, or her trip, or perhaps even the spring air, but she is restless, her nerve endings electrically charged. She throws a suitcase of clothes, some blankets and books, her laptop, a tub of canned food into the back of her car, slips the spare key under the mat, leaves a phone message for Cynthia telling her where the key is, and heads out.

She has not thought it out well, but she will survive. There is no electricity, of course; no running water. The house has been vacant since the early eighties, and had been trashed by the last tenants. She is prepared: she had seen it after that. She sees now that Walter has done some repairs: the graffiti and black paint have been erased with a few coats of white. Someone has swept the house out occasionally; mended the roof. The decay now is the decay of a dry climate: the silvered, splintery wood on the south and west sides, the desiccated putty around the window panes. Dust. Dead bluebottles and wasps.

"I cleared out the chimney a year ago," Walt says. "You ought to be able to make a fire."

He is worried; she can see that. In his fisherman-knit sweater, he lingers, not willing to leave her on her own. He has brought a wheelbarrow of firewood, a barrel of water, in his pickup. She has showed him her stash: an air mattress and folding chair and paper plates purchased at Wal-Mart on the way; her books. She has assured him that she'll only be a few days. He does not trust her, or he feels responsible for her: one or the other. Or both.

"I will be fine," she says. "Just a few days until my house dries out. It's only October. I'll be fine."

"There's still the old bath house," Walt says. "You could dip water from the well for the boiler. It's also wood-fired."

"If I feel the need to bathe, I will do that," she says. "I can always run back home for a shower. It's not fifteen minutes."

"You could always run back home to sleep," he says. She can hear that he is still worried.

"Go along, Walt," she says. "I'll be fine."

The rain begins again and doesn't let up. Even when it stops for a few hours, the air is moist; a long cloud sits over the lake, filling the narrow west valley. Since when is the valley so damp? She doesn't remember this much rain, ever. The climate must have changed.

She explores the house tentatively. She has not been inside in over twenty years. It is not as big as she has remembered it, but the rooms feel well-laid-out, pleasingly proportioned. The house seems sturdy. There is damage. But she is able to live in it. With a strong fire in the fireplace, it is warm enough, though cold at night; she must wear several layers of sweaters, and long pajama pants under jeans, even with the fire going.

She sets her cans of food on the kitchen shelves, unfolds her camp bed in what had been the parlour. It is not bad. It would be better if she could shut off rooms. The house is too big, too open.

The house was not finished until Sidonie was in her teens, because Father had planned it on such a grand scale, and using the best quality materials available, and could only build a little at a time. When she was very small, there were the kitchen and parlour on the first floor, and on the second, Mother and Father's bedroom and Sidonie and Alice's bedroom. Father showed them drawings in blue ink on big rolls of paper of the rest of the house that is to come, a ghost house. Bathrooms, upstairs and down; additional bedrooms; a dining room; an office for Father and a sewing room for Mother; a big front porch.

Old photos of the house show the main wing only, at first; then the new north wing, with its dining room below and bathroom above. The porch, on the west side of the house, overlooked the long lawn and the lake. Their house was different than other houses in Marshall's Landing at that time: bigger, more open, and less finished, somehow. Their ceilings were higher, and floors bare; they had shutters rather than drapes. Instead of a fireplace, a big porcelain stove. No wallpaper anywhere, or coloured paint, but plaster embossed with designs of curlicues and diamonds. Where the other families — those who had indoor bathrooms — had a small room at the back of the house with a toilet, a sink, a cast-iron tub, Sidonie's family had a separate WC — a narrow room with a high window, a toilet, a tiny pedestal sink — and another room with a floor patterned in small hexagonal tile, like a honeycomb, and in it a large sink with a mirror, where Father shaved, a big tub like a sleigh, and an immense shower closet, walled inside and out with white rectangular tile.

When Sidonie was very small, there was no indoor bathroom or WC. She used the outhouse during the day. At night, there was a chamber pot, a white china bowl with a rolled rim, a handle, a painted border of bluebells. Mother said that she was humiliated that they didn't have a bathroom. Even after it was built, she grumbled: they might have had a smaller, less expensive one, sooner. But Father said he would not build cheap.

When the new wing was built, the kitchen was moved into the lower part of it, and where the kitchen was became the dining room. The new kitchen had tile floors and granite countertops and maple shelves and cupboards that looked more like other people's parlour cabinets. It had two sinks, both made of zinc. Other people's kitchens had smooth, coloured countertops, with bright metal trim and painted wood cabinets. They seemed brighter, cleaner. But Father said they will make more work, and cannot be cleaned thoroughly.

Other people's houses, too, had more doors, smaller, intimate rooms, darkened parlours, with figured wallpaper and linoleum, parquet, ornate fringed rugs.

In Sidonie's house, the rooms flowed into one another, at least on the ground floor. Only the bedrooms and the bathroom and WC had doors. The windows were large, much larger than in other houses, and light flooded the house, flowing from one side to the other. From May to October, the shutters on the south and west sides of the house were closed for most of the day, because of the intensity of the sun and the heat. The porch, when it was built, provided blissful shade.

Between the kitchen and parlour, Mother had hung a curtain of a deep, wine-coloured flannel, very soft and thick. Mother said that she did not want to have people seeing her dirty dishes when she was entertaining. Both Alice and Sidonie discovered, very early, that if they sat quietly in the kitchen, they were able to overhear a great deal of what was said in the other rooms.

Sidonie girds herself against the destruction, and there it is: the scarred floor, the hacked stair railings, the stained ceiling. The kitchen is empty of appliances; where those have gone, she can't remember. It has stood empty the past few years, though someone had been living in it and working the orchard in the late 90s. A row of green plastic pots lines the deep window sill, some plant — it could have been geraniums — indicated by desiccated grey stalks. The cupboards, though, under their sloppy coat of white paint are the original maple her father had custom-milled and installed, and the granite countertop also has remained intact, though someone has smashed it at one end.

The wine flannel curtain is long gone, of course. But she finds herself spending all of her time in the kitchen, as she used to do. In the afternoons, when weak sun slants through the kitchen windows, she is able to sit and read; she has no other occupation. She had forgotten about the lack of electricity; her laptop battery is soon depleted. She has brought candles, but they give faint light and cast huge shadows. She goes to bed early, does not sleep, but dozes.

When Walt brings another load of wood, she asks if she can do some outside work, and he suggests helping stack firewood; Walt and his sons are cutting up some old trees. She hears the buzz of the chainsaw in the daytime, walks among the trees, which are in fall leaf, shades of saffron and pumpkin and wine almost unbearably rich against the charcoal and aubergine of the wet trunks and limbs. She warms up considerably; the heat from the day's work stays with her into the evening, and she falls asleep more quickly and sleeps soundly. But her appetite grows with the woodpile, and she soon gets through the soups and legumes she has brought. And she wants a bath; she has been sweating freely.

She finds the bucket Walt mentioned, and the key for the padlock on the well-cover. She drops the bucket down on its rope. It splashes satisfactorily, only twenty feet or so down. Draws up the bucket — she's found the wooden windlass still attached to the wall of the shed, just above the well opening.

But the water in the bucket has an oily scum, and smells unpleasant. She puts her face to it, sniffs. Unmistakable: it smells like raw sewage.

"Oh," Walt says, pulling a long face. "I hadn't thought of that. The underground stream must be tainted. The new development up the hill, of course. All those houses on septic." And through the trees, she can see the blight of structures clustered above.

The well is tainted. She finds herself trembling with something between cold and fury and disappointment.

She drives back to her house on Quail Circle, has a long hot bath, collects more food, plugs in her laptop, checks for email and phone messages. For a moment, as she moves around her familiar machines, she thinks she might stay. She has left her air mattress at Beauvoir, left the woodpile unfinished, but she might just stay here.

But her email has become dislodged from the listserv again, and there are no personal messages — only a voice mail from Hugh, non-urgent. Her house feels damp still. In the basement, she sees the dark has spread again; outside, the driveway has been dug up. None of the boxes has left the living room, but neither is there a message from Cynthia.

She re-stocks, heads back to Beauvoir. She stops at the IGA in the plaza, on the way, for more food and a jug of water. At the hardware store that used to be Masao's music store, she buys a cooler, a camp stove, a lantern, a second camp chair. She wonder where Masao is now.

The girl arrives on the fifth day, in the rain, walking out of the mist, down the alfalfa and knapweed-clotted driveway. The opportunists of the dry land. Robins and magpies and starlings are industrious with the displaced earthworms. If the rain continues, the earthworm population will be decimated. The girl walks up the driveway in her jeans, boots, plaid jacket, an olive-green canvas pack over her shoulder, hips cantilevered to balance the load. Improbably red hair cut jagged and high across the brow, glint of metal like a steel beauty mark, like a lepidopterist's pin, at the upper lip.

The walk is familiar, that long foal-stride before the face with its antennae-eyebrows, the straight slash of upper lip, the over-full lower lip, is close enough to see. The von Täler face. It's Steve's girl, of course. Natasha, that's her name. Tasha. But somehow disguised, transformed.

If the girl is surprised to see the door open to her, she does not let on. She swings down the pack, looks around as if to see if things have been disarranged.

She has changed somehow. The sullenness has sprouted into something else, or maybe just grown stronger. What does she want?

Sidonie says, "There's no hot water. I hope you like baked potatoes and canned tuna."

The girl puts down her pack, sniffs the air.

"What do you smell?" Sidonie asks.

"Woodsmoke," the girl says. "Apples. Pee."

They are running out of food again, though Tasha has brought granola bars and apples in her pack. They both read in the pale sun during the day, pile wood, talk at night, when it's too dark and chilly to do anything but wrap themselves in their sleeping bags. They become progressively hungrier and grubbier; after three days of this, the girl smells high, and Sidonie knows that she must too.

What do they talk of? Of the work of an orchard, of Sidonie's research. Of the girl's studies, her unhappiness with her classes, of the music she likes. The girl still seems sullen; her answers are given diffidently, possibly grudgingly, possibly warily. She is bright, though: Sidonie can see that. And well-read for a child of her generation, though her reading is eclectic, and she references books injudiciously, vampire novels tossed in with classics and various books of philosophy, biology, and psychology, apparently first-year university textbooks. She claims to have read every book in her house, including the British Columbia Home Health Reference. She confesses that she once diagnosed herself as having fatigue. Only she thought it was pronounced "fat-i-gyoo." Her father, she says, curtails their television (ah, the von Täler coming out in him, Sidonie thinks). She has had to read more than is normal, to combat boredom.

Sidonie, lying in her sleeping bag in the dawn, drifting in hypnogogic sleep, half-dreams of Alice, long-lost Alice. The grandmother that Tasha has never met.

Alice is spinning people into statues. She grasps the other girls one by one by the wrist, and whirls them around and around, her feet shifting heel-toe faster than Sidonie can see, her spine arched for balance, her pale braids whipping, her outstretched arms with a child at the end like a strange giant flower whirling in circles. Then she lets go, and the child, depending on how much smaller she is than Alice, goes staggering or even flying across the mashed yellow grass until she falls down or bumps into something else. After that, she must freeze in the position in which she has fallen.

Then Alice comes over and says what she is. This is a variation on the game, which is played by all of the girls Sidonie has met. Only Alice takes it upon herself to name the statue.

Mary Summers says that everyone is supposed to choose what kind of statue they are. But when Alice is playing, Alice chooses. Nobody argues with this, except Judy, who is new. But even Judy, after a while, stops standing by the wall with her arms crossed and lines up for Alice to spin her.

It's Sidonie's turn. She is one of the smallest and knows that she will fly far, and she does, spinning out of control, then somehow tripping and falling over the steps, which hadn't been there earlier. There is a painful knock on her forehead and nose, and then her knees and face are stinging, stinging. She is not supposed to move, but has curled up before she can think, so stays in that position. She can taste blood in her mouth. The stinging and pain of the blows to her limbs and face rise in pitch, like screaming, but she will not scream. She won't move.

"Oh, my God," Bonnie Pruitt says, bending over her. "Her face is covered with blood. Oh my God. I'm going to faint."

Coralee says, "And her knees, look at her knees. Her stockings are all ripped and there's dirt and blood!"

They have left their positions. That's against the rules. She will not cry and she will not move.

But some of the younger girls, Lily Platt and Marjorie Tanaka and Susan Taiji ask, "Are you okay, Sidonie?" Then it's hard to keep the tears away.

Alice is there. She is standing over Sidonie. The others fall quiet.

"Just a stone, obviously," Alice says, pronouncing on Sidonie's position.

Do your parents know you're here?" she asks the girl.

Tasha shrugs. Her shoulders remain up; she looks sullen. But Sidonie is beginning to read her posture. She is afraid, Sidonie thinks — but not of her parents. She is afraid of something else. She is afraid to walk through any door — afraid that it will be the wrong one, that she won't find her way through or back in.

The girl looks at her sideways. Her lip curls up over the metal pin. "How about you?" she asks. "Do they know where you are? Does Aunt Cynthia know where you are?"

She has a point. They are bolters, both of them.

Pruning and burning the branches gets the men so *schmutzing* — sooty and grimy — that Father invites them to bathe before they leave the orchard. The Japanese are fond of bathing, Father says. A very clean people. In their country, he says, they have great wooden tubs, large enough to sit several men up to their noses. They like the water extremely hot, and they all scrub down with soap and rinse off before they get into the soak-tub.

Sidonie thinks of naked bodies accidentally touching in the water. She pushes away her potatoes, which have suddenly become slippery, grey-white flesh. At the same time, Alice wrinkles her nose. "They bathe nude? All together?"

Father finishes chewing, lays his knife and fork on the plate so that they are not quite parallel. Sidonie stares at them, longing to reach over and set them straight. If they were extended two-and-one-fifth times, she sees, they would meet. The point of meeting would fall just short of her water glass. She stares at the spot, almost seeing the shadow cutlery. If her father were to pick up those long utensils, his elbows would have to thrust far out to each side. He would knock Alice and her off their chairs.

Father says, "Alice, there is no shame in the human body." Mother makes a clicking sound with her tongue: *Tsk*. They have a proper bathtub in their house, of course; the big cement tub in the wash house, rough like new stone, is for washing when one is very dirty, or washing the dogs. One person's body fits it, or two small bodies, like Alice's and Sidonie's. The wash house floor has cedar planks and a squat iron stove to heat the water. There is a green shade on the light and the soap for the bath smells green, like the sea, and the cedar, when it is wet and hot, smells green also: a smell-colour like the deep green of the orchards in high summer: thick, cool, clean.

Father says, "In Europe people understand this. There are nude beaches and camping places. People are not ashamed or jokey about bodies."

Mother says brusquely, "Well, we're not in Europe now. The girls can stay away from the wash house while the men are using it."

After supper, in the winter henhouse, Sidonie lifts the eggs into her basket. Four, so perhaps the hens have already responded to the shift in daylight, or perhaps she missed one egg the day before. She scans the henhouse for signs of intruders, checks the water and feed troughs, and scratches Number Two's lizard-like head just behind the earholes, before shutting and locking the big door behind her. The hens settle into creaks that might mean they are discussing her, but benignly.

As she walks back to the house, the pruners emerge from the washhouse in clouds of steam, fully dressed, bundling their towels and dirty clothes, exclaiming at the shock of the cold. Masao is there, shaking out his blue-black hair. When he sees Sidonie, he waves, grinning. Sidonie waves back. She had been about to retrace her steps, take the long way back to the house to avoid pressing through the crowd of pruners, but now she can't. She stops and Masao comes over to her, juggling his towel, which has become a sort of soft origami box containing his soiled clothing.

Masao peers into her basket, then jumps back in pretend surprise, throwing his arms over his head. "Grenades!" he yelps. "Spare me, lady! I'm on your side!" Then he leaps back, pulls the hood of Sidonie's coat up over her head, shakes an admonishing finger under her nose. "Now stay away from the wolf, okay?"

Sidonie laughs, forgetting her intention to slip around the back of the washhouse. Masao slips his arm through hers and begins to sashay. "We're off to see the wizard," he sings, in a high voice, like a girl's. Sidonie is worried she'll drop the eggs, but can't stop laughing. Masao can do all the parts from the movie. Suddenly, he's down on all fours, wiggling his rear end. "Woof!" he says. "Woof!" He's Toto, barking at the Cowardly Lion. But Mr. Tanaka, coming down the path toward them, is not amused. He speaks sharply to Masao in Japanese, and Masao stops playing. He looks around to see if Mr. Tanaka is watching, and then takes something out of his pocket, slips it into Sidonie's basket.

"For Alice," he says. It's another little folded box, made out of paper. Sidonie has watched Masao fold these little boxes — he can make them small as a pea, large as two fists. She has watched him square off a sheet of paper — any paper will do: a sheet of newspaper or a bit of flowered wrapping paper or silver-foil cigarette paper or even a bill or receipt — and go through the methodical steps, first the diagonal creases, then the squares, the turning back and forth, the flipping over, the final blowing the box into shape with a puff of air — but has never been able to do it herself.

This little box is made of a sheet of the pink paper used by Father or Mr. Tanaka to write down each picker's bucket weight or number of boxes or bins in the summer and fall, when the pickers line up at the scales with their metal and canvas bags. Sometimes Sidonie helps with this; she can add up all of the numbers in her head very quickly — more quickly than Mr. Tanaka with his pencil — so that he scratches his head and says "Eh?" and then gives her a caramel sweet. Sidonie and Alice are not supposed to take the pink slips — they are used for accounting, for keeping track of how much has been picked and how much each worker is to be paid, and are important. But it is winter now; perhaps this sheet is an old one.

The little box lies among the eggs. Sidonie knows that inside is a funny note for Alice, for she has delivered these before, and Alice always laughs to read them. The note will be written on the paper, folded inside it. It's a trick that Hugh taught them in the Hiking Club. They had to learn secret ways of passing messages: they might be written in potato juice or in codes, hidden in a knothole in an alder tree, tied into a bandana. When Masao had produced the little boxes, Hugh had seen right away that they would be useful for messages.

Sidonie wishes that Masao would send her a comical message. Masao and Alice really don't do much with the Hiking Club anymore, anyway, now that they are fifteen. And Graham has left it too. Only Hugh still leads them through their important lessons: Sidonie, Walt, the little Clares.

Masao turns quickly and begins to walk away after the men, but with a backwards glance at the house. He is looking for Alice, Sidonie knows. Masao is Alice's friend: not at school, where boys and girls don't play, but in the orchard.

Mr. Tanaka is Masao's uncle, and Masao lives with him, because his parents are dead. Did they die in the war? Sidonie has a vague queasy idea about this.

Masao and Mr. Tanaka are Japanese, and the Japanese were the enemy. Is that true?

She wakes; she is confused for a moment by the darkness, the hardness of the foam mattress. Then, remembering, calls out. The girl has gone. Where? But then, a minute or two later, she is back. Drink, now.

The pruning fires burn all night, with one or two of the men to tend them. The green wood burns smokily, and Father likes to get the burning over with. Sidonie, kneeling on her bed to peer out the window, sees the fires dotted across the hillside. Dark human shapes are silhouetted against the flames, moving this way and that.

It looks like a battle scene from the old newsreels. It looks like something from a fairy tale, or from one of Father's stories, dimly remembered. A sort of memory that is located not inside her head, but somewhere in the pit of her stomach. It's connected to a fear that something bad is going to happen, a sort of panic.

Something has awakened her: where is Alice? She has sensed rather than seen Alice moving around the darkness of their shared room pulling on clothing.

"Shhh," Alice had said, when Sidonie had raised her head. "Going to the outhouse." Sidonie had sunk back on her pillow. Alice sometimes went outside to use the outhouse in the night; she didn't like to flush the toilet and disturb Mother and Father, she said. Sidonie would rather wet the bed than go outside in the dark, but Alice is not afraid.

Sidonie had almost subsided back into sleep, but a stray recognition had burrowed into her consciousness. Hadn't she heard the jingling of a belt buckle? In fact, now she is more awake, hadn't she heard the entire suite of sounds produced by someone pulling on trousers, zipping them, belting them snugly? Had Alice really put on trousers to go to the outhouse?

The thought worries her now as she kneels on the bed. She feels for her lamp, for the switch. But it's impossible for her to turn the little knob; her hands shake. Instead, she waits, listening for Alice to turn the handle of the back door and slip back up the stairs to their room.

The longer she waits, the more awake she grows. Should she call her parents? How long has Alice been? The last time she had woken to Alice's absence and had fearfully knocked on her parents' door, they'd been really cross, and so had Alice, coming in from the toilet. "I've been gone two minutes!" What had seemed half a night to Sidonie. Now she can't trust herself, her own sense of time.

She tries counting to sixty five times. Sits up again to look out the window. Figures move eerily, silhouetted against the nearest fire. Is one of them Alice?

Her heart beats too quickly. What if Alice has been kidnapped, has fallen down the outhouse drop? Which would be worse: to rouse her parents again in false alarm, or to wake up in the morning to find Alice gone, dead even? She tries to imagine Alice murdered, but can only picture her lying somewhere, incapacitated by a twisted ankle, berating Sidonie furiously for not having had the sense this time to get help.

Then she remembers the belt-buckle jingle, the zipper. She must check about Alice's trousers. This time, she's able to get the lamp switched on. She pulls up Alice's blankets, rummages through the heaped clothing, through the garments hanging in the wardrobe. Ah — there's a pair of heavy gabardine legs. But doesn't Alice own two pairs of trousers?

Sidonie sits on the end of Alice's bed for a moment. Then, suddenly, she's sleepy again. The question of Alice's trousers (*trews*, Alice likes to call them, mimicking English novels) suddenly becoming irrelevant in her fuzzy brain. She thinks: I'll just lie down for a moment with the light off.

When she wakes in the morning, Alice is asleep in the other bed, her pale yellow hair tangled, obscuring her face, and Sidonie doesn't remember the middle-of-the-night sortie, or ascertain how many pairs of trousers Alice owns, until days later.

If their parents find out, the world will come apart.

She makes a deal with the girl: they will drive into town, get some groceries. They will check in at Sidonie's house (have showers, Sidonie thinks, but doesn't say). Tasha will call her parents. (She has, she says, lost her cell phone.) Sidonie will leave a message for Cynthia.

They will drive into town, and then they'll come back.

But when she tries to stand up, she cannot. She is dizzy. She vomits without having time to reach a basin. Possibly it is food poisoning. Possibly the well: she has drawn water to wash dishes in, and perhaps has not boiled it long enough.

She becomes more and more ill. Tasha is alarmed; she wants to contact someone. But Sidonie resists. It will pass. It's just a bug. She'll survive.

She drifts. Tasha brings her bottled water, ginger ale. She wakes to vomit, to struggle to a pail — she cannot reach the outside toilet.

She sleeps. The rain stops; the sun comes out and beats through the unshuttered windows of the dining room. The sun percolates through her lids to enter her unconscious mind. Too bright. She dreams of light: hot, insistent yellow light.

It's Sidonie's job to do the chickens, though it's Mother who sets a dozen eggs under the broody hens every spring when the chickens are laying extra. When the chicks hatch, they stay in a screen-covered crate in front of the kitchen window until they are pullets, because so many things would like to eat them. It's surprising how the chicks grow: they are the same, the same, the same, for the first few days: penny-brown fluff with round heads and four-toed feet and tiny serrated combs, and then suddenly one day they have pin feathers at their wing tips, and before you know it, they are not chicks anymore, but hens and roosters, and they do not seem even related to the chicks you remember, but another sort of creature entirely.

Sidonie feeds and waters the hens and chicks, and collects the eggs twice a day: morning and evening. "No meals until the beasts have had theirs," Father always says, and Sidonie and Alice must dress and go out early in the morning to feed the animals before breakfast, and then again before supper. Mother has to do the goat, and Sidonie is glad it's not her, as the goat is not friendly. Alice feeds the barn cats, though not too much, because they are supposed to catch the mice. Once they had rabbits, but a dog scared them, and the mother ate the babies, so no more. Alice did the rabbits.

When it's really cold out and the mornings are dark, nobody wants to go outside to scoop food from the bins with chilled numb fingers, to slosh water into gumboots. But then it is especially important to take care of the animals. Especially, they must always have fresh water, even when the water freezes up solid overnight in the bowls.

So by the time they wash up and have breakfast — porridge in winter, toast in summer — and make their lunches and set off on the mile walk to school, they have all done a number of chores, especially in fruit season.

Once Bonnie Pruitt said "Uggh! You smell of chicken manure!" so Sidonie washes very, very well in the mornings. In winter, her hands scab over and bleed because of her eczema, but she still must make sure that not one bit of chicken essence sticks to her.

Red Mite, Leaf Roller, Oyster Shell.
Woolly Aphid, Perennial Canker.
Crown Rot, Die Back, Drought Spot, Fire Blight.
Powdery Mildew, Codling Moth.
It's a ditty to sing walking up the hill from school. An incantation.

These are the names of some of the pests that have to be watched for vigilantly, treated for, again and again. Some are insects and some are fungi. If you do not treat them, the fruit will be lower grade or too damaged for anything but juice. Then you will get less money for the crop.

Sidonie and Father hold the white square of cloth under the tree: Sidonie holds one corner in each hand, and Father, whose hands are bigger, holds both of the remaining two corners in one hand. With the other, he whacks the branches with his walking stick. Then Father rolls the cloth up, and they take it to the shed and shake it into a white enamel tray, and Sidonie and Father sort and count the insects. And Father has other counting traps: rolls of corrugated paper wrapped around the trunks of the apple trees; sticky paper wrapped around limbs; little boxes with funnel entrances. The white cloth used to be one of Sidonie's nappies. The bugs have to be counted so that Father knows when to spray and what kind of spray to use. Sidonie asks, why not just spray every week with all of the sprays? Father laughs: some people do that, he says. But sprays are expensive. And they are not good to put into the air and the ground, so we try to use as little as possible.

Father also picks up a sheet of paper from the packing house that tells him about spraying for the coddling moth. Sometimes he agrees with the paper and sometimes not. The paper says on it: "Summerland Research Station." Sidonie knows where Summerland is: you have to take the ferry across the lake and then drive along the other side of the lake half the day. Father says: they are too far south to be accurate for us. Wait a day or two.

This is who Father is: he knows more than the scientists at the Summerland Research Station.

The girl, Tasha, is holding her head, wiping her face with a steaming cloth.

Drink this, Tasha says. The bolus of sugared water, the ginger tang of it like the bite of chrysanthemum rolling past her lips, tongue. A glittering ball, cool as glass marbles. The cells on her palate smoothed. She can smell vomit, the sweet decay of it, and something worse. Dirt. She is dirty. A hot rise of shame, but she cannot move.

Further back, yet: She is four or five, not yet in school. Spending the day at Walter's house. Mr. Rilke is running water through the sprayer to clean it. It's hot, and the children sit under the spray, the fine mist delicious on the skin, the sulphur smell seguing from repulsive to enticing. The mist running bright yellow at first, then paler, paler, until clear.

Sidonie has yellow spots on her bathing suit, and her hair feels oily. "Never mind," says Mrs. Rilke. "It'll wash out, a little lye soap and water, tell your mother."

Where is Mother?

Father appears when it is suppertime. He appears suddenly in the Rilke's orchard, where they are playing, the way grown-ups do. Suddenly and with towering fury.

"What is this?" he shouts. "Idiots, you! Arsenic of lead! You poison your own children!" Sidonie is hurried home: *schnell, schnell*. Alice is told to take Sidonie to the wash house and scrub her down thoroughly, but Alice cries. "I don't want it on my hands!" (Where is Mother?) It is Father who pours the heated water, again and again, over Sidonie's lathered head and body, his hand making a lid to keep the suds from her eyes, his anger gone now. Didn't Sidonie know that the spray is poisonous? Why, *bitte*, did she think that she was kept indoors when the sprayer came to the orchard? To keep out of Mr. Tanaka's way? Wrong! And why did Mr. Tanaka wear the big hat and the mask over the eyes and mouth? Because of the heat? Wrong again!

What lies in the soil, in the water: the transgressions of the past.

She needs a bath, hot food, clean clothes. They return to her house, Tasha driving: Sidonie does not trust herself not to pass out.

When they arrive, Cynthia is at the house. She has been sorting through some papers, is wearing glasses, over which she looks sternly as Sidonie comes in the door.

"I've arranged for a disaster company to come and fix you up," she says.

"Okay," Sidonie says.

"They'll get rid of the water, replace the drywall and carpets, deal with the mould, and paint. It'll be covered by your insurance. Your friend Hugh's been calling, trying to find you. I told him you'd get back within a couple of days."

"Okay," Sidonie says, feeling foolish. (Feeling rescued.)

"As for you," Cynthia says, looking at Tasha, "You're very lucky. You have very patient parents."

Tasha looks mulish: she reminds Sidonie, suddenly, of someone. Herself, of course.

"I'm going to drive you home right now," Cynthia says to Tasha. "You can load some of these boxes into my car for me."

The look Cynthia gives Sidonie on her way out is not pleasant.

Something has irrevocably shifted between Cynthia and herself.

LEDGER

It is a long winter of recovery. A pall of smoke hangs in this low part of valley, and at night the hillsides are dotted with fires, an uncanny, unsettling sight. The smoke is not only from the burning of the winter's orchard prunings, but the beetle-damaged pine is being burned as well.

The smell — apple wood and pine — is not unpleasant, but the smoke catches in the throat, and the night fires raise, again, those atavistic fears.

Cynthia takes to dropping by, asking if she can help with the boxes.

"No," Sidonie says. "I must do it myself."

There is a coldness to Cynthia, now, a hardness. She seems older. She withholds news, does not chat about Justin's doings. Obviously Cynthia is still angry with her. And Justin, also. Though she sees that Justin has grown surly toward Cynthia as well, so perhaps it is not personal. (A late bloomer, Justin, finding his adolescent rebellion at nineteen.)

"Have I done something wrong?" Sidonie asks. "I've apologized for the boxes. I'm really giving time to them now. Is it something else?"

But Cynthia will not say.

Has Cynthia discovered something in the boxes that she has taken away, the ones she is sorting through herself?

"Is there something I might discover?" Cynthia asks, coolly.

She has not found Cynthia so intractable before. Has she? Cynthia has always been pliant, even to the point of being too dependent. Or nearly always.

Cynthia has taken, lately, to saying *my mother, my father.* As if she knew them. As if she knew anything at all.

She herself has lost or repressed the first weeks or months after Alice's funeral at the end of 1974, the decisions and arrangements, the flight back, as a patient loses time under anesthesia, and sometimes the days following.

Her first memory of the Cynthia of that time: they are having coffee — hot chocolate, for Cynthia — at the Café Vienne on des Pins, and Cynthia. . . .

No, a little further back. It is Adam who is with Cynthia. He has met her after school, his classes — he was teaching architecture at McGill, then — having ended sooner than Sidonie's day at the Institute; they are all to meet at the café. It's one of those dark rainy November days that she likes best — perhaps Cynthia's birthday? She strides down the street toward the café, not hurried. Her favourite time of year and of day: a softened, muted time, less harsh to her overly-sensitive head. There is red ivy on the buildings; the streetlights reflect, a gentle blur, on the wet sidewalk.

She pushes open the café door and sees them before they see her: Adam leaning toward the child, across a little table. Cynthia looking at him, talking, her lips and hands and eyes alive. Sidonie had stopped still at that moment; something like happiness had come to a gentle simmer in the region of her thorax.

That she remembers. Then, after, the doubt that had kept her awake at night. Should they have had a child of their own? Clearly,

Adam is a model father-figure: patient, respectful, engaged. All of the right things. She had thought. . . . But no; he has taken to Cynthia living with them as if it were just what he had been waiting for. Now he leaves the campus by three, walks the short distance to the school for the deaf to meet Cynthia, and the two of them go home together, sometimes stopping at Café Vienne, sometimes at the park to feed the ducks, to kick through the leaves, to ride the swings. They do the marketing together, Adam and Cynthia, on these afternoons. After a time, Cynthia makes friends among the other day-children; it is Adam who then orchestrates visits, who joins the parents' advisory association, who serves tea and sandwiches to Cynthia and her friends. Adam who indulges the passions for the latest Barbie, who finds and funds the drawing and horseback and swimming lessons.

What this means for Sidonie is something complex, something it takes her a few years to work out. First there is the guilt, as always: at not being the one to parent her sister's child, that she has somehow profited at Alice's expense; then, forced to admit that the arrangement works, that she is happy, coming home to the apartment to an evening of reading journals only temporarily punctured by decorous games of Monopoly or gin rummy. No use telling herself that she has done Alice a good turn, taking Cynthia in, that Cynthia has bloomed in Montreal in a way that would have provided Alice with great satisfaction. She feels Alice's angry ghost breathing down her neck, even when she is happiest. Especially when she is happiest. *Mine, mine,* the ghost says. *You have no right. My daughter.*

And there is some humiliation in this quick adaptation too. Sidonie is capable of recognizing that. There's an argument that Adam has required this emotional contact, this companionship, for years, and she has been able neither to recognize nor to fulfill this need. Or: Adam prefers to interact with the child rather than with his wife; she has more to offer than Sidonie does. But even if those interpretations are possible, there is no reason to accept them, to take the situation personally. No need to respond with fear or jealousy. It simply is the state of things. It is good for the child and for her husband.

Nevertheless, an austerity falls over her, a stiff and threadbare cloak.

She writes a paper on emotional ataxia in children with autism. Then a book. She is invited to conferences as guest speaker. She is offered a distinguished research chair at the largest and most prestigious Canadian university, which she does consider, but turns down.

She retreats into herself, so slowly that she doesn't notice at first. When she does notice, she feels a sadness, but acceptance: the unfolding that happened in her early months with Adam has naturally reversed itself.

It is easy to step away, to let those live connections crust over, calcify.

Cynthia does bloom. When she is fourteen, the principal of her school calls a conference with Adam and Cynthia and recommends that Cynthia be enrolled in regular high school in the September term.

"That's been tried," Sidonie says, flatly. "Cynthia was in regular school before she came here. She was in the special education class with the mentally handicapped children. She didn't learn anything, and she was taunted and shunned by the other children. I don't see how returning her to that environment is a good option."

But no, the principal argues. Cynthia is ready to move through normal classes. She will, of course, have an aide who will sign for her. But there is hope that she'll be able to function on her very own, soon. Her lip-reading is improving rapidly, and the new hearing aids work remarkably well.

The principal is a woman in her fifties with improbably uniform auburn hair and a jacket with immense shoulder pads. Sidonie thinks that she has more theory than experience.

"We'll consider it," she says, discouragingly.

Adam is perplexed, a little angry even. "Isn't this what we want for Cynthia? Integration into mainstream society? The freedom and acceptance that comes with that?"

Sidonie could tell him something about mainstream society

and acceptance. She says, "You don't know what it's like, being different. Having a noticeable handicap. You don't know how cruel adolescents can be."

"This isn't Marshall's Landing," Adam says.

There's a wound there, Sidonie perceives, but she will not acknowledge it. She closes her mouth.

"If I didn't know you better," Adam says, "I'd think you were sulking."

"I don't sulk," Sidonie says.

"I know," Adam says. "But you've withdrawn. Have I offended you?"

She is lucky, lucky to be married to Adam, who will reason things out, and not respond emotionally, she reminds herself.

"I don't know what to do," Sidonie says. "I can only make decisions for Cynthia based on my own experience and knowledge, and you've called those into question. I'm lost."

Adam says, "You don't, you know, have to make decisions that way. You can trust me sometimes."

So they had argued, and she had given in, against her better judgment.

In 1985, Sidonie and Cynthia fly west for the first time since leaving Marshall's Landing. Since Alice's funeral. Cynthia is excited; after they leave the airport, driving north the few kilometres to Marshall's Landing, Cynthia presses her nose against the car window. "But I remember this," she exclaims, over and over. "The orchards and that old boat on the side of the highway. I remember that! And here's the turn — oh, and my old school!"

"Mine too," Sidonie says, and Cynthia is surprised.

They are back in the valley for Stephen's wedding. Stephen is marrying Debbie, a local girl. She is not prepossessing, Sidonie thinks; she's pretty enough, beneath the teased-out bob of hair, the bangs, the black-rimmed eyes that all of the young women seem to affect these days. But she is not — not educated or cultured or graceful. Not exceptional. Then again, Stephen himself is not exactly impressive. He has a bad haircut, bad skin. He slouches, wears cheap clothes. Is loud when he ought to be circumspect, and sullen when he ought to be gracious.

In the days before the wedding, she drives Cynthia around, and they visit their old haunts, and drop in on friends. Cynthia is seventeen, in her last year of high school. The apple trees are in blossom; the hillsides awash in pale green and white. She is enchanted.

Stephen and Debbie are going to move to Edmonton after the wedding. It's hard to get work anywhere, with the recession, but Debbie's uncle has a construction business, and Stephen with his recently earned electrical ticket will be apprenticing with his company.

Debbie's father says that Steve is a good worker. "There's nothing that boy won't turn a hand to," he says. Debbie's mother says, "I hope they won't start a family too soon. Things are so uncertain." She wants Debbie to get some training as a practical nurse or physiotherapist. Sidonie has the feeling that something is required of her, *in loco parentis*, by way of response, but she can't decide what it is. She is not sure how celebratory she ought to be acting. Stephen and Debbie have lived together for over a year, and she understands that the wedding has been promoted by Debbie's parents, as a prerequisite for Debbie moving with Stephen to Edmonton. Well, that's fair enough; they are looking out for their daughter's interests, and don't want her to be abandoned in a strange city, after investing a portion of her youth in the relationship.

"And you are completely responsible for Steve's sister?" Debbie's father asks. "You don't expect Steve to contribute?"

Completely responsible, yes. And then she understands what is expected.

She says privately to Stephen, "I'd like to give you a little cash to get started in Edmonton."

Stephen is embarrassed, to his credit. "You've done so much for us already," he says. "Taking on Cynthia too. I never would have thought she could have come so far. You've already been so generous."

Generous, no. How much less could she have done?

Two days before Steve's wedding, she and Alice's offspring meet at a chain restaurant in a strip plaza along the highway. The downtown area appears evacuated, but a few new franchises have sprung up along Highway 97 north of the city. At this dinner, Debbie is not present — she is working — so it's just the five of them: Stephen, Kevin, Paul, Cynthia, and Sidonie herself, who is paying for it, and feels a little like the unwelcome fairy godmother. The boys, adults now, are all deferential towards her, though, she feels, they are less comfortable in her presence than they would be if she were not there. Stephen is deferential and grateful, Kevin deferential and obsequious, Paul deferential and wary. Cynthia, who hasn't seen her brothers in ten years, is, naturally, fascinated by them. Her head goes back and forth as they talk, as if she's watching a three-way table tennis match. She takes a lot of trouble over her articulation as well: none of the lazy slushy consonants and gargled vowels that she gets away with at home. And the boys — Sidonie watches them closely — show no signs of their former torment of Cynthia. Stephen draws her out almost avuncularly with questions about school and hobbies; Paul falls into a conversation with her about popular music and bands (they both, it seems, have formed tastes for the same groups, independently); even Kevin sets out to entertain Cynthia, with self-deprecating stories of his work. She watches them closely. She doesn't trust any of them, these wild boys. Who are half Buck. Half Buck and half Alice.

They do not discuss or even mention their parents.

But when Kevin and Paul offer to take Cynthia with them for the evening, and Cynthia's eager face is turned to her, she assents.

"No bars," she says. "Your sister is only seventeen."

Where do they go? She hears later from Cynthia: to a stag party for Steve. Yes, at a bar. Cynthia an honourary brother for the occasion. "Were there strippers?" she asks, when Cynthia bubbles out the account of the evening.

"Just one," Cynthia says, laughing. "She taught me some moves — wanna see?"

Cynthia goes shopping at the mall with Debbie and her brides-maids (really lame, Cynthia says; stuff that was old hat in Montreal two years ago), and hiking in the hills with Steve and Paul, out in a boat with Paul and his friends. To a beach party, with a fire, but no swimming; it's April. Cynthia stays overnight at Stephen and Debbie's, and another night (without Sidonie's prior knowledge) at Paul's shared basement suite, where, it seems, a multitude of unem-ployed or semi-employed young men live.

Nobody seems to be really employed, though Paul has a job as a night cashier in a twenty-four-hour convenience store, and Kevin, Sid-onie understands, works as a fry cook in a greasy spoon at the coast.

Cynthia comes back from Paul's reeking of cannabis and glowing. "I didn't smoke," she says. But that's not what Sidonie is worried about.

It is convenient that Cynthia is occupying herself happily; Sid-onie has time to do things she needs to do. She tends her parents' and Alice's graves, in the little cemetery near the airport. She stops by the church. There is a new vicar, who tells her that Mr. Erskine has retired, but doesn't know where he's living. The church looks shabby, its roof shingles curling up, its stucco peeling. Its window frames need paint.

She goes to visit Masao, but finds him gone, the shop sold, now a hardware store.

Up and down the hills of the lake country, the cherries and peaches are in bloom. But in some of the orchards, she can see that the trees are badly overgrown, unpruned. In others, the trees are dying, and have been left to gnarl and choke, instead of being bulldozed to make room for new; in others still, a battlefield of stumps lies rotting in the glittering April sun, nobody having burned them or replanted.

She visits the Red and White, and finds the shelves stocked with dusty, sun-faded cans. Mrs. Gable is not there, only a young woman who must be one of the McCartneys or Platts, given her blank, small-mouthed face and whitish hair.

All of the stores and houses seem abandoned, even if they are inhabited. There is a general look of disrepair.

She drives up over the rainbow hill and sees, first, the Sans Souci driveway with a "For Sale" sign, and then Beauvoir with half its west slope lying fallow, so that it looks like it has forgotten to get dressed.

Walt is apologetic. "The prices," he says. Sidonie says she knows. Walt's son has gone to Fort McMurray to try his luck there. Walt is operating his own orchards and Beauvoir on a skeleton crew: old drunks, he says, and the Quebecois kids who hitchhike out here in the summer.

"Are you paying too much for the lease?" Sidonie asks. That is the deal she set up with Walt, ten years ago: he'd continue to run the Beauvoir orchards, but rather than being paid, would lease them and keep the profits. She had wanted to set up a fixed income for her nephews, and so had asked for a flat rate, instead of twenty-five percent, the usual arrangement. Now Sidonie wonders if Walter has come off worse in the deal.

"Not too much, but if you adjusted the price for inflation, I wouldn't be able to pay," he says.

The land is worth too much. But also, in 1983, too little: prices have dropped.

Sidonie wonders if it would be a good time to withdraw something from their savings and put in into Beauvoir. It is disturbing to see the land lying bare, unplanted. Even in tight times, the orchards were replanted, because it took a decade for a tree to mature enough to become productive. There was always the future. If the price of apples went up, you did not want to be waiting for your trees to mature.

Walt is apologetic about the house, too. "I have to warn you," he says, turning the key in the lock. The house is vacant, Sidonie knows. Walt had to evict the last tenants, forcibly, and hasn't put any in since. "It's a bit of a mess," Walt says, but she still isn't prepared for the interior.

A desecration. Sidonie has to will herself not to faint or vomit. She had known it would be bad; Walter had telephoned her, described some of the damage, long distance. But she had not pictured anything like this.

It is irredeemable, she thinks. Lock it up and abandon it. Set fire to it.

Walt says, "The roof is still good, the one we put on five years ago. And the frame and foundations still solid. It will keep."

She makes one more visit, to Mrs. Inglis, who's in a nursing home in town.

"Graham died too, you know," Mrs. Inglis says.

"Yes,' Sidonie says. "I heard."

Mrs. Inglis is blind. She wears dark glasses, but fancy ones, with large red frames, as if she were at the beach. She has put on lipstick, and is wearing a summer frock in a peach and jade print, and holds out her hand to Sidonie as if she's come over for tea; as if she'll come the next week, and the next.

"Did you ever go to Italy?" she asks Sidonie, and Sidonie confesses that she has not.

"I would have liked to have seen Alice's children growing up," Mrs. Inglis says, but she refuses Sidonie's invitation to Stephen's wedding. "But thank you, my darling," she says, and holds Sidonie's hand.

Into Sidonie's head, a rush of images: Mrs. Inglis's exquisitely flamboyant hats, her fruity laughing voice, her generous waist. She has been like a warm plum cake, a fire in the grate. But now Mr. Inglis is dead, and Graham. Sidonie's parents, Alice, Mr. Ramsay. Dr. Stewart. The Erskines and the Rilkes, Walt's parents. Mr. Tanaka.

All of those people who knew her and remember her gone now. And who is she then? For a person's life, Sidonie thinks suddenly, is a kind of bubble, given shape by other bubbles around it. Too fragile to survive more than an instant after the others have burst their walls and disappeared.

That is what it is like to be Mrs. Inglis.

In March of 1980, at the age of forty-three, Graham Inglis had, while apparently in one of his lucid periods, his medications working for once, unearthed a very old package of gopher bait — strychnine — in one of the orchard sheds. Hugh had told her this, over the telephone: it had been too late to come back for the funeral. It appeared that Graham had come upon the gopher bait accidentally, while looking for some kittens. The kittens had been birthed in the shed, and had fallen or crawled through a hole in the floorboards to the crawlspace. Graham and Mrs. Inglis had heard them mewing, seen the mother cat running back and forth and around the shed, calling. You know how my mother is about cats, Hugh had said. Sidonie had known: the Inglises had kept, at one time, more than thirty cats, most of the orchard or barn cats, Mrs. Inglis being notoriously unable to drown a kitten or turn away a litter left in a box on her porch.

Graham, acting as his mother's eyes and hands, had moved the rust-streaked ladders out of the shed, one by one, had pried up the trap door, and crawled down into the dry, sandy storage space beneath the shed and carried out the kittens — four of them — in the front of his sweater.

He must have found the strychnine in the crawlspace. Mrs. Inglis remembered that they had used to keep the more dangerous pesticides in there, years before. Of course, every sharp implement or poisonous substance had been removed from the house and outbuildings when Graham had become ill. But the crawlspace had somehow been forgotten, overlooked.

Graham had probably secreted it in his pocket; Mrs. Inglis hadn't been able to see much, then, but she'd have been able to see the suspicious box in his hand. Graham had said nothing. Had gone to see a movie with Mrs. Inglis: *Being There*, with Peter Sellers. He had described what was happening on the screen to his mother.

In his room later, Graham had written a short note that said only "I'm sorry. I do know this is best." He had put a rolled blanket against the bottom of the door connecting his room and his mother's — she slept between him and the rest of the house — and put his radio on, as he always did to fall asleep.

Strychnine is the sort of poison nobody would choose first. It is strongly bitter. It blocks the glycine receptors in the brain and spinal cord, causes muscle contractions, convulsions, slow asphyxia. As the poison shuts down the body's organs, it bucks and heaves for air. The final unconsciousness is the cessation of long strangulation.

Graham fell off the bed; his mother, who slept only lightly as when her children had been infants, heard, came into the room, switched on the light. It was too late to do anything for him, though an ambulance was called, and came out from town, a twenty-minute trip. Mrs. Inglis sat down in her nightgown on the floor, holding Graham's head in her lap. He said, "I'm sorry, Mum." At the hospital, they gave him morphine and pumped his stomach, but it was too late.

She sits with Mrs. Inglis for an hour in silence; she thinks that perhaps the old woman has fallen asleep. But then Mrs. Inglis takes off the big red-framed sunglasses and closes her eyelids over her milky eyes. Her upper and lower lids are bruised or stained plum-brown, as if fallen leaves have lain on them over a winter.

"My turn now," she says.

Cynthia has asked to arrive at the church early with her brothers. Paul and Kevin are standing up with Steve, and Debbie has invited Cynthia to be a bridesmaid, as is customary, but she has declined. I'm afraid," Cynthia had said, "to be in front of a group of people."

Sidonie makes sure that they do arrive early, driving through the wet April streets, and just as they pull into the church parking lot, they see the boys getting out of Stephen's car. Cynthia runs across to meet them without a backward look, careless of her new high heels and silky dress. Sidonie takes her time collecting her handbag, locking the car doors. She feels strange; out of her element. She knows nobody here, really. She has never seen this building before, though it's in a familiar landscape; will likely never see it again. It is nominally the church of Debbie's parents, though clearly they've never attended before, don't know the pastor. She watches the four of them, Alice's children, amalgamate into a kind of loose line. The three boys — men, really: Paul, the youngest, is twenty-two — almost all of a size, and Cynthia, who is smaller than they, tiny, but nearly an adult too. There they are. They are walking towards this

·unfamiliar church, which has nothing to do with them or Alice. They are nearly shoulder to shoulder; they keep pace, roughly, but do not touch. Strangers come out of the church to greet them, to draw them in, to prepare for the little ceremony. And Sidonie hangs back and watches them go in.

The parking lot, beginning to fill with cars, the asphalt shining wet from the rain, little lakes at the corners, where the earth has subsided. She would choose not to go inside, except to do so would cause a commotion, would divert attention from the bride and groom and their highly-planned day. There is no connection for her here. There is nobody she knows except these four young adults, and she does not know three of them well. There is no connection with Alice or Buck or with her parents, only space where they ought to be. She is the only connection, and she can't introduce this scene into her memories of her family; can't summon her memories into this scene.

Sitting in her pew during the ceremony, she thinks: I will put an end to it. I will wait until Sans Souci has been sold, and then I will sell Beauvoir. I will take Cynthia back to Montreal tomorrow, and I will write to Walter, and after Sans Souci has sold, I will instruct him to contact a real estate agent about selling Beauvoir. It is mine, but I don't want it anymore. It is broken; it is emptied of what made it anything at all. I will relieve myself of it. I will cut these ties, because they are no ties at all. They only draw attention to what is lost.

The visit does its mischief with Cynthia; she will not settle back into her life in Montreal. She has been a sensible, cooperative teenager, but now she rebels. She will not go to university there, though she has free tuition, a place to live, decent grades. She doesn't want to apply to universities in Ottawa or Toronto or Quebec City. Nowhere. She doesn't want to go to Europe for a year. This is Clara's suggestion, and not Sidonie's first or even third choice, but she would be happier with it than with what Cynthia has in mind.

Cynthia wants to go back to the valley and live with her brother Paul. No, not even go to the college there. She will work in a restaurant or something. Paul thinks he can get her a job. Cynthia's relationship with Adam, always sweet, respectful, symbiotic, comes apart. "You're wasting your good brains," Adam shouts at Cynthia, and Cynthia screeches back, so distraught that she's unintelligible. She begins to retreat to her bedroom, to stay out late. She dyes her mouse-brown hair jet-black, speaks rudely, lets her unwashed clothes pile up on her floor. Mrs. Schwarz, the cleaning lady, announces that she can't do Cynthia's room with all of the mess. "Fine, then," Cynthia says. "She can leave it."

One night she comes home from a party visibly drunk. Her grades start to slip, in this, her final term. "Who cares?" she says. "I'm not applying to go to university anyway." A report is sent home enumerating her absences from classes.

What can be done? There is nothing to be done.

Sidonie sleeps poorly; she is frightened. "Do you think Cynthia's depressed?" she asks Clara. "Or on drugs?"

"No," Clara says. "I think she's trying to wear you down. To break the bond. She *will* break it. You will have to decide how to negotiate the break."

"Should we just give in?"

"That's not for me to say. But you're not in a strong position. She is almost eighteen."

"We can refuse to give her money," Adam says.

"Of course. And that will give her permission to hitchhike and live in squats with strangers."

Sidonie says, "I don't understand this. Children were not so rebellious when I was young."

"Are you so sure?" Clara asks. "Look at you, coming to Montreal as a teenager. Do you mean to tell me that wasn't rebellion? I seem to remember you saying that you had run away from home."

Had she said that? Yes: when she was eighteen, Sidonie had taken delight in introducing herself as "the only person you'll know who ran away from home to go to school."

"It's different," she says. "I was running toward something worth-while. I had a plan. And I wasn't rebellious; I just waited for a weak moment and exploited it."

A weak moment, when her parents had been exhausted, knocked out, by Alice's choices.

It was Alice, of course, who had wanted to go to Montreal. Both Mother and Father had been vehemently opposed.

"No good can come of that," Father had said. "It's all jazz clubs and immigrants on the make. They have no morals. Not a place for a young girl."

And Mother had said, "It's too expensive. A waste of time. Who's to say that you'll be successful? You'll spend all of that money and then have nothing to show for it. Better get some practical training that you can have to fall back on."

"You don't want me to do anything that you haven't done," Alice had said. "You can't see beyond your own narrow life. You want me to stay here and get married and turn out just like you."

Alice had wanted to go to design school. It's all she wanted to do, she said. But it was too risky. Sidonie couldn't imagine it, even though Alice was so good at sewing her own designs, and at drawing. They had never known anyone who was a dress designer, or even a professional artist of any kind. It didn't seem possible.

"*Schmatte* trade," Father had said, dismissively.

When did Alice give up? Sidonie thinks now: even by being married to Buck, Alice was punishing Mother and Father, all of those years.

Sidonie says, finally, to Adam: "We can't win this. Let's give her some money; let her go."

Even then, she hopes that giving in will cause Cynthia to change her mind; that the rebellion will have burnt itself out, or prove to have been rebellion for its own sake. But no; Cynthia coldly accepts Sidonie's offer to subsidize her for three months and pay her return airfare, and continues to make her plans. Her grades do pick up; that's one good result. And the good scholarship she receives can be postponed a year. But Sidonie is stiff with worry. How will Cynthia make a life for herself?

Right up to the night before she leaves, Cynthia is sulky; she has wanted to go to a party with friends, has wanted to convert the airfare into cash and hitchhike, but Sidonie has insisted that she spend the evening with family. Adam is there; also Clara and her daughters, who are near Cynthia's age, and Anita.

We are not her family, though, Sidonie thinks. They are different, she sees that now. Portia and Ismene, Clara's daughters, though they share some of that teen hubris, that self-absorption, are not like Cynthia. They have — what? — a sense of possession about them already. A sense of entitlement. It's as if they have already been granted or taken a lien on their adult lives. They simply need to wait, to continue what they're doing — immersing themselves in activities, social life, music, paying not quite enough attention to their school work — and everything will unfold naturally before them, their birthright. They will go to university (Portia is already in her first year) and then into jobs and marriage and continue to do pretty well the same things. They have no anxiety, because their lives are pleasant and will not change. They will not change.

But for Cynthia, as for her older brothers, and for Sidonie and Alice as well, there has been too much gulf between their lives as children and what they want their lives to be as adults. Too much wanting, too much fear — of getting there, of not getting there. Of not choosing the right thing. Of whatever they choose costing too much.

At their dinner two nights before Stephen's wedding, Kevin had said, "I'd like to have my own restaurant. But I'd never have the start-up money. They say you need two years in the bank." Paul had said, "I'd like to go back to school, maybe do engineering. I was good at math. But what's the use of coming out with thirty thousand in student loans and no job?" And Stephen, after a few beers, had confessed, "I really wanted to travel. But I need to get married. If I don't marry Debbie, she'll find someone else."

I could bankroll one of them, Sidonie had thought. But which one would be the best bet? And it was not just the money, she knew. She probably could afford to invest — well, maybe — in a restaurant for Kevin, or to put Paul through at least four years of university. She could sacrifice some of her retirement savings. But she was quite certain it wouldn't do any good. They would waste it, or turn it down, afraid of wasting it. There would be some excuse. She could hear it, in the vagueness of their plans, in their focus on the outcome, rather than the process, in their assumed, second-hand cynicism. (It's who you know, anyway; they just beat the original ideas out of you; the government will just tax you till your business goes under.) It is wearying, how well she knows the barriers they will erect for themselves. And how well she knows the men they'll be middle-aged: worn out, ungenerous, heavy-drinking or religious or both. Angry.

What she wonders, the night before Cynthia is to turn her back on an assured and stable future, is whether it's an issue of class or wealth or geography that separates her niece, Alice's daughter, from Adam's nieces.

It's not brains, or natural ability. She and Alice could both run rings around not only the other children they grew up with, but also just about anyone she's met. And Alice's children are clearly all bright, too.

What is it?

She and Adam have a disjointed, at-cross-purposes argument. Adam chides her: they're all *our* nieces.

"I think it must be ethno-geographic," she says. "People from the West, especially the rural West; they don't have the same certainty. They don't have as much invested in certain social mores."

"She's just finding herself," Adam says. She is confused by his having changed sides; now he seems to be in favour of Cynthia taking time off. But she is always confused by this trait, this ability, in Adam, and others. She herself does not let go, once she has decided something. Does not forget. She is implacable once she turns her back.

She does not sell Beauvoir in 1985: the prices have fallen, and she can't get enough for it to make it worthwhile. After a year she takes it off the market. Walter Rilke manages the orchards for a while, then finds her other tenants.

More than two decades ago. And Cynthia has turned out just fine, as Adam and Clara had known she would: she has meaningful, interesting, well-compensated work; she has friends (though she doesn't appear to have a romantic life); she has Justin, who is also turning out to be an admirable human being. Sidonie thinks: she has succeeded without me. She has succeeded precisely because I've given her space, have not interfered.

It is a small, lonely pride, that: to congratulate oneself on having had the sense to leave another person alone, to free another person from one's own possibly damaging contact. But there it is. She had provided Cynthia with a family life of sorts; with an excellent education, a way of living in the world with a handicap; and with room to find her own way.

Surely that has been enough compensation for anything she might have taken. Or lost.

Cynthia has set her to sorting some boxes of papers: "I wouldn't know what was useful to keep," she says, as if this were Sidonie's fault.

A box of orchard records. Her father's ledger books tell their own story: a tale of diminishing returns. Profits in the 1940s, mostly rising until the late 1950s. Such small amounts of cash: a dollar a day, plus the picker's cabin to Mr. Tanaka in the mid-1950s. How had he and Masao stayed alive? Bad crops for a few years after the devastating winter of 1949. The prices of gas, pesticides, equipment, and especially labour, rise; the prices of apples, cherries, peaches, rise and fall. Sidonie looks for mistakes, extravagances, waste, but can't find any. The balance simply changes.

At Christmas she has half-finished sorting the ledgers. She reports her progress to Cynthia, feeling like a tardy grad student. Cynthia seems somewhat mollified.

"I guess it's all a long time ago," she says. "I guess it doesn't seem worth it, going through all of that old stuff."

Yes and no. Part of the past — before her leaving the valley in 1959 — deepens in her every year, part of her cellular makeup, it seems. The intervening years, except for some sharp, clear shards of memory, are grainy.

Between her honeymoon visit in 1963 and Stephen's wedding in 1985, Sidonie had returned to the valley three times: for her father's funeral, her mother's, and Alice's.

Father dies in late fall of 1970, suddenly and not suddenly. Suddenly, because there is no final illness: he sits up in bed, Mother says, clutches his chest, and keels over. A massive heart attack, Mother says. All the arteries blocked. She says this with some amazement, but also pride, with apparently no sense that her limited medical insight might be painful to others. It occurs to Sidonie that her mother has a habit of making bald, possibly inappropriate statements that is not unlike her own.

Not suddenly, because Father is seventy-four, fond of his cigar and whiskey, not to mention Mother's pies and her dairy-based cooking, and of working too hard and then not working, by turns, the way orchardmen do. Of working very hard physically in the extreme heat and cold for a few days at a time. It's not a surprise for those reasons, Sidonie tells Adam. And it's the death he would have chosen: quick, clean. No suffering.

Adam regards Sidonie sorrowfully, buys the plane tickets, treats her as if she were fragile. He offers to call her secretary and ask her to cancel all of Sidonie's appointments.

"What for?" Sidonie asks. "I don't want to fall behind with my research. I can go in tomorrow and Wednesday; I'll just rebook for the days I'll actually be away."

She believes that Adam is projecting his grief from his own father's death onto her. That she has a free pass card, exempting her from feeling the loss of her father too deeply.

But later, seeing Father's polished shoes lined up in the back entrance, grief ambushes her like a mountain lion; something ravenous, howling, implacable rips open her chest and crushes her heart and lungs. Father will never again look kindly at her over his spectacles, sing snatches of *Lieder* as she helps him lift pipes, put his hands on her shoulders in that way that situates her safely in her skin, when she feels about to come undone, when her self threatens to fly apart.

And all earlier grief rises in her memory to augment this one, and she can only crouch on her bed and rock and moan, until Mother stands over her with a dour look and instructs her to pull herself together, to not be a baby. "Some good all of your schooling has done," Mother says. "And you a psychologist! You of all people should know how to control yourself."

Psychology is not about controlling yourself, of course. But what has leapt upon her is something physical, something lurking in the world of her mind. It is wordless, without language or logic. It is not to be managed.

But Mother has no time for carrying on; she has a funeral to plan. Sidonie must drive her around, so that she can take care of all the many things that need to be done. Mother has never learned to drive: unusual for a country woman. Mother needs to be driven into town, to the florists, the funeral home, the delicatessen, the lawyer's office, the bank. All of this, Sidonie remonstrates, could be done over the telephone, but Mother says no, no, I get confused and forget things on the phone. People speak too quickly. And trailing her on her tour of stops, Sidonie realizes that Mother is making a sort of progress, a formal circle of visits, whose purpose is three-fold: one, it buttresses Mother up, receiving the many courtesies and condolences. Two, it allows her to re-establish these social and professional relationships on a new footing: Mother as independent agent, not as part of a couple. Three, it gives Mother something to do, so she need not think too much.

No darkened rooms, chamomile tea, hushed voices for Mother, as there had been for her mother-in-law, Estelle, when Adam's father had died.

Mother's dry-eyed energy is exhausting, though, and it is a relief when Alice and Buck arrive with the children.

Alice has changed again: she has thickened around the middle; her hair is darker, long and untidy. Her clothes — jeans and a plaid flannel shirt — are not very clean. Her face is tan; she wears no makeup. You would not look at her twice, Sidonie thinks. It is a shock.

But then, almost instantly, she can see that this new look suits

Alice. It is more appropriate to the zeitgeist; Alice looks like what she is, a working-class mother of four. It is a natural look. And she is still beautiful; Sidonie sees that, at dinner. The curve of Alice's chin and jaw, the straight small blade of her nose, her large grey-blue eyes: they are perfect, immutable. And though she is not as slender as she was as a girl, Alice still holds herself with that unusual grace. The angle of her neck, her arm, the turn of her waist, at any time, is always perfect, lovely. It's impossible to be in the same room and not be struck by her loveliness.

Mother seems intent on praising, singling out Sidonie at Alice's expense. Isn't her outfit lovely? What a chic haircut. And Alice ought to wear darker lipstick to give her lips some punch. And look how slim Sidonie is. It's so important for a married woman not to let herself go. When there are all these terrible girls now with no morals just waiting to grab someone's man.

Has Mother always done this? It seems understandable that Alice would be jealous, angry. "I'm so dowdy," Sidonie says. "This suit is more than four years old. It's totally out of style. And I've put on at least fifteen pounds since my wedding." She can't remember being praised to Alice, like this. Only when she and Adam came out on the train, perhaps. And remember what happened then. It is uncomfortable that Alice should be slighted like this.

But Alice doesn't rise to the bait, only smiles to herself. And then, surprisingly, she catches Sidonie's eye and grins broadly at one of Mother's pointed remarks. The gaps between her teeth are still there, Sidonie sees, but somehow they add to Alice's charm. Her hippie charm. Alice grins and raises an eyebrow, and this is so unexpected, so unprecedented, that Sidonie is unable to respond. She realizes only slowly; she is being invited to take Alice's side against Mother. Has that ever happened before?

The boundaries have shifted. Sidonie is not the outsider, but the one courted. She doesn't trust that. She knows where that leads. She must be cautious.

Buck has lost all of his earlier wildness, his sullenness and disaffection. He seems ultra-concerned with rules, propriety. He's obsessed with being punctual to church, with the boys being obedient, not just to himself but to all adults ("You listen to grandmaw, now, y'hear?") and rants about litter left on the roadside. It's as if there are only two possibilities: rebel or authority figure. Nothing in-between. Of the two, Sidonie would have chosen the position of rebel; he was less dangerous then than he is now: a small, angry man who wants to control and punish everyone.

This is before his accident with the acetylene torch; at this point, Buck is still working intermittently at things. He works at the packing house, at the sawmill, on highway construction. Is still strong and fit enough to consider himself, to be considered, a young man. He is still looking for his break. And it does seem more hopeful, at this point, because he has become more conventional, more invested in society.

But as he has grown in that direction, Alice has grown in another. They are the two little wooden figures in the Black Forest clock in the parlour: the husband comes out when it is sunny, with his newspaper and pipe; the wife when it is raining, with her kerchief and umbrella. Never the two together.

The funeral is held in a funeral home in town — a new idea, and Sidonie is surprised at Mother's choosing it. Mother says, "Your father didn't have much time for religion; it would seem all wrong to have him lying there in a church." But Alice says, "Father was Roman Catholic, of course. Can you see Mother having the funeral at the Catholic church, the way she sneers at it?"

The funeral home is not like Father, either — it's kind of like a mid-level American motel, a Howard Johnson's. But the good thing is that Masao has been conscripted to provide the music, and he brings a tape deck and fills the room with Schubert *Lieder*, Mozart's *Requiem*, parts of Handel's *Messiah*. The sort of music Father would surely have chosen for saying goodbyes to his friends. The music makes Sidonie cry, against her intent. But Alice, sitting beside her, squeezes her hand and gives her a Kleenex. At my funeral, Sidonie thinks, we'll have some dry, mathematical Bach. Nobody will cry.

And after the funeral, a lot of people — Sidonie's and Alice's friends, as well as Mother's and Father's — come back to the community hall for a reception, where there are contributions of food from many, many friends and neighbours.

"Now," says Mother brusquely, after they have gone home, "I want to talk to you about what I plan to do with the place."

Is it Sidonie's imagination, or do both Alice and Buck sit up a little straighter, but keep their faces neutral, as if trying to pretend they haven't been anticipating something?

Mother says, "Your father wanted the place to be divided equally between you two girls when I'm gone. So you can think of it as yours in the future. You may divide the land or one of you may buy the other out. It won't matter to me what you do, then, though of course I think it'll be a tragedy if you decide to sell up altogether, after all the work we put into this place.

"But I'm not dead yet, and I don't want to go live in an old folk's home, so I'm going to stay here. But the house is too big for one person and I can't manage the orchards, so this is what I'm proposing. Buck and Alice, you will come and live here, and Buck will run the orchards and you'll have the house. I'll have my own little house; we'll convert the old barn into a cottage for me."

There's a silence. Sidonie is not surprised by Mother's plan. Logically, it's the best solution. She sees that Buck looks moderately pleased, but also calculating. What more can he expect, she thinks. But Alice's expression is thunderous.

"No," Alice says, flatly.

Mother looks completely taken by surprise.

"No? What do you mean?"

"No," Alice says. "Not a good enough deal for us. For Buck and me."

Buck looks confused, so Sidonie surmises that whatever he and Alice had speculated or planned, Alice's reaction had not been part of it.

"Why would we want to move out here and work like slaves in the orchard," Alice asks, "and not even own it? Not even have it ours?"

"Well," Mother says. "Of course you would own it one day..."

"Half of it," Alice says. "We'd own half. And who knows when. Who knows how many years of back-breaking work?"

Buck interjects, "It would be all set up, right, so as to be fair? If we were running the orchard, we'd be paid, right? I mean, the value of the house, if we were paying rent, would be deducted, but we'd be paid fair and square for doing the foreman's work? A share of the profits. And then after — I mean, when we inherit, Sidonie would have to let us buy her share, right?"

"Since when do you want to run an orchard?" Alice asks.

"Since always," Buck says, aggrieved. "I grew up on an orchard, you know."

"It's harder work than you think," Alice says, "running a proper orchard. Eighty acres is a lot different than five."

Eighty? But then Sidonie remembers: Alice had been given ten when she got married. And another ten have been sold to the Rilkes.

"I know the basics, anyway," Buck says. "And if your father could do it, why can't I?"

"But it doesn't pay anymore," Alice says. "Don't you see? There wouldn't be any profit, and then we'd have to take out a mortgage just to pay Sidonie out. We'd be in debt forever."

Buck says, "But wouldn't it be great for the boys. Keep them out of trouble. Healthy outdoor work."

"Do you know what it's like to get kids to work in an orchard?" Alice asks. "They're too small to do any real work; they get hurt, or they're always goofing off when you need them. And do you always want to be working in the summer, in the heat, and worrying about late frosts, and rain and ice? Have you gone out in April and worked all night setting up smudge pots because of a late frost?"

"I could learn," Buck says. "It's better than what I'm doing now."

"And all for what?" Alice continues, as if he hasn't spoken. "So that she" — she nods at Sidonie — "can get half the pie?"

"Alice, we've explained the financial arrangements," Mother says. "I think you'll see it's fair, if you think about it...."

"You can have it all," Sidonie says. "I don't want it. I'll never live here again. You can have my half." She has a feeling that she shouldn't say this without consulting Adam, but on the other hand, Adam is far away and not very concerned about money.

There's a pause. Then Mother says, "Well, no, Sidonie, that wouldn't be fair," but without, Sidonie thinks, quite enough conviction. And Buck says, "I don't think Sidonie can make that decision. Can she?" But Alice doesn't say anything.

"I mean it," Sidonie says. "I'll telephone Adam. You can talk to him if you like. I'll be fine with it."

"I don't think it would be legal, anyway," Alice says finally.

What did Alice want?

Alice had been wild and foolish; Sidonie wise and careful, if one were to look at the outcome.

Revision, revision. It is always possible, she supposes.

Alice's life, her luck, at that point in her life, had all been aligned, maligned, by her husband Buck, who had a string of misfortunes lasting from the late 1950s to the mid-70s. The details come from her mother. Buck bought used cars that fell apart within weeks; loaned money to a supposed business partner, who vanished. One year, he decided to breed dogs, and acquired a bitch of indeterminate breed, had ended up having to shoot the pups for some reason or other — after, of course, the children had become attached to them.

After Father's death, Alice and Buck had moved back to Marshall's Landing, living in a trailer on the flats near the high school, and Buck had decided to start a business stripping junked cars and selling the parts. But he'd accidentally torched an old Chevy's fuel tank, which still contained some gasoline; the tank had vomited a fireball that had engulfed Buck's leg and left him with puckered scars from his anklebone to the top of his thigh.

All of this Mother tells Sidonie in the late spring of 1973. Mother is dying. Sidonie knows this, and Alice also, but not Mother. Or they are all maintaining a polite fiction, at least. Sidonie has been summoned, and stays with Mother in her house for a month, taking leave from her job. And Mother confides in her for the first time, telling her all of the things she has never known about their neighbours and about Buck.

He is the ruin of Alice.

Shiftless, selfish, stupid, destructive Buck Kleinholz.

After Alice's funeral, Stephen had said to Sidonie, "Grandma used to slip my mom cash, every time we saw her — five dollars or so. Sometimes as much as twenty. My mom hated it, I think. But we weren't supposed to tell my dad, or he'd take it."

She had found another ledger, this one a record of loans and repayments. And there is Masao's starting-up loan for the music store, from 1957 — more generous than she'd have thought, but paid back quarterly until 1966. No interest charged, apparently, though she knew Masao would have made frequent gifts of recordings to her father. Other entries for loans, some to BK and AK — that would be Buck and Alice, surely. Mostly not repaid. A small sheaf of IOUs, paper-clipped together, signed by Buck, mostly, but also Alice.

Never loan anything it would kill you to lose, Father had always said.

Father's will had given joint interest in Beauvoir to Alice and to Sidonie, but not to Alice's heirs.

She calculates the total of the IOUs, the money loaned with probably no expectation of return, to Buck and Alice, over the years. The ten acres Father had given them for a wedding present, later, somehow, acquired by Buck's father, Mr. Kleinholz, and sold. Another lot of ten acres sold off in the 1960s. It had been an astounding amount of money, by her parents' standards. Not so much, perhaps, by hers, or by the standards of Adam's family. Where had the money gone? To modernize the house, she sees; the building expenses are all laid out. Some for her wedding, for her parents' travel to the wedding. The cash they had given her and Adam, which they'd spent on one painting.

She had sold off forty more acres after Alice had died to Walter Rilke and another neighbour, put the money in a fund for the boys. It would see them through a few years. They had been too young to live on their own — Stephen had been fifteen — but she'd found, through Dr. Stewart, an older couple in town who would take them in.

The remaining forty acres and the house she had kept; it was only fair. They'd had more than their share, Alice and her children.

When the call comes in the late fall of 1974, it is from Walter, though the information about how to contact Sidonie in the middle of the day is transmitted from Hugh, a hemisphere away, via Mrs. Inglis. Five phone calls, Sidonie calculates, must be made in order to reach her. But she is not safe.

The phone call comes at 3:37 in the afternoon, Sidonie notes, holding the pink memo slip the secretary has brought down to her office. When she sees the phone number, she knows immediately that something has happened to both Buck and Alice. Why else would Walter call her in the middle of the day, at work? A cognitive leap, and the last one her brain will be capable of for some time.

Walt says: something terrible has happened. Brace yourself. (This, she knows, is the correct way to deliver bad news. But she also knows that Walter is sincere.)

"It's Alice," Walter says. His voice is cracked: a wind-snapped tree.

"Buck has been arrested," Walter says.

"The younger boys and the girl are still in school," Walter says. "I'm going to go pick them up before the news travels there. I'm still trying to track Stephen down.

"We don't know what happened," Walter says. "Buck saw the kids off to school and then called the doctor, and she called the police. I went over when I heard the sirens, but nobody would tell me anything. Dr. Stewart tried to tell me something, but the cops shut her up."

Sidonie is present at the inquest, which is not held in Marshall's Landing, of course, but in town. Dr. Stewart testifies that Buck had called at 9:05, saying, in a "quair" voice, that something was wrong with Alice; that Alice was dead when she arrived at 9:30 in the morning; that Alice had been dead at least four hours, but not more than ten; that she could clearly see an indent about two inches in diameter in Alice's skull, at the right temple. Dr. Stewart looks as if she is about to faint as she says this.

Sidonie does not feel faint. She feels nothing, only the parts of her brain processing very slowly, and a buzzing, like the beginning or end of a headache.

They have said that they will not call the children to give statements, but Stephen has volunteered anyway. His parents had been arguing a great deal in the past few weeks. No, he didn't know what the arguments were about. Physical violence? Yes.

Alice died of a cerebral hemorrhage, the coroner says. Would she have lived, if she'd gotten medical attention sooner? Possibly, but likely with enormous damage, paralysis, loss of faculties.

Sidonie can see the forces in the room as if the facts were all chess pieces or musical instruments, the coroner and Dr. Stewart, the players. What each is trying to do. The coroner, she sees, must make a report that will go to the Crown prosecutor. He is interested mainly in how to classify the assault, as that will determine the charge. Dr. Stewart sees this, and wants to cover all the possibilities. She wants the most serious charges possible, but she isn't sure what will count most: whether possibly having left Alice to die in their bed will count in Buck's favour, on grounds of mental incapacity, or against him, on grounds of premeditation. Whether the death will seem more accidental if it is due not to the initial injury but the time lapse. But at the same time she wants to underscore the seriousness of the damage. And Stephen, she understands, doesn't want to indict his father, so he admits to frequent arguments, to suggest a blow in a rage. But he doesn't, either, want to suggest that his mother was a brawler, a woman who gave blow for blow.

So clearly she can see their machine-like brains moving.

All else is fog.

Clara telephones from Montreal. "This is what you do," Clara says. "Call this colleague of mine who has moved out your way. I've already contacted him, so he's expecting you. Get him to evaluate your brother-in-law. We'll get him put away quietly, without a trial."

Sidonie's brain can understand, coldly and clearly, exactly what Clara is proposing. She decides, without a qualm, to carry it through.

Buck's sister and parents at the inquest, looking dazed and stupid. Buck looking shifty, his eyes narrowed, his mouth open — but that was how he frequently looked.

Stephen, saying, awkwardly, "I appreciate what you did, getting Dad out of the trial. I mean, into the hospital, instead of jail. Because he must be sick. He must be."

Kevin saying, "We should have shot the bastard. Taken him out behind the shed and shot him like a dog with rabies."

Stephen and Kevin, at this time, fifteen and thirteen. She had thought them grown up.

Paul saying nothing coherent. Should she have taken Paul and Kevin, or at least Paul, back to Montreal with her? Paul had been eleven. He had needed help. She had not made certain that he had gotten it. Steve had said, leave us together; we'll be alright. But she had not asked Paul or Kevin what they wanted.

She had been afraid of them, long-haired, sullen, rough-mannered adolescents. She had not been able to imagine them fitting into her life in Montreal. And she had fallen sway to that old valley suspicion and reluctance, that rural ambivalence. *Don't bother. Don't get involved. It'll do. It won't be great, but it'll be alright.*

Cynthia, though, had been just six, and small, and quiet, and she had taken Cynthia away.

Clara's former colleague had told her, when she had telephoned him: "He'll never get out. Where he'll be is more secure than a jail cell, and not half as comfortable. And there's no parole." He had not said what Clara had: that if Buck were not insane going into the institution, he'd likely become so.

In the hours after the funeral and inquest — packing up personal things, papers, her mother's good dishes, putting everything into storage — Sidonie finds the application forms, filled out in Buck's choked printing, for the removal of Beauvoir from agricultural reserve zoning. The signature lines are empty. The presence of the form is baffling. The only reason anyone took land out of the reserve was to be able to subdivide. There would have been no chance of Alice agreeing to this, surely. Sidonie stubbornly believed that Alice had wanted to orchard again, despite her angry arguments against Buck's pipe dreams: her roots were buried too deep. And the property is still half Sidonie's, as she and Alice had not yet got around to having a new deed drawn up. So even if Alice had signed, the application would have been useless.

But had Buck known that the property was still half in Sidonie's name? How much had he known about Alice's plans?

"Was your father unhappy about your mom asking for a divorce?" she asked the boys. Stephen had been silent: a telling silence. Kevin had laughed, hard and without humour.

Buck said in his statement to the police that he and Alice had been arguing, that they'd both been drinking, that he'd given her a slap upside the head, that he might have had something, a tool or something in his hand, he'd just come in from working in the sheds, he couldn't remember.

Perhaps she should not have left the boys. They had been fine, except for Paul — they had done better than you might expect, but she should not have left them. A sin of omission. Buck, she does not regret; he had a trail of rottenness through him, a trail of willful destruction. Buck was like a dog the Rilkes had adopted, who had been, as a pup, struck over the head and thrown in a dry well. The dog was never right: it had fits; it bit children; it chewed up the nice cushion Mrs. Rilke had given it to sleep on; it flew at cars, and had been struck and injured at least three times. Mr. Rilke had cried, she remembers Father saying, when he put it down. But he had done the only sensible thing, and shot it, finally.

A human being is not a dog: she knows that. But who had been left to mourn Buck, who had his incarceration or his death injured?

Well, his mother, for one. By the time of Sidonie's mother's death, when Alice and Buck had moved into Beauvoir, Buck's father, *that old piece of shit*, as Alice had called him, had been put out of commission by a couple of strokes: he had sat, blank-gazed in a wheelchair. Buck's mother had looked ten years younger, had been helpful and deferential to Alice. Had, Alice said, often babysat Cynthia, had doted on Cynthia. After Alice's murder, Buck's brother Gerry, his sister Lottie, had paid a call to Sidonie, to thank her for saving Buck from jail, to assure her that the children would be well cared for by the family. She had not given anything away. She had come to their house the next day, while Gerry and Lottie were not at home, with Dr. Stewart, with the lawyer, and had asked Mrs. Kleinholz to pack Cynthia's bag.

Mrs. Kleinholz had wept, but had not fought; she remembers that.

Buck had not died in the psychiatric hospital down near the river at Coquitlam; times had changed. In the late eighties he had been released, she had read in the reports; he had become a changed man, had found religion, had become a sort of lay pastor, even. Buck had not died then; he had died, a few years later, of pneumonia.

She is not sorry about taking Cynthia. A nasty place, that house, with its dreariness, its absence of toys or books or decoration, with that dirty old man still living there. She is perhaps sorry for Mrs. Kleinholz. She had been at Stephen's wedding twelve years later: looking cared for, quiet, in a dark dress. And Lottie, suddenly glamorous, her pale hair cut and styled fashionably, her dressmaker's suit. Lottie had become an airline hostess, Mrs. Kleinholz had said. She wonders if Mrs. Kleinholz is still living, if Cynthia is in touch with her, or with Lottie. Gerry had ended up doing time in jail, and John, if she remembers, had gone into the armed forces.

She does not think that any of the children are in touch with their Kleinholz uncles.

A bad, violent streak in that family. Though maybe Mr. Kleinholz's drinking and temper had been at the root of it. And the Kleinholzes had been displaced persons, she remembers: Germans who had been evacuated from Poland after the war, after the creation of the Soviet bloc. Who knows what they had suffered before turning up in Marshall's Landing?

She remembers Masao speaking to her, before the funeral. "It's a terrible thing, Sidonie. But don't hate. Let it go."

She had turned away; has not spoken to him since.

She thinks, now, that she would trade a good deal to see Masao again.

A long winter. She keeps to herself; she walks around the little half-frozen lake. She contracts bronchitis, though she has not been out in public enough, she thinks, to pick up any germs. She reads.

She has dislodged something that ought not to have been dug up. Something rank, stained, is surfacing. There is more of it. She does not want to look.

The new doctor she sees about her bronchitis insists on a complete physical, but proclaims her healthy. Her lungs are clear and capacious, her blood pressure low, her pulse strong, her colon polyp-free, her ovaries and uterus appropriately somnolent. Even her teeth are her own, though the molars are a keyboard of amalgam, the incisors becoming startlingly horse-like, she notices, as she brushes.

She is lucky; her friends are not as healthy as she. Anita, for example, has had hip replacements, and has lost some height. Anita is gnome-like, with her large round eyes, her bent posture, her long grey thistledown hair. Clara, too, walks with a stick; although she swings it vigorously and makes jokes, she needs it for even small hills. And Clara carries a little extra weight — perhaps thirty pounds, Sidonie judges, which makes her puff a little on inclines, and contributes to some prodigious snoring. When Clara and Anita and Sidonie had gone to Florida together, a couple of winters ago, Anita and Sidonie hadn't been able to sleep, and they'd had to get a second room, for Clara.

Hugh, too, has *health issues*, as Cynthia would call them. He takes an array of pills for his heart and circulatory system. His knees make cartilaginous popping sounds when he walks. He forgets small current things, though not the details of the past. He has an enlarged prostate, he says — whatever that means. She won't let him tell her anything more.

The doctor concludes that she was in remarkably good shape. "Your family are all as long-lived and healthy as you are?"

She starts to say yes, but catches herself. "My parents both died in their seventies," she says.

"And your siblings?"

"I had one sister," she says. "She died young."

"And are you married?"

"My husband died several years ago," she says. "We were divorced for many years before that." Curious, the order she has chosen.

"Children?"

"No."

"Are you retired? I see that you have recently moved here from Quebec."

"Yes. But still writing articles, going to conferences." She sees the drift of his questions; she'll head him off thoroughly.

"Ah, then you are a professional! Tell me, what is your line of work?"

Only a slight lilt, a slight over-precision in his English. She wonders how he came to be practicing here, in this small interior city.

"Plenty of family and friends here?"

"Plenty," she says firmly.

But he is persistent, this young man.

"Sometimes I find that when my patients retire, they have a little trouble with adjusting. They miss the routine of work, the camaraderie. No signs of depression?"

"No," she says. "No. Not at all."

"Good," he says. And then, "I always recommend to them to try something new, join a club or organization. I say to them, 'Try yoga.' Do you do yoga?"

"No," Sidonie says.

"Or volunteer work," he says. "There is always the need for volunteers. Ah, the life of the mind. That is a great dispensation."

What an odd word for him to have chosen. But perhaps he meant something else. Disposition? Compensation?

She doesn't ask.

A healthy mind in a healthy body; that's what people had said when she was young. What did they mean by it? She has known unhealthy minds in healthy bodies, and vice versa. It had been drilled into them, as children, though: reading improving books, eating fresh fruit and vegetables, bathing. Not thinking sexual thoughts. Or not *too many* sexual thoughts, if you had the good luck to be United Church, rather than Catholic or Lutheran.

Had it done them any good? Too difficult to tell; so many of them have not survived, even, to early old age.

The unfortunate aspect of living to be a hundred, of course, is that everyone you know will be dead.

I walk, she tells the doctor firmly, to close off his questioning.

The little lake near her house is grey-white in winter, a depressing no-colour, the ice mottled, clotted, like porridge. And the low-lying lake fog has filled the valley like a soiled bolster for nearly three weeks on end, and the sun, such as it is, sets behind the hill to the south and west by two o'clock in the afternoon. What has become of the clear bright January days she remembers from childhood?

She had skated on this little lake as a child. She learned to skate here, on sheets of ice scraped clear by fathers with makeshift ploughs of rectangles of plywood attached to two-by-four handles. Some years the ice was smooth as glass; others, if the lake had frozen up during a storm, it was pocked or rippled. Then skating was difficult, treacherous. But sometimes the lake froze perfectly, and there was only a little dry snow, which the wind blew away; then they could all skate right across the lake to the stands of poplar trees on the far side. That was like flying, or the closest you could come to flying, to glide without obstacle across the little lake, under a pearl sky, to the dark curtain of pines.

The pines are dying now; the mergansers and teal and grebes gone for the winter.

She marches sturdily along the icy, rocky path. She ought not to be walking it by herself, perhaps, even with her rubber-and-wire boot grips. But she has come to know its dips and turns over the winter; she can anticipate where she will need to bank to the left, to dig her heels in, to put a hand out to the black-and-ochre bark of a dying pine.

The trees had been thicker, the snow deeper, fifty years ago, she thinks. She has heard that the winters really are warmer now; that warmer winters are the cause of the pine beetle epidemic, in fact. She feels that this winter *has* been warmer than those of her childhood. There have not been the deep snowfalls, the punishing cold. Only this continuous fog and the freeze, thaw, freeze that glazes the roads and walkways. When she was a girl here, not only this lake, but even the bigger, deeper ones had frozen so thoroughly that people had driven their trucks out on them. She remembers driving in her father's truck right across this lake, right to this side from the other. The ice thick as a rock wall. But you would not drive on it now.

Winter here had been more vigorous in her childhood: the roads snowed in, the fruit trees dormant, sometimes cracking and losing limbs under heavy snowfall, sometimes losing blossoms to late frost. The beaches abandoned, the tourists flown south. And now, winter in the valley seems so much milder, more like what is called winter at the coast.

And yet, the climate has apparently changed only a degree or so. It is curious that such a small alteration should make so much difference. And also that warming should bring such destruction with it. It is this warming that has killed the pine. All along the valley, where the cool blue-green of the ponderosa, the dominant species, swathed the dry hills, there are now only streaks and patches of rust-colour. The hillsides seem to be in decay.

A beetle the size of a grain of rice has wreaked this. The slight increase of warmth has allowed a tiny fraction more of larvae to survive the winter, and these additional larvae, like compounding interest, have swelled the numbers of beetles to unimaginable hosts. So curious (and of course alarming) that these minute changes have had such dramatic, perhaps catastrophic results.

She strides along on the thin, slippery snow. Red-osier dog-wood, saskatoon berry, Silverberry, Soopolallie. The edge-shrubs, the encroachers, always looking for an opening in the thin dry forest. How does any plant survive here at all, with the scarcity of moisture? These, perhaps, send their roots down to the level of the little lake and draw up water. She had forgotten their names, had not thought of them all of these years, and here they are on her tongue. They are bare-branched now, silver and taupe and wine-barked. Possibly they are as beautiful now as they ever are, for they are not lush or promising shrubs. They have small, sparse leaves, unprepossessing flowers, dry, bitter berries. But now, just as it sets, the sun ekes through the low-lying cloud, and the shrubs are suddenly touched with subtle colour, silvery-sage-green and plum-red, stark and lovely, in their narrow branches, as etchings.

She stops for a moment. Around the base of a dogwood, where the glossy red stems branch out, the snow has thawed into multiple overlapping circles, and among the circles are the cross-hatchings of bird tracks. She waits; one more moment, two, and then the chickadees come back as silently as they must have left at her approach, landing in the bright ruddy branches, then hopping down to forage in the leaf litter.

It is serious business, foraging for food in the wild in January. Claw and bill, they sort and seize, only a slight toss of their throats showing that they have found sustenance under the withered leaves. How diligent they are, how resourceful, their sleek grey bodies and black-and-white hoods moving quickly, purposefully, economically.

And then she moves her hand in its white fleece glove, and they scatter upward and into the brush like blown leaves.

Two hours to circumambulate the lake; that breaks the back of the afternoon.

She returns to her house after her walk along the lake path, a little less heavy. Succored. Is that the word? She says it aloud, hears the pun. Suckered. Suckered into carrying on for another day, another evening. Though it's not as if there's much choice.

FISH GIRL

When Sidonie was born, she got stuck. Her head was very large, and she was a large baby altogether. Dr. Stewart estimated at least ten pounds, though they didn't think to get the scale from the shed. The district health nurse, visiting a week later, said her scale weighed Sidonie at ten pounds and four ounces. Mother was in labour for seventy-two hours, she says. Though Sidonie knows how babies are born — Alice and Hugh have enlightened her, and anyway, she has watched the cat have kittens — when she imagines her own birth, she sees Mother pulling her out of a hole in the ground.

The hole would have to be somewhere on the outer edge of the garden near the rhubarb and asparagus patches, where the orchard grass started. It would have to be smaller than the well, but larger than a marmot's tunnel. Mother would have pulled for three days. That was labour: Mother bent over double, grunting, sweat flying from her forehead, darkening her dress beneath her armpits and breasts. Mother pulling Sidonie by the hair, which sticks straight up like beet or carrot tops. It is not painful, but a pleasant sort of pressure. And then, finally, Sidonie bursting from the earth, head first of course, and Mother flying backwards, head over heels. Heels over head. Arse over teakettle, as Mr. Inglis would say. But ending up sitting right-side-up, turnip-headed Sidonie lying in her lap, naked except for a fine dark fur over her private parts. And blue as a saskatoon berry.

Mother says that Sidonie was blue when she was born. Blue and limp. "I was quite sure she was dead," Mother says. "After three days of that. But Dr. Stewart put her across her arm and massaged the life back into her. And then she stitched me up, because her shoulder came up at the last minute and ripped me from stem to stern. I couldn't sit without a cushion under me for six weeks."

Stem to stern: what does that mean? But Sidonie can't ask, because she hears this narrative from behind the wine flannel curtain. She is not supposed to have heard it.

Sometimes Mother will say about Dr. Stewart, "Without her, neither of us would be alive today." And sometimes she will say, "Doctors — hang you up on a meat hook and carve you up, just as soon as look at you."

This is women talk: conversation that takes place in hushed voices when there are no men or children around. Sidonie extracts from what she overhears that childbirth and pregnancy are battles played out on women's bodies: fierce, violent, unnatural calamities. The cat has her kittens silently, slipping them out, little wet packages, into the hay, bending her head around to nip and lick off the caul — which she then neatly eats — and, with her Turkish-towel tongue, licks the kittens into blind mewing life.

Once Sidonie hears someone ask Mother if Sidonie had been quite all right after being without air for so long. Mother says, coldly, "Without air?"

"You said she was blue."

"Oh, yes — well. She only needed to start breathing. A good slap on the backside would have done it, I daresay."

"I knew a woman in Calgary," this woman says, "whose baby wasn't breathing when he was born. And the doctor got him breathing finally, but he was quite handicapped, poor child, though he looked normal. I wondered if it would have been kinder not to interfere."

Mother says, "Well, there's nothing wrong with Sidonie. She's just always been awkward."

She remembers herself at eleven or twelve. She and Father are doing the dishes. Father says "Time and motion!" and "One-two-three-hoopla!" and whistles Bach, which is very good washing-up music. Sidonie cleans the table knives as her father taught her: put them in the sink all facing the same direction, grab them by the handles, fan out the blades, pass the wash rag back and front, swish, drop onto the drain board. The rhythm of the whistling moves her hands, gives her brain a chance to think, but not think itself into the usual tangle.

Father says, "Forks next," and begins whistling again. Sidonie drops two forks on the floor, finds the rhythm, washes them again.

Then her father asks a surprising thing. "Would you go to school in town, if you were driven?"

Sidonie shakes her head.

"Why not? Is it the school or the bus you are afraid of?"

Father has never questioned or discussed her school life: not in her hearing, at least. It's her mother's job to see about the children's schooling, he says. So Sidonie is surprised. She doesn't know what he knows about her. To start in seems like diving into the lake when it is dark. But he goes on whistling, and in a moment her voice, like her hands, gets pulled along free of her.

"I don't want to go to the high school," she says, "because I'd like to stay at my school. I know where everything is."

While she says this, it is as if she is inside her school, with its long rectangular shape, its echoing wide central staircase, its pleasing safe symmetry: two storeys, two wings for each storey, three class-rooms for each wing, one each side of the hallway, and one straight ahead. She can smell the Javex and the rubber sheet on the sofa in the sick room, the chalk, the tempura paint, the decayed grass smell of boots and wet wool in winter. She can smell the hot soup smell of the teachers' lounge. She thinks of the balance of the school:

the rows of windows with their perfect, pleasing rectangles, the fire doors at the back of each classroom, each opening at five minutes to three every day, as the chalkboard monitors step outside to shake the chamois and bang the felt brushes together, the balance of the principal's office, teacher's room, and sickroom filling one of the classroom spaces (top right-hand wing), while the library fills another classroom, in the bottom left-hand wing. She thinks of the balance of the teachers: Miss Stewart, the primary teacher, small and plump and kind; Miss Beattie, the intermediate teacher, thin-haired, bony and mean; Mr. Ramsay, the principal, blunt and direct in the hallway, and Miss Duthie, the librarian, quiet and tactful among the books.

Her father says, "I noticed that you can add up the accounts in your head. Do you find the mathematics at the school easy?"

Sidonie says, "I do my own math. Mr. Ramsay gets me a different book."

"And what level is it that you do, in this book?"

"I don't know," Sidonie says. In fact, she does: the book says *Journeys in Algebra II*. It is a book for high school: she has seen students walking home from the bus carrying it. But Mr. Ramsay said she shouldn't tell people that she was doing this level, or they would all want to.

"Hmmm," Father says.

And after that, in the evenings, she does exercises with Father. Every evening. Father puts music on the gramophone, and Sidonie must practice writing, or stitching, or walking on a line on the floor. She must read to him, standing in front of him, forming her words properly. She thinks sometimes that she will burst with impatience. But Father finds her more music, and buys her a violin, and teaches her to play it.

"Order and rhythm!" Father says. "That's the way we do this!"

Alice whispers to her across their bedroom at night: "Retard. Spazz."

But she had been lucky: rescued, again and again. And how had she repaid that?

It had been a difficult existence, one in which many children had not thrived. She knows something about that from her work, her studies. She knows about the tender, branching brains of children, about poverty of body and spirit, of the seed sown on barren ground. It is her field. Her ground. But she had been lucky. She had been nurtured. She had been extraordinarily well cared for, given the time and place.

And how had she repaid that care?

Turnip child. In this summer of 2007, she is still pulling herself out of her deep hole.

When Mr. Defoe comes to dinner, Sidonie, who is fourteen, makes the salad. It is June, so there are lots of fresh things in the garden: some new lettuce and peas, which Sidonie's mother plants in May and June and again in August; peppercress, green onions, radishes. Alice tells Sidonie what to cut, and brings her the vegetables herself, washing them and checking for snails, which Sidonie can't be trusted to do, because if she finds snails, she will have to take them out to the orchard and release them at strategic points, and will forget to come back. Alice is making a dressing for the salad out of honey and mustard and apple-cider vinegar, which are all very odd things to think about putting in salad, but which taste very good together, like the notes in music. Sidonie wonders if Alice can hear the different flavours, how they will work together, before she mixes them, but when she asks her how she knows, Alice just says in a bored voice that she saw it in a magazine.

Alice is good at knowing how to do things like that; has won blue ribbons for her cakes and pies and flower arrangements in the junior division of the exhibition part of the Regatta, and is always chosen to be in charge of decorating the hall for Teen Town dances and the Hospital Auxiliary Fair, and got the Domestic Science award from the Women's Institute when she graduated from high school. And, of course, she was Lady of the Lake, elected last year, 1957, at the Regatta, beating out a dozen contestants from up and down the valley.

Sidonie cuts the vegetables very accurately for the salad, because she has remembered that Mr. Defoe is to marry Alice. She has almost said this to Alice three times, but has remembered, just in time, not to. Anyway, Sidonie thinks, Alice already knows, because her electricity is humming more loudly than usual. Of course Alice hums, appropriately, on the inside, her outside remaining cool and silvery white, not like Sidonie, whose electricity, when she is anxious or excited, leaks out inappropriately in a sort of buzzing hum, and makes her arms flap.

Alice knows because she has ironed her blue dress and made a cake that is covered with white icing, but not in peaks; instead, in a thick blanket that has no edges. And on the blanket she has put crisscross blue lines, so perfect that even Sidonie can see no wobble in the size of the diamonds. The cake with its blue lines, Sidonie sees, is the same as Alice's dress, with its ribbon trim, only opposite. And then Alice has put, in some, but not every diamond, a tiny blue and yellow Johnny-jump-up flower, which she has dipped in egg white and sugar, so that the colours shine through mistily.

"Do you think it's too much?" Alice asks herself out loud, and Sidonie sees that the cake, with its blue lines, is a kind of net, and the net is to catch Mr. Defoe. Will it work?

Mr. Defoe, whose first name is Gordon, arrives at 5:30 on the dot. Father introduces him to Mother. Father and Alice converse with him in the parlour, which is open to the dining room, so Sidonie hears parts of the conversation as she lays plates and cutlery out. Something very strange: Father and Mother and Alice are all pretending, it seems, that they haven't met Mr. Defoe before, that he had Father haven't shouted at each other across the driveway, that Alice hasn't already climbed into Mr. Defoe's truck and ridden off down the road.

Alice says, "Don't you think our little lakeside community is charming?"

Mr. Defoe says, "Oh yes. But tell me, why is it that. . ."

Father says, "I suppose you will be starting to cut out the new Spartans in the east orchard this fall?"

Mr. Defoe says, "Yes, Inglis has mentioned they are full of. . ."

Alice says, "One must go into town in the winter, of course, for any sort of culture. . ."

Mr. Defoe says, "Are you fond of music, Miss Von Täler?"

Father says, "The sulphur sprayer needs an overhaul: when I borrowed it in spring, it was losing pressure. You'll need to order new coupling joints. . ."

Mr. Defoe says, "I plan to have the equipment serviced. . . ."

Mr. Defoe is like a tennis ball that Alice and Father are playing with, Sidonie sees. Poor Mr. Defoe. But he seems, to her sidelong glances (she is not able to look at him when introduced) not too sub, as Alice would say. He has good shoulders and back, and thick reddish hair, no moustache. He has an accent: not apricot-jam-sticky like Mrs. Inglis's, or full of rushing air, like Mr. Inglis's, or lilting like Father's, but an accent like rocks sliding down a metal chute. A funny thing, too: though the hair on his head is reddish, the hair on his wrists and the backs of his hands is black, as though his body and head belong to two separate men.

At the dinner table, Sidonie reverses her earlier thought. Mr. Defoe, she sees now, is not the ball, but another player, taking on both her father and Alice (and now her mother as well) all at once. He does not drop the ball, she sees, though he's often cut off in midsentence. He doesn't say anything that Father would see as arrogant or boastful, or that Mother would say was coarse, or that Alice would complain was uneducated. *He acquits himself well*, a voice inside her head says, as if reading from a book, and she smiles, privately. So she is caught off guard when he addresses her directly in the lull brought on by the chewing of pork chops.

"And where do you go to school, Sidonie?"

She swallows too hastily through a perhaps constricted throat, chokes, knocks over her water glass, and bumps the table leg hard with her knee. Alice's eyes narrow: she will make Sidonie pay, after. *Spazz*, she will say, meaning spastic.

Sidonie says, not looking up, that she goes to school in town.

"And will you go to the new high school when it opens?"

Yes, she says. But she cannot drag her eyes to Mr. Defoe's face, as she knows is polite. She glances wildly at Alice, but Alice's face is set, remote. Will Mother rescue her? But Mother is busy with the gravy boat.

Father says, "We shall all be glad to have the high school here in Marshall's Landing. Too long have our youth been drawn out of the community."

Now Sidonie feels irritated instead of awkward. Does Father always have to sound like he's intoning Goethe? Mr. Defoe must think they're comical. She must do something to mend the net, or Alice's minnow will escape and it will be her fault.

She raises her eyes to their visitor's face, as nearly as she can. A million sparks of conversation flicker and die on her tongue. When she speaks, her voice sounds tremulous to her own ears.

"What do you like to do for fun, Mr. Defoe?"

Is that what she had said? Something like that. Whatever it had been, it hadn't been the right thing, though nobody had apparently noticed the long calculating look Mr. Defoe had given her before turning back to his plate.

Father's cherries, which are a different strain, ripen later than the Inglises', so there is no shortage of pickers. School is out, and Sidonie and Walt and Masao, and Alice on her days off, all pick for Mr. Inglis, or rather, Mr. Defoe, and then for Nakamuras, and then in their own orchards.

"Pick clean!" Mr. Defoe says, as if they haven't been picking cherries all their lives. He treats them no differently than the other pickers, though he has been to their house, and comes by every few days to pick Alice up. ("Where do you go?" Sidonie asks, and Alice says, "None of your beeswax.") But once, when he shouts at Alice to clean more of the stones and leaves out of her bag before she dumps it, Alice mutters, just loudly enough for Sidonie to hear: "Oh, go hump yourself."

It is better when they are picking their own cherries. Then Sidonie can eat as many as she wants — her mouth and fingers and the soles of her feet are stained purple for that whole week.

In their own orchard, too, they have Masao to goof around with.

Mr. Defoe had put the men from the camp down in the Hare Road orchard, so they never saw him. Masao is here with his hijinks, his jet-eyed grin. He carries Alice's bag sometimes, and arranges to work in the tree next to hers. He helps Sidonie, and jokes with her, too. But it is Alice who is Masao's friend.

In August there is time between picking cherries and picking apricots and peaches to spend the whole day at the lake, and the younger set converge there by late morning, parents driving down the hill in the late afternoon, bringing picnics and folding chairs. Mother packs egg salad sandwiches or potato salad (the hens laying superbly now) or sometimes an entire cold fried chicken (the expendable roosters), crisp and paprika-scented, the way Father likes it. (Paprika, Sidonie thinks, is made of ground red earth from some exotic, tropical country; it imparts to food the tang of palms and dust and sun and wild music played on long-stemmed string instruments, and the taste of some fruit that she will only many years later identify as mangoes.) Also there are rolls and butter and cake and fruit — apricots or raspberries. Mr. Tanaka and Masao and some of their friends come along as well. Mother and Father and Mr. Tanaka will plant their unfolded chairs on the shallow beach, and ceremoniously, ritualistically, disrobe.

Sidonie used to find this process terrifying, but now it's only embarrassing to see the adults in their bathing suits. Mr. Tanaka with his thin, ribby chest, his little pot, his smooth, hairless body like Masao's, only slacker, stretched out like an old sweater; Father with the blond pelt on his chest, as if the hair from his head has migrated to his torso, his white legs and upper arms contrasting startlingly with his sunburned neck and forearms; Mother, with her skirted bathing dress (Out of the twenties! Alice protests) and the blue spider veins like cryptic messages on her legs.

They swim in the little bay, next to the pier and pilings and great red hulk of the packing house. The camp road, if you follow it to the hill's crest, past the reservoir and down again, zig-zags in hairpin turns down the steep slope to the lake. At the end, the road plunges straight down like a boy running across a field on the last day of school. The hillside between the orchards is dotted with ponderosa pine and balsam-root and saskatoon bushes, but along the narrow shoreline, cottonwoods grow, providing shade and shielding the beach from the view of the road and hills, so it seems a separate, discrete world.

Alice spreads her mat and arranges her things, slowly taking off her shorts and shirt. This year Alice's bathing suit is a two-piece: red bottoms, a red and white halter top. She looks, Sidonie thinks, like a candy cane. All the boys and men look at her; they don't try to disguise that. How can Alice bear it? She, Sidonie, would hate it. But Alice seems oblivious, unconcerned.

Sidonie wears one of Alice's old suits. It's navy, and has faded to an uneven purplish shade, and the white piping has turned grey. Sidonie has worn it for two summers already. She likes it, despite its ugliness: it feels comfortable, familiar. Mother tried to throw it out this year, but Sidonie is glad she has kept it. It fits her better than it did before, sitting becomingly on her chest and hips now, instead of hanging in folds. She feels vindicated in saving it: it has become a second skin.

The small flat stones that line the beach change colour at the water's edge: the dry ones are dull: grey, fawn, with little contrast, while under the water, they gleam like semi-precious gems: jade, tiger-eye, jet, quartz. Sometimes she finds translucent agates: at home she has a small bag of these that she has been collecting for years.

Overhead, the sky is cloudless, a deep, even saturated blue. The lake is a darker blue, and the hills on the far side a different shade yet, though of course they're not really blue, but dark green from the pines and firs, and gold from the sunburned grass. And the lake is not really blue: only in the distance, where it reflects sky. At the shore, it is clear, like glass, and a little deeper, a light, shimmery green: beyond that, deeper green, though still translucent.

She wades in to her knees, her thighs, then stands transfixed, watching the play of light and colour in the water, which has become a layered, moving thing. Minnows materialize, nibble at her shins.

Alice says from the beach, from under the brim of her hat: "Sidonie, don't flap."

Has she been flapping? Yes, and humming, too. She holds her arms down by her sides, wades further in, drawing the minnows after her. Now her feet find the cold layer, and the surface, rising up her thighs, is also cold, but not as cold. The differences in temperature and the tickling of the minnows make her aware of her feet and legs as different regions: she is segmented. She pauses a moment, then lets herself fall into the lake sideways, lightly, so that there is no splash or sound.

Submerged, swimming with her eyes open, she sees the water is clear — not like glass, but like something else she has never seen, but can imagine — something viscous, but so bright that light is refracted stronger, intensified by it. For as long as she can hold her breath, she is free in this medium — free of gravity, of the gaze of others. She arches her back and swims, seahorse-like, along the smooth bottom stones. They are black, white, ochre, rose, green-grey. They form a mosaic of a kind: random, abstract, but with a sense of pattern, a pattern she could discern, if only she could stay under long enough.

She launches herself upward for a few lungfuls of air, and is under again. Now she noses along the bottom, waving her legs from side to side for thrust, fluttering her fingers for equilibrium. The small ripples she leaves on the surface are reflected on the lake bottom, a net of light. She swims in the net, banking and rolling to catch her own shadow, which, infant-sized, darts along with her.

She surfaces again, gulps in more air (oh, how delicious, how taken for granted!) and plunges in again. This time she follows the splintery stump of a piling to its root, pulling herself down hand over hand, climbing in reverse. At the base of the post she finds a strip of algae, lank, like a hank of hair. All at once she is afraid: it will wrap around her ankle, drown her.

Towards shore is brighter. She swims hard, under the water, using her strong long legs and arms, froglike. When she is in the shallows, she sees that Masao has come into shore as well, and is flicking water at Alice and laughing, and that Alice launches herself into the water, grabs his ankles.

But Masao turns, lithe as a water snake, and seizes Alice's wrists. Now he's pulling her into deeper water. He locks fingers with her, pushes her under, but Alice wraps her legs around his waist and drags him down with her. They grin at each other, face to face in the churned water. Masao's hair floats upward: he's an attenuated troll. Streams of silver bubbles float from his nose, his ears, his hair and shoulders. He twists to free himself, but Alice clings, locking her ankles.

Then all at once Masao scissors his legs together, shooting them both upward. Alice's legs unlock, she gasps air. Masao is gasping too, and laughing. He shakes out his hair, so that brilliant gleaming drops fly around them.

Masao unlocks his fingers from her wrist, arches his back. Alice lets herself float away, starfish like, on the lake's silky surface. Only her face, her toes, and her breasts in their red and white nylon shell emerge above the surface.

On the beach, Masao prostrates himself next to Alice. He doesn't have a towel; he lies on the bare hot rocks. Sidonie sits on the edge of the water so that her legs are in the water, leans back into her arms, lets the sun fall on her face and throat. It's like a shower of warm honey, only not sticky. Walt digs a pool in the gravel with some younger children. The water is cloudy where they dig, full of the silt and yellow pollen that lie buried under the clean, smooth river gravel, and they laboriously bail it clear, fill it with clean.

Then Walt and the McCartney twins, hatted and shirted for protection of their almost translucent skins, stand in the shallows, waiting to scoop up somnolent minnows. Sidonie remembers this activity: how building a pool and system of canals could fill a whole day. How the pleasure of it would draw you inexorably in. How Mother would say, you'd *never* stick to shelling peas or picking raspberries that long.

How you could lose yourself an hour at a time collecting white stones or the conical, screw-shaped snails that lived on the larger, algae-covered rocks at the far end of the bay.

While her feet cool in the water, her head and shoulders heat; she feels the metals in her tissue become charged, liquid with heat. She is two beings: the molten Sidonie absorbing the sun; the cool fish Sidonie waiting, chill, unawakened, under the lake water.

Walt calls to her from the pier, and executes a perfect back flip. Near perfect. Sidonie can do better. She stands and plunges into the water, suddenly, noisily, arousing murmurs of protest from Alice and Masao, is momentarily alive to the sudden swirling of cool water around her heated head, and strokes quickly out to join Walt.

She pulls herself up to the ladder slats, walks wet-footed across the silvery, slivery wood planks to the edge. Toes pointed to the open lake, heels on the wooden edge, she finds the position that will catapult her perfectly in an arc extending from the earth's centre, then springs. The forces of gravity, of momentum, of centrifuge; the pull of stars, the leap of molecules all gather in her legs, her arched spine. The crown of her head lifts her up, up, over; she feels her spine and legs now follow, a lariat, a flung chain. Her fingertips part the surface of the water; then her head and torso and toes. She feels each cell of her skin join with the water. It takes no time at all.

Then she arcs up through the water, her limbs smoothly building on the propulsion of the dive. The lake parts for her, supports her, lifts her. (How is it, Alice always says, that Sidonie can swim like a fish, but can't walk across a room without tripping over her own feet?) But she is a fish, a fish girl, all sinuous eely tail and trunk, strong supple arms. She is fish girl, cool, mailed in chitin, slippery, gilled. She is sleek, she hides in shadows, she watches from her cool refracting element, she moves without hindrance or hesitation.

She pulls herself through the water, waving her tail-legs behind her.

On some evenings and on Sundays, the Inglises also arrive at the beach, which is an occasion, a procession. First Mrs. Inglis, swathed in a flowery dress — a robe, really — and large white-rimmed sunglasses, an enormous straw hat, and carrying a straw bag; then

Mr. Inglis with at least two hampers, one of which clinks, and finally Graham and Hugh, laden with chairs and umbrellas and floating mattresses. They always set up in the same place, where the beach is widest, the cottonwood shade deepest. If anyone is there already, they always move, give up their place to the Inglises. Then Mr. Inglis takes the umbrella and plants it in the river gravel like a flag. Once, Alice asked why the Inglises always had the best spot on the beach, and Mother said it was because Mr. Inglis had paid to have several barge loads of fine river stone brought in and poured on the shore; that the beach was pebbled and gradual, rather than steep and muddy, was due to his beneficence.

The wooden and canvas chairs are unfolded and placed in front of the umbrella, then various unguents and towels spread over the Inglises themselves. Mr. Inglis, under his straw fedora, lights a cigar, pours clear fluid (gee and tee, Mrs. Inglis calls it) from an ice-packed flask into a glass, and opens a newspaper. Mrs. Inglis, after calling silvery hellos and waggling her fingers to all of her acquaintants, settles with a magazine or a book. Hugh, who is pale as a white rabbit, with a white rabbit's colourless lashes and pinkish eyes, stays in the shade with his parents and a book; Graham sometimes joins the other young people, sometimes swims far out into the lake until his head is a tiny blob.

Seeing her next to him on the beach, Hugh says, "Is this *Sid*? Sidonie, what happened? You've metamorphosed from a darling little girl to a heartthrob! Legs! Betty Grable, look out!"

Graham says, "Down, boy."

Sidonie knows Hugh is kidding. She's not at all like Betty Grable. Her hair is still in fuzzy braids, her chest almost flat, her face all pointy chin and straight slash of mouth and eyebrows. But she looks at her legs stretched out in front of her. Are they nice? She doesn't know; she's never thought about it. But for the first time, she feels that it would be good to have nice legs. She hopes that they are nice.

She says, "*Alice* is the belle."

"Oh, she speaks," Graham says. Sidonie blushes.

"Alice," Hugh says, "could have launched the whole goddamn sixth fleet."

Sidonie blushes again: not because swearing isn't nice, but because she is afraid Graham or Hugh will think that she thinks that. Hugh is allowed to swear, she thinks; he's been at university. Also, now that she is fourteen, she is old enough to know that only old maids object to swearing. She wants Hugh and Graham to know that she, personally, doesn't.

She wants too, to let Hugh know that she has picked up his reference to Helen of Troy. That she has read a little of *The Iliad*, even if it was in an English translation. But it would be abrupt, strange, to say that obvious thing. Instead, she makes a leap, blurts out something that's meant to be provocative, but that falls even on her own ears gauchely.

"Alice is going to marry Mr. Defoe," she says.

Graham laughs, but Hugh frowns. "Why?"

"Why not?" Graham says. "She could do worse."

"Defoe isn't a gentleman," Hugh says. They seem to have forgotten she's there, Sidonie thinks. Hugh has flushed darker than Sidonie does.

"Gentleman?" Graham mocks. "No, if that word means anything, which I sincerely doubt, I suppose he isn't. But he is a goer."

"He's rather a little fascist," Hugh mutters.

Graham laughs again. "So are you, if I remember some of your rants a year or two ago. But if you mean he's going to change the way things are done around here, you're probably right, and they probably need changing. And what more would you want for a girl like Alice than to be married to someone who'll be a name in the community?"

"Alice should go to college," Hugh says. "Get some training."

"What for?" Graham says. "She'll only marry some local and keep house, run the WI teas, that sort of thing. Her face and her manner will be all she needs."

"She's more than pretty," Hugh says, in the stubborn way Sidonie recognizes.

Graham narrows his eyes. "Think so?" he says. Then, "Maybe you're right."

Later, later, Sidonie will watch Graham and Alice sitting together, and will see that they look alike: they have the same high-nosed, symmetrical profiles, the same full lower lip and curved chin, the same expression — one that is self-contained, what Mother would call snooty. They could be siblings. It occurs to her at once that they look aristocratic, and that she understands what aristocratic means: it is the assumption of ownership (of the beach) coupled with a disdain, a detachment. For neither of them really cares, she thinks. They take the beach as their own, but do not love it, as she does, with her affinity for the water, her ability to become inebriated in the intensity of blues, or as Masao does, with his boy's enjoyment of play, or even as sociable Hugh, despite his sensitivity to the sun.

And Sidonie will wonder, for the first time, why it hasn't occurred to everyone (meaning her mother and Mrs. Inglis) that Alice might marry Graham. Not Hugh: he's too young, too boyish, too enthusiastic, too bumbling. But Graham: he'd be perfect. And now that he has come back, he seems older, tougher. All that searching for a husband for Alice, and there was Graham right there all the time.

It hasn't occurred to Sidonie, yet, that Mrs. Inglis and Mother, let alone Graham and Alice, must have thought of the possibility, and for their own reasons, decided against it.

But on this day on the beach, Sidonie is aware only of the rightness of Graham and Alice making a match. Alice, the most beautiful girl in the community: smart, stylish, graceful, respectable: a princess, if there ever was one. And Graham Inglis: privileged, educated, owner of Meccano sets and encyclopedias, hardened, mysterious: a seasoned knight.

She had not known then that Graham was ill. Had that been the impediment?

One day Mr. Defoe appears on their beach; up to that point Sidonie has never noticed his absence, taking it for granted that the beach is exclusive to the few Marshall's Landing families. But one day he is there, in baggy chinos, white shirt.

"Now I know your secret," he says. "I've been going to Wood Lake; I didn't know about this little Shangri-La." He isn't speaking to anyone in particular, but Sidonie feels like he's making an accusation. Alice looks at him with her eyes slightly closed, like a sleepy cat, and he spreads a tartan car blanket and sits down between her and Mrs. Inglis. Alice, Sidonie notices, seems suddenly a little smaller, and the red-and-white bathing suit somehow frivolous, silly, with Mr. Defoe there.

Mr. Defoe doesn't take off his street clothes for a long time. When he finally does, he steps out of them almost shyly, as if he wished someone would hold a towel around him. But once he's standing in his trunks, she notices that the hair on his chest, like the hair on his forearms, is black, all the way up to his throat. She wants to giggle again at the incongruity: the black body hair, like a bear's pelt, the sandy crop that glints red-gold in the sun. Mr. Defoe is bigger, too, than he looks clothed. His legs and chest are full and muscled: he makes Graham and Hugh both seem mere boys. It gives Sidonie a funny feeling when he pulls Alice up by the hand and leads her to the water. Alice looks frail, childish, in comparison. And Sidonie has the sudden impression that Alice is being abducted; she has to resist the urge to fling herself at Alice's ankles and cling to her heroically.

There is no horseplay with Mr. Defoe. He swims out strongly, like Graham, but not so far, slowing now and then so Alice can catch up with him, but not slowing enough that she can keep pace. Out in the lake, they stop swimming and tread water, facing each other. They're talking, but softly; the words don't carry. Walt wades in from practicing somersaults and stares at them curiously.

"They're going to *kiss*," he says. They don't kiss. But Sidonie thinks that there is something in the way they're talking — or rather the way Mr. Defoe is talking to Alice, and Alice is holding her head slightly averted, her gaze downturned submissively, that seems more intimate, more revealing, than kissing would be. She thinks of how, the first evening he came to dinner, she had imagined Mr. Defoe as a rather fierce and prickly creature to be caught in the little net made by Alice and Mother and Mrs. Inglis. Now she feels a shiver, as if something tentacled and clawed were coiled about Alice out there in the water.

But silly. It's only Mr. Defoe.

In the evening, Alice goes out with Mr. Defoe, dressed in her blue poplin with the tiny pleats and crinoline. Alice in the cab of Mr. Defoe's truck, her full skirts spread over the seat, her white hands clasped in her lap, her pale golden waves of hair shining.

Late August: on the way up the hill from the store, Sidonie hears a truck pull up behind her. Hop in, Mr. Defoe says. Sidonie jumps up, steps on the running board, swings her legs in. She is wearing pleated shorts, a white cotton shirt tied at the midriff. She leans back in the seat, admires her own long tanned legs, her flat stomach. She is as tall as Alice and slimmer. Sometimes, not looking at herself in the mirror, but glancing down at her own legs or catching sight of her profile, her own lean shadow reflected in a shop window, she thinks: I am almost beautiful. I have as pretty a figure as Alice. She is golden brown and her skin shines. She leans back into the seat and takes up with her long legs the space that Alice's skirts usually occupy. Pushes her shoulder blades into the seat back, leans her head back.

When she rides with Mr. Defoe and Alice, she has to scrunch near the door but today it is *her* seat. The sun comes in the open door windows and makes white patches on her thighs, glints off Mr. Defoe's arm hair. Mr. Defoe drives as all of the men do, left arm hooked over the door through the open window; right hand resting lightly on the steering wheel. When he steers, he uses the first two fingers only; it's a gesture the men have, to drive with as little apparent effort as possible.

When Mr. Defoe turns off along Bond Road instead of following the usual route to Beauvoir, she only assumes that he has another errand to run, one that will take so little time that he doesn't bother asking her if she minds the detour. When he turns into the old Enderby place, she assumes only that he's taken the wrong driveway.

Nobody lives here, she thinks, but doesn't say. Grown-up men don't like to be corrected by young girls.

The truck stops between the house with its smashed windows and the leaning shed. She sits, still trying to guess what Mr. Defoe's errand is. Doesn't think. Doesn't think to be especially afraid. Doesn't think to run, though she could still likely have jumped out of the truck cab and bolted down the Enderby's long lilac-lined driveway, at this point. She is the fastest girl in grade nine. Doesn't wonder, when Mr. Defoe gets out of the truck and comes around to her side. Doesn't run when Mr. Defoe opens the passenger door and pulls her toward him with a quick yank on her wrist and knee, so that she slips sideways, her head and shoulders lurching into the driver's end of the bench, her legs falling off the passenger end, out the open door.

Struggles, then, because she's being touched, a hand slipped up under her shirt, squeezing her breasts, the tender tips of her breasts where the growing is. She squirms and struggles, but she's bent backwards over the edge of the seat, off balance. Tries to scream, but Mr. Defoe's mouth is over hers, pressing her lips painfully against her teeth. His mouth right over hers, and his — oh, disgusting! — his tongue pushing into her mouth.

She tries to kick and claw and bite, but his hands, his mouth, the weight of his body are all so much stronger than hers that she feels only her own puniness. The more she struggles, the harder she is held. Her wrists are gripped in one of his hands; she thinks the bones will be crushed.

But even then, even then, she does not feel alarmed enough: doesn't guess what is coming, while the button of her waistband is plucked from its opening and her shorts are tugged in two moves down her legs.

Then, being touched *there*, the leg opening of her underpants stretched out and herself touched there, and then a swift impaling, a sharp little twist somewhere she hasn't felt sensation before. She thinks: that is his *finger*. Mr. Defoe's finger *inside her*.

The world slipping sideways: how can she walk in it again, so invaded? How can she walk out in the world again, now that Mr. Defoe with his dry red skin and his grin has put his finger inside her? She will shrivel and die with the shame, the exposure.

She thinks that she will faint, but she does not faint, and it all takes a long time, perhaps because she continues to struggle. Her underpants and shorts are yanked down further, and off. She is pulled out of the truck, struggling, yelping, onto the grass (thick with pineapple plant and daisies, for it has not been mowed in years) and then there is more of tongue in her mouth and sucking of her breast tips (ugh, ugh: she thinks of grown-up women feeding babies, and is appalled at this perversion) and more of the finger thrusting in her vitals, and slaps and her pigtail yanked hard, once, when she tries to get her knees up, and then blunt warm flesh against her private parts, *pushing*, and then inner sharp tearing like being cut with scissors over and over.

How long that takes: the pain over and over. And then a kind of groan from Mr. Defoe, and the stopping, and hot wet between her thighs like her period, and his saying: "There, you've been asking for that for a long time, haven't you?"

She had gotten up and walked home then, and he had not tried to stop her.

After that she could not think, and then she had begun to think too much.

She had thought: that is why girls aren't supposed to catch rides with strange men.

She had thought: but Mr. Defoe isn't supposed to be a stranger.

She had thought: Mr. Defoe must have felt very safe, to do that. And she herself must be very powerless: much more than she would have guessed.

All the hints and innuendoes she had not understood fell into place. She thought: what if I have a baby? And then, after she knew she would not: that was lucky.

She thought: that is what Mr. Defoe will do to Alice when they are married. (Perhaps he already had? No; if he could do that to Alice, he surely would not have bothered with herself.)

She thought — no, felt — how will I walk out in the world, now that Mr. Defoe has done this to me?

She thought: well, it is not the end of the world. The world makes a big fuss about this, but it is not the end of the world.

She felt intense pity for Alice, who would marry Mr. Defoe, and belong to him, and not know what he was. It did not occur to her that Alice might not want to know. She herself would want to know.

She saw that the world was not as it had seemed, and she began to think very carefully about how she must *be* in the world, and that changed things for her completely. She saw that a literal world existed under the one that people spoke about, and that this world was both more and less dangerous than the one represented in words. She saw that people were unable to speak directly about the literal world, and that they spent a great deal of their energy speaking about it indirectly, and pretending it was not as it actually was, while at the same time creating a detailed coded picture of it, and not letting each other forget about it.

She felt sorry for Alice, and decided to tell her, but could not. The day of the wedding drew closer, and she could not. She saw little of Alice, now, in avoiding Mr. Defoe: that was one reason.

She decided that she would write a note to Alice. She wrote it carefully, composing it all first, using her best Alice-style handwriting. She tried to use a grown-up way of speaking.

Gordon Defoe raped me, she wrote. She had first written "Mr. Defoe," but that sounded childish.

There: clear and concise. She put the note into Alice's apron pocket: why? Because she was about to press it into Alice's hand in the kitchen, and lost her nerve. When Alice finds it in her pocket, it will be detached, somehow, from Sidonie. Alice will get the message, but it will be somehow separate, authorless.

The message will be the thing Alice gets, not the connection with Sidonie. Alice will read it and know what to do.

Only Alice doesn't find it: Mother does, borrowing Alice's clean apron, for hers is sticky from canning. Mother finds it, and thinks it is from Alice.

Mother calls Sidonie down from her room, where she is reading. "Why are you hiding away? We have company." But it is only Mrs. Inglis, who often walks over in the evenings to chat for a few minutes on the porch or in the sitting room.

Mother is agitated: she rubs her hands, feints to the left and right, finally seems to come to a decision. "Let's sit in the kitchen," she says to Mrs. Inglis. "I'm baking a sponge and want to keep an eye on it. Sidonie, you may stay here in the sitting room and read, but I want you near if I call you for help." By which Sidonie understands that she is to watch for anyone coming through and alert Mother in time. Mother and Mrs. Inglis go through the wine flannel curtain. Their voices are even more audible in this direction than when Sidonie eavesdrops on the parlour from the kitchen. Mother doesn't know how the sound carries; perhaps Sidonie's ears are just much sharper than Mother's.

"What should I do, what should I do?" Mother wails.

"What does she want?" Mrs. Inglis asks.

"What does she want?" Mother sounds bewildered by this question.

"Well, does she want to lay charges?" Mrs. Inglis asks. "Does she feels this was an attack? Or has she been inviting it, as girls do, only not wanting it so precipitously? There's some grey area there. Or maybe she's pregnant and doesn't want to admit she's jumped the gun?"

Mother says, "No, no. . . . I don't believe Alice would. . . . She's a sensible girl."

Tears in Mother's voice now, incredibly. Sidonie would almost say she sounded frightened.

"What do I do?"

"What do you want to do, Frances?" Mrs. Inglis asks, calmly, and Sidonie thinks: how rarely it is that she hears adults addressed by their first names.

"I don't know. . . . I don't know. It's so terrible! After all my hard work, that it should come to this, that I should have to have this in my face. . . ."

"It may not be as terrible as you think," Mrs. Inglis says. "I think you must have a heart-to-heart with Alice. See what she meant by that note. Do you have it still?"

A crackle of unfolding paper, a pause.

Mrs. Inglis says, "Are you sure Alice wrote this?"

Mother is indignant. "Do you think I don't know my own daughter's handwriting?"

"Well," Mrs. Inglis says. "I'd talk to Alice, before anything else. Find out what really went on."

"I will," Mother says.

Sidonie is awakened by rough shaking, a slap. She has been waiting for Alice to come home, to come upstairs, to intercept Alice and warn her. But she has, impossibly, fallen asleep. Her first sensation is astonishment. For the past few days she has felt herself drifting, never fully conscious, but not sleeping, either. But here! She has been asleep after all. And it is Mother shaking and slapping her.

"What have you done," Mother cries. "Stupid, dirty girl!"

There are a number of things she might have done: tracked chicken manure into the house, left the frying pan unscoured, forgotten to put her sanitary napkin in the outhouse drop. But she knows: her stomach a lump of cold pie dough, she knows what it is. She begins to cry.

Mother flies at her, boxing her ears, pulling her hair. "Stop that! Pull yourself together and tell me what you've done!"

She cannot speak the words to Mother; it is Alice, slouching in, pale and mean-lipped, who gets it out of her. Alice is cold and dry, and Sidonie is able to speak, to tell everything, to not break down.

"Well," Alice says, matter-of-factly, as if she's been sweeping up a broken dish, "That's that."

Mother's expression changes. "Do you think it's so bad?" she says to Alice. "What if — what if she were to go away. She could stay with her aunt Mary in Harwood maybe. Nothing would have to. . ."

They've all been speaking in hoarse whispers, but now Alice shouts, her face screwed up and red: "*Gaaah*! What are you, retarded?" and bangs out of the room, slamming the door, thumping down the stairs.

Sidonie can her Father move in his bed, call out sleepily: "*Was ist los?*"

A terrible empathy between herself and her mother: a terrible shared understanding that Father must not know. At that moment, she would have stabbed herself in the heart to sever that connection.

Mother walks out into the hallway. "Everything's fine, Peter," she says. "Girls having a little argument; that's all."

Please please please let this not be spoken of again, Sidonie wishes, and it is not, at least within her hearing. She feels reprieved, lucky.

She had wished never to hear of it, and she had not. She had wished never to see Gordon Defoe again, but he had stayed on as the Inglises' foreman. She had understood that to be the price of the silence.

And Alice had put away her Lady of the Lake frocks, and had begun to spend time with Buck Kleinholz, to whom, before, she would not have given the time of day.

She had wished for the wrong thing, of course. She had buried not only herself, but also Alice, with undeserved shame. How had they not been protected, how had they not been defended?

Always going at things slant-wise; always drawing near but missing the point, that was herself. She had entered the field of psychology, searching, obviously, for some connection, some understanding of what went on in other people's heads, but had slid off on the tangent of experiment design, always at an arm's length from the conclusions she wanted. She had chosen Adam as a lover, then married him, condemning both of them to decades of dissatisfaction. She had adopted Cynthia, her sister's child, and yet turned her over to the primary care of Adam, never stepping into the role of female parent. Never letting herself take Alice's place.

She had moved back to Marshall's Landing, clearly following a deep, intuitive longing for home, and had been sidetracked by logical considerations (or the fear that often takes logic as its disguise) and had landed down in this house just kilometres from where she really wanted to be.

To be whole; to see wholly: those have always been her goals. But how often in her stochastic approach has she missed the mark? It is not good enough: there is not time for this, now. She must learn to listen, to be still and listen. To get it right.

On the other hand (and there is always, it seems, another hand), the stochastic is perhaps all there is. There is no knowing; all that can be hoped for is that something will hit the mark. Or perhaps there is no mark, no centre: and where the arrows hit most must be declared the intended bull's eye.

LADY OF THE LAKE

In July 2007, Walter's son Jack calls: Walter has had a heart attack. "We're short-handed," Jack says. "We're going to have to leave the fruit on the trees at Beauvoir, unless you want to hire someone to do it. Thought I should let you know."

Oh, it happens: fruit left on the trees. She has seen it happen. It is only a small tragedy. But the waste. A small chance that Alex, who is unemployed again, might be interested. Possibly he might have some friends. She'll ask him.

But surprisingly, half an hour after her phone call, she has a whole army of pickers: not Alex, who's away, but Tasha and Steve and Debbie; Cynthia and Justin, who profess to having always wanted to pick fruit, and even Kevin, who will drive up from the coast, taking time off work, bringing his former wife, his stepsons.

So they have become orchardists: they have camped out here, ten of them, all weekend. Kevin's former wife is Native, or, as she should say, First Nations. She remembers Cynthia has told her that Kevin had been with this woman the longest — perhaps seven or eight years — of all of his relationships. But Sidonie has never met her, and nobody had mentioned Celeste's background. The boys, Cashiel and Fearon, who look about eleven and thirteen, are lighter-skinned than their mother.

"Celeste has picked cherries before," Sidonie observes, watching the woman sling her bucket over one arm and hoist a ladder, balancing it on her shoulders.

Kevin says, "Oh, yeah — she grew up around here, and did some picking as a kid, didn't you, Celeste?"

"I did," she says. She has the soft, slightly guttural voice of one who has spoken a native language as a child, Sidonie notices, surprised.

"She's one of the Cedrics," Kevin says. Sidonie remembers the family, remembers Dolores and Sam, who were not much older than her. "Dolores," Sidonie says aloud, and Celeste says, "She was my auntie. She's dead." Celeste is a little reserved, wary.

"What's the story with her and Kevin?" Steve asks Cynthia, and Cynthia shrugs.

The boys seem easy with Kevin: joking, looking at him with open faces, though they are, perhaps naturally, very shy with the other adults. The boys pick slowly, for the first couple of hours eating more than they put into their pails, and then slacking off their picking, complaining of tiredness and boredom. But Steve and Kevin are both easy on them. She remembers now Mr. Rilke and Mr. Tanaka and Father would holler at her and Alice and Walt, holler at and drive them. They were incompetent, slow, rough on the fruit, moved their ladders carelessly.

Perhaps it was necessary. Everyone's livelihood depended on the older children, the adolescents, working as hard as adults. But how they all, almost all, grew to hate the constant reprimands and corrections. And to hate, perhaps by association, the trees, the monotony, the extremes of weather, the physical labour.

They work through the rows steadily, a small swarm of human locusts. Debbie brings tubs of meat sandwiches, ice chests of water and pop. They work all Saturday; at three, in the heat of the day, Kevin takes the boys and Celeste, Tasha and Justin, down to the lake in the back of the truck. The rest of them lie down in the shade of the spruces.

Steve says, "I should have brought my generator; I could get the pump working and we'd have water in the house."

Cynthia says, "Where's Alex?"

"Don't know," Steve says, a little angrily. "He took off a few days ago in his car with his sleeping bag and a few clothes."

"I'm thinking he might have gone to Whistler to visit Jessica," Debbie says.

Sidonie had asked the same question, when she arrived at the orchard earlier, and Justin had said, with a sidelong look at Tasha, that Alex had gone to look for something he needed, which somehow didn't sound quite as legitimate as Debbie's explanation. She hopes he is not engaging in some risky enterprise. He has been restless since spring, unsettled, at times almost sullen.

It is too bad that they can't manage to pull off Alex's idea. But there are too many impossibilities.

When they're too tired to pick any more that day, they all go down to the lake again. A light evening breeze ruffles the water, and the wavelets lap and shuffle the small polished stones. A hiss, a drag, a click: *shellac, shellac*, the pebbles say. The breeze, blissfully cool, smells of sage and dust, of mud, of cool wet leaves, of iron, of fruit esters, of limestone, of the lake itself. Sidonie has brought her bathing suit. "You're going to swim?" Fearon asks, and Cashiel scoffs, "Put her toes in, just. You know old ladies."

Sidonie swims out into the lake in a wide arc. The water in the evening light waves green and gold around her, vanishing both to the north and south in rounded blue points. The hills curve, deeper blue, on both sides. The lake is a blue-green egg, herself the centre. That's a trick of perspective, though, thinking the lake is oval; it's really a long, narrow, hundred-kilometre snake, slightly curved, between a kilometre and five kilometres in width.

She swims out a hundred metres or so, then begins looping back, toward the cluster of pilings, which rise perhaps three metres from the water. There is still a ladder. She climbs it, not as quickly as she had done as a girl.

"Be careful, Miss," one of the small boys perched above says to her. "There's broken pilings under the water."

"Yes, there are," she says.

When she pulls herself up, the boys leap from the posts. One plunges head first, another feet first, into the green and gold mirror below. In a few seconds, which seem longer, they emerge in little silver explosions of spray.

She knows she is showing off. But there is a point of honour here. She measures the distance, glances back at the others on the shore. Only Justin and Cynthia are watching her, though Justin nudges Tasha to look. She focuses on the clear jade surface, flexes her feet, raises her arms over her head, arches her back. The boys below her are quiet. She springs outward and upward. The air rushes by her only briefly (fifteen feet per second, she thinks) before she cuts cleanly into the water. The rush of water against her skin, the slowing, in the dim depths. Deep here, but she turns, thrusts with her feet, her thighs perfect machines in this element, follows her own trail of silver bubbles back into the light.

The next day Sidonie wakes with her arms and shoulders at once locked rigid and on fire from the repetitive motion of the picking. She can hardly pull a T-shirt over her head. But here is still a day's worth of cherries to pick.

The day is even hotter than before. She considers opening up the house to give everyone a place to escape the heat and to rest, but decides no, no. Everyone complains of sore shoulders and arms. Under the trees, she sees from her ladder Kevin massaging Celeste's wrists, pressing his lips to them.

Celeste laughing.

When they're picking in adjacent trees, Steve says to her, "I picked up this interesting book at a flea market. It's called *The '60s: Montreal Thinks Big.* Do you know it? It's about architecture."

She knows it, though she hasn't thought about it for years. She is not surprised by Steve's comment; Cynthia has told her that he buys and reads his way indiscriminately through boxes of second-hand books.

"It's really theoretical," Steve says. "I can't get my head around a lot of it. But it mentions your husband — your late husband, I should say. Adam St. Regis. That's him, right? Same last name as Cynthia."

Yes.

"I didn't know he worked on Habitat," Steve says. "I've always been interested in that. I'd like to see it."

"I lived in it," Sidonie says. "From the time it was built until, oh, the mid-eighties. Adam lived there until he died."

"I didn't know that!" Stephen says, and she thinks in his voice is something of the regret of a possible life. Her fault: she had abandoned him. As she had others. Will they continue to ambush her, these losses?

Coming in for a break, she finds the boys stretched out on the lawn, under the trees. "You can come up onto the porch," she says. "It's cooler." The younger boy, Cash, shows the whites of his eyes. "I'm scared to go near that house. I heard someone was murdered in there!"

"Where did you hear that?"

"My dad told us. My other dad."

"Is it true?" the older boy, Fearon, asks. He is going to be good-looking, Sidonie thinks, with his clean jawline, his high cheekbones and deep-set, almond-shaped eyes, which are green, not black, and his dark hair and long thick eyelashes.

"Yes, it's true," she admits.

"Who was it?"

"My sister," she says. "Steve and Kevin and Cynthia's mother. Her name was Alice." And as she says this, she feels a sigh, a release of air from the open front door.

"Did her old man do it?" Fearon asks, knowingly.

"Yes."

"Did you used to live here, then?" Cash asks.

"Yes," Sidonie says. "I was born in this house. And my sister too."

"Did you have electricity?"

"Oh my goodness. Yes."

"My grandma didn't, in her house," Fearon says. "It must have been boring without computers or TV."

"We had a record player," Sidonie says. "And a radio. And we read books and magazines, and drew a lot. And spent a lot of time outside."

"Fearon can draw," Cash says.

"Not really," Fearon says, but he is pleased.

"My dad, my real dad, is from here too," Cashiel says. "Do you know him?"

"What is his name?"

"Greg Clare."

"I know the Clares," Sidonie says. "I went to school with Richard Clare."

"He's our grandfather," Cashiel says. Then looks at her sideways, warily. "He doesn't know us, though. He doesn't like that our dad got together with our mom."

Fearon, next to him, scowls.

"I see," Sidonie says.

Cashiel says, "He's rich, though. Our dad says. He's a property developer. He's made, like, a billion dollars. But we don't get any of it, eh."

Fearon says, "I wouldn't take it anyhow."

Something is expected of her. But what? She gets up, dusts off the seat of her khaki walking shorts, smooths the legs down. An old woman's shins, between the hem of the shorts and the tops of her grey socks and hiking boots. The skin translucent, the sharp bone shining through, the calves puckered and rope-veined. Whose old body?

"There are no ghosts in this house," she says. "Many happy things took place here, and the house has stood empty a long time. It's not haunted, only empty."

"You can have it," Sidonie says. "You can have Beauvoir. The land and the house." She has made this offer before, when Father died, and Alice had rejected it. "I don't want it," Alice had said. But now Sidonie makes it again. "It's yours if you want it."

"I want it," Alice says.

They have climbed up the granite outcropping to the north of the orchard, and are sitting on the sun-warmed rock. It's June and the trees are ranged below them in their rows of green foliage: the cherries dark, large-leafed; the peaches a bright sharp glossy green, tinged with pink; the leaves of the apple trees matte, a more countrified light green.

The lake below, a long pool of pale cool blue today — cornflower blue. Alice used to wear that colour. A glitter of wavelets drifts like a diamanté spray corsage. The mountains across the lake are a curtain of purple.

Alice says, "I do want it. But how will it work? How can we do this?"

"It's simple," Sidonie says. "We get a lawyer and I sign it over."

But Alice doesn't answer. She must have meant something else by her question.

It is 1973. Sidonie has come home to help Mother die. They do not say that: they say that she has come to help Mother. But Mother is dying. A nurse has come to stay with her so that she can die at home. Sidonie is paying for this. The hospital would be free, but on the day when it becomes apparent that Mother's pain has increased to a point of unmanageability, Mother weeps, and says that she doesn't want to be moved, doesn't want to go into hospital where everything will be strange.

"Mother has never been in the hospital," Alice says. "She doesn't want to spend her last few days in there."

Can this be true? But Alice is right; she and Sidonie were born at home, and none of them has ever gone to the hospital. Even Sidonie's broken ankle, when she fell from the shed roof, was set by Dr. Stewart right on the kitchen table.

"We were brought up in the nineteenth century," she says to Alice.

On that day, Mother moans and moans and Alice, coming outside to where Sidonie is hoeing the garden (for it has all gone suddenly to weeds, with the last stage of Mother's illness), puts her face in her hands and rocks and moans as well, as if she were connected by strong but invisible threads to Mother. Dr. Stewart has been there earlier and given Mother a morphine shot, and there have been a few hours of respite. But it doesn't last, and Mother needs another one quickly, and the sheets need changing and washing.

"We need to call the ambulance," Sidonie says sensibly. "Mother needs to be in the hospital now."

But Alice cries and bangs her head against the porch posts, and Sidonie says: "Alright. A nurse."

The nurse needs a hospital bed for Mother, and also an IV stand, various dressings and pads and disinfectants, which Sidonie brings home from town in the truck.

So now Mother lies in a light doze, and Sidonie and Alice are able to escape from the house. Alice goes home to do her own housework and feed her children, and Sidonie continues to work in the garden. Peas, lettuce, strawberries, radishes all to be picked. Watering and hoeing.

Alice comes up to Beauvoir every day, while the children are in school, and she and Sidonie clean and sort cupboards and take walks, long walks, through the orchard, to the lake, up through the bush, to the south, to the old gold mine, and to the old reservoir, which is shrinking: a new irrigation system has been constructed, one with underground pipes, and the reservoir, no longer in use, has diminished to a small pond, ringed with cattails and upstart poplars. The small ponds near the reservoir have already become dry marshes, and the water pipe, along with the glade of rainforest flora that ran alongside it, has completely disappeared.

There is a deep, peaceable silence between Sidonie and Alice, now. It is as if, with Mother dying, they have been born fresh into new, less irritated skins. Sidonie doesn't say this, doesn't comment or speak much. What is there to say? She has stepped out of her life temporarily, and has slipped into this one with such ease that she is only aware a sort of surprised gratitude. She goes days without thinking of Adam or of her job. When she does think of them, it is as if they are faraway places, stories she has been reading and may return to or not.

Alice, though, talks. She says, "Remember the year we had all that snow, and we made the big fort? And remember the storm, and the beach ball? Remember canning, all that work, and always so hot? Remember Hugh's hiking club?"

She says, "I am angry that it took so long to find out what was wrong with Cynthia. I got measles from the kids, you know, when I was pregnant with her. Her eardrums were damaged. The doctor up in Horsefly was practically useless, an old drunk. Dr. Stewart knew right away, when we moved back here. Cynthia's quite bright, you know. She's not retarded, like everyone says."

Alice says, "People don't like Buck. He's so difficult. But he's a good man in some ways. He had a hard childhood—his father used to beat the crap out of him. But he tried to look after his brothers and Lottie, you know. And he's really patient with Cynthia."

Alice and Sidonie pick and slice up the strawberries and put them in freezer bags in Mother's freezer, which will be Alice's freezer. Alice says, "You'll visit, won't you? You and Adam. You can come and stay with us any time."

She says, "It'll be so good for the kids, to have this space. They'll be able to roam in the hills like we did."

They climb Spion Kopje, and sit near the peak on the west slope, overlooking the range of mountains, the lake spread out below like a puddle of some rare liquid metal. Alice says, "I wasn't very nice to you when we were children. I can't explain why, but I regret it every day," which is somehow horribly embarrassing for Sidonie to hear.

Alice says, "I'm sorry for what I said about Gordon Defoe. I know what happened. It wasn't your fault."

She says, "I wanted to be an artist, you know. I wanted to go to art school. But Mother and Father didn't think that was a good idea. They thought I'd be corrupted, become a Bohemian, get pregnant and have abortions and die of TB in some squalid ghetto. And I didn't think I was good enough to make it."

Alice talks about her failed year at college, her 1957 year in the education program at Victoria College. She says, "I never had enough time. Mother had set up for me to board with these people who made me work as an au pair every afternoon and evening and weekend, as well as pay rent. She thought it was a good deal, that we were getting a reduction on the rent. I found out from the other girls that I was being exploited. But Mother thought it would be a great thing; the husband was an officer at Naden and they had a hyphenated last name. I never had any time to study or have a social life. Even then I didn't do that badly. I failed my practicum because the examiner was an old biddy who took off points for me not drawing the window blinds to the same height, and my skirt being an inch too short."

She says, "I'm going to take some art classes at the new college. Did you know that? Some drawing and painting classes. This fall, now that Cynthia's starting school. Do you think I'll be good enough?"

You've always been good enough, Sidonie thought.

She does not remember if she said this. She hopes she said it, but she cannot be sure she did.

One evening, that summer of 1973, Hugh, who is home for a visit, and his brother Graham come over with a pan of lemon bars that Mrs. Inglis has baked, and Masao and Walt drop by as well. The six of them sit on the porch in the long bright June evening, watching the bats and nighthawks, listening to the crickets, talking. Graham is in a good state. He makes his old dry elaborate jokes, and is gallant, mildly flirtatious towards Alice. Courtly, that's the word. And Hugh has stories about Brazil, where he is working now. Masao talks about the store and music, and Walt about the orchards, and all of them about politics. (The NDP: a good thing, on the whole, though the older folks don't think so.)

They play music on Masao's tape deck: BTO, Led Zeppelin, Cream, The Stones, CCR, Cat Stevens. Masao sings along: *And if I*

ever lose my hands, lose my power, lose my land/ Oh if I ever lose my
hands — I won't have to work no more.

"I thought it was *plow*," Alice says. "Lose my *plow*."

"No; *power*," Hugh says with certainty.

(Now, she thinks: *Moonshadow*. She had never made the connection with the Schubert song before.)

The June air is like warm milk. When the light finally begins to wobble, at 10:30 or so, Alice brings out a tray of drinks: "Long Island Iced Tea," she says. "Sort of. It's all I could make with what was in the house." But miraculously, a flask of rye appears out of Masao's car, and Hugh produces a bottle of rum, three-quarters full. "The loaves and fishes," Masao says.

"It's a good thing liquor doesn't go off," Graham says, reading the label of Alice's bottle. "This is about twenty years old."

"I recently drank a bottle of one-hundred-year-old sherry," Hugh says.

"Was it a bribe?" Graham asks.

"Yes," says Hugh. "The Brazilian government is very generous with Canadian engineers. But I can tell you, that sherry had gone off."

"Maybe it's hard liquor that doesn't go off," Alice says, mediating, and Hugh scoffs. "Who says *hard liquor* these days?"

"I do," says Sidonie. "I say it every day around five o'clock in the imperative mood."

Walt chuckles, a deep, liquid chuckle that reminds Sidonie of his father, Mr. Rilke, and that seems part of the summer night, like the crickets and the occasional call of the nighthawks.

Lying back in the big wooden chairs on the porch (they are called Adirondack chairs, Sidonie knows now, though she never heard the term in her childhood), lying back in the dusk with their scavenged drinks, their light conversation, Sidonie thinks: we could be all teenagers again, or maybe young adults. It is a night out of time, an evening that we never had, that we'll never have again.

They have each gone back to their younger, essential selves. They have shed twenty years, and returned to an earlier time, but a time that didn't exist. For the six of them, twenty years ago this dynamic wasn't possible. Hugh and Graham were almost never home; Alice was aloof, burning; Sidonie still an awkward adolescent; Walt tongue-tied with anger and self-consciousness, and Masao wary and on edge. They couldn't have managed it. And yet what they have made this evening, natural and sweet as it is, is only illusion. It's an illusion because they do not meet like this, because each of them has had to shed a thick shell of everyday being to meet like this. It's an illusion because they are not, as they appear, a witty, charming, affectionate group of young people, but rather a random meeting of middle-aged strangers. Graham, the oldest, is thirty-six; Sidonie and Walt, the youngest, are twenty-nine. They do not see each other often in their everyday lives. Though they played together hours on end, day after day, as children, though they are siblings and neighbours, they are still strangers.

They are disconnected thoroughly from their earlier lives: only Walt still works the orchards. But this, this illusionary evening, has produced their essential selves. What does that then say?

Graham says, "Are you still with us, young Sidonie?" And Hugh says, "She's addled by the hard liquor."

Sidonie says, "I was wondering if we'll ever all be together again," and Graham says, "That is the one question you're not allowed to ask," while Alice simultaneously says, "We're always together. None of us have really left." Which was not true; which was only Alice being poetic, under the influence. But which Sidonie has always remembered.

It is then that she realizes what Alice is planning. How Alice has delayed taking Beauvoir on, assuming the responsibility all this time, not because she has not wanted Beauvoir, but because she has not wanted to let it fall to Buck. How Alice has become stronger, how she is planning to remove Buck from the picture. She will ditch him, in the phrase used in Marshall's Landing. Mother would not have countenanced this; Mother, tight-lipped, drawing herself in visibly when the subjects of divorce or remarriage were mentioned.

In the milky half-darkness, she sees now Masao's head on Alice's lap, and something drops into place with geometric perfection, lucidity, beauty. She will move back: she and Alice and Masao will run Beauvoir. It is as simple as that.

But the next morning, parking in front of the IGA in the plaza, having driven down for milk, bread, she sees a familiar-looking figure get out of the truck parked next to hers, walk into the store without glancing back at her. She is frozen to her seat: a little death. It's Gordon Defoe.

She flies back to Montreal two days later.

Hugh on the telephone again: "Can't you put a stop to this? It's just not reasonable. It's not what I intended at all. They just won't listen to me. It's a disaster." And more of the same. She knows by now that Alex has absconded with Hugh's daughter Ingrid; that Alex's mysterious trip the month before had been to Toronto: he had driven there and brought Ingrid back. She knows that Ingrid is staying with Alex, refusing to enroll in the engineering program in Toronto, as Hugh had planned she would. That Alex and Ingrid are planning to live in Alex's parents' basement, to start looking for some land for an organic garden. Tasha has told her all this: Stephen and Debbie, apparently, are too annoyed to talk about it.

"What can I do?" Hugh asks, plaintively.

"Give them a dowry," Sidonie says.

They are all so angry. But what of it? Grown children are for letting go of. There is no binding or pruning them into shape without horrible consequences.

In the fall of 1986, after Cynthia leaves, Sidonie asks Adam for a divorce, and moves, temporarily, into a hotel. He refuses for about six months, then asks her to meet him to discuss how they will proceed. He has fallen in love with someone else, he says. He tells her this in person at dinner: not at one of their usual haunts, but at a new hotel restaurant. It's ostentatious with black marble and art nouveau décor. Around them women gleam in big-shouldered satin pleats, shiny mounds of hair. It is the Age of Shiny Things. Adam wants to partake. Why shouldn't he? He has worked hard, has used his brains and charm and connections to move ahead in his career. Has not stinted at home, either. Has given Cynthia a decade of indulged, loved childhood. Has given Sidonie two decades of a comfortable home, of the most interesting of the culture and conversation that Montreal has to offer.

And she has been perhaps too austere to receive it. It has all fallen on stony ground. The parched, baked landscape of her unyielding self. She has not intended harm, but harm has come from her.

She refuses alimony: "I have my salary," she says. "My own salary and pension." Adam offers to let her have the apartment, but she knows that he wants to keep it, the apartment in the striking building that he helped design.

She finds herself another place back in their old neighbourhood, where they had first lived. And she is happy to have it, and what is left of their furnishings after Adam has claimed his piano, his van der Rohe chairs and Saarinen tables, the grotesque sculptural pieces he has acquired. "Marc likes them," he says. He is half ashamed, half intoxicated with his freedom.

With little furniture, with bare floors, her new-old apartment is pleasingly bleak. Sidonie comes home from her lab sometimes to lie full length on the wood floors, to listen to recordings of Bach and Sibelius in the dusk, in the almost empty space. And feels safe, free. She remembers how, before Alice's death, she had determined to leave Adam; how she had scoured the city for an apartment. She hadn't been able to find one; she had been, she suspects now, too attached to the one she was living in. Lucky, lucky, to have a place to herself now.

"It's a bit monastic," says Clara. She shows her loyalty to Sidonie by not speaking to Adam for a year after their separation, as if she's in mourning. Anita is more detached: it is better, she says, to be true to the body. To not live with lies.

Sidonie is still young: forty. She is introduced to friends of friends, some of whom she agrees to have dinner with, or more. She doesn't form any deep attachments. She works, gives papers, travels.

She undergoes therapy, and smooths out some of her more notice-able social wrinkles.

In 1993 Clara calls to say that Adam is dying: he has cancer. his liver is shutting down. He is conscious, but not expected to live more than a week. He is asking for her.

When she finds him in his hospital room, she sees a mummy: his flesh has dried up, and he is deep yellow, gilded like a mummy.

"Sidonie," he says. "Ah, Sidonie. My beautiful lost girl."

It is only nostalgia: a sentimental longing to experience some real or imagined former pleasure.

"Don't, Adam," she says.

Arid, stony ground. Though she knows something about what can grow, what can bloom from the dry limestone earth.

A strange sight, their cars all lined up in the driveway at Beauvoir as if the von Tälers were home and entertaining. As if they had never left, but were having a family celebration: Peter and Frances, Alice and Sidonie, their children and their children's children. "So this is what your place was like, Dad?" Ingrid asks, and Hugh answers, "More or less, though I always thought Beauvoir has a better view. The land is steeper."

They all stand on the verandah, looking down at the lake.

"You can smell the fruit growing," Alex says, inhaling.

"Do you want to go inside?" Sidonie asks, though she hopes that nobody will. But they all do want to, so she produces the key and opens the front door.

A rush of stale but cool air; already the land outside has absorbed the morning sun and warmed the air, but the house is shaded by the stand of spruce, now massive, at its southwest end. She had always known that she wouldn't live here, that she would be the one to leave. The uselessness of nostalgia: shut the door on it.

Hugh and Cynthia stand at the dining room window, looking out, but the others move from room to room, and climb the stairs to the second storey. What do they want to see it for? They all look inward, speculative, as if trying to see this as a home. Debbie is studying the big tile stove and mantle. Justin and Tasha are, like children, trying out the old switches. (They don't work, of course; the electricity has been off for years.) Steve taps on walls, sniffs.

Sidonie, mounting the stairs, glimpses, through the open doorway of her parents' old bedroom, Alex and Ingrid simply standing by the window, embracing.

Alice and Sidonie's room. It had always seemed luminous to Sidonie. But now, with the spruce grown up outside the window, the room is less bright; instead, aqueous, glimmering blue-green.

Justin and Tasha have come in to investigate Alice's old room, and Sidonie moves back out into the hallway. Steve comes up the stairs — she hears him also pause for an instant and then resume his tread, as he passes her parents' bedroom — and coming down the hall, says, "By the shape of the ceiling downstairs, there was a leak in the bathroom. Can I take a look?"

Sidonie moves aside to let him enter, and then looks in herself. The honeycombed tile, with its pattern of white and aqua, has been torn up, and the stained floorboards are exposed. Steve squats, reaches out, taps the wood.

"Not so bad," he says. "No rot."

Is he thinking that it can be saved?

Downstairs, Hugh says to Ingrid, "Well. Enjoy the tour?" and she raises an eyebrow at him, doesn't answer. Alex and Debbie have gone into the old garden. Alex is poking at the soil with a ballpoint pen, crouched, intent, very like Stephen had been upstairs. Then he puts his hands into the soil, scoops up a double handful, lets it fall. Surprisingly, touches his loamy finger to his tongue, tastes it. All around him the pigweed, knapweed, thistles sending up their determined little shoots among the dry stalks of last year's weeds.

A mess. Mother would be heartbroken. But no: a foolish thought. Mother is dead. She has no thought for this.

Alex, sitting in the garden, running the dry soil through his hands. "This is good soil," he says. "It's been built up."

Forty years of digging in compost.

Steve says, "What happened to all of the flowers? I remember flower beds, perennials, around the house," and kicks through the dried weeds to reveal the stalks of peonies, upthrust clogged corms of iris, the rampant unkempt tentacles of the roses.

"All still here," Sidonie says, in wonder.

Then Debbie comes over with a cry of triumph: in her fist a dozen red raspberries. There is a clamour as they all gather to take one. They are a little small: not enough water. But the sun in them fizzes on the tongue.

Where needs must, needs will, Sidonie's mother had been fond of saying. Now Sidonie thinks this, surveying the drawings Kevin has unrolled on her dining room table. The others are coming later for dinner, but Kevin had something to show Sidonie first. He leans over the table, beefy, shaven, tattooed; she notices his straight, thin mouth and eyebrows for the first time as familiar. He has gone to some trouble, using full-sized drafting paper, proper scale, a neat draughtsman's printing. She's seen enough of Adam's work to read the plans. It's Beauvoir, with an addition to the northeast angling off the kitchen: a large open room, glassed on two sides, with a fireplace at one end, tables, washrooms. A wide verandah. And here, plans for a refit of the kitchen: two long work areas extend the entire span, with oversized rectangles for ovens and refrigerators. Or rather, it's not Beauvoir, but a new version of it. The old house re-envisioned as a house and restaurant.

Kevin turns over another sheet, and there's the whole upper part of Beauvoir, the bench with additional buildings labeled "greenhouses," "storage," "market." Garden areas are marked off. The symbols architects use for deciduous trees indicate a small orchard, and other symbols denote a perimeter of conifers.

And a third sheet, with an addition to the southwest end of the house: an upper storey with bedrooms and bathrooms, a lower storey labeled "spa."

"Did you do all this?" Sidonie asks. "It looks professional."

"My ideas. And Steve's and Alex's. Cynthia drew it up."

Of course: Cynthia at Adam's side in front of the slanted board, all those evenings.

"So, what are we looking at here?" she asks, but she already knows. It's as if these drawings have existed in her own brain for months now, or years, dormant, hidden, and have just been brought to light.

On the telephone, Clara says disapprovingly, "You know that this is patriarchy, don't you? Primogeniture. Alex getting the lot."

"There's really not enough to divide up," Sidonie says. "The curse of farming."

"Ha!" Clara says. Then: "Did you know that Adam left Cynthia money when he died?"

She had not known.

"It wasn't official," Clara says. "There wasn't time. It was a verbal request to Anita and me, which I'm ashamed we have not yet followed through with. But there is a fund. Should we give it to her now, or wait until the boy is old enough to have some sensible ideas?"

Dinner, Sunday night, at Stephen's. Surprisingly, the television is on; someone wants to catch a story on the news. The babble of it forms a distracting counterpoint to the conversations at the table, and Sidonie, whose chair is nearly facing the TV, who can see it through the doorway between dining room and living room, is distracted, irritated. When the news comes on, it catches her attention, in spite of herself. There's a segment at the end on the new bridge construction, and out of the tail of her eye, just as the presenter is saying something about the dedication of the original bridge nearly fifty years ago, she catches sight of Alice.

Everyone stops chewing and talking, and she realizes that she has gasped Alice's name aloud, and is pointing at the screen with her fork, as if it were a remote control. Stop! Stop! But the program has moved on; they're now showing what looks like giant concrete pontoons.

"Alice!" she has said.

"Where?" Cynthia and Stephen exclaim in unison, their heads swiveling, their voices unguarded.

"Where? Why was she there?"

Sidonie has to think. There had been a crowd of people in out-of-date clothes, some long-vanished public faces, a shot of the old bridge with its moveable span. "It must be old film footage. Alice was at the opening of the first bridge; yes. She was part of a group of people who greeted Princess Margaret — yes, that's it."

"Why Grandma Alice?" Tasha asks.

Sidonie says, "She was Lady of the Lake the year before. They wanted someone presentable to introduce to the princess."

"What is Lady of the Lake?" Justin asks, and Alex says, "Local beauty pageant. Like being Miss Okanagan," and Tasha says "Yuck!" but Justin says, "Grandma Alice was a beauty queen? Awesome!"

Yes, Alice the beauty queen.

There is discussion: can a copy of the tape be acquired? Who would have it? Would it be on the internet?

It has been a shock: Alice walking a little at a diagonal, her face arranging itself into a smile as she became aware of the camera. The swish of her white dress around her knees almost audible.

Somewhere, this — and perhaps more — exists on black-and-white photographic film. It can be copied — perhaps digitally — and they all can see it over and over.

SAGE AND PLUM

By spring 2008, the house has been mostly renovated. Steve and Alex have been working on it almost full time; still, parts have to be subcontracted to trades, and between labour and materials, there has been a hemorrhaging of cash. Both Steve's and Sidonie's houses have been colonized by stacks of architectural and organic farming magazines and books. The house is re-wired and plumbed and insulated. Everyone had agreed on keeping the old plastered walls, so holes have been drilled, new wiring threaded through. The electricians had grunted and sworn; it would have been much easier, they said, to have pulled off the wallboard, put up new dry-wall. The old copper and lead plumbing has been removed and replaced with new synthetic, and Steve has sold the copper for enough to pay for the new pipes. The insulation has been blown in from the outside between the posts and beams, the holes resealed. New windows have been bought, the old too fragile to re-glaze. Sidonie had argued for aluminum — less expensive — but Steve and Cynthia had insisted on custom windows made to look like the old. The roof tiles have been replaced where needed, the tile works in

Vancouver, from which the originals had been ordered, still owned by the same Italian family.

They have all put in hundreds of hours of labour collectively: sanding, painting, varnishing, re-pointing, scrubbing, scraping and polishing.

Sidonie says, "It probably would have been cheaper and simpler to rebuild," but Cynthia argues that the existing house is stronger, better, than what they would have arrived at.

"We have earned the house," she says. "We have all got our fingerprints all over it." And it is beautiful: the wood floors gleam, the granite slab in the kitchen, trimmed off and polished, reflects light from the windows during the day and the hanging linen-shaded light fixtures at night. Restaurant refrigerators and a gas range fill the old kitchen, and the dining room contains a few tables and chairs; an addition will house the rest, as they expand.

Some of what Cynthia has called serendipity has occurred with the furniture: visiting Walt in his convalescence, Sidonie is surprised by his offer of two dressers, a dining table, a suite of chairs. "They're from the house, from your house," Walt says. "You gave them to me when you closed it up, back in 73. Also some beds and tables, but they haven't survived our boys. You gave us all this."

"You can take them," Christina says. "We're getting new for our condo. These won't fit."

Steve, seeing the chairs, is excited; they have been made by a craftsman; they can be copied, he says, for the restaurant.

Kevin, Celeste, and the boys will live in the old house for now, it has been decided. It will be more convenient, with Kevin cooking, Celeste running the restaurant. A second house will be built later. Sidonie has some ideas about this: she has the beginnings of an idea of a small house, a Craftsman-style house in a copse of ponderosa. She sees, in prescient flashes, herself working at a wooden kitchen table, sees warm pine, a small deck, a door opening to a herb garden, window boxes with scarlet geraniums.

Anita visits. Sidonie drives with her out to Beauvoir, where the foundations for the restaurant addition are being poured. She waves to Steve and Alex, who, hard-hatted, are working the stony porridge down between the forms with long paddles. They wave back. She leads Anita out of the way of the trucks to the porch. She has not planned to go inside — it is not her house, now — but Kevin is in, sees her from the kitchen, opens the door for them. He is trying out a soup, he says: if they wait, he will let them test it for him.

They walk around the garden and orchard. Anita says, "It *is* a little like Italy. Lake Maggiore, maybe. But the light is different — more northern. It's bluer and throws harder shadows."

Sidonie has loaned to the restaurant the art that doesn't work in her new house; here, against the older plaster, the lower ceilings, the oils and photographic prints come alive.

"You've kept the Prudence Heward," Anita says. "That's good — I've always thought it was a good likeness."

"It isn't me."

"It is, though, in a way. Look. The hair, the colouring, the shape of the face. The way the model is looking at the space in front of the viewer, as if she's paying attention to something nobody else can see."

Along the inside of the dining room, half a dozen of Anita's photographs are lined up in their copper frames — black and white shots of rooftops, ironwork, textured walls. Anita looks at them critically. "Some of these aren't bad," she says. "I remember taking them — I was trying to make a narrative of the Plateau district. But they still look too European, don't they? I didn't see that at the time."

They are served Kevin's soup, which he is refining in preparation for the menu. Anita laughs when she tastes it. "A good joke," she says. "The story of the homely borscht, deconstructed." Sidonie is bewildered, but Kevin leans over the table eagerly. "You picked up on that? The way the ingredients have been incarnated as references?"

"Oh, yes; the chiffoniered pickled beet and cabbage on the floating latke," Anita says. "Very witty. And the soup is so light, like a broth."

Kevin looks very happy. "And did you catch the apple?"

"Apple cider for the pickling, correct? And a little apple butter on the latke?"

"You should move out here!" Kevin says. "You'd be an amazing consultant. We should have you write the menu for us. Hell, we should have you write reviews. A plant."

Anita laughs. "Maybe I will," she says, "if Sidonie won't move back to Montreal with me. You've no idea how much I miss her."

They are flirting, Anita and Kevin. She is amazed, as always, to notice this, to understand that people are capable of simultaneous awareness of these attractions, that they have the energy and will to enact them. From the outside, it is like watching the ballet of iridescent, scintillating birds. Only they are *her* birds: they are beings otherwise familiar to her, otherwise known.

Would Anita move here? Live with her, perhaps? But it is difficult to imagine Anita away from her galleries, her network of artists and café owners and denizens of urban parks and streets.

They drive down the hill to the lake, and sit on Sidonie's tartan car blanket over the small flat oval stones. The lake is glass-clear, and glimmers with the ochre and cream and charcoal of the pebble bed.

The little throb of the water at the shore. The damp rustle of new poplar leaves. The taste in the air, of limestone and green sap. The sun and sap-smell and colours run through the veins, up through the skull, down through the soles of the feet, sewing her to the earth, to the overarching sky. She breathes, is conscious both of her own breathing, of the air and water and stone around her. An unfolding, a settling.

Anita is looking through her camera, taking shot after shot. The camera makes an almost mechanical shutter sound; an add-in, Sidonie thinks, to make the camera sound like an older one, to make its action more tangible, more connected.

Alex and Ingrid move into the Quonset hut where the ladders and machines used to be housed, for the summer; Alex is looking for a second-hand mobile home that can be towed onto the property. They share the corrugated half-cylinder with their new tractor, their rakes and hoes and harrows, bins and crates and plastic sheeting and tubing. They have a little stove and a bar fridge running off a long extension cord from the house, a sink with cold water only, a cast-off sofa and bed. The hut smells of loam and sex and occasionally of marijuana. Sidonie visits them, bringing a bottle of wine, which she and Alex share, and bottles of blackcurrant syrup and soda for Ingrid. Alex has shaved his head and beard, for the heat, and also for ease in washing, he says. Sidonie thinks that he resembles her father now, and says so. Ingrid says, "I think so too: Cynthia showed us some photos. He'll be a good orchardist like his great-grandfather, yeah. He is studying all the time, when he isn't working in the orchard or on the house."

She sees that Alex has tacked up charts and graphs with spray schedules: spraying has now become a fine science, with applications timed to emergence of insect species, to mean temperature readings, to traps. Alex shows her some of the tools: the pheromone traps, the wrap-around bands, the degree-day charts. He talks about the sprays: they have names now like Sniper, Assail, Confirm, Intrepid, Admire. "It's very complex," he says. "I never was one for memorizing stuff at school, but this is interesting." He talks about toxicity, about chloro-nicotinyls and organo-phosphates. He says, "I thought we could do it all with pheromones and stick insects and chickens, but I don't think we can. Not with our labour pool and the concentration of orchards in this area."

Sidonie remembers her father tapping the limbs, and tells Alex about the white cloths, the insect counting. His eyes glow. "Thanks, yes! That's just the sort of thing I need to know."

Hugh and Sidonie take a break from being carpenters' assistants and lie on the lawn in the shade of the spruce cluster. A group of finches hops and twitters in the spruce branches; one of the males tips back his crimson head and warbles a spiral of high, clear notes.

"Purple," Sidonie says.

"Highly unlikely," Hugh says. "Probably House."

"No; that warble is Purple. And he has a little point to his head — it's not flat. And no streaks on his belly."

Hugh sits up. "You're right. What are they doing here? Used to be all House here. The bird population is decimated."

"The birds are coming back," Sidonie says. "We had a flock of goldfinches in that bit of fallow field the other day. And Steve gets three different varieties of hummingbirds at his feeder."

"Are we going to just lie here and argue about birds?" Hugh says.

"Yes. I think so."

Justin tumbles off the roof of the restaurant addition and breaks his ankle. After a few days Cynthia drives him to Sidonie's and dumps him off, unceremoniously.

"I've had enough of him," she says.

Now Justin talks to Sidonie again, but his discourse is a long note of complaint. "I want to be out of here," he says. "This terrible small town. I want to see something else."

"Well, go," she says.

"I can't. I have to finish my degree. I have to take care of my mom."

She sees, for the first time, his grandfather Buck in him. A shiftiness, a snarl that has usurped his innocence.

And then she sees Alice too. What is it? It is the look of an animal gnawing off its own trapped limb, that's what it is.

Driving him back home later, they pass, between the cemetery and the beginning of the industrial strip, a new billboard that reads *Resist the New Fascism. Information 765-2321*. "I'm going to call that number," Justin says.

"You are?"

"Yes." He turns his face, and she sees the fierce mischief in his expression.

She thinks of Cynthia, of Alice, of their sullen, self-defeating gestures.

"You can go anytime," she says to Justin.

"No," he says. "I can't."

She says, "You can. You will." Imagining his absence, though: an amputation.

Sidonie and Hugh go shopping among the stores of the sprawling plazas and strip malls for a crib for Alex's and Ingrid's expected child. "My grandchild is not going to sleep in a laundry basket on the floor of a Quonset hut," Hugh says.

"My great-grandnephew. Or niece," Sidonie says. "You know they're going to move into Steve's basement for the winter."

"Still, bloody irresponsible."

"They seem happy, Hugh. They seem committed to this."

"Why do they choose to undertake such a hard life?"

"Because they've never had to. Because they can."

"They seem," Hugh says, "to be very much in love, anyway. Whatever that means."

Sidonie laughs. "I think that's my line: whatever that means."

Hugh looks sideways at her. His mouth moves under his moustache.

"We could have made it together, don't you think? We jog along pretty well, you and I."

She says, not very gently, because she has noted his use of the past conditional, "Hugh, we'll always be good friends."

He looks away, but nods.

Sidonie comes upon Fearon and Cashiel shooting small birds with a pellet rifle. She is angry: frighteningly angry, must control an impulse to break the rifle over her knee or to smack them around the ears with it. Then she has a day of lying low in her townhouse, trying to breathe herself out of a pit into which she has fallen.

A huge mistake, this undertaking. They will all be ruined. None of them has the moral or intellectual wherewithal to make it a success.

She walks around the little muddy lake near her house. The spring flowers in their waves have come and gone; the grasses are already bone-coloured, rustling around her ankles. The heat of the late June sun has a force, like weight, on her head and shoulders. Like a hand emanating heat and light, anointing her.

She finds binoculars, a field guide, drawing pads and pencils, drives back to Beauvoir, leaves the package with Celeste; the boys have been banished to their grandmother's for the week.

Sage and Plum opens in time for the tourist season. On the

opening night, there is soup made with yogurt and watercress, tournedos of farmed wild boar wrapped around an asparagus-hazelnut pâté; breast of duck glazed with red currant wine and honey; squash and sunflower seed ravioli; trout with Oregon grape confit. Local wines; a chocolate and hazelnut torte from a recipe of Sidonie's paternal grandmother's that had been made only on birthdays; a tart of strawberries and marscapone. Nearly all of the ingredients come from within fifty kilometres of the restaurant: the cheeses, the fruit and berries, the meats.

Alex says, "By fall we'll have all your vegetables growing here. And your eggs and cheese, if you'll have goat. Ingrid is afraid of cows."

Cashiel and Fearon drive the three-quarter ton over the lip of the gully. It is winched up, unharmed, and under it (cushioning its fall, somewhat) is Hugh's mother's old Anglia, which has hitherto been hidden by a tangle of feral blackberry bushes.

The new bridge is opened in July of 2008. The hollow floating concrete tubes that supported the old bridge will be towed out and sunk into the lake, much to the heated discussion of the von Tälers and Kleinholzes. Hugh, it turns out, has been a consultant for the demolition of the old bridge, not the building of the new. He defends the plan: less environmental impact overall, he says, than trying to airlift or truck the huge cylinders to a landfill somewhere. There might be some leaching, he says, but it won't be much. The lake can handle it. Cynthia and Steve are vehemently opposed, they say, to filling even the deep fissures of the lake with garbage. Sidonie finds herself torn between Hugh and her nephew and niece. Who is right? Both sides angrily mount arguments, facts, statistics.

In August, Ingrid miscarries. The midwife says it's common; one out of four pregnancies ends this way. But Alex believes that the trouble is with the soil floor of the Quonset hut, into which decades of pesticide drips must have seeped from the stored sprayers. Alex and Ingrid move temporarily into Alex's parents' house, and Alex has the soil floor of the Quonset hut dug out and replaced at a cost of two thousand dollars.

Cashiel and Fearon's father visits, and Sidonie, rashly, invites her old playmate and enemy Richard Clare to come by, to meet his grandsons. Richard's hair has faded to a sort of peach colour from its original carrot. When he meets his grandsons, he cannot speak; Sidonie watches his chin wobble, his knees shake. She says to Fearon, show you grandfather your drawings. She leaves them on the porch, the three heads bent together. A scene of redemption, of tender reconciliation. But before Richard leaves, he and his son Greg, the boys' father, somehow get into a shouting match in the parking lot that is only resolved when Kevin strides out of the kitchen, flexing his frescoed forearms. The von Tälers laugh and laugh.

Ingrid's mother visits from South Africa; Hugh brings her out from Toronto. Sidonie finds her completely unlikeable: high-handed, insensitive, narrow-minded. Watching them together, she is annoyed by Hugh as well; he defers to Ingrid's mother unnecessarily, is unnecessarily friendly.

After she's put on the plane, Hugh stays a few days. He and Sidonie climb down into the gulley to see the Anglia. It's camouflaged in patches of dull green, that particular green of very old cars that almost seems natural, and patches of rust. The doors hang open, and the windows have been shot out — diamonds of shattered glass littering the seats and the earth around. Squirrels or porcupines or some other animal — is that a whiff of skunk? — have colonized it, tearing the brittle, flaking seat leather, chewing the wooden knob of the gear shift. The sealed instruments of the dashboard, though, are intact, still showing their gauges and dials. The ivory-coloured plastic knob for opening the trunk says "Bonnet." Hugh and Sidonie climb in the vehicle gingerly, because of the crumbled glass. Hugh takes the driver's side, and they sit as if they're driving somewhere. Hugh, Sidonie sees, has teared up; what is he remembering, what body-memory is flooding into him from this old wreck? He does not say. She does not ask. She puts her hand out, and he grasps it as a line.

Clara visits, and buys a set of lounge chairs and tables for the patio; they are wicker and iron and glass, not at all like the old Adirondacks, which have long since disappeared. Everyone likes them very much. The seat cushions are a silvery blue-green, a paler shade of the spruce trees, and remind Sidonie of Alice.

Justin drops out of school two weeks into classes in the fourth year of his degree. There is some warning that this is going to take place: one night when Cynthia isn't present, and a little drunk for the first time in his family's presence, Justin demands, "Is anybody going to tell me who my father is? Because my mom won't. But one of you has to know."

Nobody answers. It's Debbie who asks, gently, if it matters.

"Of course it fuckin' matters," Justin says. "I have a right to know. I have a right to choose who I am."

It's a few days after the conversation that Justin disappears. He simply goes, carrying only a small bag (they surmise) of clothing. He does not answer his cell phone, and Cynthia finds it finally, turned off, stuffed in a drawer. She goes around with bruises under her eyes. Sidonie herself does not sleep. There are posters of missing young people at various gas stations and cafés; posters with very old dates. She does not want to think of Justin disappearing. It is not likely, she tells herself, and tells Cynthia, that Justin will not remain AWOL for very long. But they are both thinking of Paul, of course.

Sidonie has never let herself wonder too much about Justin's father. She remembers Cynthia returning to Montreal, after she had run away, to live with Adam, at first — she had grown up in that apartment over the river, after all — then turning up a few months later on Sidonie's doorstep, sullen, pregnant. She had said nothing. Sidonie had asked nothing, had not remonstrated, only made up the spare room bed. It had been a silent winter — it was just after Sidonie had moved into her own apartment — but not a happy one, for herself. Cynthia had volunteered nothing, had grown larger, more withdrawn, in the warm red nest that Clara and Anita had made of Sidonie's apartment. Sidonie had dreamed disturbing dreams, had felt she was choking.

But when Justin had been born, Sidonie had walked with him night after night while Cynthia slept, her tiny nineteen-year-old body curled up, curled around what inner bruising and tearing Sidonie could not bring herself to contemplate.

When she thinks of Justin, she can still feel the weight of his eight-pound body in her arms, the warm damp of his head in her palm, the rise and fall of his ribs against her wrist. The smell of him, which was the smell of sun on spring earth. His whorled hair, the tiny compact creases and folds of him, like the intricacies of a wild blossom.

She does not speak of this.

She must attend a meeting of the local residents one evening; the meeting, her neighbour has told her, delivering the flyer, is not only about the flood damage, but also about establishing a development plan. There is a rumour that the resort people are planning to build a large marina, and that's not a good idea, given the narrowness of the access road which winds among their houses, not to mention the noise of the increased boat traffic, the pressure on the wildlife of the little lake. Everyone is to attend: the house owners and the mobile home owners as well. Strength in numbers, Sidonie's neighbour says.

Sidonie doubts that any development of the little lake, undesirable though it may be, can be inhibited — that there is really any recourse against planned development in this valley — but she attends the meeting. She is surprised to see the number of people present when she enters the large room — the meeting is being held in a community hall on the nearby reserve — and to see that they are not all the elderly residents that she sees on her walks or retrieving her mail, but younger people too, some with babies, and a large and articulate contingent of residents of the reserve itself.

Surprised, too, that the group is very organized and well-informed, and presents rational arguments and information. What had she expected? Something like the vociferous tenants' meetings she had witnessed when she had lived in the apartment. She will tell Hugh: she is impressed and amused. And heartened; she will say that. It is a gleam of rationality.

She does not speak during the meeting, but at its end, a short, ample woman with an untidy white bun and a small chin approaches her.

"Sidonie? Sidonie von Täler?"

It is Miss Erskine. Daphne Erskine. So she is still alive.

Her old Sunday school teacher, Brown Owl, now lives in one of the trailers by the lake's edge — one of the smaller, shabbier ones. She has never married. She has been a missionary for many years, she says, in Africa, but is not strong enough now to be useful. She keeps busy, though, with her work at Lazarus House — an addictions centre, Sidonie knows.

"I saw your name on the owner's association list," Daphne Erskine says. "I wondered if it was really you, come back to the fold."

She says, "You know somebody who will be very pleased to hear that I've run into you? Father Mas!"

Father Mas?

Masao.

"I was so pleased when he took ordination," Miss Erskine says. "He had a special clarity and glow about him, when you were children in my little Sunday School group. A long time ago. Do you remember?"

When had Masao become a priest? It's surprising news.

"He works with street people in Vancouver," Miss Erskine says. "With the most forlorn and abandoned. He has a gift, I think. But I wish he would not work so hard."

"I was so sorry about your sister," Miss Erskine says then, touching Sidonie's arm. "Alice was a beautiful girl. It was a great loss."

She says it as if Alice's death has happened recently, not over thirty years ago.

"I will tell Masao that you are back here," she says. "He comes for visits once or twice a year or so, you know. To see old friends. I'll tell him that you are here."

Cashiel is suspended from school for fighting with his cousin, Gabe Clare.

Ingrid becomes pregnant again.

"Do they not know about birth control where she comes from?" Tasha asks, delighted.

A coyote gets into the henhouse, and kills seven of Ingrid's hens. Ingrid cries; Sidonie remembers Colette and the numbered hens of her childhood. Cashiel and Fearon make a marker for the mass grave, all of the hens' names burned on with Fearon's woodworking set.

Alex and Ingrid net approximately twenty thousand dollars in the summer and fall in produce sold wholesale to the restaurant and at the farmer's market. Alex says he needs to have the greenhouses by next spring, and a fruit and vegetable stand of his own. He and Hugh and Stephen begin to look at the bottom land to the east of the valley, where the vegetable farms have always been.

Debbie starts her own business making artisanal jams and salsas for the restaurant and for sale in the gift stores up and down the valley. In her first two months, she clears five thousand dollars. Tasha works for her: she puts on a natty suit and sells to other restaurants. Sidonie, along for the ride, sees Tasha assume a kind of polish, charm, that she had not thought possible.

"It's a costume," Tasha says. "I can do this but I'm really only *me* when I'm in my jeans, working in the trees."

She looks at Sidonie sideways, and Sidonie nods; something in her own body has loosened, opened. Her skin rearranges itself, slips more comfortably over her jaw and her shoulder joints. Yes.

She is walking with Hugh; they've decided to attempt their old trail up the Kopje, retracing their childhood hiking route, but carrying a bottle of local *plonk*, as Hugh calls it, wine from right next door, but really quite good — an award-winner; some crackers and Camembert and grapes, instead of their old waxed-paper twists of jam or egg sandwiches. Sidonie climbs slowly, steadily, while Hugh makes little surges and then stops, panting. They do not comment on their modified pace.

Sidonie tells Hugh that she has met up with Miss Erskine, thinking that Hugh will be surprised. But Hugh has already found her, visited her himself.

"I am not a religious man," Hugh says, "nor do I believe that churches should take up the job of governments in helping the poor. But it seems to me that she has got hold of the right idea of religion — she is extraordinarily aware and kind, you know. And she has taken on thankless work with the most despised of humans in our country."

"We all thought she was hopelessly sappy and embarrassing, as children," Sidonie says.

"Yes," Hugh says. "Of course. But I suppose she was extraordinary then, too. Her brother, the reverend — he was pretty run-of-the-mill. A closeted queer, of course. An adequate clergyman. But Daphne — she had something unique, a kind of conviction."

"I suppose so," Sidonie says, astonished at Hugh.

"She stopped me from trying to kill someone," Hugh says. "I probably wouldn't have succeeded, but I'd have got myself into a lot of trouble, if I'd gone through with it. I was only nineteen or twenty. I'd have ruined my life."

An eclipse of astonishment. "You were going to try to kill someone? *Who*?"

But Hugh is silent.

Sidonie does the math. "No," she says. Then: "How did you find out?"

"Alice told me," Hugh says. "Though my mother knew too, and I suppose your mother told her. I don't think anybody else knew, though of course it shouldn't have been a secret. He should have been arrested. But people thought differently then. And he was making so much money for Dad's orchards."

A piece falling into place. There had been so little brouhaha, after Mother had found that note. Alice shouting, but not when Father was within earshot. The engagement broken off. But not much attention on herself. She had been left, for better or worse, to recover in privacy.

"Of course," Hugh says, "my mother wanted to make sure he was fired and never worked again in the valley. But that wasn't practical: he was a good manager. My father couldn't have done without him."

"What happened to him?" Sidonie asks.

Hugh says slowly, "He bought the place, you know, when Mother died. I was overseas — I didn't realize he was the buyer. The lawyers were handling it for me. It was Defoe who got the land out of the ALR and sold it for development. He must have made millions, even in the 80s."

So: the end of a story.

Hugh says, "That was wrong, of course. For him not to be charged. He should have been charged. It shouldn't have been hushed up. My — all of our — mistaken sense of gallantry was not the right thing, in hindsight."

Something shifts: something loosens inside her mind. It is the image, perhaps, of young Hugh, small Hugh, always ahead of her, always turning back to rescue her, to urge her along. She has shut herself off from that solicitous, tow-haired boy for so long.

They are on a grassy, flattened part of the slope: perhaps a cirque, scooped out by some ancient glacier, or perhaps just a ledge formed by a rockslide. A few stands of rabbit bush and some little prickly-pear cactus dot the still-green grass. Before them, the lake spills, a generous libation, between the long blue knuckles of the hills. How many gallons, how many molecules, of water? Sufficient and more to water the trees and vines, to wash the rocks of dust, to temper the summers and winters. The deep blue absorbs, contains, gentles the gaze. It parts and rejoins, seamlessly. It reflects the hills, drawing their blue down; it mirrors the sky.

"Shall we stop here and eat?" Hugh asks, "rather than go all the way to the top? I'm afraid the wine is getting warm."

Though it is fall, the sun is warm; the rock outcroppings, with their colonies of lichen, are still radiating heat.

"Let's," Sidonie says.

Ingrid urges them all to sign up for yoga once a week at the community centre. Tasha signs up and persuades Sidonie to do so as well. "I don't," Sidonie says, "do well with terms like chakra and third eye. I'm a scientist. I really don't speak that language."

The class is hard: she finds herself grunting and stretching, struggling for balance. She notices that what is required is a strong feedback loop, the sort for which she has been developing therapies. Has anyone done work on yoga, in her field, she wonders, and then falls over yet again. The breathing, the focus on the position of her body: that is the challenge, the exercise. Can she train her mind to develop those paths? She will try; she will be her own experiment. There are moments when she experiences something different, something like highly improved reception, in herself. She will keep at it.

The class conflicts with the one of the nights Tasha waits tables at Sage and Plum, but Cynthia offers to take on that night. A food critic from a local tourism magazine visits Sage and Plum, and on his third visit asks Cynthia out. The family is abuzz, Sidonie sees: there is much speculation as to why Cynthia has remained single for two decades (the consensus is that she hasn't wanted to saddle Justin with a stepfather), and much discussion over the worthiness of the food critic. He is not prepossessing; he is in his fifties, balding; he wears thick-lensed glasses. He has fine, small hands, rounded shoulders. But he signs and is a teacher, like Cynthia, and when he speaks, in a voice quieter than any Kleinholz's or Inglis's or von Täler's, everyone stops and listens. All of them, Steve and Debbie and Kevin, Hugh, Sidonie herself, go around saying to each other, *I like him.* Sage and Plum gets a rave review in *Valley Life* magazine.

And then he is gone, and Cynthia is climbing up into the cab of Jack Rilke's pickup truck to go down to the Legion for a beer.

"Do not play around with Jack Rilke," Steve says. "The Rilkes have been our neighbours for sixty years."

Our neighbours. Sidonie grins to herself.

The restaurant traffic is slower in the winter, but Kevin makes a pitch to a couple of wineries and the ski hills, and busloads of lunch customers help keep things afloat. Sidonie has taken to dropping by the place, to lend a hand on busy evenings, or to watch the boys. It makes a change from the little lake with the ducks.

Cashiel says, "Want to hear my myth?" He has been bouncing, literally, off the walls; Kevin and Celeste are too busy to pay him attention. Sidonie has been about to leave; she takes off her coat and goes upstairs instead to sit on Cashiel's bed (her old bed-space!) while he reads out his assignment.

"It's a creation myth," he says. "We had to make one up."

"Go ahead," she says.

"A boy created a video game. He made an avatar, and then he made a world for the avatar to roam around in. He made a quest, so the avatar wouldn't be bored, and he made monsters and traps, so that the avatar would get stronger."

"Yes," Sidonie says.

"The boy made some other friendly characters to help the avatar, so he wouldn't be lonely or despairing."

"Very good."

"But then there was a storm and the boy's computer got fried, and the avatar and his friends and all of the monsters got boosted up a million levels, and they escaped the computer and became real."

"Oh, my!"

"So then the boy got his computer fixed, and tried to *unmake* them, but he couldn't. They were all loose in the world. In a different world, not this one. And the boy worried about them, but he couldn't help them. He only had to hope that they remembered all the rules and cheats that he had built into the game."

"Yes, well: I guess that he would."

"Do you like it?

"Very much. Tell me about the monsters. What they looked like. What powers they had."

Cashiel shows her pages of tiny sketches, lists of attributes: pages of tiny drawings and crabbed writing. He has almost a book-sized manuscript of his drawings and lists. She thinks: And Cashiel is constantly in trouble at school for not writing enough, not doing the work. She contributes to his list of monsters, *Lastrygonians, dracanae, hydrae, medusae, Cyclopes.* Cashiel is impressed.

"But there are more monsters than these," she says. "Talk to your grandmother."

He opens his eyes wide. "You mean those old stories? I could put those into my myth?"

Fearon says, taking an interest from his own bed, "This could be a new kind of game. Not a platform or a maze game, but a web game. The screens could connect. . ."

"In three dimensions!" Cashiel says. "Or add in interface, there's another dimension."

"Yeah, it's all about the connections, then."

Around the two of them, energy: light.

Kevin says they've decided to close down the restaurant on Christmas Day and do a family dinner. "We'll lose some business, yes," he says, "but there haven't been a lot of calls for reservations. It's not like in the city, where so many people live alone."

"Live alone and can afford to eat dinner out," Sidonie corrects.

They will all come: Cynthia, Justin, who has finally returned from his walkabout, Steve and Debbie, Alex and Ingrid, Tasha, Sidonie. Hugh is flying out as well. Cynthia's beau, as her brothers refer to Jack Rilke now, will not come; he will have Christmas with his parents and his ex-wife.

"Do you think it's strange," Cynthia asks Sidonie, "for a man to spend Christmases with his ex?"

"I do," Sidonie says firmly, swallowing her own alarms. "Strange and wonderful."

Tasha announces that she will be bringing a friend: "A person called Don," Debbie says.

"Or Dawn," Alex suggests, winking.

"Oh, dear," Debbie says. "I know it's really common now, but I hope. . ."

Sidonie, who has some idea, says nothing.

And Celeste's auntie Edith will come, though no other family members. "There's a better party going on at my uncle Roy's,"

Celeste says. "But Edith and Roy are on the outs."

There is a vote, and turkey is not on the menu. "Thank you!" says Kevin, who has been cooking for staff Christmas parties all month. Instead, there is moose — a great rib roast, donated by Celeste's dad — and quail.

"Not the little jobs with the topknots that run through the orchard!" Ingrid says, alarmed, and Kevin explains that they will be domestic quail. But he has a gleam in his eye, at her comment.

And crab, which is to be delivered, fresh off the boat, by a friend of Kevin's who is driving up from the coast Christmas Eve.

Everything else will come from the farm or orchard: tiny Andean button potatoes in various colours, which seem to like the valley soil; grilled peppers, cherries and rosemary for the sauce for the moose, currants and walnuts for stuffing the quail (the currant bushes and walnut trees discovered in the tangle of brush at the north edge of the property, by the gulley); pickles and chutney with Debbie's label: Sage and Plum Moveable Feast.

A cake thick with dried fruit and nuts.

Only the chocolate, the cheeses, and wine are not from the Sage and Plum Gardens, though the cheese and wine are locally produced. "But I bought the chocolate where it was made," says Justin, who has returned with several pounds in his backpack. And a beard.

Sidonie dresses for the dinner. She puts on, after her usual narrow black jeans, a thin black dress, which is quite lightweight, really. It falls to her thighs; the sleeves flutter. A pleasing dress, comfortable on the body. Tags cut out, as they scratched. Adam had bought it for her in 1967. She is pleased with the roll of the collar, the tiny, neat pockets and placket.

Then the tunic: this one patterned in a spectrum of oranges that she particularly likes: the colours of an Indian spice market, perhaps. Also, originally, a dress. Bought in 1972 for Adam's parents' fiftieth wedding anniversary party.

And last, the vest, which she is even fonder of than the dress and tunic. This a fine, cabled wool knit, narrow, with deep armholes. It had been Adam's: he had thought it too conservative, and she had taken to wearing it, in the late 70s, over large flannel shirts or turtlenecks: the Annie Hall look.

Such a strange assortment of garments; she would never, before this year, have considered wearing these things together. But she can see that the effect is salubrious, the sizes and colours of the rectangles made by the various items form a pleasing arrangement. And leaving her bedroom, she sees the zebrawood beads, a peace-offering, a traveller's present from Justin, hanging from the row of hooks. Their satin texture, their warmth and weight pass through her imagination: dare she? She puts them on. Yes? Yes. There. She feels somehow robed, hallowed.

They have had by Christmas of 2008 much more than the normal amount of snow, and much colder temperatures. By all predictions, this winter of 08/09 will be more intense than those of the last ten or twelve years. Sidonie, wading through the new drifts from her car, feels buoyant, elated. It is a winter from her childhood, clean, airy, a clear demarcation in the year. She tries to form a ball in her driving gloves, but the snow is too dry to stick; then Fearon, who's shoveling the courtyard, forms a loose missile with his bare hands and heaves it at her, overhand. She has to hold up her bag of wrapped presents to gain safe passage.

The gifts have been mostly for the children, a custom of both von Tälers and Kleinholzes. But there are some gifts for the adults too: practical and promissory. A goat for Ingrid: it will arrive in spring, but she receives a card with a photo of its mother, a pretty black-and-white Nubian. A separator for Debbie, to make cheese; also represented by a photo cut from a brochure.

Four large filing cabinets for Sidonie: these represented by a bill of sale from the auction house. A black iron object, called a spider, for Kevin, who handles it almost reverently.

"It's an antique," Alex says. "From Quebec. I found it on eBay, after six months of looking."

For Tasha (whose friend *is* Dawn, not Don), keys to the elderly three-quarter ton pickup that Alex has used to take vegetables to the market all summer and fall.

"Since you've been driving it for the past few months anyway," Alex says. "But I'll need it to haul manure in spring."

Sidonie has not known what to give anyone, and has resorted to distributing a pair of thick wool socks to each person. She has found out that her neighbour, she of the flat-faced dog and the casseroles, possesses a large bureau full of socks that she has knit, and that she sells for charity: for Stephen Lewis's African grandmothers, she says. Sidonie has chosen for each family member: heavy grey merino, self-striped, lacy and patterned. A pair for everyone.

It would have been better if she had knit them herself, she thinks, but she has not. She never learned how to knit, though she had been given yarn and needles as a child, shown over and over. Her hands refused to pick it up; she had never got past awkward. And Alice had been so adept that Sidonie had been let off the hook. It is her brain wiring, really, she supposes, that has not got that aptitude. She does not use that layer of processing as well. She had traded it early for the ability to manipulate abstract things. Could she have learned, if she had tried harder? Would her brain have developed differently?

It is Cynthia who has given the best gift: she has found a company that will print and bind books, and provides a computer template to put them together, and Cynthia has, over the last year, created a scrapbook of photographs (captioned, dated) out of the albums in Sidonie's files, the albums that Justin has painstakingly reassembled, and had a copy made for each of them. "But how did you do this?" Sidonie asks, and Cynthia explains about scanning the photos, choosing the coloured borders and titles. But the books are very professional-looking; Cynthia has a gift.

Here are Mother and Father, looking, at last, like what they were; an intelligent and disapproving Scotswoman, an expansive and indulgent middle-European burgher. And another photograph, looking like what they also were: North American orchardists of the mid-century. There are photos of parties, of children — Alice and

Sidonie, Hugh, Graham, Walter and Karl, Masao. There are photographs of the house, of small trees, of pets. Photographs of groups of people at weddings, at dedications of buildings, on the beach.

And here is Alice, in a white dress and tiara, shaking hands with Princess Margaret. How funny; Sidonie remembers that dress so distinctly that just seeing this image of it she can feel the texture of the cotton whipcord, the batiste lining, bought in Vancouver; hear the sound of the shears, the rumbling whir of the Singer. She sees the dress growing slowly on the dining-room table. Alice pressing out seams, picking out basting, for hours and hours. The bodice recut three times before the fit satisfied her. It had been almost bridal, the most perfect thing seen in Marshall's Landing. Mrs. Inglis had loaned Alice a pair of white kid slingbacks; Miss Robinson, a strand of real pearls. They had all looked at the dress, not touching it, awed. Mother had put on a white glove and turned the dress hem up to show the perfect stitching, the secret finished seams.

And Alice, wearing the dress, the short white gloves, her hair a smooth blonde chignon, her little hat, her slim white perfect self, her attending princesses, standing on the carpet to wait for the real princess.

In the photo you don't see this. You see a very pretty slim girl, with an uncertain smile, a wisp of escaping hair, a homemade dress that strains a bit at the armhole seam. A provincial beauty, dimmed by Princess Margaret's professional coif and couture, her formal bearing.

A little death, though she knows photographs do not always tell the truth.

They have all become a little older, a little more worn, in three years, Sidonie sees, looking around the table. Alex has lost his baby face, looks grimmer. Ingrid has put on weight, carries a lushness that for the first time truly recalls her paternal grandmother. Justin, just off the plane, is very thin, as well as bearded. (He's picked up some intestinal parasite, Cynthia tells Sidonie.) He looks harder: he is harder.

He does not make such an effort to be polite. His hair has darkened, too: she does not see in him her golden boy. She is punctured with loss, but she does not speak of this. Justin is not hers; has never been.

But relief, mixed with the loss.

Steve and Debbie, Kevin and Celeste, look simply tired. They have worked hard for people in their late forties. The enterprise has, overall, lost money. They will not see a profit for a year or two yet.

Only Tasha looks pleased with herself, paying exaggerated attention to the short, sulky, red-haired young woman sitting beside her: a ruffian if Sidonie ever saw one. Dawn. What had her parents thought, naming her that? She is dressed with exaggerated butchness, her hair aggressively spiky, her speech deliberately tough. What dreams of femininity has she disrupted, or is she demonstrating against?

There are arguments, after the joviality of the gifts. Hugh accuses Alex and Kevin of working Ingrid too hard; Debbie and Cynthia exchange words over Justin's appearance; the boys squabble over a new electronic game; Kevin yells at them and Celeste yells at Kevin.

Sidonie, sitting between Celeste's aunt Edith and Tasha's friend, has to hold up the ends of two conversations, which, she begins to realize, would be volatile if mixed. Edith is telling a slightly obscene and mocking story about her transgendered nephew, while Dawn is complaining about the line-ups at the liquor store where she works on "Indian cheque day." Sidonie is human insulation. She is tickled. It is an amusing job.

Kevin cuts into the luscious dark cake, which is distributed in great, heavy slices: they are a family of fruitcake-eaters, rare, perhaps, in the world. The cake, Sidonie thinks, is like a geological sample, a chunk of earth, rich with geological time, or at least historical time: a midden of what their families have desired, found, made, over half a century or more. There are walnuts from the Sage and Plum tree, the Beauvoir tree; there are almonds and raisins from Italy; there is good wheat from the prairies, and the whole soaked in Bosnian apricot brandy, a gift from Debbie's parents.

They toast with a thimble each of ice wine, Hahnenschrei's first vintage of ice wine, a gift from their neighbours George and Katya.

"*Late Bloomer*," Sidonie reads from the label, and Steve asks, "What is ice wine, anyway?"

"It's made from grapes left on the vine until after the first frost," Kevin says. "The frost concentrates the sugars, which are high, anyway, for the grapes being left longer."

The wine is satin, cool, sweet as lilies.

"It tastes purple," says Cashiel, who, like his brother, has been given a thimbleful.

"It tastes like I imagined wine would taste, when I was a child," Cynthia says.

"A toast," Debbie says, surprisingly, "to late bloomers."

There is a knock at the house door, but nobody hears it for a while. In the end, it is Sidonie, getting up to use the washroom, who hears and answers it. She moves through the sea of boots that lie dripping, scattered, on the new tile floor in the hallway, stooping to line up a few pairs, to clear a path. Through the sidelight, she can see that there are no additional cars in the drive, but that someone has made a path on foot down the driveway. She can hear stamping on the other side of the door, snow being cleared from boots. A throat-clearing cough: a man's. Through the patterned glass of the sidelight she can see the blurred figure of a man of around medium height. Light, or grey hair. Not bulky enough to be one of the Rilkes. Who is it, walking up their drive on Christmas Day?

The old door sticks at the tile, swollen a little with the snow. Stephen will need to plane it a little, just on the lower left. She tugs at it. "Just a second," she calls. "The door is stuck."

She kicks through the jumble of Kodiaks and Columbias, braces her foot against the jamb, gets a better grip. Now. Now. She pulls harder, and the door bursts open.

ACKNOWLEDGMENTS

Thanks to Evalyne Hillaby Smith and to Harold Rhenisch for their stories and details of life in the Okanagan in the 1940s and 1950s. (All factual errors are my own.) Thanks also to Carolyn Ives, Leigh Matthews, Rachel Nash, Patsy Alford, and Annette Dominik, who read early versions of the manuscript, and to Peg Hasted and Susie Safford for talking me through first chapter revisions late in the process. Anne Nothof refined the book with her clear editing skills.

A sabbatical leave from Thompson Rivers University gave me time to complete the first drafts. The Lake Country Museum provided many story triggers in its collection of artifacts and archives.

JULIA TOMKINS

Karen Hofmann lives in Kamloops, B.C. She has been published in *Arc, Prairie Fire, The Malahat Review*, and *The Fiddlehead*. Her book *Water Strider* was shortlisted for the Dorothy Livesay Prize at the 2009 BC Book Awards, and "The Burgess Shale" was shortlisted for the 2012 CBC Short Story Prize. *After Alice* is her first novel.